THE BOTTOM
OF YOUR HEART

Maurizio de Giovanni

THE BOTTOM
OF YOUR HEART
INFERNO
FOR COMMISSARIO RICCIARDI

*Translated from the Italian
by Antony Shugaar*

Europa
editions

Europa Editions
214 West 29th Street
New York, N.Y. 10001
www.europaeditions.com
info@europaeditions.com

Copyright © 2014 by Giulio Einaudi Editore SpA, Torino
Published in arrangement with Thesis Contents srl and book@ literary agency
First Publication 2015 by Europa Editions

Translation by Antony Shugaar
Original title: *In fondo al tuo cuore. Inferno per il commissario Ricciardi*
Translation copyright © 2015 by Europa Editions

Library of Congress Cataloging in Publication Data is available
ISBN 978-1-60945-293-3

de Giovanni, Maurizio
The Bottom of Your Heart

Book design by Emanuele Ragnisco
www.mekkanografici.com

Cover photo: Ex-voto. 19th or 20th century. Musée du Coeur
(Doctor and Mrs. Boyadjian Collection). MRAH, Parc du Cinquantenaire, Brussels

Prepress by Grafica Punto Print – Rome

Printed in the USA

For Paolo Repetti's big,
hidden heart.

THE BOTTOM
OF YOUR HEART

I

The professor is falling.

He's falling, and as he falls, he spreads his arms wide, as if trying to embrace the scorching summer night that stretches out to catch him.

He's falling, and since the brief struggle knocked all the air out of his lungs, his body now pointlessly demands that he take a deep breath, even though the new lungful of oxygen won't do him a bit of good, won't even have a chance to make it into his bloodstream.

For that matter, his nose won't even register the scents from the blossoms on the trees and the flowers blooming in their beds, the smells from the open kitchen windows throughout the neighborhood, which is immersed in the blistering heat as if in some curse.

He falls with his eyes closed, ignoring the lights still burning in the windows of those unable to get to sleep despite the lateness of the hour, or further out, beyond the roofs of the apartment buildings that slope down to the sea, the streetlights lining the boulevard that marks the end of the network of narrow lanes, the *vicoli* of Naples.

The professor is falling. And as he does, his thoughts shatter into a thousand tiny shards, flickerings of consciousness that will never again construct one of those well-turned phrases for which he is so justly renowned in the lecture halls of the school of medicine. By now those flickerings are like so many fragments of a broken mirror, reflecting what little they can catch in the fall, yearning for the days when they could assemble a single, harmonious picture.

One of those shards catches a flicker of love.

If he only he could linger over the topic, the professor would muse on the strangeness of love. It makes you do such strange things, things you would never usually do; love sometimes makes you ridiculous, and other times fills your life with color. Love creates and love destroys, he would say, employing one of his proverbial figures of speech. Love can even throw you out a window.

But the professor is falling, and when you're falling you can afford nothing more than a few scattered shards of thought. And so, the fertile scientific mind accepts the fear of pain.

Pain is something you can study, the professor would declare, if he had the time and the leisure. Pain is a symptom, a sign that the complex machinery of the human body, about which we know so much and yet so little, is not functioning as it ought to be. A signal, a flashing warning light that demands attention: hurry, come running, something's wrong. With children—the professor would tell us if only he weren't falling—this is the problem: they can't tell us where it hurts, they don't understand the things they feel. They sob, they weep despairingly, but they say nothing; and the poor physician trying to cure the little devils has to blunder around in the dark, palpating here and there until a shout louder than the rest gives him a clue. You're cold, cold, you're getting warmer, hot!

If only he weren't falling at dizzying speed, the professor would reflect for the thousandth time about the strangeness of life, which can lead you to involve yourself professionally in matters you'd usually steer clear of. He, for instance, could never stand children; not even when he was a child himself, the morose only son of a work-obsessed provincial businessman and a weepy schoolteacher whose unctuous hugs he avoided like the plague. But there's not much you can do about it, he would have said with a shrug, if he hadn't been so busy windmilling his arms through the warm night air; a job is a job, and since women produce children, and his profession involved women, he necessarily had to work with children.

The professor is falling. And in a flash he realizes that there is no more time, even though the fall is lasting much longer than he ever would have expected.

There's no time to get back into shape, in the hopes of surviving the struggle that culminated in his being tossed out the window with such laughable ease, which is, after all, the reason he's now falling. And to think that he was proud of his smooth, sensitive surgeon's hands, so different from the rough, calloused hands of the many seekers who begged him to treat them, hats in hand and pockets empty; he was even proud of his flaccid flesh and double chin, clear signs of opulent dinners and highly placed friends, the envy of his jealous colleagues.

If only he'd been a little more muscular, if only he'd continued the long uphill climbs that once took him from his home to the hospital—before he purchased the gleaming new Fiat 521 C, its dashboard equipped with speedometer, clock, and fuel and oil gauges, its bodywork two-tone, black-and-cream, his pride and joy, now standing motionless on the pavement seventy feet below, presumably indifferent to its owner's flight through thin air—it might have kept him from falling. And now perhaps he'd still be presentable, his shirt wouldn't be torn, his suspenders wouldn't be unhooked, his gold-rimmed spectacles wouldn't be askew on his twisted face.

Still—the professor might be thinking, if the fall wasn't practically over by now—a person doesn't expect to have to fight for his life while he's sitting in his office planning out tomorrow's schedule. He expects, at the very worst, some unexpected visitor he can dismiss with a few caustic jokes; he certainly doesn't count on a hasty, desperate bare-fisted brawl, which caught him by such surprise that he didn't even have a chance to shout for help. Not that there would have been many people to hear him at that time of night, but a male nurse, a janitor, some intern with a vulgar, athletic build, the physique of a laborer, might have heard and come running; and now, instead of plummeting toward the pavement at dizzying speed—a speed he could have calculated if he weren't falling—he would be filing a criminal complaint for assault and battery.

It's strange the way time dilates in moments of extremity, the professor would have thought if he'd survived the fall. And he'd have described the way the brain, as it observes the fragments of thought flying through the air, lingers on some things but not all, by virtue of the wonderful rapidity with which this fantastic product of evolution is able to make certain connections and exclude others. The professor would explain how untrue it is what people say, that your whole life flashes before your mind's eye; for instance, there's not a trace of either his wife or his son in his rapid-fire thoughts, as they explode like fireworks, blazing and brilliant against the dark backdrop of night. Nor is there any sign of any of the numerous individuals who, in a convulsive choreography, populate the working day of a prominent professor of medicine with an endowed chair and plenty of hospital duties. Duties that he performs with zeal; in fact, let it be said, if he had only taken them a little less seriously, he'd now be sleeping comfortably in his bed instead of flapping through the darkness like a bat.

But what he does see, behind the lids of his closed eyes and the grimace on his face as he braces for impact, is the cheerful, vivid image of Sisinella.

Sisinella with her white teeth gleaming in the sunlight, or her red lips pursed in that tiny pout that drives him crazy. Sisinella laughing in the wind, holding her cunning little hat with both hands as they zip along at top speed with the top down in his magnificent automobile, purchased, basically, just for her. Sisinella as she takes him to a special and highly personal paradise, in the feather bed hauled up by no fewer than four porters to the new apartment in Vomero. Sisinella who makes a boy of him, he who never really was a boy, not even in his youth. Sisinella with her soft hands, Sisinella with her long legs, Sisinella with her strawberry-and-cream flesh. Sisinella.

The professor is falling, and as he falls he thinks about how much he would have liked to see her face, her expression as she unwrapped the package he was going to make sure she found, as if by accident, under her pillow. The jubilation that would have ensued, how she'd have been as excited as a little girl, her cheeks still red from lovemaking, her small nose wrinkled with joy, and her sumptuous young breasts heaving with pleasure. The reward she would have confered upon him for that gift. A pity. A real pity.

The professor is falling, but all things come to an end, and so does his fall. And that magnificent machine, evolution's most extraordinary creation, the brain that has produced so many acute, brilliant thoughts, taking its owner to the very peak of his profession, is largely ejected from the bony container that held it for more than fifty years and which now shatters like a walnut on its sudden impact against the ground, not much more than two seconds after the professor's foot first left the floor, seventy feet overhead.

In one final, immense flash, the giant fireworks display is extinguished in the memory of a childish, lustful smile.

II

They would meet at the Palace of the Immacolatella, and there was never any need to make a date. They met every time word got around that a steamship was about to set sail, those huge ships with twin stacks and a horn that would split your eardrums and shake your chest, if you stood too close.

They'd meet in the late afternoon, when he had an hour off from his work as an apprentice and she could get away from her housework, while his master napped, snoring openmouthed in the chair behind the workbench, breath reeking of wine, and her mother sat sewing until she started yelling for her again, at the top of her lungs, to come and help make dinner.

He was twelve, but he had the eyes of a centenarian, the filthy ravaged hands of someone learning to master a trade, and a skinny, wiry body wrapped in a tattered jacket that had been turned inside out, a jacket that had once belonged to who knows who, who knows when. She was eleven, but her mouth, clenched tightly against hard work and tears, was that of a hundred-year-old woman; her nose was razor-sharp and her lips were thin, her eyebrows furrowed in her determination to survive.

He always got there first, and he'd always sit in the same place, between the mountains of coiled hawsers that were each the thickness of one of his arms. A carefully chosen observation post, from which it was possible to see the ship and the wharf, and the barges loading crates and bales full of things to transport far away. And you could also see *them*, sitting on the ground or stretched out, still asleep from the previous day, waiting for a departure they'd longed for and dreaded, a departure they'd secured by scrimping and saving for years. Some of them slept, others looked out to sea as if they'd never seen it before, garbed in the cheap clothing they'd washed and ironed almost as if for a party. The big ship awaited them, two sailors guarding the gangway, suspended in a long pregnant pause, waiting for the whistle that would signal the beginning of boarding.

The ship. A black beast, colossal, with its immense belly that would gobble them all up, take in everything, objects and people, leaving nothing behind it but the usual, terrible emptiness.

He sensed her as she approached, silent and lithe as a stray cat, and crouched behind him. He didn't turn around, didn't take his eyes off the line of people awaiting their fates just a few yards away. There was a surreal silence as the sun set, filling the July sky with flame and color. She stared out, over his cap, at the greasy seawater and the dinghies milling around the big ship like flies around a horse.

"I wonder where they're going," she murmured.

He shrugged.

"To America. Don't you know that they're going to America?"

"Yes, to America," she replied, still whispering as if she were in church. "But where? America is so big. And then, once they get there, what are they going to do? Where will they go? What are they going to eat? They have children, you can see them. The children have to eat all the time, or they'll starve."

He said nothing for a while. He was chewing on a blade of straw.

Then he said: "Before anywhere else, they'll go to Palermo, to Sicily. They'll load more people, more or less as many as they're loading here. And the ship came here from Genoa; if you look carefully, you can see there are already other people on board, every so often one of them peeks out, see? The people who boarded in Genoa have taken all the best places, then the Neapolitans take the places that are left over. And the Sicilians just have to take what they get."

"How do you know all these things?"

"Gennarino told me. His father's a stevedore, he loads crates onto the ship. The people who are leaving give him a little something extra, to make sure nothing gets broken. He's wearing a black hat, you see him? At the far end of the ship."

She gently caressed a hawser, as if it were an animal.

"That's not what I wanted to know."

"Then what?"

"What I meant was . . . I mean, they're leaving. They're not coming back. What are they going to do? What language are they going to speak in America? What are they going to eat?"

He shifted suddenly, in annoyance.

"Is that all you ever think about, food? They're leaving to get rich, to get a better life. What do you think: they don't eat in America? They sure get more to eat there than here. These people are beggars, miserable wretches, whatever they find there is better than what they're leaving behind. Because what they're leaving behind is nothing. Nothing at all."

She didn't react. She just went on stroking the hawser. A large rat poked its head above the big coil of hawsers she was crouching next to. She stamped her foot on the ground and the rat turned and ran, with a faint squeak.

"Food's not all I think about. I think about those children and those women following their husbands who are following who knows what. And I think about the ones who stay behind. Just look at them."

Right behind the departing passengers was another group: children, women, and especially old men, dressed in more ordinary garb.

Parents, wives, sons and daughters who would wait, probably

in vain, for the emigrants to put aside enough money to send for them, or else until they admitted defeat and sailed home, hungrier than when they left.

"I'd never make you sail away alone. I'd come with you. Either both of us, or neither of us."

He turned his head slightly, seriously.

"I'm learning a profession. And I'm good at it, you know I am. I'll always have plenty of work, and we'll have enough money. We don't have to leave, if you don't want to."

The silence was broken by a short blast of the ship's horn. One of the sailors whistled, and those who had been sleeping sat up with a jerk.

A little boy burst into tears; his mother took him into her arms. An old woman, standing in the crowd of those who weren't departing, plunged her face into her apron. From this distance, you couldn't hear her sobs, but you could see her shoulders shaking.

He went on: "But wouldn't you want to go? To see what America is like? To see if we can do it too, if we can go live among the Indians? They say that it's a place that's bigger than any other, that there are strange animals no one has ever seen before."

The sun was setting fast, but the air grew no cooler. She wiped away a drop of sweat.

"No. I want to stay at home. The people who are leaving are weak, they're the ones who can't make it here. But *I* can. I want to make it."

He was silent. He spat out the straw and picked up a rock.

"Then why do you come down here, when the ships set sail? If you don't want to leave, why do you come?"

"Because you come. Because I know you like it."

"That's the only reason?"

A man and a woman were embracing at the foot of the gangway. They weren't crying, they spoke no words of reassurance or tenderness. They clung tight to each other, in despair.

She whispered: "No. That's not the only reason. It's also to remind myself that I'm not going to be forced to leave here so I can find something to eat. That I'm going to live well here, at home, where I belong. Because I'm not weak. I'm going to make it."

She was just a girl, and she'd spoken so quietly that it was almost impossible to understand the individual words; but he turned to look at her as if she'd shouted in his ears.

"If people are happy together, if they love each other, if they have a family, then any place can be their home. There's no reason to fight, is there? You just go wherever you're happiest, that's all."

She said nothing; she just went on staring expressionlessly at the couple embracing in silence and the black hull of the ship looming behind them.

"I'm going to be happy," she murmured. And she started to nod, slowly and forcefully, as if she were listening to a voice from within telling her just how to do that. "I'm going to be happy. I know I will. I have it written in the depths of my heart."

III

I'm going to be happy, thought Enrica. I'm going to be happy.

The air in the closed interior of the steamer was unbreathable, so she'd stepped out onto the deck. But the hot wind brought no relief, and the smell of diesel fuel coupled with the rolling of the deck made her seasick; for the thousandth time she wondered whether she'd made the right choice.

I'm going to be happy, she repeated to herself firmly. She even whispered it, without realizing it, and a fat woman looking green around the gills stared at her curiously.

The last few months hadn't been easy. Shy by nature, she'd had to force herself to build, painstakingly and patiently, a friendship with Rosa, the childhood governess of the man she'd fallen in love with.

Had she fallen in love? Yes, no question. She was more than certain. Because love, Enrica thought to herself, is a physical thing more than a state of mind. You can measure it by the beat that your heart skips every time he lays his eyes on you, and by the extra little surge in the next beat, when you realize that there's a tenderness welling up in those eyes. Love is the heat that you feel on your face at the idea of placing your lips against his. Love is the sinking feeling in your belly when you spot his silhouette at the window, on a dark winter evening, glimpsed from across the street, through the rain.

Love is something physical. And she was in love.

The absurd thing was that the whole time she'd always

sensed, in her heart, on her skin, in her gut, that he loved her too. And during the long months in which he had watched her from the window and she had awaited a single gesture, a word, she'd wondered why he hadn't declared himself. Was there another woman?

The only way to find out was to talk to those who knew him, and there was only one person who fit that description, namely his elderly governess, his old *tata*, a modest woman, only apparently bad-tempered, who'd welcomed Enrica's desperate appeal with pragmatism, telling her how much she hoped Enrica's wish would come true, and sooner rather than later, too, because Rosa was tired and afraid that her young master would be left alone, once she was no longer around to look after him.

Now, on the deck of the steamer, as Enrica clasped her hat to her head with one begloved hand, and pressed a scented handkerchief to her nose with the other, she struggled to remember the enthusiasm and trepidation she had felt when she first set foot in his home. At Easter she had felt she could sweep aside any obstacle, that—with her innate calm and patience—she would be able to claim her desired place, beside the lifetime companion she had chosen in silence, in the privacy of her bedroom, reading and rereading the first awkward letter that he had sent her, in which he asked her permission to greet her when they met.

She had cooked for him. With Rosa's help, she'd put together a meal with all the dishes he loved best. She'd picked out a dress, a perfume, a pair of shoes. She'd even planned out the topics of conversation. She was ready; she felt like the woman she most wanted to be.

She gulped back a sob that was rising in her chest. She felt sorry for herself when she thought back to that night. He'd never shown up at all, and there she had sat, stiff and silent, while Rosa, embarrassed and sad, watched her from the kitchen door, not knowing what to say. Finally Enrica had gotten up and gone home. Later, when her fear for his safety won out over her mortification, she'd stood watching at the window until she'd heard a car pull up in the street below, and she'd seen him step out of the car with a chauffeur holding the door; she'd been able to make out a silhouette in the car's cab and, in the silent night, she'd heard a woman's laugh. That woman.

That was when she'd made up her mind to be happy in spite of him.

If he preferred the other woman, she could hardly blame him. She'd seen her once, at the Gran Caffè Gambrinus, and she could hardly ignore her beauty, her style, and her elegance. Rosa had said in a contemptuous tone that she was a fallen woman, one of those who smoke in public and flirt with everyone, but Enrica knew how difficult it was, for a simple schoolteacher like her, to complete with someone like that other woman.

Enrica's mother—who never missed a chance to point out that when a girl reaches the age of twenty-four she can officially call herself an old maid, that her younger sister (younger!) had not only been married for over two years but already had a son, while Enrica seemed fated to a future of miserable loneliness—watched her with unconcealed and growing concern, and this pained Enrica intolerably, especially now that she couldn't even lay secret claim to a love she believed was reciprocated. Her father, so similar in temperament to Enrica, quiet and gently determined, understood that if he spoke to her about it he'd only wound her further; and so he watched her surreptitiously, helplessly, sympathetically sharing in the sorrow that he could see on her face.

Shielding her glasses from the sea's spray, Enrica told herself that yes, she'd made the right decision. She couldn't stand the prospect of a long hot summer, of having to duck her head every time she walked past his window; struggling to keep from looking across the street on afternoons when she tutored students forced to take makeup exams in the fall; doing her best to side-step painful chance encounters with Rosa in the grocer's shop downstairs. What could she tell the old woman? That she didn't think she was up to fighting for the man she loved? That the weapons of seduction, which that other woman seemed so expert in, weren't part of her arsenal? That she was so cowardly and resigned that she was willing to step aside, so long as it put an end to her suffering?

And so she'd stopped by the teachers' college where she'd taken her degree and inquired whether they knew of anyone who might be looking for a teacher. Was she running away? Yes. She was running away. From him. From herself. From what she wished had happened and hadn't. From the stagnant life she hadn't been able to escape.

She'd thought it over long and hard, and decided that this was the best solution. They called them "temporary climatic colonies"; they were designed to ward off tuberculosis, one of the diseases that threatened children's health. Give a sick child to the sea, and the sea will give back a healthy child, ran the slogan; who could say if that were true. In any case, it was a way to offer fresh air to those who couldn't afford it, and an opportunity for the Opera Nazionale Balilla, the Fascist youth organization, to do some summertime proselytizing. The director of the college, who remembered Enrica as the best student she'd ever had, had given her a hug and promised that she'd make sure she was first in line if any openings presented themselves. Sure enough, a few days later the director had sent for her.

Enrica's father had objected; he'd rather have kept his daughter close. But her mother had supported her, in the hope that a new setting might offer a chance to meet new people.

So now Enrica found herself aboard a ship steaming toward the island of Ischia, twenty miles across the Bay of Naples, where a summer colony was currently missing one of its teachers; the last one had been discovered to be scandalously pregnant, though unmarried. Apparently fate wanted to second her decision to put as much distance as she could between herself and those sorrowful green eyes that appeared to her every night in her dreams—when, that is, she finally managed to get to sleep after tossing and turning for hours.

She squinted into the sunshine, gulped, and tried to distract herself by admiring the view. She recognized Pizzofalcone, the Charterhouse of San Martino, Castel Sant'Elmo standing atop its brilliant green hill; along the coast, the handsome façades of the palaces of Santa Lucia and Castel dell'Ovo, which stretched alongside the water like a long stone finger. Further back, Posillipo tumbled downhill toward the bright blue waters of the bay, with its court of a hundred fishing boats returning after a night out on the water. The city, teeming and treacherous, assumed a stirring beauty from that vantage point, and she felt a twinge of homesickness. Enrica wondered what people who are forced to emigrate must feel when they sail away and turn to look back at that spectacular view, knowing they may never set eyes on it again.

A knot of despair swelled in her throat. The green-gilled woman, who'd been struggling against an overwhelming urge to vomit, found the strength to ask her if she felt well. Enrica nodded with a tight smile, then turned back toward sea to conceal the ocean of tears that had filled her eyes.

I'm going to be happy, she said over and over again to herself. I'm going to be happy.

And she silently wept.

IV

O nce a year, in this city, the heat comes. The real heat.
Of course, one might say that there are plenty of times
when the temperature is too high, that, generally
speaking, it's never really cold here. But that's not entirely true.
One might also say that, even in other seasons, there are days
when the south wind—the sirocco—brings hot air out of
Africa, driving people mad, making them do things, say things,
think things they would never have otherwise even imagined.
And true, that does sometimes happen. But heat, the genuine
article, only comes once a year.

It's never a surprise. People begin bracing for it in spring-
time, when the sweet scent of flowers spreads through the city
and men loosen their ties in the sunshine, when it becomes
more pleasant to stop and chat on the street or out an open
window, conversing across the narrow streets and the *vicoli* of
the center of town. The heat'll come any day now, say the
housewives, cheerfully pinning sheets onto clotheslines that
might stretch between the balconies of two different buildings;
the woman say this with a smile, but in their voices there's a
faint note of concern. Because they all know that the heat, the
genuine authentic heat, is a serious, terrible thing.

When the real heat comes, it doesn't arrive unexpectedly. It
has its fixed dates, and it moves like a naval flotilla, crossing
the sea in procession. It sends a few clouds on ahead to give
word of its arrival, and perhaps a sudden cloudburst, just to
create an illusion, a diversion on the eve of the final onslaught.

Dogs sniff at the air, occasionally emitting an uneasy yelp. The old men sigh.

Finally there's a night that offers no cool respite from the heat of the day, as it usually would, and that's the first signal. The men wander through their homes searching in vain for some combination of open windows that will provide a semblance of a crosscurrent. The young mothers watch over their sleeping children, unable to forget the stories they've heard of newborns found dead, in their cribs, at dawn.

The dreaded sun rises, bringing the first day of heat. It rises into the sky like a warship sailing into port, menacing and aflame. And it shows no mercy. The strolling vendors are caught unawares, already out in the streets, and they immediately find themselves dripping with sweat under the burden of their wares; if the goods they're selling are perishable, they'll desperately try to protect them and keep them appetizing, but they will inevitably be unsuccessful: everything begins to look withered, poor, and ugly. Much like the vendors themselves, as they strain to attract the attention of the women they sell to with their hoarse cries, women who are careful not to step out onto their balconies, if there is any way they can avoid it. Things are even worse for the shopkeepers, waiting anxiously, motionless at the thresholds of their stores, while the interiors grow so hot that they're uninhabitable unless equipped with slow-turning ceiling fans.

The churches are still safe, and their cool naves and aisles are soon invaded by regular churchgoers as well as by those who, in cooler seasons, are busier sinning than seeking redemption. The women bathe the smallest children with damp rags and keep them in the shade, while for the older ones they ready a basin of cool water which, though it will soon turn hot, at least gives them a chance to have some fun, splashing and screaming.

From the earliest morning hours the beaches are swarming with people, but they seem almost motionless. Because the heat, the real heat, is another dimension altogether in which time swells, like legs in stockings. Words and sounds change, and trains of thoughts run along different tracks when the real heat descends. The boys no longer play tug-of-war, the girls no longer stroll in pairs or quartets along the shore, showing off their cunning little hats or their striped swimsuits which have fake belts at the waist and leave half their thighs uncovered; no one does daredevil flips off the diving boards on the wharfs. It's too hot to move much in a sea that doesn't even cool you off for long. All prefer to loll in the water like walruses, carrying on slow conversations interrupted now and then by a brief dunk of the head. The big-bellied captains of industry half-sprawled on the wet sand look like so many beached whales, as they chat about business and politics and sleepily read the morning papers.

Gradually, as the hours go by, the sun shows less and less pity. The customary topics of conversation—the events of the day, the winning lottery numbers, the American economic crisis of a few years earlier and the resulting depression, recounted in apocalyptic letters from emigrant relatives—are swept away by the heat, the real heat. People look each other in the face, pale and miserable, from across the street, exchange a slow, wan wave, mouth an appropriate cliché ("Hot enough for you?"), and then trudge on, dragging their feet across the cement. People make dates to meet in the Galleria, as if trying to form disheveled salons under the glass ceilings, in search of a little shade, muggy and unsatisfying though it is, and they talk about how long the heat can last.

A specific body of lore flourishes: buddy, last night just to get a little cool air I slept on the floor; that's nothing, buddy, I went out and slept on my balcony in nothing but my underpants and undershirt, and the mosquitoes practically ate me alive, alive they almost ate me, look here at the bumps I have on my arms. Straw boaters are waved over the face like fans, and young men in two-tone shoes talk down the charms of the young *signorine* who walk past slowly, to spare themselves the effort of attempting to strike up conversation. The many over-weight gentlemen and the many oversized matrons bemoan, in the presence of the heat, the genuine authentic heat, the bygone years when they strolled light-footed, their toes barely touching the ground as they floated along on the feathered wings of lost youth, but they console themselves with the thought that this heat has killed their appetites, even as they eat the fourth gelato of the day to soothe their parched throats.

The outdoor café tables, sheltered under broad white awnings, are the objects of rustic duels, and the winners linger, nursing their drinks with tiny sips while those waiting for a spot to open up observe them with ill-concealed hostility, wishing all manner of painful deaths upon them. The coachmen, waiting in vain for paying passengers, battle for a place in the shade of the buildings lining the piazza, nod off seated in their carriages, mouths open, hats pulled down over their eyes.

The trolleys that rattle and screech up into the hills and down toward the water are loaded with families in search of even a the-oretical whiff of cool air. Sweat and stench prevail inside the trol-leys, and everyone envies the freedom of the street urchins, the Neapolitan *scugnizzi* hanging off the outside of the streetcars in clusters, enjoying a free ride, as naked and dark as African natives, shouting and cheerful as clowns. The driver, snorting in annoyance, will stop the streetcar from time to time and step out to chase them off; the *scugnizzi* scamper away like a flock of swallows, laughing at his threats, calling back insults, only to assault the vehicle as soon as it gets moving again.

When the heat comes, the real heat, it lowers a blanket of silence and fear over the city, because everyone is certain it will never end. Every item of clothing, no matter how light, seems like a thick woolen blanket, intolerable, and dark haloes of sweat soak the cloth under the armpits and on the chest. Forced to wear suits and ties, office clerks walking up and down the stairs of the buildings where they work sigh as they realize they'll have to have their garments washed ahead of time, and they dread the cleaner's bill, while marriageable young women try to go out less often in order to keep the wave the beautician, who made a house call, has set in their hair—for in this heat, the wave will wilt quickly.

People look down from their balconies, scanning the street for the appearance of the iceman, calling out his wares with a shout. The ice will be more expensive than usual and there will be loud angry protests, but no one who can afford it will go without a hunk of cold, to which he will entrust his hopes that sooner or later the heat, this honest-to-goodness heat, will end. The negotiations with the iceman are different from those with any other strolling vendor. In fact, there are no negotiations at all; he knows his customers' need and desire, and he refuses even to stop unless he hears the clinking of coins, in part because he knows that to stop means to allow some of the white gold that he carries in his cart, insulated by blankets and rags, to melt. Once he has received the price demanded, he extracts the block of ice with an iron hook and, before the entranced gazes of the children, cuts off a chunk using a hooked black cleaver, while a *scugnizzo* triumphantly collects the fragments that fall to the ground. Given the weight of the ice, no one will be able to buy it from the upper floors of an apartment building and lower a basket on a rope to haul it up, the way people do with fruit and vegetables; but carrying it back home, up the dark, steep stairs, will be more enjoyable, with that cool bundle in one's arms.

Heat, the real heat, lasts only a few days and, with a few rare exceptions, those few days fall between the beginning and the middle of July. Days without rain and without peace, blasted by a harsh light made milky by a shroud of mist that hovers in midair, like a curse floating over the city. Days in which the elderly become taciturn, their eyes lost in the empty air, with no stories to tell, no complaints about their aches and pains, no venomous criticisms of their neighbors or acquaintances in the *vicolo*. Labored breaths become a sort of lugubrious sound-track; not even monosyllabic responses to the worried questions of their children about how they feel.

Heat, this real heat, sneaks in through the pores and ransacks the rooms of the soul where memories are kept, and old people have more of those than anyone else. Events from long-ago summers will appear before their eyes, smiling faces and forgotten love songs, strolls along the shore of a sea that was even bluer than it is now. Toothless old women with drool on their chins will, in this heat, turn back into tarantella dancers at long-ago parties, waiting for their beloveds to invite them into the shadows of an apartment house doorway, as cozy as any sheltered bower; and old men forced to sit idle for years will once again be sun-bronzed young fishermen, speaking of love to their fair companions in a boat rocking on the water by night, under a moon hotter than the noonday sun. Heat, the real heat, knows how to be treacherous and cowardly, and it takes it out on the weakest members of society, preying on their melancholy.

There are only a few days of heat, real heat. But in those few days the atmosphere changes, and the city becomes another place. It tastes like ice and smells like the sea, but it can also have the black color of death.

Heat, real heat, comes straight from hell.

V

Another twenty steps and he'd see him. Not even thirty yards, as soon as he turned the corner. He drew a breath and quickened his gait.

When he could, he'd take another route, unless that meant unacceptable delays; and if it was absolutely inevitable, then at least he tried to pass by as quickly as he could, to shorten the moment. The moment in which the chilly fingers of suffering would run through his skin and clutch at his heart.

Once he reached the spot he lowered his gaze; his hands in his trouser pockets, a light jacket unbuttoned over a white shirt, the narrow strip of dark fabric secured over his belly with a gold tie clip, his sole concession to an offhand sartorial elegance. If he'd been wearing a hat, he'd have looked exactly like the other young office clerks or businessmen walking the streets of central Naples, forced by work to go out into the terrible heat of that season. But Luigi Alfredo Ricciardi was no office clerk, nor was he a lawyer, though he had studied the law. He was a commissario, an officer of public safety, and he was heading for his office at police headquarters, as he did early every morning.

Along the way, though, someone was waiting for him. Someone who had, at least in his physical form, been taken away some time ago by two overheated city morgue attendants before the sorrowful eyes of a small crowd sadly accustomed to events of this sort: a little boy run over by a trolley. Unfortunately, it happened frequently; orphans arguing over a heel of stale bread, a *scugnizzo* chasing after a rag ball, a child escaping the grasp of a distracted mother. Or any of the countless children who traveled, dangerously and illegally, clinging to some projecting part of the streetcars themselves, until they lost their grip and fell, to be cut in half by the heavy wheels.

And that was exactly what had become of the little boy who was waiting for Ricciardi just inches from the spot where he died. Though he didn't look up, the commissario's doleful eyes received the horrible image of an unharmed face, a head shaved bald to ward off lice, shoulders covered by an oversized smock of a shirt, and arms lopped off clean at the elbows.

The black mouth emitted a gush of blood and the words came, mumbled but still quite clear: *I'm falling, I'm falling, I can't hold on any longer.* A handhold that had failed, arms that lacked strength. The torso, cut in two, was floating in midair and telling Ricciardi that the poor creature hadn't died instantly, that the boy hadn't been spared any suffering.

With a knot in his stomach, Ricciardi broke into what was almost a run, lifting his handkerchief to cover his mouth. God, how unbearable this was. An old tramp, half-asleep in the shade of an apartment building, raised his bleary eyes at the sound of the commissario's quick steps and watched him with unfriendly curiosity; something about that young man in a hurry upset him, and he recoiled against the wall. There are people who can see it in my face, they can see my curse as I go by, thought Ricciardi.

Lately, his misery had been more intense than usual. He couldn't even count on the sweet relief of looking at Enrica through the window. She had vanished, and the only fleeting images that appeared behind the panes of glass in the apartment across the way were those of her family. He couldn't blame her; if anything, rationally, he was happy for her. What could a man like him possibly offer her? Perhaps she'd met someone, or she'd made up her mind not to grant the pleasure of seeing her to a man who lacked the courage to take the initiative.

If you only knew, my love, if you only knew the inferno I have in my heart, how much I wish I could be at your side like any ordinary man, and love you and smile at you and embrace you and make love to you the rest of my life. If only you knew how badly I want to be normal, and have the thousands of worries and petty concerns that everyone else has, and not have to listen to the severed torso of a young boy as it vomits blood onto a street corner.

The young woman's absence left a much bigger hole in Ricciardi's life than he ever would have expected. Even Rosa, who up until Easter had referred to Enrica as a newfound acquaintance in a way that almost seemed to hint at an invitation to the apartment, had stopped talking about her for some time now. Ricciardi had been tempted to ask her why, but now Rosa herself was a source of growing and increasingly urgent concern.

Rosa was not well. More than once he'd caught her leaning against something or other, suffering from a dizzy spell that she stoutly denied, or else opening and closing her right hand as if it had gone to sleep. Now and then she'd sit down and remain seated even when he walked into the room, breaking a habit she'd maintained since Ricciardi was just a child. She dropped things, even light things like a fork, and sometimes she'd just stop in the middle of a sentence, having lost the thread. He had tried to persuade her to go see Bruno Modo, the doctor at Pellegrini Hospital who also served as the medical examiner, one of the very few people the commissario trusted, but she had refused the suggestion so vehemently that Ricciardi was discouraged from pressing the matter. It's completely out of the question, she had told him. Why don't you worry about yourself, you're getting skinnier and paler every day. Sit down right here and make sure you eat every last bite.

It had never occurred to him that he might someday lose Rosa. As far back as he could remember, and even before that, the woman had always been by his side. Much more than his own mother, who had often been sick and had died young. And he couldn't imagine no longer hearing the usual string of complaints, the litany of worries, and scoldings, that his old *tata* unleashed concerning the way he lived and the loneliness he imposed on himself, a loneliness she found absurd. Still, if she was unwilling to see a doctor, there was no way to force her to.

The night before, Rosa had told him that she had sent for her niece Nelide to come help her, as he had so often asked her to do. At least he had gotten her to do that. Perhaps if she could just get some rest she'd get back on her feet and everything would go back to normal.

The temperature was turning red-hot, though it was still early. Out an open window came a woman's well-modulated singing voice. His thoughts jerked him suddenly to Livia, who had once been a singer and had more than once obliged him to take her to the opera. He didn't dislike going out with her; if nothing else, those carefree evenings helped him get his mind off his work, his worries about Rosa and, most of all, Enrica's absence.

He knew that Livia cared for him. She herself had confessed that fact. And Ricciardi wondered why she should choose him, with all the men she could have, wealthy and attractive as she was. Perhaps, he thought to himself as he faced the last stretch of road, it was precisely because he was so uninterested in courting her that she found him intriguing; this trait must have offered a welcome change of pace.

For that matter, he had a clear understanding with Livia: their friendship entailed only evenings at the theater or the movies. No social occasions, no dinners, no aperitifs, no get-togethers. They weren't a couple, nor would they ever be. They shared a few pleasant hours, discussed the show they'd just seen, and made a little light conversation as she accompanied him home in her car; all this, one night every couple of weeks. She asked for nothing more, and he would have been unwilling to offer any more even if she had. The ritual never varied:

her chauffeur would come to police headquarters and hand-deliver an envelope containing the tickets, the time and the date of the show; if he agreed, on the scheduled day the car would come by to pick him up at his office.

He suspected that Rosa disliked Livia, so he avoided mentioning her. As for him, he was well aware of her allure and knew how difficult it was to take his eyes off her magnificent body sheathed in the very latest fashions, off her perfect face, and her eyes, which glittered gleefully; and there was also a certain satisfaction to walking into the theater with Livia on his arm and noticing how his companion attracted the adoring attention of the men and the sullen glares of the women. But if he were ever going to bestow his heart on anyone, if the curse of madness hadn't been laid on him, he would have chosen sweet Enrica, whose beauty was unparalleled, at least in his eyes.

While, in spite of himself, he shuttled, in his mind, from one woman to the other, he fetched up at the entrance to police headquarters, where he found an imposing and familiar bulk dressed in a brigadier's uniform waiting for him in the shade.

"Maione? What are you doing here?"

The man touched the visor of his cap in a rapid salute: "What can you do about it, Commissa'? The holidays have played havoc with the shifts, and I don't mind a little overtime with the way things are these days. I traded shifts with Cozzolino, he's a bachelor and he needs his vacation time to find a girlfriend, though who's going to take him I can't imagine, with that face of his, like a snarling guard dog's. Anyway, it was a good thing, because something happened at the general hospital, a phone call came in just a few minutes ago. I sent Camarda and Cesarano on ahead; and I stayed here to wait for you, because I knew you'd get here early. What do you say, shall we get going?"

VI

The general hospital of the royal university of Naples was at the center of a dense welter of narrow *vicoli*. It had been built on the grounds of an ancient monastery, on the same grid, and it occupied a fairly vast area.

It loomed up unexpectedly, with its high gates, right after a tight curve that, like all the others, seemed to lead into an innocuous little piazzetta which was no doubt going to lead to another narrow lane which would run until it hit another piazzetta and so on, ad infinitum. Ricciardi thought to himself that that's just the way the city had been planned, senselessly, one *vicolo* after another and one piazza after another, as construction spread from the sea toward the hills; then he would find himself face-to-face with one of those aristocratic palazzos, with flower beds arrayed behind an imposing front gate. As he did, it dawned on him that everything had a purpose after all.

Outside the gate stood a small, silent knot of people held back by two custodians. Maione's stature and uniform ensured that the assembly parted widely enough to allow them to pass. The older custodian, a heavyset man with a large mustache and a work shirt a couple of sizes too small, greeted them and without another word turned and started off, waving for them to follow.

They walked down a tree-lined lane that was relatively cool. The flower beds were well tended and the grass had recently been mown. Ricciardi and Maione looked around: the structure consisted of a number of buildings all the same height, four stories plus a mezzanine, in good shape. There were people looking out the windows, some men in white lab coats, several female nurses with white caps. There was a distinctly expectant air, the kind that could only be shattered by the arrival of the police. It was as if their irruption were the signal for the beginning of a theatrical production of sorts, to the enormous relief of the spectators.

Near one of the pavilions, several people were gathered in a circle. Not far away, a single automobile with a black-and-cream paint job stood parked sideways. Maione recognized the officers he'd sent ahead, and summoned one of them over.

"Well, Cesara', here we are. So, what have we got?"

The man walked toward him and snapped a sharp salute: "Someone seems to have fallen. From up there, apparently."

He waved vaguely in the direction of the building. Maione snorted in disgust and said, parroting his subordinate: "Someone seems to have fallen. From up there, apparently. Always sharp as a steel trap, aren't you? Get out of here, go on. Let me find out who I need to talk to if I want any information around here."

They drew closer and saw what lay at the center of the small knot of people. The corpse, facedown, of a man no longer young, to judge from what was possible to see at a glance. He didn't have a jacket on, his shirt was torn at the bottom, and one of his suspenders was unclipped. One of his shoes had come off, and a slightly hiked-up pant leg revealed a beige sock held up by a black garter. Ricciardi nodded his head toward Maione, and the brigadier told Camarda, the other officer, to phone headquarters immediately and tell them to send over the photographer, and to have Dr. Modo come over, if he was on duty, from Pellegrini Hospital.

The people closest to the corpse were two female nurses, one of them in tears, a laborer with a rake in one hand and boots on his feet, a custodian wearing the same kind of work shirt as the man who had walked them over, and a man in a white lab coat. Maione asked them to step back, and moved away with them a short distance: he knew that in the first phase of the on-site investigation, Ricciardi always wanted to be left alone at the scene of the death.

The commissario noted that the position of the corpse was compatible with a fall, probably from the highest possible elevation: the window on the top floor was open and at least seventy feet from the ground. The man must have also taken a bit of a running start, because he'd sailed out past the bushes that lined the edge of the path directly beneath the building's wall. He'd jumped or he'd been thrown. Ricciardi concentrated, then swiveled around sharply.

Off to one side with respect to the location of the corpse from which it had originated, sheltered by the scanty shade thrown by the trees on the far side of the narrow lane, Ricciardi recognized the image of the dead man, standing upright. The torso was askew, twisted away from the pelvis, as if the body had been cut in two; the same impression of a split prevailed as he examined the figure vertically, because one half of the head was virtually intact, while the other half was ravaged by its impact with the ground. The commissario did a preliminary physical inspection of his own, prior to the arrival of the medical examiner. He noted the fractured spinal cord and skull. On the phantom's forehead there was a large wound from which gushed a fountain of bright red blood, bathing the right side of the face, which was crumpled and deformed: the cheekbone was stove in, and instead of a mouth there was a black hole. There was no trace of the eye. The left side of the face, however, displayed a dreamy, almost tender expression: the eyelids were half-closed, the lips parted in a half smile. The incongruity of the thing made for a ghastly effect.

Ricciardi noted that the head was pressed against the ground on its right side; that was caused by the direction of the fall. He shifted his attention back to the image, and for the thousandth time was wounded by the pain of others. The corpse was repeating gently, in a voice little more than a whisper: *Sisinella and love, love and Sisinella, Sisinella and love, love and Sisinella*. The absurd last thought at the end of his fall and the beginning of his death. The commissario ran a hand over his face, which was covered in a veil of sweat, and in spite of the heat was unable to control a shiver.

He went back to Maione, who had in the meantime collected the particulars of the people who had been standing around the corpse a moment earlier. The brigadier made the introductions: "This is Commissario Ricciardi, officer of public safety, and I'm Brigadier Raffaele Maione."

The man with the rake snapped to attention, holding the rake straight at his side as if it were a rifle: "Corporal Vitale Pollio, Signor Commissario. Reporting for duty!"

Maione looked him up and down with a smile: "At ease, corporal! That's just crazy, this guy thinks he's still at the front! Signor Pollio, here, is the gardener. He's the one who found the body."

Pollio turned to the brigadier with a look of confusion.

"Forgive me, Brigadie', but once you've been a soldier, a part of you stays one. I went to war, you know, and life at the front weighs on you like an overcoat. Yes, I was tending to the flower beds over there. I saw what at first I took for a heap of rags. I thought to myself: what are they doing in the middle of the lane, those dirty clothes? Then I went over, and I had my rake with me, just to see if it was something I needed to pick up and haul away. That's when I saw it was a corpse. You know, Commissa', when I was at the front, I had to climb out of the trench to recover them, the dead bodies, so I've seen plenty. I remember one time, after an Austrian attack, at . . ."

Maione broke in firmly: "Yes, Pollio, that's fine, we understand.

And once you'd deduced that it wasn't a pile of dirty rags, what did you do?"

The gardener blinked.

"Excuse me, Brigadie'. I called the custodian immediately, Signor Gustavo, here. And I didn't touch a thing."

Ricciardi spoke to the man in the workshirt, a lean and wiry fellow who kept looking around him, as if he feared the imminent arrival of the enemy troops evoked by Pollio.

"And you intervened, Signor . . ."

"Gustavo Scuotto, at your service, Commissa'. I went outside and saw . . . I saw what had happened. So I went to get someone in the clinic. But rest assured, I never touched a thing either. I thought that maybe . . . that there was a possibility that something could still be done for him."

Ricciardi nodded.

"Who did you call?"

The older of the two nurses stepped forward, a corpulent woman of about forty with a brusque demeanor.

"He called me is who he called. Ada Coppola, Commissa', the ward charge nurse. They always call me for everything, so they called me this time too." She glared at the custodian, who lowered his eyes.

A forceful woman, thought Ricciardi.

"So what did you do, Signora?"

Coppola flexed her muscular arms beneath her ample bosom.

"I went downstairs, I saw this shattered wreck of a body, and it was clear that nothing could be done for him, and that he'd been dead for some time. At that point I reported upstairs."

Maione broke in: "What do you mean, he'd been dead for some time? Who did you report to upstairs? And where upstairs?"

The woman turned on him, speaking harshly: "Don't you see that he's stopped breathing and the blood is dry? I went upstairs and made a phone call from the room he fell from, his office, on the fifth floor."

"From his office? Then you know who he is."

The younger nurse, who hadn't stopped sobbing the whole time, now wailed loudly, earning an angry glare from Coppola, who told Ricciardi: "Forgive me, Commissa', my colleague is still in shock. She's still pretty tenderhearted."

The young woman snapped through her tears: "What does that have to do with it? It's one thing to care for a sick person in a bed, but this . . . this thing here is quite another matter. My name is Maria Rosaria Zupo, Commissa'. I am . . . or I was the nurse assigned to the director. Now I have no idea who I'm assigned to."

The man in the lab coat spoke up, with a sad smile. His features were sharp, his hair was slicked back, and he had a narrow mustache; he was no longer especially young.

"Don't worry, Zupo, we'll find something for you to do. *Buongiorno*, Commissario, I'm Dr. Renato Rispoli, the head assistant of the chair of gynecology in this university. I came to work early, it was still dark out, and I'll tell you the truth, I didn't notice a thing. I came straight in on the ward side."

Ricciardi motioned with his head.

"Do you know who the dead man is?"

Rispoli turned his melancholy eyes toward the little heap of rags and bones that lay on the ground.

"Certainly, Commissario. That is, or rather was, Professor Tullio Iovine del Castello, the director of the chair of gynecology."

VII

Ricciardi decided to wait for the medical examiner's arrival before searching the upper floor and the room from which the professor had presumably fallen. He conferred with Maione, who sent Camarda upstairs to prevent anyone from entering and possibly removing some object or altering the scene. Then the brigadier told the nurses and the custodian they were free to go, since they had already told them everything they knew.

The photographer arrived and began his dance around the corpse. The gardener, Pollio, observed the bursts of light from the magnesium flash and the rapid replacement of bulbs and plates with the ecstatic fascination of a child in an amusement park. Rispoli told him, kindly: "Pollio, you can get back to work, as long as the commissario says it's all right."

Ricciardi nodded and the man delivered a comical military salute, and left.

The doctor commented: "They're good people, Pollio, the custodian, and the nurses. They work with the sick and the dead every day, but Zupo's right: this is quite another matter."

Ricciardi waited long enough to give Rispoli's observation its due, then asked: "What do you think happened here, Doctor? Did he jump? Was it an accident? Or do you think someone pushed him?"

"I have no idea, Commissario. We worked together for many years, but we weren't so close that . . . In other words, I doubt that he'd have confided in me if he'd had any reason to do this kind of thing."

"Had you noticed any changes in his personality in the past few days? I don't know, long silences, moodiness . . . any signs of worry?"

Rispoli gave the questions some thought. Then he said: "No, Commissario. Nothing comes to mind. Tullio was highly respected, a leading light of his profession. He was in charge of the instructional side of one of the most important academic chairs at a medical school that was itself considered top-flight, both in Italy and worldwide. His publications, the research he supervised, they were landmarks in the medical field. He was a successful man, from every point of view."

Ricciardi nodded pensively. He kept his hands in his pockets and his eyes fixed on his interlocutor's face. Behind the man's back, the shade of the corpse went on murmuring his love, over and over, for some woman named Sisinella.

"I imagine he had a family."

Rispoli nodded with a guilty air, as if he'd only just remembered something important: "Certainly, a wife and a daughter. We'll have to inform them."

"Isn't it odd that he should have been here so early?"

The doctor shook his head firmly: "No, Commissario. It was normal for Tullio to stay late, or come in at the crack of dawn. Ours isn't a nine-to-five profession, there are special cases that demand constant close attention. Women, as you know, are unpredictable by nature: and the same holds true in the medical field. Most likely he never even went home last night, that often happens."

Well, he won't be going home now, thought Ricciardi. The Deed, the horrendous phenomenon that poisoned his existence, was a lurking, cowardly enemy. It forced him down twisting, fruitless paths, chasing some last illusory thought that most of the time had nothing at all to do with whoever had helped the deceased along to his death, nor with the instant in which that death had occurred. Tullio Iovine del Castello's last thought was one of love. People kill themselves for love, people kill others for love. Or perhaps he'd simply fallen over the windowsill, as he leaned out with a sigh to gaze on the first star of the morning.

The commissario spoke to Rispoli again: "Please supply Brigadier Maione with all useful information. The professor's address and other essential particulars, his employment history with the university. We'll take care of informing the family."

After Rispoli was gone, Dr. Modo emerged, out of breath, from the lane. His too-long white hair hung down below his hat, and his loosened tie allowed his shirt collar to flutter freely.

"Ah, here you are," he panted, relieved. "This time I really was worried. Are you both all right?"

Ricciardi and Maione exchanged a baffled glance. The brigadier said: "*Buongiorno*, Dotto'. Excuse me, why shouldn't we both be all right?"

"Because your officers don't know how to do their job, that's why! A phone call comes in from the switchboard at police headquarters to the switchboard at the hospital. A nurse comes running to call me just as I walk in, as I'm putting on my lab coat, and she says to me: Dr. Modo, you need to run straight over to the general hospital at the royal university, because Commissario Ricciardi and Brigadier Maione are there. They need you right away."

Maione confirmed: "That's exactly right. And where are we, in fact? At the general hospital."

Modo stared at him, dumbfounded: "And it doesn't occur to you that if some poor wretch gets a phone call of that sort he might naturally assume that you'd been involved in, I don't know, a car crash, for instance? Which might after all be a good thing, because then you'd stop calling me all the time. Then I got here, I asked what ward you were in, and they told me: downstairs in Gynecology. And if I wasn't worried before, I started worrying then."

Ricciardi smirked: "Bruno, you even kid around first thing in the morning, and with this heat. We're here for work. Just like you."

Modo mopped his brow: "I suffer from the heat more than you do. Look at you, natty as always. But of course, I was forgetting, you're a reptile with ice in your veins, you never sweat. To sweat you have to have blood and a heart to pump it. Not you, you just make me run back and forth at all hours. Well, so what have we here?"

Maione gestured, as he moved to one side, toward the corpse on the ground. The photographer was done and was putting his equipment away in his bag. The doctor knelt down and began his inspection. Once again, as he watched him work, Ricciardi admired the delicacy and respect with which he performed his examination: as if those poor remains, crumpled on the ground, were still a living body deserving of care.

Suddenly Modo turned around, visibly shocked: he had turned the corpse's head so that the face was fully in the light.

"Why, this is . . . this is Iovine, the director of the ward."

Ricciardi nodded: "Yes, that's what they told us. Did you know him?"

"Of course I knew him. We're practically the same age, I think he might have been a year or two older than me."

Maione commented, under his breath: "Damn, I would have guessed he was younger."

Modo shot him a venomous glance.

"You worry about yourself, Brigadie', because that gut of yours is going to send you to an early grave, is what it's going to do. We went to medical school about the same time, and occasionally we'd run into each other when he'd come in to do some consultation at the hospital where I was working. We'd say hello, no personal relationship. He was a . . . well, let's just say that he struck me as an ambassador, always standing straight as a board, a bit of a know-it-all. It didn't make me want to be friends with him, is the truth of the matter. Still, poor guy. What an ugly way to go."

He continued his examination for a few more minutes, then he stood up, wiping his hands on his handkerchief. Ricciardi walked over to him.

"Well, Bruno? What can you tell us?"

Modo pushed his hat back off his head in a typical gesture, and scratched his forehead.

"Well, it seems pretty clear. He fell from high up, very high up. I'd guess the top floor, if not the roof. He's broken to bits, even his spinal column, you can see that his pelvis is out of alignment, in at least one place if not two. He landed on his head, and he died on impact. But there is one thing that puzzles me: one of his fingernails is broken. Surgeons take special care of their hands, and in fact his are very nicely groomed. But he has a broken nail, on the ring finger of his right hand. I'll have to look more closely, I'll know after the autopsy, but I'd guess that he tried to grab something. Did he jump, or was he pushed?"

"We still don't know anything. I wanted to wait for you before going upstairs to look for evidence, maybe a suicide note or signs of a struggle. Could you tell me, broadly speaking, when it might have happened?"

Modo slipped both thumbs in the belt loops of his trousers. He looked as if he were making up his mind whether or not to go out for a sail in a boat.

"Well, it's hot out. Very hot. And it was hot last night, too. Hard to establish the exact time, but I'd say no later than midnight."

"So not this morning?"

"The hypostatic marks on the stomach don't lie. It must have happened late at night."

Ricciardi wondered how a man could fall out a window onto

a lane in a general hospital, fail to go home to sleep, and have nobody notice, either at his place of work or in his family.

He turned to Modo once again: "Please, Bruno, try to get the autopsy done quickly."

The doctor snorted.

"Well, surprise, surprise, you're in a hurry. Nothing's ever leisurely with you and the good old brigadier. Fine, I'll let you know when I'm ready."

He turned to go, but Ricciardi called after him.

"Bruno, one last thing, and this one is personal. Rosa, my *tata*, you know . . . has been suffering from some health problems for a while now. She forgets things, she tends to drop things."

"She drops things? Always with the same hand?"

"I couldn't say for sure, but that sounds right."

"Does she have dizzy spells?"

Ricciardi tried to remember.

"Sometimes she has to sit down. She doesn't tell me much, she doesn't want me to worry and she refuses to be seen by a doctor."

"How old is she?"

"She recently turned seventy-two. If sometime when you have a minute, you could come see me, some evening . . . pretend you're just dropping by for a visit and take a look at her, I'd be grateful. You know that you're the only one I trust."

"And that's my cross to bear, unfortunately. All right, I'll let you know the minute I have an evening free. From what you tell me, I'd say that your Rosa has some circulatory problem. Not to be taken lightly, especially at her age. And trying to keep up with you, she must be leading a miserable life, the poor woman. Especially now that you've started up with the high-society set . . ."

Modo was referring to a chance encounter at a movie house, when Ricciardi and Livia had turned around to see him sitting in the row behind them, with an irritating smirk on his lips.

Embarrassed, the commissario shrugged.

"What high society are you talking about, I had to keep a promise . . . Let's just say I lost a bet."

"Tell me the name of the gambling den where if you lose a bet they force you to go out with a woman like her, and I'll go lose my whole salary there. The widow Vezzi gets more and more beautiful, and that night on your arm she was radiant. You were the most envied man in the movie theater, including the actors kissing actresses."

Ricciardi cut his friend off.

"All right, I get it, let's get back to work. The morgue attendants are on their way, and I'll have them take the corpse to the hospital; and remember, I'll expect you to come by sometime to take a look at Rosa." He turned to Maione: "Come on, Raffaele, let's go upstairs and take a look around."

The brigadier sighed: "At your orders, Commissa'. The doctor certainly has a point: with this belly and in this heat, the ideal thing is to climb four flights of stairs."

VIII

Inside the pavilion there was an unnatural silence. As he climbed the broad steps on his way up to the top floor, Ricciardi guessed that the place must normally be much livelier; but that morning the building seemed deserted. The doors lining the hallways were nearly all closed, and you could barely hear the occasional murmur.

They crossed paths with a nun carrying a metal container; Maione raised his fingers to his cap and the nun replied by bowing her head, but continued hurrying down the stairs. On the last landing, they found Rispoli waiting for them with the young female nurse, who had finally stopped crying, though her eyes were still red.

Rispoli said: "Unfortunately the news is starting to get around. When something of this sort happens, people get upset, it's inevitable. Come this way, please. Allow me to lead the way."

They turned down a hallway at the end of which stood a desk and a large closed door. The nurse said: "That's my desk. I greet people and send them in as soon as it's their turn."

Ricciardi pointed at the door: "That's the professor's office, right? Has anyone been in here since you arrived?"

"No, Commissario. I didn't even go in. It's too upsetting. I left last night at ten o'clock and the door was shut, and that's the way I found it when I came in at six this morning, after I saw . . ."

She was about to start crying again, but mastered the impulse.

Ricciardi asked her: "Did you say goodnight, yesterday,

before leaving? Did he speak to you? Did he seem agitated to you, or worried, or . . ."

"No, he was the same as always. The director . . . wasn't a man who talked a lot, and understandably he didn't confide in me. I asked him if he needed me, whether he'd be staying much longer, and he told me: No, Maria Rosaria, you can go. I'm expecting someone. And I left."

Maione perked up: "Expecting someone? He didn't say who?"

"No. That's all he said: I'm expecting someone."

Ricciardi nodded.

"So he had an appointment. After ten o'clock, which is the time when you left, Signorina. Was that normal for him, to receive visitors at such a late hour?"

Zupo seemed uncomfortable; from time to time she'd shoot a glance at Rispoli, who remained impassive.

"The director worked very hard, you know. Basically he was always here. So yes, sometimes he'd have someone come in very late. And not just for professional matters, friends would come too. When you stay in the office all day, that happens."

"I understand. All right, let's go in."

On the other side of the door was a very spacious room; the most noteworthy piece of furniture was the desk, a veritable mahogany catafalque, elaborately inlaid, a venerable antique that emanated power and prestige from every ounce of its bulk. Behind it stood an office chair with a broad backrest; to afford ease of access to the work surface, the chair stood atop a dais. Sitting in front of the desk were two more chairs; behind them was a bookshelf loaded with volumes that occupied the whole wall. Next to it was an examination table that terminated in a pair of stirrups. Ricciardi, pointing to the equipment, asked the nurse: "Did the director examine patients here?"

The nurse shrugged: "Not usually, there are rooms in the

wards downstairs for that; but sometimes, if he wanted to get a quick impression, yes, he might."

Facing the desk, against the wall with the office door, were a sofa and two small armchairs and a coffee table. On the remaining wall was the window.

It was wide open. There was no wind, and clearly there had been none during the night, because there were no signs of disarray on the desktop, which was piled with papers. Ricciardi walked over to the window. The sill was low, but still it seemed unlikely that the doctor had accidentally tripped over it and fallen out because he was himself so short. He'd have had to climb onto the sill intentionally, and it would have taken some effort, because there were no step stools; unless someone had moved the step stool after using it.

Maione went over to the desk; Ricciardi walked toward him with a quizzical glance.

"No, Commissa'. Unless I'm mistaken, I don't see any letters of farewell. But he might have left them somewhere else."

Ricciardi noticed that at one corner of the table sat an object that seemed out of place amongst the papers, folders, and books. A small, closed case. He picked it up and opened it. Inside was a gold ring, an exquisite piece of craftsmanship, with a large diamond in the center. The commissario moved over to the sunlight pouring in through the window and looked down: the drop had to be more than sixty-five feet. The morgue attendants were loading the pine crate containing the remains of Tullio Iovine del Castello, director of the chair of gynecology at the royal university, into the van. All that remained of him now was a dark stain on the ground and, for Ricciardi's exclusive personal use, a dolorous image that kept repeating a phrase, in all likelihood senseless.

Riccardi lifted the ring into the light and saw that there was something engraved on the interior, but the writing was too small. He looked around and, as Maione continued searching for notes that might contain a suicide's last thoughts, he spotted a magnifying glass next to a roll of blotting paper.

He picked up the lens and was finally able to read: "Maria Carmela." He turned to Rispoli: "What is the director's wife's name? Her given name, I mean."

Rispoli seemed uneasy. Perhaps he didn't like seeing people rummaging through his boss's office, or maybe it was something else.

"Signora Iovine del Castello's first name is Maria Carmela."

"In that case," Maione added, as he went on opening desk drawers, "in a few days it will be her name day. Today is the 8th; the feast of the Madonna del Carmine, Our Lady of Mount Carmel, is the 16th."

Ricciardi said: "And this is her name day gift. Her name is engraved in it."

Maione, who had just pulled open the last drawer, said: "And here's another one, Commissa'."

He pulled out a case identical to the first. Ricciardi opened it and found an identical ring, with a slightly larger diamond. He held it up to the light and with the aid of the lens, read: "Sisinella." Bingo, he said to himself. So that's who you were thinking about when you hit the ground, Mr. Director.

He turned to look at Rispoli, who was staring at the floor, displaying an incipient bald spot on the top of his head. Nurse Zupo was blushing like a schoolgirl caught smoking in a school bathroom.

"Signorina," said Ricciardi, "go ahead back to your desk and close the door behind you. We'll talk again soon."

Once the woman had left, he turned to the physician: "Doctor, spare us some pointless effort. Were you aware of some . . . particular friendship on the director's part?"

"No, Commissario. I didn't know anything about any of the director's friendships. I only spent time with him in his working environment, here at the institute, and I know nothing about his life outside of here."

Maione was done searching the desk and had moved on to the bookshelves; the temperature was rising by the minute, and the brigadier huffed and puffed, occasionally mopping his brow.

"Do you know of anyone who might have held any grudges against him? Any reasons to want to do him harm?"

Rispoli hesitated. His mustache quivered, as if the doctor were about to reply, but then he said nothing.

Ricciardi said: "I beg of you, Doctor. If we were to discover that you were hiding something from us, we'd have no choice but to report you for failure to cooperate with the law."

Rispoli thought quickly. Then he said: "The work we do here is strange, you know, Commissario. We're physicians and we're teachers, we have to work with sick people, and what we try to do doesn't always work out the way we hope. It's hard to explain to others. People think that, because we're at a university, everything's always going to turn out all right, but in fact . . ."

Ricciardi waited. Rispoli went on: "I'm not telling you anything that isn't public knowledge, nothing that didn't happen in front of witnesses. Last month the director had to perform a particularly challenging operation, because of complications that ensued following a primiparous—a first—childbirth. I was present during the operation, and I can assure you that every step was taken to save the newborn's life as well as the mother's but . . . I'm sorry to say that the woman didn't survive. We did save the life of the baby, a little girl. The husband . . . From time to time, faced with great grief and sorrow, people say things that they'd otherwise never even think. The man tried to attack the director. He told him that . . ."

Ricciardi pressed him: "What did he tell him?"

Rispoli finished his sentence all in a rush: "He swore that he'd kill him."

IX

You swore to me, Rosine'. You swore an oath to me. And an oath is something you can never break. When you swear an oath, that's a promise you have to keep.

You swore to me, swore you'd never leave me. Do you remember the first time you said it? No? Because I do. We were in Posillipo, on that narrow little beach. It was hot, just like it is now. So, so hot. But who ever noticed the temperature, hot or cold, when the two of us were together?

And the moon was out, that night. I come from a family of fishermen so I know it, when the moon is out. When the moon makes that highway of silver down the middle of the sea, and the city lights seem like so many stars fallen to earth, and it doesn't matter that they've fallen because there are so many, many more in the sky above. That night, Rosine', there was no one on that beach but you and me. I remember every single one of our kisses. My heart was banging away in my chest like windows swinging in a high wind, like waves slapping against the hulls of the boats, *thump thump thump*. Do you remember, Rosine'? Of course you remember. You were thirteen years old. And I was fourteen.

I never let my hands wander down between your legs. You weren't just some girl to have a good time with. You were the one I wanted to spend the rest of my life with. And you knew that, you knew that what was between us would never end. Everyone in the neighborhood understood that you belonged to me and I belonged to you. Even though my power and my strength grew as I grew older; even though people came to me, little by little, more and more, in search of justice and respect, and you became more and more beautiful. Yes, everyone understood that you were my woman and I was your man, and no one even thought of laying eyes on either one of us.

Do you remember the time, Rosine', when some guy from another neighborhood saw you coming back from the fountain with your girlfriends, loaded down with freshly washed laundry, laughing that laugh of yours that always turned my insides upside down and inside out? Do you remember how, since he didn't know who you were, he walked right up to you, and your girlfriends looked at him, terror on their faces, because they knew exactly what was happening? Do you remember that a *scugnizzo* who was playing nearby came running to get me, and not five minutes later I was there with ten of my friends? And how he ran, I can still see it, with his shirt untucked, and the blood from where I'd stabbed him dripping from his hand. And if he hadn't run for his life he would have been lying dead on the ground, even though you were begging me not to hurt him, because he hadn't done a thing to you. And before nightfall that very day his father, his uncles, and he himself with a bandaged hand had all come to me, to beg for forgiveness and mercy. Do you remember that, Rosine'?

Everything, everything I've ever done in my life I did for you, Rosine'. The business, the apartment, the respect of my friends. Everything. For the dreams we dreamed together, side by side overlooking the water, that night I tasted the flavor of your mouth for the first time, the flavor that poisons me tonight, with the same moon in the sky, and the same mute stars gathering to weep with me. All of this, because of the oath you swore that night. We were children, but your voice was a woman's voice. *I'm not going to leave you, Peppi'. I'll never leave you.*

Oaths are meant to be kept, Rosine'. Oaths are serious

business. If you fail to keep an oath, you make a mockery of respect. And respect is the basis of life.

Do you remember the day of our wedding, Rosine'? You were twenty years old. The sun, the sea, and the green of the hills rising before my eyes—none of these are enough to say how beautiful you were that day. It would take the sky reflected in the water, shattering into glittering sparks so they do harm to the eyes and good to the heart, it would take the calm mountain, resting and watching, it would take the trees tossing their branches in the breeze as if to applaud, and the waves breaking white on the rocks to say just how beautiful you were. The neighborhood girls insisted on being your ladies-in-waiting, you were the princess about to become a queen, and they walked one step behind you. And they were laughing in the sunshine when they arrived at the little church of Mergellina, by the sea, the one with the painting of the dragon with a woman's head, the place you had chosen to tell me yes. I was waiting, uncomfortable in a suit I'd never worn, and I was thinking about my father who I'd never met, my father who died at sea, and I was also thinking that I would never, never again be as happy as I was then.

I'll tell you today, Rosine', that you broke the oath you swore that night by the sea: I'd never seen anything as beautiful as your eyes and your smile, as you arrived with the court of your girlfriends at the little church with the woman-headed dragon. And we swore once more, before God, that we'd never leave each other.

An oath is something you never break, Rosine'.

And that night, do you remember that night? I thought I knew everything. My father's brother had taken me up to that place where they teach you. But I didn't know a thing. Your hands, my hands, our skin. With the moonlight pouring in through the window, the moon that had stood by us as our godmother, the same moon. You gave me life, smiling even through the pain, life, and tears of joy. And I wept too, Rosine'. Me, Peppino the Wolf, the boss of the quarter at just twenty-five; Peppino the Wolf, the man who incited respect and terror; Peppino the Wolf wept that night into his pillow, while you slept, happy in my embrace, your lips curving into the half smile of the woman you had become. And while you slept, I chased after the fears of the future. When a man is too happy, he cries, Rosine'. Now that you're gone, now that you've broken your oath, I can tell you.

What good is love, Rosine'? Can you tell me what good love is? Why be happy, if after happiness comes despair? What is a year worth, a miserable year of light, if after that you have to spend the rest of your life in darkness?

Do you remember when you told me, Rosine'? Do you remember how long it had been since the day at the church with the woman-headed dragon and the sun that shone in your face, since the night with the moonlight and tears of happiness? Two months, that's how long. Two months exactly.

And one night, when I came home from a day of hard work, so tired I could barely stand, you took my hand and you put it on your belly. And then you told me: this is what love's good for. I looked heaven right in the face. And I could hear my heart in my ears, *thump thump thump*, like I had that night by the sea when I was fourteen, and that day in front of the church. But I'll never hear it again, my heart. My blood, yes.

Those months flew by. I felt like a god, and I said to myself: I can never die. I can never, ever die. Because I have to take care of my flesh and blood, and if I'm dead I can't do that. I can't do what my father did, when he went to sea one night to keep me from starving and never returned, and I, just a year old, never saw him and can't even remember him stroking my head, and I look at the one yellowing picture of him that I possess, with a round hat and a long mustache, standing next to the chair in which my *mammà* is sitting, no more than a girl, with me in her arms. I've devoured it, that portrait. I can never die, I told myself in those months.

Your labor pains began early, too early, a full month before your time had come. Your fear, my despair; I ran back and forth, I went to get the doctor, the one who comes down into the *vicoli* with his black bag in hand, and I took him by the collar: Dotto', tell me who the best one is, the best doctor in town. Tell me, or I swear as God is my witness I'll gut you like a fish. He saw in my eyes that I meant what I said. And quick as a flash, without taking a breath, he gave me the name of the doctor who was better than all the others, none other than the boss of all the doctors who teach at the university.

I waited outside his gate for two days. Two days, then I saw him, driving a black-and-cream car, wearing gold-rimmed spectacles. I stopped him. I talked to him. At first he snorted impatiently, he told me he didn't have the time. Then he too looked in my eyes and understood. Professo', I told him, there are no problems, no problems with money or anything else. But if you tell me no, *then* there are going to be problems, and they're all going to be yours.

Do you remember when he came to our home, Rosine'? All the people standing in silence outside our *basso*. His car could barely even make it through the *vicolo*. He said: everyone out, and I left the apartment and only my *mamma* and yours stayed behind with you. Then they called me, and I went back in.

He told me that the situation was difficult, but that it could be solved. He told me that he'd take care of things, but that it wouldn't be cheap. He gave me a figure, and it was a year's salary, but what the hell did I care? All right Professo', I told him. Do what you need to do.

I took you every day, Rosine', do you remember? Every day. I'd filled the inside of the van with straw and cotton, because the professor said it was important for you to lie down, that you should never get up. And then I carried you up the stairs in my arms; I'm strong, you know it, and you were light, even with the baby in your body you were light, Rosine', and pale, and still you smiled, and when you smiled you were like that time on the beach at Posillipo, and you made the sun come out, even in the middle of the night, Rosine'.

The professor would examine you in his office, on that reclining chair with stirrups. That room was the antechamber to hell, as far as I was concerned. He never said a word, he just shook his head no and said nothing. Nothing ever scared me in my life, Rosine', I'm Peppino the Wolf. But that white face, with the double chin and the spectacles—it terrified me.

Then one night, Rosine', the blood began to flow. Your blood, and so much of it, it seemed like liter after liter to me, and the bed was dripping blood onto the floor. I took you straight to the general hospital. I didn't want to leave you, so I sent two of my boys to get him, but the professor wasn't home. No one knew where he was. Your blood kept flowing, pouring down, and my boys turned the city upside down, and this worthless man was nowhere to be found. You were white as a sheet. You said to me: Peppi', my baby girl. Because you knew it was a girl. And you fell asleep.

They found the car up in Vomero, no less. Near the new apartment houses. It had been five hours since I took you there, to the general hospital. Five hours, and the doctor on duty, just a kid, didn't know what to do; he was sobbing with fear, because he could see my face, and he ran back and forth with armfuls of bandages.

He showed up in the end, his collar buttoned all askew, his double chin trembling. He was with his whore while you were falling asleep, you understand that, Rosine'? With his whore. If not for his new car, we'd never have found him at all.

After two hours he came out of the operating room, dripping

with your blood. He looked down at the floor. He said nothing.

And behind him came the nurse, and she had the baby in her arms.

You know when you're losing your mind, Rosine'. You know it because the future vanishes from your head. You look ahead, and where there were once days and nights and months and years, now you see nothing. All it takes is an instant, and suddenly there's nothing. They say it's like dying, and maybe that's right. After all, what's death, if not when they take away your future?

For me it was like waking up in hell. And again I heard my heart in my ears, *thump thump thump*. Then it stopped. And it hasn't beaten since.

I don't remember what I did. Or what I said either, for that matter. They had to take her out of my arms, that much they told me, and it took two male nurses, an assistant, the custodian, and three of my own men to do it. I remember the little baby wailing. God, how I hated that baby. The baby and he, the professor, had taken my future away. They were in on it together, the devil himself had sent them both to carry me down to hell.

I went into the operating room.

The place looked like a slaughterhouse, there was blood everywhere. On the operating table were your flesh, your bones, but not you. If the moon had been out, maybe you would have stood up and smiled at me. But there was no moon that night, and there never will be again.

I swore an oath, Rosine'. I swore an oath. Foaming at the mouth, my eyes bulging out of their sockets, the veins standing out on my neck. I swore an oath, with all my body and all my soul, but without the heart that you'd taken away with you. You broke your oath, Rosine'. You swore that you would stay with me for the rest of our lives, that we'd grow old together. And you broke that promise.

I spent two days locked indoors. Not sleeping, not eating, not even thinking. Two days, because the Wolf doesn't sleep or eat when he's thirsty for blood. And after two days I came out.

My mother was there. With the little girl. Outside the door, for two days, they'd never once stopped crying, grandmother and granddaughter. I came out. My mother knows me, and she took a step backward. She read the death in my face.

I went over to her. I don't know what I wanted to do, Rosine'; I reached out my hand. I touched her, and the little baby stopped crying.

She felt my hand on her swaddling cloth and she stopped crying.

The air outside stood still, not even a fly buzzed; you could hear Crazy Antonietta, you remember her, Rosine'? The one who sings all the time, even at night, who lives at the end of the *vicolo*. Hers was the only voice that could be heard. '*Dimme, dimme a chi pienze, assettàta . . .*'

I looked at her, Rosine'. Just once, I looked at her. She has a nose, a tiny little button of a nose, exactly like yours. Do you remember, Rosine', when I used to pretend I was hunting for your nose, that was so small I couldn't find it? The baby has a nose like yours. Just like yours.

You swore that oath, Rosine'. You made a promise and you broke it. I swore an oath, too. And oaths aren't something you break.

Her nose, Rosine'. You ought to see her. She has an adorable little button nose.

You ought to see her.

X

Sitting at her vanity, Livia was brushing her hair and absentmindedly singing

There once was a Vilia, a witch of the wood,
A hunter beheld her alone as she stood!
The spell of her beauty upon him was laid,
He looked and he longed for the magical maid!

There'd been a long period during which singing had been an important part of her life. From her earliest childhood, in the quiet city of Pesaro, Livia's voice had grown up with her, turning rich and nuanced. As her voice grew, so did her beauty. Her parents, wealthy aristocrats, quickly realized that, given the varied talents that had been bestowed upon their daughter, who seemed every day more like a princess in a fairy tale, the sleepy little city on the Adriatic coast would be too small for her; and so they packed her off to Rome to study under an aunt who was an opera singer.

It was then that singing became her passion and her profession. As a contralto, Livia toured the world, embarking on an extremely promising career. Then she met Arnaldo Vezzi, and she had sung no more.

Certain men, Livia thought to herself as she continued to brush her hair, burn everything they touch to the ground. They're like uncontrollable fires. Certain men cannot have anything but themselves in life. Vezzi was a genius, perhaps the greatest tenor of his time, and a genius's wife couldn't have a career of her own, or even a personality of her own. She had to be the wife of a genius and nothing more: smile, be beautiful, and keep her mouth shut.

But Vezzi's life had ended as perhaps he deserved, with his throat cut in a theater dressing room, there, in that city whose torrid heat was now pouring in through her open window. And it was in that same city that she had decided to live.

Of course that was strange, and she realized it. Some of her girlfriends, in the phone calls from Rome during which they updated her on the latest gossip from the highest social circles, circles in which Livia had once traveled and which she didn't miss in the slightest, had informed her that this decision of hers had generated its fair share of bafflement.

As she sang, she reconstructed the chain of ideas that had led her subconscious mind to select that aria:

For a sudden tremor ran,
Right thro' the love-bewilder'd man,
And he sigh'd as a hapless lover can
A never known shudder
Seized the young hunter,
Longingly he began quietly to sigh!
"Vilia, O Vilia! The witch of the wood,
Would I not die for you, dear, if I could!"

Not a romanza for a contralto, but for a soprano. And it wasn't from an opera, but an operetta. Sung by Hanna Glawari, Franz Lehár's *Merry Widow*, from the start of the second act.

"The Merry Widow."

Livia knew perfectly well that that had become her nickname in the drawing rooms of her new city, where her arrival had caused an uproar. The fact that she had refused to dress in mourning, in spite of her recent loss, had caused a scandal.

The protocol of grief was a rigorous one. The first year, black dresses and hats, with no ornamentation of any kind, except for a horrible string of beads in dark wood, with the addition of a black veil for the first six months; no jewelry except for simple earrings, best if they were pearl; in the summer, white with black accessories; no luncheons or dinners, no theater, no movies, no concerts. In the second year, a few small concessions: tea was acceptable, and some color could be added to one's dress, provided it was relatively drab.

Livia thought it was awful that tradition should force a woman to sacrifice two years of her life just because her husband had gotten himself killed, and that it was unbelievable that the loss of a child wasn't treated in a similar way. When diphtheria had taken her infant son Carletto six years earlier, and she herself had felt as if she were dead inside, no one had expected her to wear black; the death of a newborn baby didn't call for mourning, perhaps because it was such a common occurance.

After Arnaldo's murder, she hadn't felt it necessary to observe the appalling local customs for even a day. After all, they hadn't been husband and wife for years. They were just two strangers bound by habit and convenience, by his prominent social standing and her beauty, which he showed off like a trophy. Thinking back, Livia was disgusted with herself, with her willingness to live like that.

The merry widow, then. With her fashionable clothes, her valuable jewelry, the elegance of her lithe, feline gait that caught so many eyes. The merry widow, whose entrance into her box in the Teatro San Carlo was greeted with an intense silence, followed by a sudden buzz of conversation that rose like a tide. The merry widow, who smiled at everyone but confided in no one.

Many men claimed, as they chatted in salons and foyers, that they had enjoyed her charms, but they were all considered braggarts because none of them had been seen out and about with her, and none of them could claim to have seen the interior of her lovely new apartment on Via Sant'Anna dei Lombardi.

But now someone claimed to have run into her on the arm of a strange fellow with green eyes. And that someone had investigated further, and the rumor had circulated through word of mouth, much as the flames might leap from a burning curtain to the wallpaper. The green-eyed fellow was a certain Commissario Ricciardi, an officer of public safety, no less.

Livia was certain that this subject was the talk of the town in the most exclusive cafés. She didn't mind it, either, because those green eyes had been the very reason she had moved to this town.

After a lifetime of watching men come as soon as she called, she found the role of suitor strangely intriguing. To hang on a man's lips, to try to fathom his thoughts and foresee his wishes, was something absolutely new for her.

It was hardly easy. Ricciardi was a tough nut to crack. When she was with him, Livia felt as if she could hear a sort of buzz, a background noise that spoke of memories or perhaps of regrets, of ancient sorrows. Livia didn't rule out the possibility that these regrets concerned another woman, but from that point of view she feared no one. She was Livia Lucani, not just any woman. She'd turned the heads of princes and cabinet ministers; for two weeks a Florentine count had flooded her hotel room with bouquets of roses. She wasn't about to be defeated by a phantom.

Moreover she sensed that, even if he didn't show it, Ricciardi enjoyed being with her. When they discussed a play or a movie they'd watched together, she glimpsed a flicker of interest and a tranquil enjoyment otherwise absent in those eyes the color of waves crashing onto a rocky shoal. The man was beginning to thaw.

After that November night last year, there had been nothing

more between them. It seemed a dream, when she thought back on it. The rain, his fever. His pain, his hands, his shivering. The enchantment. Who could say if it had really happened at all?

For the first time in her life she had imposed upon herself an abstinence that, in the full maturity of her body and her heart, weighed on her. But if a woman is in love, she's hardly willing to settle.

"Vilia, O Vilia, my love and my bride!"
Softly and sadly he sigh'd.

Standing at the door to her bedroom, holding an armful of fresh linen, Clara the housekeeper stood listening raptly. Livia saw her in the mirror and gave her a level, inquisitive look.

The young woman couldn't contain herself.

"Signo', I can't help myself, I have to tell you: you are marvelous when you sing!"

Livia burst out laughing: "Oh, come on, Clara . . . I thought I was singing to myself, I didn't even realize that . . ."

"What are you talking about, Signo'? People in this neighborhood come to the windows of the buildings across the way to listen to you! Don't you realize what a stupendous voice you have? If I had a voice like yours I'd do just like the goldfinches do: I'd sing and never stop."

"Thank you, my dear. Thank you. It's been so long since I sang that I'm out of practice. I loved to sing, when I was young. But now that time is gone . . ."

Clara interrupted: "Are you kidding? I've never heard a voice like yours. And in this city we all sing from morning till night, and even from night till morning. You know what we like to say here? That a heart in love or a heart in despair has no choice but to sing. It can't do without."

A heart in love, thought Livia. A heart in love has no choice but to sing. That's why when I was with Arnaldo I lost all desire to sing. A heart in love.

She turned to look at her housekeeper, who was now making the bed: "You know what I say? Let's give a party. A party, in celebration of the wonderful summers that you have here."

"Signo', I've always thought it was a deadly sin to have an apartment like this, with a drawing room that opens out onto a terrace, and never have anyone over."

Livia stood up and clasped the young woman's hands in hers: "Yes, a wonderful party under the stars. We'll invite two hundred people. I want everyone to be there. And we'll have the piano moved out onto the terrace: you say that the people who live around here like to hear me sing, no?"

"Of course they do, Signo', it's all they can do to keep from clapping, when you're done."

Livia broke into a little dance step: "We'll have a masquerade party. Let's think of a theme, something fun, I want everyone to be happy. What theme can we come up with? Help me out."

Clara thought it over, wrinkling her nose in comic concentration. Then she said: "Why don't we pick the sea, Signo'? Here, for us, summer means the sea."

Livia was delighted: "You're a genius, Clara. The sea. Nothing could be better. And once again I'll sing in public. We'll call a maestro, I need to practice, I can't come off looking like a fool. I want my audience to be amazed. It's going to be a wonderful night. And I'm going to introduce the man I desire to everyone who attends. You said it yourself, didn't you? A heart in love has to sing. I have to sing."

Clara was caught up in Livia's happiness.

"Signo', listen, you have to sing a song with the words of our land, a song we can understand. A serenade, a tarantella, something that when the people hear it they'll say: ah, the signora sings like an angel. An angel in love."

"Yes, Clara, you're right. I have to sing a song that everyone, absolutely everyone understands. Even those who pretend to be deaf. It has to be an enchanting song. And I know just where to get it."

She went to her wardrobe. What she needed was an outfit that would take people's breath away: in that garment, the merry widow would dance her waltz.

XI

Not even the heat could distract Lucia Maione from her worries as she walked briskly toward the market.

A few nights earlier, from the darkness of the hallway, she'd spied on her husband as he sat at the kitchen table. The light of a candle cast a large shadow of his silhouette on the far wall. He was drenched in sweat, an undershirt covered his chest, and his head was bent over a sheet of paper on which, Lucia felt certain, he was adding up columns of numbers.

She knew that because the same scene always repeated itself as the end of the week and payday drew near. She knew it because the following morning she would extract the sheet of paper from the trash and read it: always the same numbers.

Always the same money.

After the very last of the children had been trundled off to bed and fallen asleep, he would tell her to go to bed, that he was going to have a last espresso and then he'd join her: he just had some work matters he needed to think about. Lucia would pretend to retire and then, barefoot and silent, she'd tiptoe to the kitchen door and watch her husband worrying.

Until the government had decided to cut salaries, a year and a half earlier, they'd been living comfortably. They weren't wealthy, but they could afford to go out to the park for a stroll on Saturday afternoons and buy a spumone for the children, and once a month the whole family went to the movies. Now even the supplemental payments for especially large families weren't enough to make ends meet.

Raffaele didn't talk about it. Every morning he gave her as much as she needed to buy groceries without showing any sign of worry, but Lucia knew perfectly well what was going through his mind, what he kept to himself to spare her the anxiety.

She tried to be as frugal as possible, but the kids were at the age when they were as ravenous as wolf cubs, and God be praised they were all growing up hale and healthy, constantly outgrowing their clothing, which meant she had to test the limits of her remarkable skills as a seamstress and take in outfits to fit the smaller children as their elders grew bigger. She felt a pang in her heart when she saw how much Giovanni, at sixteen, resembled Luca and how proud the boy was to wear the clothing of his older brother, who had been killed in the line of duty. Still, she inevitably had to buy some new outfits, and that always brought her face to face with the harsh reality of constantly rising prices. And so Lucia was forced on long journeys to the market, where there were savings to be had. She always returned home loaded down like a mule; sometimes she made the older children come with her—they always saw the trip as an exciting adventure, which cheered her up.

Then there was Benedetta.

The girl had been orphaned by the brutal murder of her parents, a murder committed by her only living relative, one of her mother's sisters. She was an only child, and Raffaele, in a surge of sorrow and pity, had brought her home at Christmas; now they had begun the proceedings to adopt the child. She was wonderful. Benedetta and their eldest daughter Maria were practically the same age and had become inseparable. And even if that meant that there was now another mouth to feed, and another small body growing with dizzying speed to be clothed and shod, they would never, because of the money, have given up the opportunity to give that marvelous creature a family of her own; she'd already suffered too much in her short life.

Lucia slowed to a halt. Before her eyes the picture of her husband's broad shoulders appeared to her, as he sat in the dim light of the kitchen, and those shoulders rose and fell in a sigh, a sign that meant once again the figures didn't add up.

Raffaele subjected himself to endless overtime, taking on shifts for colleagues who were bachelors or well-to-do. He was killing himself with work, and no one knew better than she did, she who loved him and knew him well, how little of himself he held back in the daily battle against the wrongdoers who infested the city.

It had been, from the very beginning, his way of reacting to Luca's death, Luca who had decided to become a policeman just like him: even more honest, even more inflexible, even more attentive, even more tireless. But now it wasn't just because of his mission that her husband was working so hard, it was also so that his family could live better.

When Raffaele had stood up, gently pushing back the chair, and gone out onto the balcony, Lucia had taken advantage of the opportunity to peek at the sheet of figures that lay on the table with a pencil stub. As always, it contained a list, laid out in her husband's large, neat handwriting:

Bread, 12 kilos: 16 lire.
Pasta, 4 kilos: 9 lire and 50 cents.
Rice, 1 kilo: 1 lira and 50 cents.
Milk, 5 liters: 11 lire.
Potatoes, 5 kilos: 2 lire.
Meat, 1 kilo and a half: 10 lire.
Anchovies, 2 kilos: 7 lire and 50 cents.
Salt cod, 1 kilo and a half: 3 lire and 50 cents.
Eggs, 1 dozen: 4 lire and 20 cents.
Fruit and greens, 15 kilos: 15 lire.

Olive oil, half a liter: 2 lire and 60 cents.
Sugar, a quarter kilo: 1 lira and 60 cents.
Coffee, 150 grams: 1 lira and 90 cents.
TOTAL WEEKLY EXPENSES
86 LIRE AND 30 CENTS.

On top of which, Lucia thought to herself, you had to add sixty lire for the landlord and ten for the weekly rate for electricity and heating. Plus at least thirty lire more for various expenses: cotton, clothing, notebooks, medicine. Too much.

Too much, my poor love.

She'd looked up at Raffaele, who stood looking out at the quarter dotted with streetlamps. In the distance she could hear a man and woman fighting and, closer in, the sound of a piano playing. In the heat, windows opened to let out life and all its passions.

In the silence of the apartment, which was broken only by the regular breathing of the children in their bedrooms, Lucia decided that she wasn't going to stand by and watch her man work himself to death for her and her children.

You, she had said without speaking, addressing her husband's back, you're there at the bottom of my heart, and I'm going to do everything I can to put a smile back on your face. Then, careful not to make the slightest noise, she finally went back to bed.

I'm going to do everything I can to put a smile back on your face, Lucia repeated to herself, firmly. And she started toward the market again.

XII

The address that Nurse Zupo had given Ricciardi wasn't far away: he needed only to walk down a long *vicolo* until he reached Piazza San Domenico Maggiore, then walk down Mezzocannone, teeming with university students hurrying to summer school classes, and then follow Corso Umberto I until it took him to Piazza Nicola Amore, a square formed by four perfectly symmetrical buildings arranged in a semicircle, so that it had also come to be known as the Piazza dei Quattro Palazzi. Professor Iovine del Castello had lived there before he fell—or was pushed—seventy feet to the ground.

It wasn't far, no, but before they'd gone two hundred yards Maione was puffing like a steamboat and mopping his brow.

"Commissa', if you ask me, the professor threw himself out the window to get a little fresh air. *Mamma mia*, it's not even nine in the morning yet and already you can't breathe. If things keep up like this, by noon we'll all be on fire."

Ricciardi was walking beside him, as usual without sweating.

"True, Raffaele, it's hot. The heat is dangerous around here, you know. It drives people crazy. As well as taking away what little inclination they might have to work."

"Eh, you've got that right, Commissa'. For example, I'd be glad to sit at home in my underwear; in my apartment, if you open the kitchen and bathroom windows, there's a steady breeze that's pure poetry, believe me. I'd stretch out on the bed, ask Lucia to make me a cup of coffee, and I'd lie there reading the newspaper, following the news the rest of you make, the work you do, the cases you crack."

"But you work twice as hard as anyone else at police head-quarters. You wouldn't be able to stay home, even if you had a broken leg."

A shadow passed over Raffaele's face.

"Everyone knows their own business, Commissa'. Believe me, if I could I'd happily take some time off. Just remember: we work to live, we don't live to work."

Ricciardi practically stopped in his tracks: "Now you've become a philosopher, too. Tell me, though, what's going on: are you having problems? I don't know, the kids, or else . . ."

"No, no, don't worry about me. Maybe it's just that this heat brings evil thoughts. But to get back to our flying professor, there were no suicide notes. Instead, we found two gifts ready to be given, to two different people. The professor was another hard worker, but he managed to find the time to do lots of other things, eh, Commissa'?"

Ricciardi thought it over.

"Apparently he had his problems on the job, too. You got the details on the guy who threatened the professor's life, didn't you?"

"Of course I did, Commissa'. And if you want to know the truth, the name rings a bell. I must have read it somewhere: Giuseppe Graziani. I even have the address. As soon as we get back to headquarters, I'll run down to the archives and talk to Antonelli, you know yourself that he has an incredible mem-ory, he never forgets a thing."

"There's something about the mechanics of the professor's death that remains unclear to me. There are no supports in front of the window, and on the windowsill there are no traces or signs on the layer of dust. Either he fell from somewhere else, or else he jumped with a running start, or else . . ."

Maione finished his sentence for him: "Or else someone

threw him. The professor struck me as on the heavy side. It must have been someone quite muscular, in that case. And no matter how it happened, Commissa', I checked into it: he can only have fallen from there. Above that window there's a terrace, but the access door is locked and only the custodian has the key; from the rust on the bolt, I'd have to guess that no one's been up there in who knows how long. On the floor below there's a ward with thirty beds, someone would certainly have seen him. From the floor below that, he wouldn't have done himself the damage that he did: he might have gotten off with a broken leg. No, he fell from his office."

"In other words, we're going to have to wait for Bruno to complete the autopsy. Now let's go talk to the widow. We're going to have to give her some sad news."

A skeptical smirk appeared on Maione's face: "Are you sure, Commissa'? If he really did die last night, and they called us this morning, it strikes me as odd that his wife still knows nothing."

They'd reached the piazza, at the center of which stood the statue of a famous mayor of the city who had died forty years earlier. The professor's apartment house was at the corner of Via Wilson, which turned into Via Duomo. It was one of the aristocratic neighborhoods of the city, and like all noble neighborhoods it stood adjacent to a large run-down area, the area that extended along the waterfront.

At the entrance, surrounding a fat woman in tears, stood a small knot of people dressed for work. One of them stood next to a crate full of broccoli. Ricciardi and Maione exchanged a glance; the brigadier sighed and spread his arms wide.

"What did I tell you, Commissa'? This isn't a city where things can happen in a normal manner. Here everything happens either faster or slower than normal. News, for example, travels faster than lightning."

Ricciardi went over to the group and asked: "Could you tell

me where I can find the apartment of Professor Iovine del Castello?"

The fat woman emitted a strangled moan. Then, looking around at the others for comfort, she said: "The professor, I'm sorry to say, has tragically gone to his reward. And if you care to know, I hear that he fell out of his office window, at the general hospital. Poor professor, just yesterday morning he stopped and spoke to me. I can't believe it, the man looked so well . . ."

Maione snorted: "Signo', the man didn't die of an illness, he fell out a window: of course he seemed fine when you saw him. And just who are you, I'd like to know?"

At the sight of the policeman's uniform, which had at first escaped her notice, the woman composed herself instantly: "Ines Renzullo, Brigadie'. I am, if you please, the concierge for this building."

Maione touched his finger to the visor of his cap: "And I do please, Signo'. And could I know, if *you* please this time, how you knew about his death?"

The woman sniffed: "Signora Carmela called me, the professor's wife, half an hour ago, and told me: 'Ines, I'm afraid my husband's dead. Please, I don't want to see anyone; anyone who calls, ask them to come back some other time. And please, don't tell anyone.'"

Ricciardi looked around: there were at least ten people between deliverymen, tenants, and mere passersby, standing listening to the concierge's story. Maione figured she must have told that story at least a dozen times by now, and he was willing to bet that with each retelling the story was embellished with new and intriguing details.

"And you, obviously," he said, pointing to the rapidly swelling crowd, "kept your oath of silence."

"What does that matter, I only told a couple of my girlfriends, they saw I was upset and they asked me what happened. Is that my fault, if stories get around as fast as they do?"

Ricciardi sighed, discouraged.

"How did you know, if it wasn't Signora Iovine who told you, that the professor fell out his window?"

"I sent my grandson to the general hospital, he's twelve years old and fast as lightning, and he heard it from the people who were standing around there. In ten minutes he was back and he warned me that you were on your way. We were expecting you."

Maione gave himself a slap in the face: "What the hell was I ever thinking the day I decided to become a policeman in a city like this one? But still I say, will there never be a day, one single day, when we can just calmly go about our jobs? I'd like to be able to pull off a raid, an inspection, a surprise arrest: am I asking too much? Once in my life, and then I swear, I'll retire."

Ricciardi nodded his head toward the woman, now clearly bewildered: "Pay no attention to him. And, if you please, take us up to see Signora Iovine."

XIII

It took almost a minute before Maria Carmela Iovine del Castello came to the door. She shot the concierge a harsh glare, but then looked past her to Ricciardi and Maione and, seeing the brigadier's uniform, she understood. She turned and went back into the apartment, leaving the front door open behind her. Ines threw her arms wide and trotted away.

The apartment was shrouded in shadows; the shutters were closed. There was a scent of lavender in the air which, along with the heat, gave Maione an immediate headache. Since the only partly illuminated space was the living room, they headed there, where the woman stood waiting for them.

Signora Iovine was of average height, elegant, about forty. Her oval face was longish: there were faint lines on either side of her mouth and on her forehead.

As Ricciardi introduced himself, he extended his own and Maione's condolences, then stepped closer: "Could I ask you how you learned of your husband's death?"

"They phoned from the general hospital. The ward charge nurse, Coppola."

Maione recalled the large female nurse who had been in the knot of people gathered around the corpse. How diligent, he thought to himself.

Signora Iovine gestured to two chairs: "Have a seat. Can I get you something? An espresso? A rosolio cordial? Forgive me, but in this situation I'm afraid I'm hardly a perfect hostess."

The two policemen politely declined and sat down. She perched on the sofa.

Ricciardi heaved a sigh.

"We're very sorry, Signora, to disturb you at a time like this. But as you can imagine, time is of the essence. Still, if you don't feel you're up to answering a few questions right now, we can certainly come back some other time."

"No, Commissario, I understand the urgency and I intend to do what I can to help. I'm the first to want to know what happened."

Her voice was calm; only her hands, white-knuckled and clenched in fists in her lap, betrayed grief-laden tension.

Ricciardi went on: "We searched your husband's office but we found neither a letter nor a note that might suggest . . . that he had decided to end his life. Do you know of any reason or situation that might have pushed him to . . ."

"No. My husband was a powerful, wealthy, respected man. He had no debts, he didn't gamble, there was no shadowy past of poverty and desperation, he had no relatives in dire straits. His family was well-to-do: his father was a prosperous merchant. I'd rule out any motivations for . . . for an act of that kind."

Maione cleared his throat: "All right, Signo', money wasn't a problem for your unfortunate husband. But money isn't the only thing there is, don't you agree?"

"What do you mean by that?"

Ricciardi broke in: "My colleague is trying to ask whether there might be reasons of some other kind, not economic in nature. A state of excessive exhaustion, some disagreement at work, or at home, perhaps with you yourself. The brigadier is trying to reconstruct your husband's psychological state."

Signora Iovine pursed her lips and furrowed her brow in an expression that must have been a habitual one, given the wrinkles they had noticed previously.

"Commissario, as I told you, my husband is . . . was an

untroubled person. He worked hard, but he always had. A university career, and he'd reached the very highest peaks of academia, means keeping to a demanding path and it involves rivalries and conflict, but he'd clearly achieved his goals. Here at home, too, there was no reason for conflict."

Ricciardi nodded. It was time to explore new territory: "We understand that you have a son. Is that right?"

"Yes, Commissario. His name is Federico, and he's eight years old. I sent him out to play in the park with his nanny as soon as I heard the news. I haven't told him yet: he's very close to his father, and he's quite a sensitive child. I'm going to have to find a way."

"Certainly . . . Excuse us if we insist, but it's our job to take into consideration any possibility, however remote. It does happen that people who commit such an extreme act do so without leaving a note or any written message, but it's pretty unusual. Do you happen to remember anything strange he might have mentioned? Did your husband say anything that surprised you?"

"No, really, nothing. My husband, Commissario, was away from home a lot. For that matter, that was the nature of his job: pregnant women can hardly plan the timing of their medical needs. Lately, he'd been very busy, and he was definitely tired, but nothing out of the ordinary."

Maione sighed. They'd come to the crucial point.

Ricciardi resumed: "In that case, since we have no reason to suspect this was suicide, we need to take another possibility into consideration: that someone might have pushed your husband out that window. Do you know whether the professor had recently had any disagreements or quarrels, even a petty argument, and if so with whom?"

The woman fell silent. Hers was an expressionless silence that Maione found unsettling. She sat staring into empty space, practically without blinking, and slowly twisted her hands. Then she looked up and said: "You're asking me a difficult question, Commissario. My husband was beloved, but he was a surgeon and a university professor. He took both responsibilities very seriously, he was exacting; as demanding with himself as he was with those who worked with him or studied under him."

Ricciardi and Maione waited. After a brief pause, during which she took a sip of water from a glass on the side table, the woman went on: "When it comes to work at the hospital, Dr. Rispoli, my husband's assistant whom you no doubt already met, is better informed than I am. I can only tell you what went on here, at home."

It was clear that Maria Carmela Iovine was thinking about something and trying to decide whether she ought to mention it.

Ricciardi had to proceed with all deliberate caution.

"You see, Signora, in this phase anything can be useful in guiding our investigation, and we're going to have to investigate in any case. Any information provided to us would not be considered an accusation against the person in question, but simply a piece in a larger puzzle. Don't worry, we can assure you that anything you say will be held in the greatest possible confidence."

Signora Iovine seemed relieved by those words. She got up from the sofa and said: "There's something I want to show you."

Both men leapt to their feet. The woman walked away and, a short moment later, returned with a sheet of paper in one hand, which she gave to Ricciardi.

"Go ahead and read it. It came by mail last week, here at home."

Ricciardi unfolded the sheet of paper.

Tullio,

I imagine you will be surprised to receive this letter of mine, after nearly twenty years. It is true, I had hoped that our paths would never cross again, but as you can see destiny,

which works in ways impossible for us mere humans to fathom, has decreed otherwise.

You no doubt clearly remember everything that I remember, but please understand that I bear no grudge for what you did all these years ago; you've always been a master at eliminating your adversaries. For that matter, when all is said and done, your vile act actually laid the cornerstone of my good fortune. Being unable to undertake a university career forced me to find partners so that I could open a clinic, and I like to think that our clinic's success hasn't eluded your notice, and even that it's prompted some feelings of anger and envy, two emotions that, I might add, have always been part of your character.

In the past two decades I have never made any attempt to exact revenge for your betrayal, even though I might have done so; we work in the same field, and more than once I've been forced to remedy an error made by you or one of your assistants at the general hospital: I know that you like to surround yourself with incompetents so that your own supposed skill can stand out even more sharply. And yet, let me say again, I never have. Not because of I never wanted to, but because launching an attack against you, out in the open, would have triggered your retaliation or, even worse, might have led you to ask for help from one of your many political allies. Still, I've saved the documents, and I could track down all the necessary witnesses. I'm not saying that I'd be able to ruin you, but I could certainly undermine that image of probity and competence that you've built on the ruins of those you've destroyed.

Why am I writing you all this? You know why.

I'm a sick man, Tullio. Nature has its way even with us physicians. I'm treating myself, but little by little my strength is ebbing away. My son, my Guido, needs to take my place as soon as possible, otherwise my two partners will succeed in ejecting me from my position at the clinic, nullifying the work of an entire lifetime.

You know very well that my son is a good-hearted young man, though I recognize that he is hardly brilliant. But he studies hard, and he's passed nearly all of the required examinations. He should by rights have earned his medical degree a year ago, which would have given me time to instruct him in those rudiments necessary for him to replace me as director of the clinic, so I could wait to die in peace. But fate has placed you in my path once again: you have flunked him, directly or through a subordinate, three times now. You did it in a way that was ostensibly irreproachable, by tripping him up with complicated questions and clinical hypotheticals that no one has ever seen in reality. I know that, you know it too. But I don't understand why: after all, I'm the one who suffered from your treachery all those years ago. It's clear that your wickedness, your thirst for blood, lives on. But this time you're playing with something that matters far more to me than my career: you're playing with the life of my son, and that's something I won't allow.

Understand that I'll stop at nothing. At nothing, I tell you.

Guido will come to see you outside of your usual office hours, far from prying eyes. You two will decide on the questions together, and you will let him pass the exam. He will take his degree and you will safeguard your reputation, because he will bring you, in the same meeting, the documentation concerning your bungled operations which I had to remedy surgically, in some cases leaving the patients sterile.

I'm sure that only fear can persuade you to give in. I know you.

I'll wait for your response, and then I'll let you know when my son will come to see you. I imagine that late at night might be best, at your office. And if you fail to ensure that you are alone when he comes, then I'll take it that you're not interested in this trade, and I'll take action accordingly. As the saying goes, let Samson die with all the Philistines.

                                        With my very worst regards,
                                        Francesco Ruspo di Roccasole

Ricciardi handed the sheet of paper to Maione so he could read it, and turned to look into Maria Carmela's pale face. Extortion, no doubt about it. And a tacit threat: I'll take action accordingly.

So there was more than one person who had it in for Iovine. The image of the professor that was emerging was quite different from that which had at first appeared.

"Signora, do you know the man who sent this letter?"

"Yes, Commissario. I know him, but I haven't seen him for more than twenty years. He's the director and part owner of the Villa Santa Maria Francesca nursing home, the one in Mergellina."

"And do you know what he is referring to when he speaks of your husband's alleged unethical behavior toward him?"

"I do remember that he was competition with Tullio for a position as university assistant, and that my husband was selected, and he was not. But I couldn't tell you why, nor could I say why Ruspo was denied a career at the university."

Maione, who was done reading, turned to the woman: "Excuse me, Signo', but did you receive this letter? Did you read it first and then talk about it with your husband?"

The woman stared at Maione. Such direct questions irritated her, but she had to answer them.

"Yes, Brigadier. I received it. I thought it must have been . . . I thought I'd received it by mistake, that it had been sent to the wrong address. My husband never receives correspondence at home. Never. I read it and I waited for him to come home. I was upset. He skimmed it and told me not to worry. He started laughing."

Maione exchanged a glance with Ricciardi.

"He started laughing?"

"Yes. He said they were the ravings of a man on his deathbed, but that out of respect for days gone by, he wouldn't report the matter to the police or to the council of the physicians' guild."

Ricciardi pressed on: "So he didn't seem worried to you? You didn't get the impression he was afraid?"

"No, Commissario. He didn't give any weight to the matter at all. But I wasn't as calm as he seemed to be, and I urged him to be careful. And as you can see, I decided to hold on to the letter."

Ricciardi nodded.

"I'm going to have to ask you to let us take it. I assure you that, once we've checked it out thoroughly, we'll return it to you."

"Are you going to talk to Ruspo? You'll need to investigate in depth, I'd imagine . . . But if it were to turn out that my husband . . . anything that might sully my husband's memory . . . Certainly you must understand, I have a child to protect, if his father's integrity were called into question . . . I'm all alone now, I have to look after him."

Ricciardi reassured her: "Signora, the only thing we want is to find out whether someone is responsible for the professor's death. Anything not directly related to that matter is of no interest to us and will not be divulged. Not by us, at least."

After a moment's silence, Maione said: "Signo', forgive me, but we do have to ask you this. Where were you yesterday evening? Could your husband have tried to contact you by phone, or I don't know, might somebody else have tried to contact you on his behalf?"

"I went to dinner with my son, here in the building, at the home of my cousins. I go quite often, when my husband doesn't come home. We stayed out late, listening to a program on the radio. We didn't get back until after midnight. As of eight o'clock, when we left for dinner, no one had called; and if some-one had called after that, my housekeeper would have come to inform me. So I'd rule out that possibility."

The last few words were uttered in a whisper; the woman's gaze was wandering around the room as if this were the first time she'd seen it. Ricciardi and Maione knew that expression, they'd seen it many times before on the faces of family members of people who had met violent deaths: they didn't understand right away what had happened, then the reality began to lap against them like a series of waves, until, like a tsunami, the awareness of their loss buried everything, stripping away rational reasoning and mental equilibrium.

Signora Iovine's lips began to quiver; she put her hand on her forehead.

Ricciardi asked: "Do you need anything? Can we do some-thing for you?"

She emitted a long racking sob and covered her face with both hands. After a moment, she recovered and, apparently calm now, stared at the commissario.

"We had plans, my husband and I. We had plans. In August we were going to the countryside, where it's nice and cool. The countryside is so good for the boy. He's delicate, extreme heat isn't good for him. We had a new car, did you know that? You can put the top down. Federico couldn't wait to go on vacation in a convertible. I don't know how to drive. Now how can I take him to the country? I'll have to learn to drive, won't I?"

Ricciardi dropped his gaze to the carpet. Maione coughed softly. At last, Maria Carmela Iovine del Castello began to cry.

XIV

Nelide was making *ciccimmaritati*. It was Rosa's belief that if a woman of Cilento had any pride in her birthplace, that dish had to form part of her repertoire, and she intended to put her niece to the test. No one could ever have guessed that there was satisfaction in the way Rosa watched her, because she resembled nothing so much as a pillar of salt. In fact, truth be told, her expression was more of a frown than anything else.

For that matter, Rosa had no particular reason to be cheerful. Alongside the usual worries provoked by her young master, who seemed unwilling to settle down and start a family of his own, now there was a new problem on the horizon.

Her own state of health.

Rosa had no fear of dying. She was a pragmatic person, a farmer's daughter, raised in a sunbaked, hostile land. She knew that death was part of life, that in fact it's as necessary as the seasons; it comes so that the new can take the place of the old. But could anyone really take Rosa's place?

Nelide hesitated as she ran her rough hand over the formica counter, so smooth in comparison with the coarse wood to which she was accustomed. Rosa appreciated that mistrust in the presence of such a highly unnatural material, and she was pleased when she saw that her niece immediately found her footing and returned to the gestures of that ancient ritual, arranging the ingredients on the table: dark durum wheat, corn, fava beans, grass peas, round white scarlet runner beans, *tabaccuogni* beans, small and brown, chickpeas and *mimiccola* beans, and finally lentils. Each heaped in a separate pile, to make sure the quantities were correct. A bowl held the *janga* chestnuts, previously dried and peeled, which would serve to give the soup its sweetness, an essential function.

Nelide worked neatly and methodically. She might perhaps have moved a little faster, but that would have been at the expense of precision; speed would come in time. After all, the girl was just seventeen, though at first glance you'd say she was anywhere between sixteen and thirty. A solid, healthy Cilento woman, from Rosa's point of view.

Ricciardi's elderly governess had eleven brothers and sisters, and more than seventy nieces and nephews. And though every one of her siblings had baptized one of their daughters Rosa—in honor of the one sister who hadn't produced children, and who had always helped out by sending small sums of cash, gifts her young master permitted with a disinterested smile—when the time came the niece that Rosa picked was Nelide, the third-born child of the seventh-youngest sibling, her brother Andrea.

Alongside the small piles of beans and grains, the girl arrayed spices and condiments: garlic, olive oil, salt, the absolutely necessary *papaulo*—the fiery-hot dried chili pepper—as well as the tomato purée spooned out of the *buatta*, the metal can that stood, covered with a rag, on the highest shelf in the pantry. Now I want to see what you can do, thought Rosa from the chair pushed against the wall in which she sat, her fingers knit over her ample belly. Up till now, the girl had remained safely within the bounds of strict orthodoxy, but the time had come for a personal touch. Either you have it or you don't.

Nelide had been to the city other times to visit her aunt. Ever since she was a little girl she had proven to be much more similar to Rosa than were those female cousins who bore their aunt's name. Almost as wide across as she was tall, extremely strong, she was stubborn, resolute, and taciturn, with a perennially scowling face; she was neither a model of attractiveness nor particularly good company. She could barely read and wrote only with great difficulty, though she did have an extraordinary, instinctive familiarity with numbers. To make up for whatever qualities she may have lacked, she possessed others that Rosa considered absolutely essential. She was loyal and obedient: when she took on a task she gave herself no peace until she had completed it. She was tireless, indifferent to the time of day, incapable of distraction. She was honest and hard on herself, clean and a homebody. Rosa had tested her, setting small traps every time Nelide visited, visits she encouraged using as an excuse events for which she would need the girl's help. And meanwhile, she had introduced her niece in all the shops and the market stalls where she did her shopping. The young woman had proven herself alert, quick to learn, with a sharp, precise memory. Even Ricciardi had gotten used to having her around, and was happy that, thanks to Nelide, his old *tata* was having an easier time of it.

Toward the young master, Nelide felt a mixture of fear and veneration: precisely what Rosa wanted. On her niece's rugged, square face, marked by narrow lips under a faint mustache, she could see the germ of the same protective sentiment she felt toward that melancholy, unhappy man, whom she had looked after for a lifetime with a missionary zeal.

Now, therefore, yet another of the countless examinations to which Rosa subjected her unsuspecting niece was underway: the Cilento cooking test. Rosa was convinced that tradition was crucial to a healthy stability, and she stubbornly continued to cook according to the rules she'd learned from her mother and grandmother, and that she had absorbed from the very air she'd breathed as a child and as a young woman.

Nelide wiped her palms on her apron. She stared grimly at

the piles on the tabletop: everything was there, but she still wasn't satisfied.

Good, thought Rosa. Her left hand, fingers knit, sensed the tremor in her right hand. It was as if, every so often, it went to sleep. She knew what this was. She knew because this was how her father had died, growing weaker day by day and then falling asleep, until he finally just stopped breathing. She hoped that it would be as gentle for her, but that's not what scared her.

Her biggest worries were for Ricciardi. What fate awaited him? Who would look after him? Nelide was certainly fine when it came to immediate necessities: seeing that he ate regularly, pressing his clothes. But relations with the sharecroppers, making sure that payments were collected as they came due, managing the family's estate? The young master had never taken any interest in such matters, and if it were left up to him, the entire estate to which he was sole heir would dwindle away.

Her thoughts went to the Baroness Marta di Malomonte, Ricciardi's mother. Ah, Baroness, she thought, you too spoke so little. Why didn't you explain to me what your son is like? Why didn't you tell me how I ought to act with him?

Nelide scratched her cheek. Perhaps, Rosa thought to herself, she ought to place her trust in this young woman. Perhaps Nelide could take over from her. After all it was a simple matter of sticking to certain deadlines and picking up the threads of what she had done month after month for many years. She had more confidence in that grim-faced seventeen-year-old than in all the men she'd met in her lifetime.

Of course, it would have been preferable to hand over her responsibilities to a woman who had entered the family by the front door, not the service entrance. She had hoped, she had insisted, she had begged her young master to open himself up to the natural evolution of a man, to an engagement followed by a wedding.

That Enrica, the daughter of the Colombos, had struck her as the perfect one. She had a kind heart, she was gentle and sweet but also, and Rosa had sensed this intuitively, determined and strong. What's more, she was in love.

The absurd thing, to Rosa's uncomplicated mind, lay in the fact that Ricciardi, too, beyond the shadow of a doubt, was in love with Enrica. And yet he hadn't lifted a finger since the day he realized he was losing her, that she was distancing herself from him. For that matter, how could she blame Enrica? The years pass and a girl has a right to a future.

One thing was certain: if he wished to set up housekeeping and start a family, that woman from the north, the one with a car and a driver, wasn't right for him. She was fine if you wanted a good time, perfect for going out to the theater or the movies, but not as the mother of his children.

Who could say, perhaps they'd find each other again, Enrica and her young master. Only then it would be too late for Rosa to pass along her knowledge.

Nelide nodded vigorously, as if someone inside her head had just given her a peremptory order. She headed to the pantry, grapped a jar, and added to the concoction a tablespoon of pork lard. Yes, now all the indispensable ingredients for making *ciccimmaritati* were present, and she could proceed to cooking. She glanced at her aunt for her approval, then grabbed a cookpot.

After all, Rosa decided, Nelide deserved a chance. She was a reliable young woman.

And there wasn't time to come up with any other solutions.

XV

Ricciardi and Maione returned to police headquarters after receiving confirmation from a mistrustful female cousin of Signora Iovine that the professor's wife and his son had both been her dinner guests the previous night. This woman too had been told, only hours before, of the professor's untimely death.

"I just can't get over it, Commissa'," said Maione as he slammed his fist down on the desktop, "the way that everybody around here seems to know about things even before they happen. What do they have, a wireless network in constant operation? Now, for instance, if we were heading out to arrest a murderer or a thief, the guy would already know hours in advance that we were on our way, and we'd come up with a great big handful of nothing."

Ricciardi threw the window open to let in a little air and flopped down in the chair behind his desk.

"You've been too touchy for some time now. Hasn't it always been this way? And remember, this is how you manage to get all that information from your secret girlfriend."

"Commissa', you're just playing with me, and if you want to play, let's play. My secret girlfriend is actually my secret manfriend, or not even *that*, what are you tricking me into saying, she's nothing to me. She's a *femminiello*, a transvestite who I decided just once, out of pure pity, not to throw in jail, and ever since she's shown her gratitude by telling me the gossip that she hears."

"You see how on edge you are? Will you tell me what's got into you?"

The brigadier heaved a deep sigh.

"What can I tell you, Commissa': I must be a little tired. I do work too hard, I know that, but we need the money, with all the kids I have at home."

Ricciardi turned serious: "Raffaele, you aren't short on cash, are you? I have plenty of my own, if you want I can . . ."

Maione held up a hand. "Why no, Commissa', if you start talking like that you'll offend me, and I won't even be able to tell you anything anymore. I earn a good salary and I have no trouble making ends meet. It's just that now we have the little girl from Mergellina, you remember her, Benedetta; and Lucia and I would like to adopt her. We could use a bigger apartment, too; we have little boys and little girls living together in the same room, and now that they're growing up, they're going to need a place to study. So I'm setting aside a little money so we can move in a year, that's all."

Ricciardi decided to explain his intentions: "Please don't be offended. I have a good salary, you know that, and aside from Rosa I have no family. You have children, and what you've done for Benedetta is admirable and does you honor; you ought to let your good friend help you out. Have you talked it over with Lucia?"

"Good lord, no! She'll immediately start worrying and we'll never hear the end of it. No, no, I've just been doing a little budgeting, that's all. But Lucia doesn't know a thing, and I don't want her to know a thing. As for you, Commissa', thanks, but it's really not necessary. After all, since you stubbornly continue not to get married, you already pay the mother-in-law tax. How much has it risen to by now?"

The reference to the ironic name given to the tax on unmarried men that had now been in effect for five years made Ricciardi shake his head: "I'm more than happy to pay that tax.

I already have Rosa who serves simultaneously as both mother and mother-in-law: however substantial the cost, I avoid much worse consequences. Still, all kidding aside, promise me that if you are ever in need you'll let me know. Don't give me something else to fret about."

Maione burst out laughing: "Don't you worry about that, Commissa'. Now let's get busy. Shall we go pay a call on the clinic of this doctor who sent a letter to the dead man's house?"

"It's too early for that, we don't even know whether he jumped or if someone else helped him out the window. Let's wait for Modo to finish the autopsy and see if he finds anything. Instead, let's find out something more about the man who swore he'd kill him, the one whose wife died in childbirth. What's his name?"

Maione pulled his notebook out of his pocket and read aloud: "Graziani, Giuseppe. I'll hurry down to Archives and talk to Antonelli. Shall I bring you an ersatz coffee, Commissa'?"

"No, no, thanks. With this heat, a disgusting ersatz coffee like the ones we drink here would kill me. Bring me news instead."

Ten minutes later Maione had returned: "May I come in, Commissa'? There's another piece of news that I just got from the wireless telegraph."

Ricciardi looked up from the report that he was drafting concerning his on-site examination of the scene of the death at the general hospital: "Well?"

"There's a strange guy outside in the hall. He says that he saw the professor last night. And when he heard that he was dead, he came in of his own volition."

"You see? It's not always a bad thing for news to travel fast. Send him in."

The man did have an unusual appearance. At first glance he was short, but that impression was accentuated by the fact that he had an unmistakable curvature of the spine; he wore thick-lensed eyeglasses, and his arms and legs were disproportionately long compared with his torso. His hair, thinning on top of his head, grew thick along the sides in tangled curls; his skin was a sickly pale white. He seemed uneasy; he worried the hat he held in his hands, and looked as if he expected to arrested any minute.

Maione winked at Ricciardi, in an acknowledgment of the odd character.

"Commissa', this is Signor Coviello, Nicola by name. Signor Coviello, Commissario Ricciardi, who's in charge of the case of Professor Iovine. Come right in."

The man took a step forward, hesitantly. Ricciardi waited a few seconds then, since the man seemed unable to make up his mind, asked: "Did you want to speak to me?

Coviello opened his mouth, shut it, and then opened it again, as if he were a fresh-caught fish. At last he said: "Commissa', *buongiorno*. I . . . I heard that this misfortune had taken place, that Professor Iovine is dead. That he fell out his office window."

Maione butted in firmly: "Excuse me, but how the hell did you know about it?"

Confronted with the brigadier's sudden aggressivity, Coviello flinched, almost as if he expected to be punched: "No, you see," he stammered, "I have a cousin who runs a shop near the general hospital. Since he knows that I know the professor, this morning as soon as the custodian . . ."

Maione interrupted, in exasperation: "Yes, yes, I understand. You received a paperless telegram. Let's continue."

The other man was now more bewildered still.

"What telegram? No, Brigadie', it was my cousin's son who brought me the news . . ."

Ricciardi decided to put an end to that unproductive line of questioning: "Forget about that, Coviello. Tell me, why have you come in to see us?"

The man dragged his foot back and forth across the floor,

worrying his cap in both hands all the while; he was already regretting his act of good conscience.

He spoke in a low voice: "Commissa', I'm a goldsmith by trade, I have a workshop down in the *borgo*, you can ask any-one, they call me Mastro Nicola."

After identifying himself in this manner, he fell silent. After a short while the brigadier said, impatiently: "Covie', you came in of your own free will, no one subpoenaed or arrested you; we don't have a lot of time to waste, would you mind telling us why you're here?"

The man seemed to snap out of it.

"No, it's just that I was thinking about where to start."

"Try starting from the beginning," Maione suggested.

"Right. *Grazie*, Brigadie'."

Maione looked him up and down grimly, trying to decide whether the best thing might not be to toss him bodily out the window, and have him meet the same end as the profes-sor had. Luckily for him, Mastro Nicola snapped to. "All right then, as I've told you, I'm a goldsmith. A month or so ago, the professor came into my shop, introduced himself, and . . ."

Ricciardi interrupted him: "Hold on a second: was he already a customer of yours? Did you know him?"

"No, no, Commissa', I'd never seen him before. But he'd heard I was good at what I did and told me he wanted to com-mission two pieces. Actually, at first just one; then, the second time, he asked me to make another."

Ricciardi asked: "What kind of pieces?"

Coviello spoke animatedly: "Well then, Commissa', this is the way I work: either my clients bring me the material, the stones, the gold, and the silver, or else they commission the items and I ask for a down payment so I can buy the materials I need; or else a little of each, that is, they bring me some old object to melt down, or loose stones to set in something that I make myself, and then they give me the money to purchase the materials, or else . . ."

Maione snapped: "Coviello, what did you come in here for, to deliver a lecture? Commissario Ricciardi asked you about the professor and how you came to know him, not the story of your life. Go on, and stick to the facts."

Ricciardi shot him an angry look, then turned to the goldsmith: "Go on, Coviello. If you please."

The man gave Maione a brief glance. His ears were bright red.

"Forgive me. The professor had no materials of his own, but he wanted to give a gift to his wife, because her name day was coming up. He didn't even really know what he wanted. I told him that one of my suppliers had a few nice diamonds at home and I suggested a ring. We agreed on a price and he said that would be fine."

Maione asked: "Did he haggle?"

Coviello shook his head, his eyes still fixed on Ricciardi. Maione's tone of voice clearly made him uncomfortable: "Not much. He said that he'd expected it to cost less, but he immediately gave me the deposit so I could give my supplier a partial advance payment. My suppliers give me credit, because I always settle up on time, so I can . . . in any case, we made a deal. He wasn't even in a hurry, as long as it was ready in time for the Festival of the Carmine, Our Lady of Mount Carmel; he'd asked me to engrave the name Maria Carmela on the inside of the ring."

Ricciardi pressed him: "And the second time?"

"He came back about ten days later, at night, when I was just about to close up. I work late sometimes in my shop. He said that he needed a second ring, identical to the first. I told him that it wouldn't come out exactly identical, every stone is different from the others, and he replied: well then, make it better. With a bigger stone. And I need you to deliver them both to me at the same time."

The last part of the story was told in a tone of voice that was clearly meant to reproduce the professor's own: imperious, stentorian.

"Did you ask him to make a new deposit?"

"Certainly, Commissa'. I can hardly afford to do the work otherwise. It was a higher price, but he didn't object. In fact he paid the entire amount in advance."

Maione broke in: "And did you have to engrave a name this time too?"

"'Sisinella,' he wanted me to write 'Sisinella.'"

"And you didn't ask him anything? Like just who this Sisinella might be?"

"Brigadie', that's none of my business. If I start asking questions like that, I'm going to scare all my customers away."

Ricciardi nodded, absentmindedly.

"Let's talk about yesterday. Where did you see him? Did he come to you, in your workshop?"

"No, I went to see him in his office. He'd insisted I deliver the rings that day, even late, he'd wait for me. I worked fast, but with precision. You know, that kind of ring isn't easy to fashion, it's a labor of love: you have to make a sort of knot in the metal, it symbolizes a union, and in the middle you set the stone. Setting the stone is hard, because the gold doesn't offer a flat surface, still . . ."

Maione emitted a muffled snarl. Coviello snapped his mouth shut.

Ricciardi asked: "So you went to call on him at the general hospital?"

"Yes, Commissa'. It took me a little while to find him, that place is a labyrinth and at that time of night the custodians had all gone home. The professor had explained that he was on the top floor."

Maione cut in: "How did he look to you? Did he strike you as angry, upset, worried?"

Coviello thought it over, then said: "No, Brigadie'. He was just like the other two times. Brisk, even a little brusque, but calm. I wanted payment in full for the first ring: he inspected my work, read the engraving, and paid. The bigger ring, the one with the engraving that read 'Sisinella,' he put in a desk drawer. He set the other one down on the top of the desk."

Ricciardi leaned forward: "Do you remember anything particular about the office? Was the window closed?"

"In this heat? No, Commissa', it was open. And that high up there was even a bit of a breeze. Climbing the stairs I'd turned into a sweaty mess, and I remember that the five minutes I spent up there gave me a little bit of relief."

"And he didn't say anything to you, the professor?"

"No, Commissa'. He didn't even compliment me on the work I'd done. Maybe that wasn't his style. But he must have been satisfied, because the rings had turned out well."

There was a pause. Ricciardi was trying to reconstruct the situation. Then he asked: "What time was it when you left?"

"Hmm, it must have been ten thirty, or a quarter to eleven. The church bells near my house rang eleven o'clock just as I was arriving; it takes about twenty minutes to get back from the general hospital, so right around that time."

"Did you get the impression that he was still expecting someone else?"

"We just said goodbye, nothing more, but yes, I think so."

Maione took a step forward.

"And what made you think that?"

"There was someone in the hallway."

Ricciardi sat up straight in his chair: "Could you be a little more specific?"

"I didn't get a look at his face, it was really dark, the lights were off, but when I walked out of the office he was sitting on the bench. A man, for sure. And a big one, too. He looked like the mountain at night."

XVI

P apà? How are you, *papà*? I don't even know if you're sleeping or you just prefer to lie there with your eyes closed, fighting your battle.

I don't know anything. I don't understand anything.

You know, *papà*, I just sit here watching. Watching how useless I am. How helpless.

Don't you think, *papà*, that this is a fine piece of irony? Someone like you, who has always battled against disease, who has conquered it so many times, been beaten only by a few, but who has never given up, never stopped searching for new solutions and new paths, now has to lie here, in the shadows, doing nothing. Nothing at all.

Motionless, waiting for nightfall.

I'd like to ask if you're thirsty, but I hear your regular breathing.

If you can't do anything, you who are a genius, the smartest man I've ever known, then what use am I?

Me, I'm nothing, no one. All I know how to do is disappoint you.

You never told me that I disappointed you. You were stern, no question, you always wanted me to do my best. But I expected you to show me the way, so that all I needed to do was walk.

Now what should I do, *papà*?

I tried. I'm not like you, I'm not a genius like you, but I'm stubborn, and I'm strong. Physically strong, strong in my heart.

If I get it in my head to do something, I do it; if you tell me to do it, I do it. With all my self, with all my soul.

Medicine, for instance, was never easy for me. I don't understand it right away, I have to read it over and over again. And maybe I could have asked you for some explanations; but you know I would never have done that.

How are you, *papà*? I hear you struggling to breathe. Perhaps your lungs are giving out too.

With all the studying I did, I'd almost made it. God, what I would have given for your last smile. It would have been the best reward; but I just wasn't good enough.

Still I tried.

I burned plenty of candles, studying. When everyone else was out enjoying themselves in bordellos, cabarets, gambling dens, I was studying. When everyone else was asleep, I was studying. When the others were giving up, I kept trying.

You don't necessarily have to be a genius, you know, *papà*? It's enough to try, and keep trying, and try again and again. In the end, you almost always succeed. Almost.

I know, there were times when it helped to have your same last name. They all love you, I could tell from the smiles on their faces when my name came up at roll call. All except for one.

And yet I knew it, *papà*. From the very first time. I know that it's the most important subject for me: it's the area of your expertise. I know that you cared about that subject more than any other, and I knew that you were worried, but you wouldn't tell me why. I couldn't understand why he wasn't satisfied with that answer: I told him what was written in the book, word for word, and he still didn't like it.

And he didn't like it any better the second time.

Or the third time.

It was a race between him and your illness, you busy dying and him busy flunking me, a race to see who could hold out longer. I could see the fear in your eyes, and I felt I was losing my mind. I'd have smashed his desk in half, I'd have taken him by the throat in front of everyone. You know it, *papà*, I'm strong. So very strong.

The last time, I didn't even want to come back home. I wandered around for hours. I took a carriage and told the driver: just go. I was sobbing with rage, sorrow, helplessness. The city streamed past me: the sea, the churches, the monuments. I was crying the tears that I didn't want you to cry.

For me, the only thing in the world is you, *papà*. It's always been just you. I never talked to *mamma*, I don't have friends: just you, you alone. And I disappointed you, even if you say that it's his fault, that there was disagreement between the two of you years and years ago, that he has nothing against me, but against you. But I know it, *papà*, that if I'd been good, really good, I'd have passed all the same, and you'd have been able to die easy, without fighting, without having to take on this terrible battle, this struggle to last long enough to see me take your place.

I know, *papà*. I know I disappointed you.

To go see him. To look him in the eye, not in front of the other students, not in front of his assistants. Man to man, face to face, force against force. To go see him and ask him why, what do I have to do, what else do I have to study. I'll paint the sun if he asks me to; I'll do anything to keep from disappointing you. To go see him and beg him, if necessary.

Papà? You'll wake up, won't you, *papà*? I'll be able to look at you and make a sign so you understand that everything's all right now, that I finally succeeded? That's the way it'll go, isn't it, *papà*?

There are times when I think I can hear the sound of the beast that's devouring you from within. Gnawing, slowly, relentlessly, at your flesh. It's as if I can actually hear it.

I don't know what's going to happen. If he doesn't understand, if he doesn't realize. If it weren't for him, you know, *papà*, I'm sure that everything would turn out all right. It would be the way it's always been. All I'd have to do is burn more midnight candles, listening to my classmates call me a crazy elephant, enormous and silent, who doesn't know how to have fun. They never say it to my face, I know they're afraid of me, but I can hear them mutter it under their breath as I go by.

I don't have time for fun, *papà*. They don't know the things I have to do. How I have to work, to keep from disappointing you.

To go see him, that's right. That's what I have to do. Because if it weren't for him, everything would turn out fine, and I'd be able to see your gaze, contented and reassured.

And then you'd be free to go.

I don't want you to go, *papà*. But I especially don't want you to go without having forgiven me.

And you know that's why I don't just press a pillow down on your face, *papà*. Because before that I want your forgiveness.

I need to go see him. Talk to him man to man.

Because if it weren't for him, everything would be all right.

XVII

Cavalier Giulio Colombo was about to do something that went against all his instincts and the core of what he considered to be a businessman's ethics: he was about to eject a customer from his store.

To tell the truth, Signora Carbone wasn't doing anything out of the ordinary: when the weather took a turn for the worse, and that morning the July heat really was something fierce, she liked to spend a few hours in the Cavalier's nice shop, at the corner of Via Toledo and Piazza Trieste e Trento, close to the church of San Ferdinando, a shop which specialized in hats, umbrellas, walking sticks, and gloves. It wasn't because she had any intention of making a purchase, though there were days when she finally toddled out the front door with a package or two in her hands. It was because she found the Cavalier and his sales clerks to be such lovely company, the finest company a lonely, wealthy woman could enjoy before teatime.

That day, though, there was something Giulio Colombo had to do, and to do it he had leave his shop for a few minutes; and that would be impossible as long as Signora Carbone continued clutching at his arm with her crooked fingers as she chatted away.

". . . and so you see, Cavalie', since I don't perspire the way I used to, the heat makes my head spin and now and then I lose my balance. I just don't perspire the way I once did, Cavalie', because I've turned into an old woman. A decrepit old woman."

As he mulled over his own affairs, Giulio replied in accordance with the standard shopkeeper's script: "What on earth are you saying, Signora! Why you're still just a young thing, you know!"

Signora Carbone smiled, toothless and coquettish: "No, no, Cavalie', I've grown old. You're such a gallant gentleman that you pretend it's not true, but if you only knew the aches and pains in my back. There are mornings when I can't even get out of bed. Just today, for example . . ."

Colombo's gaze chanced to meet that of the old woman's housekeeper, who was standing by the door. It was an exchange of reciprocal suffering. He did his best at least to bring the conversation back to the subject of shopping: "Signora, why don't you take these gloves here? They're light and translucent, you see? The air passes right through them, you'd think you weren't wearing gloves at all."

Signora Carbone felt them suspiciously: "You think so? But you can see the skin right through them, and from a distance they hardly seem black. I wouldn't want people to think that Signora Carbone has put off mourning. You know very well, Cavalie', I've made up my mind to wear black for the rest of my life, ever since the day my poor husband died, thirty-one years ago. That's how it ought to be for any woman whose husband dies, not like it is now, when the poor man's body is still warm and these sluts are already out dancing with some other man. What a world we live in! There are times when I wonder if I shouldn't have been born in another century, not in these modern times where there's no more morality, no sense of decorum, no more . . ."

Colombo couldn't afford to wait for Signora Carbone to complete her ethical analyses, which would customarily be followed by companion pieces on politics and social mores. He summoned Marco, one of his employees and the husband of his second-oldest daughter, Susanna, and told him: "Oooh, *madonna santa*, I just realized I forgot to take my medicine! I have to run out to the pharmacy. Do me a favor and just look after Signora Carbone, make sure she has whatever she needs, I'll be back soon. Forgive me, Signora, it's just that you're so utterly charming that you make me forget everything, even what time I'm supposed to take my medication. With your permission, I have to go."

The woman, torn between disappointment and the urge to learn more, tried to ferret out some information: "Don't you feel well, Cavalie'? What seems to be your trouble? Because if you need it, I can recommend a different doctor for every kind of malady . . ."

Marco, who was a sharp, intelligent young man, perhaps a shade overambitious, but above all else quick on the uptake when necessity called, strode over to the woman with a dazzling smile: "At last I can take over and serve this lovely signora; the Cavalier likes to keep you all for himself. How can I be helpful today?"

Annoyed though she was not to have been given a full report on the Cavalier's state of health, the woman felt flattered by this shower of compliments and curled her lips into a smile, with an aesthetically horrendous effect: "I don't know, I'm not certain. In your opinion, how do these gloves look on me?"

Colombo picked up his hat and his cane and, as Signora Carbone's housekeeper shot him a conspiratorial glance, he excused himself again and left.

He had to admit that his son-in-law, with whom he engaged in extended, combative arguments about politics on a nightly basis, was becoming increasingly invaluable in the running of his business. His skills were such that he could almost be forgiven for his fervent support of the Fascist Party, and for his belief that the Mussolini government would restore Italy and Rome to their place atop the world, which to the Cavalier, an old-school liberal, constituted an absurd pipe dream, as false as it was dangerous to the future of international relations. As he headed off at a brisk walk toward Gambrinus, he was surprised to realize how pleased he was at the young man's enterprising spirit, even if he had detected a glint of curiosity in his eyes. He certainly wasn't about to confide in him what he was about to go do. He wouldn't tell that to anyone.

As soon as he had taken a seat at a small table inside the café—which was half empty because nearly all the customers were crowding the veranda, where there was at least the illusion of cool—and ordered an espresso, he put on his spectacles and pulled a sheet of paper folded in four out of his pocket.

He had five children, the Cavalier Giulio Colombo did. He loved them all tenderly, and he adored his wife. All he knew was his work and his home, he'd never allowed himself distractions and he'd never kept any secrets.

This was the first time.

Children, he thought as he smoothed out the sheet of paper and placed it in the shaft of sunlight that poured in through the plate-glass window overlooking Piazza del Plebiscito, are all the same in a father's heart, so what's wrong with having a special affinity with one of them? Maybe it's just because one resembles you more than the others, because you see your own thoughts reflected in her eyes. For him, that's how it had always been with Enrica, the eldest child. Since the day he'd first taken her in his arms as a newborn, by now nearly twenty-five years ago, he'd felt something melt inside him: this was his little girl. All his. Even more than she was her mother's, and more than would be the case with all the others, she was his baby.

He missed her. He'd had to accept the decisions of that determined, silent young woman, and he knew it was pointless to argue, but he missed her badly.

His concern stemmed from the fact that, while the girl had written home regularly to inform her family of what she was doing in the summer colony on Ischia, where she had gone to teach during the summer session, that day a letter had reached him at his shop. That meant the letter was for him alone. Why had she felt the need to do such a thing? What could have befallen her? He began to read quickly.

Dear *Papà*,

forgive me if I've frightened you by writing to you at the store. Let me begin by telling you that I'm doing well, that nothing new has happened, nothing different from what I tell you in the letters I send home. Life here in the colony is calm; a few of the children are rapscallions, but I have no difficulty keeping it all under control.

This letter was sent to you because I owe you an explanation. There have never been shadows or secrets between us, dear *papà*. You know that we have always understood each other, even without words, with nothing more than a glance: perhaps because we are so similar, perhaps because you have the right sensibility, or perhaps because, since I was the firstborn, I've had more time with you.

Let me be perfectly clear, I love *mamma* dearly. She is a wonderful person, and I'm sure that the things she tells us, the advice she gives us, are intended only for our benefit. But you know how pedantic she can be at times, and how lately the only things she has to say to me are focused on the topic you know all too well: finding a husband. I'm well aware that most young women my age are already married and have more than one child, and that I ought by rights to be at least engaged by now, with someone you approve of, and be planning my wedding. Maybe even you, dear *papà*, would rest easier if that were the case, even though you'd never admit it, and simply smile patiently at me behind *mamma*'s back when she starts in on one of her tirades.

But there's something I want to tell you that, on the one hand may cause you some pain because of how much you love me, but on the other hand may reassure you: I'm capable of feeling emotions, I'm not a strange or cold person, and my hopes and dreams are simply to have a family, a wedding, a husband, a home, and children of my own. And the truth is that I have a place in my heart for one special person.

I'm in love.

There, I've written it. It may not be the same as saying it out loud, but at least I've written it. And I've written it to the person I'm closest to in the world: you, *papà*.

The man I'm in love with lives in the building across the street. His windows overlook our own and I met him without anyone introducing us, just like that, on long winter evenings when he stood motionless and watched me embroider; we were separated by the rain and joined by our eyes.

His name is Luigi Alfredo Ricciardi; he's a commissario, an officer of public safety at our city's police headquarters. He works just a hundred feet or so from our shop, and to think of the two of you so close, you two who are so dear to me, warms my heart.

We've practically never spoken. We've only had two or three occasions to meet and exchange a few smiles. But I love him with every ounce of my being, and for some time I was certain that he loved me. I made friends with his *tata*, Signora Rosa, with whom he lives alone, and I waited calmly for him to seek me out.

But he never did. In fact, I learned, and saw with my own eyes, that he sometimes goes out with a beautiful wealthy woman, possibly not from our city. How can a man who has the opportunity to spend time with a woman like her be interested in me? Me, nothing more than a simple homebody, certainly neither beautiful nor desirable, devoid of the allure that so captivates men?

I sat wallowing in my disappointment for days on end. I saw the worried look furrowing your brow, dear *papà*, and *mamma*'s as well. I needed to put an end to this situation, I had to get back on my feet. If I stayed there, embroidering by the window, waiting for him to look at me, I'd never go back to really living.

So I decided to accept this teaching position to put some distance between me and him. I know that you, dear *papà*, didn't understand the reason behind my unexpected flight; for that matter, how could you have? You were missing a fundamental piece of information, and to keep you from worrying I decided that it was necessary for you, at least, to know.

I wish I could tell you that all it took was putting the sea between me and the city, that I no longer think about him, that my days pass in joy and serenity and that I'm having the time of my life. But I don't want to lie to you. I'm still suffering, and my mind is stuck to that window, it hasn't moved a yard. I still suffer as I did the night I decided to board the ship that brought me here. I still suffer, and I imagine that that's the way it has to be, because love can't be erased by a few miles of water.

I don't know, my dear *papà*, if I'll be able to muster the courage to send you this letter. I hope so, because knowing that I have you close to my heart gives me a bit more strength.

I know that you're in the habit of personally opening the mail that you receive at the store, so I'm confident that these words of mine won't be seen by anyone else. I beg you not to change your routine, I'll continue writing you about the things I feel in my soul, while I'll talk about the things that happen around me, in quite another tone, in the letters I send home, in which I'll also be writing to *mamma* and my dear brothers and sisters.

Farewell, my beloved *papà*. Hold me tight the way you did when I was a little girl. I need it now more than I ever did back then.

Yours,
Enrica

*

The waiter, standing with the demitasse of espresso in his hands, looked down at him with concern: "Cavalie', do you feel all right? You have a look on your face . . ."

Giulio Colombo nodded, thanking the waiter for his concern with a gesture. There was a knot in his throat. Once he was alone again, he reread the letter. His Enrica. His sweet little Enrica, the child who used to listen to his fairy tales for hours, while the other children played tag in the Villa Nazionale. His sweet little Enrica with her big, romantic heart. He couldn't stand the idea that she was suffering so for love.

He would write back to her with a short letter, urging her to go on sending letters to him at the store, and not to fret, because her words would remain locked in her father's heart. He'd tell her that he loved her with the tenderest and most powerful love on earth, and that he'd stand by her no matter what decision she made. He'd tell her that suffering seems endless but that it's not, that a smile will return, bigger and brighter than ever before, and that she was beautiful, the most beautiful of them all, and that she wasn't to dare doubt it, that she was not to dare think that she was less attractive than any other woman. He'd write her all that, because that's what he really thought. Because he was sure of it.

Taking a sip of his espresso and looking out onto the sun-baked piazza, he thought to himself that if he could ask a favor of the Madonna del Carmine, Our Lady of Mount Carmel, whose name day and festival were very soon, he would ask that she give a little peace to that wonderful daughter of his. To bring a little joy into her heart.

XVIII

Modo's phone call came into police headquarters in the afternoon. Maione went straight to Ricciardi's office to inform him: "Commissa', the doctor called from Pellegrini Hospital, he says that he's completed the autopsy and wants us to come right over. I asked him: Dotto', can't you tell us over the phone what you want us to know, and then you can just send us the complete report? It must be 140 degrees outside, it looks like an African desert, do we absolutely have to go to the hospital? And do you know what he said to me?"

Ricciardi looked up from the report he was drafting and said: "I'm just amazed he spoke to you at all, old grouch that he is."

Maione imitated the doctor's deep and irreverent voice: "He told me: and the two of you, when you make me run all over the city, in the rain, in the heat and the cold, do you ever bother to take my comfort into consideration, and I'm older than either of you? That's what he said to me. And he added, with a laugh: after all, Brigadie', I'm doing you a favor, the morgue is the coolest room in the city. You get what a sweetheart he is?"

Ricciardi was already putting on his jacket: "Well, let's get going all the same: he's a joker, but if he's bothering to call it means he's got his hands on something important."

It wasn't far to Pellegrini Hospital, but in that heat even a hundred yards was an arduous trek. They got there not ten minutes later in very different shape than they had been in when they left: Ricciardi was white as a sheet, Maione drenched with sweat and rumpled. When Modo came to meet them, the brigadier told him: "Dotto', as God is my witness, you'll have me on your conscience. I'm going to die any second and you'll have to carry the weight of knowing you murdered me; you'll have to take care of my family for all eternity."

"Brigadie', if the punishment will be to enjoy Lady Lucia's cooking for all time, I really will kill you one of these days. Come, I have something that may interest you."

The morgue was located in a building outside the hospital, as was common practice. Ricciardi thought to himself that the doctors and the builders who constructed medical facilities disliked the idea of keeping the dead near the living at least as much as he disliked the idea himself. Death, to a physician, was an error, something that he had been unable to prevent, a reminder of his own fallibility and the inability of science, of scientific tools, of books and university lessons, to put off the inevitable indefinitely.

Ricciardi feared those places, because they were steeped in pain, and pain—as no one knew better than he did—always brought more pain. As he walked behind Modo and Maione toward the morgue entrance, he glimpsed a faded translucent image through which he could see the parched hedge surrounding the building. A stout woman, not young, her face twisted into a mask of pain, was vomiting dark blood and murmuring: *I'm coming to join you, I'm coming to join you, I'm coming to join you.*

The commissario asked Modo: "It does still happen, Bruno, that the bereaved commit senseless acts, doesn't it?"

The doctor turned around, as he sorted through a ring of keys hooked to his belt, looking for the right one, and said: "Why, of course. A couple of months ago, right here by the door, a woman whose son, a bricklayer, had been killed in a construction accident, drank half a liter of acid and was laid out next to her son for one last night. We do all we can to heal them and then they go kill themselves. It makes you want to give up, I'm telling you."

I'm coming to join you, thought Ricciardi. The black heart of grief engenders more grief. What madness.

The interior of the morgue was refrigerated, but the heat outdoors was so intense that it undermined the effect of the immense quantities of ice hauled there by the attendants. The result was a faint stench that wafted its way up their nostrils.

Maione lifted his handkerchief to cover his mouth: "*Mamma mia*, how disgusting, Dotto'."

Modo shrugged: "That's one more reason I wanted you two to hurry over: we try to process them as quickly as we can, the corpses, at these temperatures. There's not enough ice in the world. Now come here. First let's take a look at the articles of clothing, I placed them on this countertop."

He went over to a low cabinet with a pile of garments on top. He picked up a shirt with a large brown stain on the front: the dried, clotted blood of Professor Iovine.

"Look closely, the buttons on the collar and the top two buttons on the shirt, at the throat and the chest, have popped off. You see? There are torn threads. And the tie was yanked down, almost unknotted."

Maione peered closer: "And what does that mean, Dotto'?"

"Hold on a minute, Raffae', then we'll be ready to draw some conclusions. Now look at the bottom, in the back. The fabric, it's true, is delicate because this is a very fine piece of clothing, but it's very clear: the cotton is practically torn."

Ricciardi and Maione were able to make out four round marks, slightly darkened on the white fabric.

"And now the trousers," said the doctor, lifting another item of clothing from the countertop.

At the center of the dark fabric, in the rear, just under the belt loops, there was a deeper mark than those on the shirt.

Maione murmured: "Just one. And right in the middle."

Modo smiled, like a schoolteacher before a diligent pupil.

"Exactly. And I'll remind you that the suspenders had been

unhooked in the back: on the left from both buttons and on the right from just one. While in the front they were still in place. Last of all, I'd remind you that our Professor Iovine landed on his head."

Ricciardi nodded: "I'm starting to understand."

Modo gave him a wink: "Good boy. But now let's move on to the main course."

He went over to the marble slab, where a body lay under a sheet. The doctor uncovered it with a theatrical gesture, like a chef revealing an elaborate dish. Maione grimaced in disgust: "Dotto', *madonna mia*! Just being in here is ghoulish enough, but when you start acting the magician with the dead—just a little bit of respect for my stomach, if you don't mind!"

Modo raised an eyebrow: "Maione, you're too delicate for this line of work. Or else, and this is the explanation that I prefer, you're getting too old: time to make way for the new generation, take it from me."

The corpse on the slab was naked, belly-down. There was no missing the fractures of the spinal cord and the dent in the skull corresponding to the point of impact.

Maione shook his head: "Poor man. With all the power and wealth he had, he still winds up on a marble slab in the morgue, exactly like everyone else."

Modo threw both arms wide: "That's exactly right, it's just like the philosophical brigadier says. You all wind up coming to me, sooner or later."

Maione made the sign of the horns with both hands, index finger and pinkie pointing downward to ward off evil: "For the love of all that's holy, Dotto', I'll come take you out for an espresso whenever you like, but as for coming in here feet-first, try to understand: I'd just as soon put that off as long as possible!"

Ricciardi was eager to get to the point: "If you two are done with the warm-up act, let's proceed."

Modo raised one hand: "Well put. The dead commune with the dead, so our cheerful commissario wants to know what poor Iovine has to say to him. Look down here."

And he pointed to the area just above the corpse's flaccid gluteal muscles. Ricciardi leaned forward to look closer and so did Maione, after a moment's hesitation. Following the doctor's finger, they saw four lines on the skin, running parallel and vertical, some five or six centimeters in length, and reddish in color.

"What are those?" asked Maione.

"Scratches," Ricciardi replied before Modo had a chance.

The doctor nodded approvingly: "Exactly. Put that together with the marks on the trousers and the bottom of the shirt, and it tells us that someone came up behind him, grabbed him by the belt and in so doing tore loose his suspenders. And with the other hand, the same person grabbed him by the throat, ripping the buttons off his shirt. He almost choked him, just look here."

He turned the corpse's head ever so slightly, producing a soft sound, like broken crockery.

"Those are the fractured cranial bones, don't let them distract you. What we're interested in is right here."

On either side of the neck was a deep red stripe, produced by the chafing of the shirt collar and the tie.

"Now do you see the dynamics of what happened?"

Maione scratched his forehead: "*Mamma mia*, in that case he didn't jump. Someone else threw him, and it must have been someone . . ."

Modo gave him a slap on the shoulder: "Good work, my intelligent brigadier. It must have been someone very, very strong. A real giant."

XIX

For Ricciardi and Maione, the walk back to police headquarters was a chance to review the scenario suggested by the autopsy findings. Night was starting to fall, but the air gave no sign of cooling. There was almost no one out on the streets; a few families trudged wearily home from the beach.

Maione said: "To be honest, Commissa', I never believed that a man like Iovine would throw himself out the window. First of all, there wasn't so much as a goodbye note; and then, what reason would he have had to do it? He had plenty of money, he had risen to the top of his profession, he was married, with a beautiful house, a wife and a son . . . And if the inscription in the second ring means what I think it does, well then he even had a *cummarella*, a sweetheart on the side. Why on earth would someone like him ever commit suicide?"

Ricciardi was reluctant to agree: "You know better than I do, Raffaele. We've seen so many who've been given wealth and comfort and taken from it nothing but loneliness and a sense of emptiness. People do lots of stupid things: the professor's lover, whoever she was, might have been blackmailing him, or perhaps he had some secret vice that was ruining him. In any case, the marks on the body and clothing are unequivocal: someone murdered him."

Maione was huffing and puffing from the slight uphill climb.

"And it was someone very strong, Commissa'. For that matter, Coviello, the jeweler, told us that he saw someone in the shadows who was immense, in fact he said the man looked like a mountain. This someone picked the professor up and tossed him out the window. And he did it so quickly that the poor professor never even had time to scream, because if he had someone would surely have heard him, since the hospital is full of patients and nurses."

Ricciardi stopped suddenly: "By the way, did you check to see whether Antonelli remembered that guy . . . what was his name . . . Giuseppe Graziani?"

Maione slapped his forehead: "Oooh, *mamma mia*, Commissa', you're right, I completely forgot to tell you; I was coming to see you when the doctor called. I was right when I thought that name was familiar. Giuseppe Graziani is none other than Peppino the Wolf!"

"Should I recognize that name?"

"No, Commissa', he hasn't passed through your hands yet; but if you ask me it's only a matter of time, guys like him never escape their fate. He's a *guappo*, a low-level criminal who's building his career, he runs the Pendino quarter. We've already had a couple of tips about him: he's expanding his territory. He controls fruit and vegetable shipping, the pushcarts that sell in the streets all around town. Everyone's afraid of him, according to Antonelli, but he doesn't know much else about him."

Ricciardi started walking again.

"That's one lead. And the threatening letter is another. That makes two. And another thing we need to figure out is just who this Sisinella from the second inscription is: what the goldsmith told us might suggest it's someone who had power over the professor, if he was in such a rush to have the ring made for her. Experience tells us that where there's a lover, there's always danger. Emotions are excellent motives for killing someone or getting yourself killed."

Maione commented bitterly: "Commissa', to hear you talk, you'd think a man would have to live blindfolded, gagged, with both hands tied, locked up alone in a windowless room. That way he'll never suffer for sure."

He'd barely finished speaking when he caught a fleeting movement out of the corner of his eye: someone had just walked out of the door of an apartment building and slipped into a side street, a narrow *vicolo*. The brigadier furrowed his brow and said to Ricciardi: "Commissa', excuse me, would you wait here for a second?"

He took a few steps, leaned out into the small cross street and narrowed his eyes: in the crowd he spotted a blonde head he'd have recognized out of a thousand like it.

He felt a twinge in the pit of his stomach. What was Lucia doing in an apartment house on Via Toledo at that time of day, when she ought to have been home getting dinner ready?

As he turned around, he made a mental note of the building's street address. He'd have to look into this.

"Something wrong?"

"No, Commissa', I just thought I saw . . . But I must have been mistaken. You were saying?"

The commissario went on: "I think the time has come to find out a little more about the three situations. First: this Peppino the Wolf. A gangster, but a smart one, it seems to me. I doubt that he'd have done something as foolish as going to the general hospital, which would have been too risky; why not lie in wait for the professor somewhere else? Next, the colleague who sent the letter: he says that he's sick, actually on his deathbed. How can someone in such a condition find the strength to hurl a man bodily out a window with his bare hands? And then last of all, we need to track down this Sisinella and question her."

Maione, still distracted, replied: "Maybe not for the sick doctor, because this wouldn't be his stomping grounds, but for the lover and the Wolf, we can ask around a little."

They'd reached police headquarters. Ricciardi said: "Now

you get home, you've been here since this morning. As for the information . . ."

The brigadier sighed: "I know, I know, Commissa'. I'll have to climb all the way uphill, in this heat, to San Nicola da Tolentino, and walk into that room full of certain perfumes that I don't even like to tell you about. But a job is a job, isn't it? Have a good night, Commissa'."

Ricciardi started up the staircase that led to his office.

At the top of the stairs, Livia was waiting for him.

XX

This time she hadn't come, to the Immacolatella. He was siting in his usual place, surrounded by the coils of hawsers, at a certain distance from the boarding area.

It was hot. Terribly hot. The air felt like what pours out of a blast furnace full of molten metal. The more the wind blew, the hotter it got. A wind out of Africa.

A few of the passengers waiting to board were laughing out loud. It wasn't the way it had been just a few years earlier, when you could read a terror of the unknown on the faces of the poor waiting to emigrate, and tension quivered in the air, a fear of sailing into the maw of death.

He could remember that scene: it was like a stage production of fear itself. There were some who feared the ocean, across which they would venture after steaming for a day or two through the Mediterranean Sea; they feared that black expanse of water that no doubt harbored horrible monsters ready to gobble down the steamship in a single gulp. Or else they were afraid of the water itself, and the waves of the stormy seas, towering above them like mountains, only to thunder down without pity upon their heads, their hands, their open mouths, crushing them under, drowning them and breaking their bones. And they were all afraid of the new land toward which they would be sailing, an unknown incomprehensible place, inhabited by all manner of ferocious animals, as violent as it was inhospitable. They were driven by hunger, and they trembled at the thought that perhaps that same hunger would be waiting to greet them when they arrived. They were leaving in the spirit in which you reshuffle the deck after an unlucky hand, or pick a number to play in the lottery, placing your hopes of a new destiny at the crossroads where you met the old one.

It wasn't like that now. Now there were people smiling as they looked up at the belly of the huge black ship. The letters had started to come. At first there were just a few, haltingly written and read even more haltingly in evenings around the fire: a voice that struggled to decipher the large awkward letters as wide eyes glistened, listening in silence. Then there were more and more of them, letters written in a language contaminated by the mewling speech of those other people, in that land across the salt water. And the news, which had been terrible, started to become good. The relatives who'd sailed for America were getting organized, doing business, everyone putting himself in contact with everyone else; they were working, establishing partnerships and alliances. Desperation was a powerful force, they'd found, and if it was carefully husbanded it became determination, and then success. Money came back, but no one spent it. They set it aside, for the day they too would set sail.

He liked it better when there was fear. Fear justified staying, his being on this side of the wharf, far from the densely packed crowd and the household possessions wrapped in knotted, tattered sheets. He used to feel wealthy and strong, because he didn't have to leave. But now he had doubts.

He wondered why she wasn't there. She'd never missed their unspoken appointments. She was important to him. Very important. It was for her sake that he'd decided to stay, it was for her that he'd worked so hard to find this apprenticeship, for her that he'd begun building a future of possible happiness. Because he sensed her ambition, her determination to be different from the people they knew.

A shiver swept through the crowd of passengers about to

depart, like a gust of wind in a field of high grass; a few people stamped and jerked, uneasily. A sailor was coming down the gangway with a sheaf of paper in his hand: the passenger manifest. The moment was about to arrive.

He sensed someone moving behind him. His heart leapt in his chest, but he gave no outward sign. She crouched, as always, a foot or so from his back.

"They're leaving," he murmured. "That sailor is about to begin calling them."

She let a few seconds go by before answering: "I see that. But I don't want to come here anymore, I don't want to watch the ships anymore. I came here to tell you so."

He swiveled around suddenly: "Why don't you want to come anymore?"

"I don't like it. I used to feel I was lucky to be able to stay. Now I'm not so sure anymore."

He was surprised to hear her confirm the doubts that he felt in his chest. But these meetings belonged to them and them alone, and he didn't intend to give them up.

"You're the one who always said that you'd never leave, that you wouldn't give in, that all those people were doing was running away. Now what, you've changed your mind?"

One seagull flew up to another; the two birds exchanged a series of cries that sounded like a baby sobbing.

She replied: "I'm not running away. I'm just doing what's best for me. You know my aunt, the one who could never have children?"

He was bewildered: "Which one, the aunt who married the businessman who's making money by the truckload providing construction material for the new train stations? Sure, you told me about her a thousand times."

"That's the one. She's finally given up, she always says that if God doesn't want to send her children, she has to accept His will. But she's lonely because her husband is never at home, and she cries and feels sad. My mother says that there are people who have plenty of money but still aren't happy."

He'd gone back to looking at the crowd of men and women, but he was listening sharply.

"And so?"

"I'm her favorite niece, because she says that my face resembles hers. I can't see this resemblance, to tell the truth, but she insists on it, and since she has all the money, everyone in my family says she's right, and they all say: it's true, it's true, you're like twins, two drops of water, exactly alike; I can remember Titina when she was a girl, the spitting image of you."

She imitated the voices of her relatives so well that he couldn't stifle his laughter.

"Well? So what's it all mean?"

"It means that I'm going to go live with her. In her husband's town."

He started and turned his back on the wharf, on the ship, on the passengers waiting to board, on the sailor calling out names.

"What do you mean, you're going to leave? What about me? What about us? What about all the promises we made?"

His questions were greeted with silence. The seagulls went back to telling their stories, their cries piercing the sky. She stared out to sea. Then she said: "You have to wait for me. Work hard, work well. Become the best you can. Then I'll come back, with my aunt and uncle's money, and we'll stay together forever, rich, with plenty to eat, no wants and no fears. We'll buy a whole apartment house; we'll even buy ourselves a ship. You'll be able to make it set sail and come back all you want. You just have to know how to wait for me."

He felt a stab of pain in his heart. He hadn't been ready for this. He'd never thought of his life without her. Boarding had begun. Among those left ashore were some who wept, but he realized, to his horror, that none of those who were leaving shed a single tear; at the very most, as they went up the gang-way, they'd turn and look back, raising one arm in farewell. The ones who stay are the ones who cry, not the ones who leave, he thought to himself.

The ones who stay are the ones who cry.

Sorrow squeezed his throat.

"And what will I do? What should I do, while I wait for you? In the morning, when I wake up, and at night, when I can't get to sleep, who should I think about? Tell me that: who should I think about?"

The last few words came out in a choking voice, practically in a sob. They'd come out in the voice of a child.

She continued to keep her eyes, expressionless, on the point where the harbor opened out into the sea.

"You need to think of me, like you do already. Because I'll come back, with what we need. Promise. Promise that you'll think of me and the future we'll have together."

He followed her gaze and realized that she was already gone. Without letting him say goodbye with one final embrace.

"I promise," he said.

And she smiled, at the sea.

XXI

Ricciardi wondered how Livia did it.

How she managed to get inside police headquarters and all the way up to the landing outside his office, evading the checkpoints manned by police officers and clerks of the court that were placed every ten feet.

How she managed to know with such precision when he would be returning to work, since that never happened at any fixed time.

How she managed, in that heat, to be dressed, made up, and bejeweled as if she were about to attend a gala banquet without displaying the least sign of discomfort.

From the top of the stairs, she smiled down at him, cheerful and captivating: "Ciao, Commissario. You're back, at last. Come on up, I have something important to tell you."

Ricciardi sighed. He had extensive experience of the considerable difference between their concepts of what was important.

Not that Livia wasn't an intelligent woman, and not that she hadn't suffered enough in her lifetime to develop a certain emotional depth, but still, she had never had any direct experience of real need, of want, in anything from food to medicine. She had no knowledge of the kind of desperation that was linked to survival. The kind of experience that Ricciardi, on the other hand, dealt with, painfully, from sunrise to sunset. It was inevitable that the scales on which they measured importance were not the same.

The end of the main daytime shift was approaching, and the corridor lined with office doors was emptying out. The police officers, lawyers, clerks, and even magistrates who happened to be passing by slowed down, pretending they'd forgotten a document, a sudden appointment, or else rummaged through their pockets in search of a cigarette: anything to prolong the sight of Livia or to allow them to catch her eye. It was a scene that Ricciardi was becoming accustomed to, now that they were seeing each other more frequently.

That evening she was dressed in white. Her dress hung to mid-calf and left her arms bare; over her belly button hung a composition of artificial flowers. She wore a silk shawl over her shoulders and on her head was perched a cunning little cap garnished with small stalks of wheat; her hair hung over her neck in soft curls. A court clerk attempted an acrobatic walk along the wall in order to observe her from behind, and came perilously close to tripping over a step.

"Come into my office, Livia. Otherwise we're going to a cause a traffic jam here."

Livia accepted Ricciardi's invitation, took a seat and crossed her legs, then lit a cigarette. She looked like a little girl about to be given a present.

"Are you tired? Have you had a hard day? You look exhausted."

He sat down at his desk with a shrug.

"The usual. There's no work for anyone in this city, except for us. Unfortunately."

She tilted her head to one side: "Yes, you look tense. Would you like to take in a show tonight? At the Botanical Gardens they're offering open-air entertainment; I've heard the orchestra is first rate. What do you say? Would you care to take me out?"

"No, Livia, I'm afraid I'm in no mood for it. I've told you about Rosa and how worried I am about her health. Just think, she sent for one of her nieces to come up from our hometown to give her some help. That really must mean she's not well. I want to get home and see how she's doing; I don't want to come back when she's already asleep."

Livia gave him a cunning smile: "One of her nieces, you say? A pretty country girl, young and strong. I bet that's the reason you're so eager to get home early."

Ricciardi snorted: "I'd be glad to let you have a look at her, this Nelide. I've seen more attractive chests of drawers and shapelier armoires. Don't make me laugh. But she's an excellent housekeeper and I'm glad that Rosa can get some rest. Was there something you wanted to tell me?"

"Yes, and it's something very important to me. I'm going to throw a party. A wonderful party at my apartment, with the living room doors thrown open onto the terrace. You see what I mean, yes? I want there to be tables with food of every assortment, these wonderful dishes that only you Neapolitans know how to make, all local delicacies. And I want an orchestra, not a big one, let's be clear: six or seven musicians who can keep us dancing into the wee hours, until our feet are so swollen that we won't be able to pry our shoes off."

Ricciardi lifted both hands into the air to halt that chaotic flood of words.

"All right, all right. But why are you throwing this party? Is there some special occasion coming up?"

Livia exhaled a stream of smoke in her annoyance: "Does there necessarily have to be some special occasion to justify a party? Don't be so backward and old-fashioned, Ricciardi! In the time I've been here, as you know, I've never once been able to host a party. Once, as you'll recall, I tried but . . . let's not bring it up, let's just say that it put me off parties for awhile. But now I've made up my mind. We ought to celebrate this summer. The summer and its scents, its songs."

"It will most certainly be a success."

Livia clapped her hands: "It will be unforgettable! You know, I have to repay all the invitations I've received, and I want the city authorities to attend, as well as people from Rome. I'm not sure, but some very important guests might be attending. I have a dear girlfriend who's not having a particularly easy time at the moment, and I'd like to see that she has some fun."

"All the way from Rome, no less. For a party. Quite an event."

"That's right, an event! And it's going to be a masquerade party, with a maritime theme. The guests will have a choice of dressing up as fishermen, sailors, or gods of the deep. And the food, too, will be made to match. I have a housekeeper who's a wonderful cook, I'll make sure she has at least two assistants. Isn't that a fantastic idea?"

Ricciardi looked at her, baffled: "A masquerade party? But aren't masquerade parties supposed to be for Carnevale?"

"You see what a Neanderthal you are? Masquerade parties are extremely fashionable, and they have them all year long. Disguising yourself is fun and it stimulates people's creativity! You, for example, what costume would you choose?"

Ricciardi decided it was time to make things very clear: "Livia, please, I fight against disguises every day of my life. People are constantly trying to seem different from what they actually are, and to do so they do ridiculous things you couldn't even begin to imagine. I haven't the slightest intention of donning a mask, even for fun."

Livia shrugged.

"As you prefer. You'll feel out of place, but that's not my problem. All I care about is that you come. You have to promise me that you'll be there, because you know that you . . . you were a very important part of my decision to come live here, in this city."

Such an explicit declaration stirred something approaching pity in Ricciardi's heart.

"Livia, don't start, you know I've never asked you for anything. If you're here it's because you choose to be, and I believe that you made a good choice, because from what you tell me, in Rome you were always and only Vezzi's wife. But I don't want you to put the responsibility for that choice on me."

The happiness in the woman's eyes misted over, leaving in its place a veil of sadness.

"Don't worry, Ricciardi. I know that you don't want to be at all emotionally responsible for me. But you can't deny that I've never concealed my feelings for you. And even though you aren't willing to admit it even to yourself—actually, especially to yourself—you like being with me. It relaxes you, you even smile sometimes, without realizing it. And you'll have a great time the night of the party, too. If you promise me you'll come, I'll tell you something else. Well? Will you promise?"

Ricciardi's expression was almost a gentle one.

"All right then, I promise. I'll do my best to be there, unless circumstances beyond my control prevent me, of course. I told you about Rosa, and the work I do, as you know, makes it impossible to plan sometimes . . ."

Livia waved her hand dismissively: "Yes, yes, of course. That's all I want: that, unless forces beyond your control prevent you, you'll attend. And now do you want to know the other thing? The surprise?"

"No, I don't. If you told me, what kind of surprise would it be?"

Livia thought it over, then stood up: "You're right. I'm not going to tell anyone, it's going to be a surprise for everyone. I'd better run. If you won't come to the show at the Botanical Gardens, I'm not going either. I'll stay home and plan my party, there isn't much time. I want to have it next week, the night of Our Lady of Mount Carmel, so we'll be able to watch the fireworks from my terrace. *Ciao*, Ricciardi."

And in a cloud of white, she left his office.

Ricciardi went over to the open window. Night was falling and the lights were flickering on all over the city.

In spite of the heat, the commissario felt a shiver of obscure premonition run down his spine.

XXII

Climbing slowly uphill toward his home, Maione continued to ask himself whether the woman he had seen come
out of the apartment house on Via Toledo had really
been his Lucia.

In all those years, his wife had never ventured so close to
police headquarters without stopping in to say hello. He'd
dropped by the front guardroom and asked if anyone had
come by looking for him, but they'd told him no. Not satisfied,
he'd gone up into the offices, on the off chance that Lucia had
come at a time when there was no one at the front entrance,
but once again he came up empty. No one had asked for him.
Certainly not his wife.

There was no way he had been wrong. Lucia—with her
golden blonde hair, so unusual in that part of the country, her
brisk confident gait, her handsome body clad in black, the
color she'd worn since Luca's death. And then he could sense
her in the air, Lucia. He could feel her on his skin like a breath
of wind, in his nostrils like a delicate perfume, in his ears like
a snatch of sweet music. He didn't need to look her in the eyes
or hear her voice. Yes, the woman who had left that building
was Lucia.

But why, he wondered, as he trudged up the last stretch of
road, why had she gone there? Had something happened? Did
she need help? A doctor for one of the children? No, impossible. She would have turned to Modo, and before doing that
she would have let him know.

He walked into the apartment and was overwhelmed by the hugs of his three youngest: the two boys leaping onto him in a pretend ambush, and the little girl who began laughing the minute she laid eyes on him. He stopped to play with them, tousling their hair and pretending to be a big baboon. Then he went into the kitchen.

The first thing he ought to have said was: *Ciao*, my love, why were you in Via Toledo a couple of hours ago? Why didn't you stop by to say hello? Of course that's what he ought to have said. But, he thought, I'm a cop.

And so he played the cop.

"Mmm, what an appetizing smell," he said. "What delicious treats are we cooking today, my fair ladies?"

At the table, Maria and Benedetta were mixing flour and water into a dough as carefully as a couple of elderly housewives. They even look alike, thought Maione, they really could be sisters.

Lucia raised her face, reddened from the steaming cookpots, and blew him a kiss.

"Don't worry, we won't throw a single morsel away. Go get changed and let us work in peace."

Was he mistaken or had she been a little brusque? Wasn't she a little behind schedule today?

He feigned disappointment: "What, dinner isn't ready yet? I'm so hungry . . ."

"Don't worry. Dinner will be served at eight, like always. Go get changed like I told you to, you're dripping with sweat, worse than your children. Get going!"

Raffaele headed for his bedroom roiled by an unpleasant sensation. The dress, he thought. The dress that the person he'd seen was wearing. The black dress embroidered with roses of the same color.

He pulled open the armoire: there it was, in its place, on a hanger. But not on the usual hanger, in the middle of the curtain rod, where his wife kept her best dresses. Instead, it hung on the first hanger, the one closest to the bedroom door. As if it had been put away in a hurry.

He tried to distract himself by stopping for a chat with his oldest boy, Giovanni, who wanted to hear all about his work. The boy's mother worried about the fact that her son wanted to be a cop like his father and his murdered brother, so certain conversations were better held far from Lucia's ears, in undertones, like a couple of conspirators.

Maione told him about the professor who'd fallen out the window, without lingering on the more macabre details. He didn't want to encourage the boy, but he was pleased that he wanted to carry on the family tradition. And after all, becoming a policeman was better than becoming a criminal like so many other young men from the neighborhood, who chased after rewards both easier and much more dangerous to come by.

The dinner table was cheerful and loud, and Maione joined in the confusion; he didn't want to give his wife the impression that anything was bothering him. He waited until the kids were in bed and the dishes and pots and pans were in the drying rack, and when Lucia, exhausted, finally let herself drop into the chair next to his, he said to her in a neutral tone of voice: "*Mamma mia*, this heat makes everything so laborious. Just walking a few feet in the street outside is torture. Lucky you, that the only reason you have to go out is to buy groceries; and this evening it was hotter than it was in the middle of the day. But here at home there's a bit of a breeze, don't you think?"

"Yes, with the windows open on both sides of the apartment there's a slight draft. Anyway, it was hot this morning at the market too, believe me."

Raffaele nodded. He stared at a point outside on the balcony because he knew all too well his wife's ability to read his thoughts in his eyes, and he didn't want to give anything away.

"I really wouldn't want to have to make that uphill climb home more than once a day. I think I'd die of a heart attack."

Lucia was convinced that he wasn't looking at her because he was distracted by his worries. My poor love, she thought to herself, if only you could make up your mind to set aside this absurd pride of yours and confide in me. I'd reassure you, because I know there's always a solution to be found. But if you won't talk to me, then how can I talk to you?

"What are you talking about! Don't even joke about a thing like that. No one dies of a heart attack because of a little heat. Don't worry."

"Sure," responded Maione laconically. Then, after a pause: "Still, it really is hot, and tomorrow Mistrangelo—he's the one who takes the crime reports—tells me it's going to be hotter still. Don't ask me how he knows, but he always seems to get it right. You don't have to go out tomorrow, do you?"

"No, this morning I did the grocery shopping for tomorrow as well. You won't even have to leave me money. We don't need a thing."

Maione nodded.

"And today? You only went out this morning, right?"

Lucia stared at him, surprised: "Say, what are all these questions for? Of course I went out this morning, I told you that I went to the market. And yes, it was hot. You keep asking me the same things. But do you even listen to me, when I answer?"

Maione raised one hand in apology: "Of course I listen, why wouldn't I? I was just worried that the heat was too much for you, the way it gets you down."

"Truth be told, the one who suffers when it's hot out is you, what I hate is the cold. And in fact I'm not minding the heat all that much."

"No, it's just that you always dress in black, don't you?" Maione went on, as if pursuing a train of thought. "And black attracts the heat. It's not a good idea to go out in bright sunlight if you're wearing black. So really there'd be nothing wrong with doing your shopping in the late afternoon, or even in the evening, when the sun isn't straight overhead, in other words."

Lucia didn't know whether to laugh or to ignore him and just drop the subject: "Raffae', have you gone out of your mind? Now you're saying that because I wear black, I should do my grocery shopping in the evening? Then when would I do the cooking, at night? And then you'll have to go tell the people who sell groceries at the market to change their hours, have them open up in the evening. You can tell them: Excuse me, I'm Police Brigadier Raffaele Maione, would you be so kind as to put out your stalls in the evening instead of the morning, otherwise I'm afraid my wife might break a sweat?"

"No, I wasn't saying that, just . . ."

"Or else," Lucia went on, continuing to imitate him, "would you do me the favor of simply bringing the groceries to my home, so my wife doesn't even have to use the stairs? Sure, that would be great, thanks, just choose the finest fruit and fish, that way she doesn't have to tire out her little hands by squeezing them."

Maione sighed: "So now it's a crime if somebody worries about his wife. It doesn't matter, tire yourself out, sweat yourself silly, you can even faint in the street, just don't come crying to me about it. Today, for example, you went out in the morning, didn't you? So too bad for you."

"I went out this morning, and I'm fit as a fiddle. Now let's go to bed. Tomorrow, you'll see, I won't go out at all, that way you'll be happy."

XXIII

The dialect of this city, a city that sings songs of love and tells tales of passions, has a special word to describe a gust of wind.

The word resembles another in the mother tongue, in Italian: but it's feminine, not masculine, so its meaning is profoundly different. And the word doesn't describe gusts of wind in general, but *one* gust of wind. A very special one.

Rèfola.

Not the Italian word *refolo*, which is just a silly drizzle of air, a draft that can last for a while, bringing you nothing more than a brief sensation, the feeling on the skin scarcely registering in the mind. Nothing like that at all.

There's something magical about the *rèfola*, a short enchanted breath that vanishes even before you notice it's there. A faint awareness, perhaps the echo of a memory or the premonition of some future regret.

It presents itself as a sigh of cool air. It brings relief, it speaks of airy lands and snowy peaks, almond trees in bloom and foamy waves crashing on the rocks.

But it's merely an illusion.

I should have been there.

I should have been there, while you were falling to earth. While you were abandoning your life, all your memories, all the people, the faces, the sounds, the flavors.

I should have been there, while the ground was rushing up

at you at dizzying speed, as you were embracing death, you who had always lived every breath in full, as if you were immortal, as if there were nothing that existed outside of you.

I should have been there, to ask you while you were falling whether there was a a thought in your mind of the harm. Of all the harm that you might have done, with those arms wind-milling through the air, with that brain that was about to be smashed open on the stones in just a second or so.

And I would have relished the show. I'd have laughed at your pain and your death. I'd have danced around all that was left of you, in the moonlight. I'd have spat on your corpse, a hundred times, mingling my disgust with your blood and your brains.

I should have been there.

That's what it does, the *règola*.

It arrives when everything is stagnant, airless, when it seems as if nothing will ever change again, and that the world and the entire universe are going to sink into a sea of heat. When you feel, keeping vigil throughout the night as if wrapped in a boil-ing shroud, as if you'd been hurled down into the inferno, and that in just a moment Beelzebub might come to ask you to account for your sins.

But the *règola* brings a smile, vanishing before a single thought can be completed.

I love you, you know. I love you.

I'll say it to you in the silence of this night I'm passing else-where, far from my bed and my things, far from the thoughts that I now know were those of a little girl. Far from you and your gaze through the window.

Perhaps one needs to go far away, in order to understand love. Perhaps one needs to get away from the books on the bookshelf, from the glass of water on the nightstand, from the dresses neatly hanging in the armoire, to understand how much one might want a kiss, how much one needs a hand, in the night.

I love you. Not because of an image behind the glass, not because of the color of your eyes in the half-darkness, not because of your lips, grazing mine in a strange snowfall.

I love you because I want you in this bed, here and now. Because I'd like to take you against my breast and in my arms, because I don't know the flavor of your skin and I'd like to taste it.

I love you in the flesh and in the blood. That's what distance has taught me, and I wish it had taught me the opposite, that it had told me of a silence to be filled with other music, of empty spaces to be furnished with other wood and other glass and other silver. I wish.

But I love you. Now and yesterday and tomorrow. I love you.

The *rèfola* tells, in a fleeting second, all the stories that we'd tell ourselves, if only we had the courage.

It doesn't have the time to carry things through to the end, and it wouldn't even want to. It suggests the beginning, the first notes of the song, the opening strains of a well-known symphony.

Our soul does the rest.

I'm not sleeping, no. And how could I sleep?

Death isn't a joke. Death is an enormity.

It's one thing to struggle, to stand up for your convictions, to affirm your will to survive. Death is another.

Death means you no longer exist. That by your hand, a person who once loved, hated, felt pleasure and pain, from one moment to the next becomes a heap of bloody rags, without breath and without emotions.

Death means that by your hand a creature that till then had been at the center of a spiderweb of feelings and passions, someone who might have been a father and a husband, a friend and a son, disappears from the list of the living and becomes a name engraved on a headstone, the phantom of a memory.

I'm not sleeping. I can't.

Because death isn't a game, something that you can patiently reassemble, with nimble fingers or careful eye. Once you've dealt it, you can't take it back. Death is definitive. From death, there's no returning.

Then why do I see you here, sitting on my bed? Why do I hear your voice, why do I still see the surprise in your eyes?

I'm not sleeping. I can't.

Someone who's dealt out death can't sleep.

Ever again.

Since it's feminine, the *rèfola* always knows what it's doing. It never wavers from the task it has set itself.

Since it's feminine, it seduces intentionally, never by chance. Who knows how much time it takes, in the cool depths where it originates, choosing the right plunging neckline, the right swivel of the hips. Since it's feminine, it knows the right buttons to push in the fraction of a second it will have available to act. Since it's feminine, it knows the power of a touch that barely grazes, apparently by chance, to churn the blood gone stagnant against the heat.

Since it's feminine, it knows how much destruction lies concealed in a passion. And how much fun it is to trigger that destruction and then stand to one side, observing its terrible effects.

And now? What will we do now?

We'd gotten used to the prosperity, the tranquillity, as if they would never come to an end. To the gifts, the money, the clothes.

We'd gotten used to them.

Because they came from those womanly hands, smooth and restless, and from the desire to receive compliments and smiles. We thought they'd never end.

Of course, he could also be repulsive, with that body of his that had only ever had the vaguest semblances of manliness about it, with that double chin, that flat, hairless chest, that flaccid gut: an instant of imaginary masculinity after a few seconds of feeble agitation. He could be revolting.

But then he'd dole out his power, his wealth, in exchange for a smile. And in the end, it was a good price for a smile. And even for the glimmer of a moan, a heavy sigh.

Who knows how he could ever fool himself into believing he gave pleasure, with that horrible belly, that old man's face, those girl's hands. People always find ways to fool themselves.

But now it's over. And we'll have to find something else.

For that matter, we should have expected it.

We should have expected him to die.

He was bound to die, wasn't he? He was bound to die.

But you have to be ready for it, for the *rèfola*.

An open window, a door left ajar. Because the *rèfola* may touch your soul, but it's something physical, concrete, real, it needs space and time to reach you, it requires a moment's attention from the body.

Provided you want the *rèfola* to hit you, naturally.

I can smell the breath of death.

I can smell it in the air. A heavy, lurking stench, that lingers in your mouth more than in your lungs. Death lies in the heat; its stink befouls the air down in hell.

A transition, nothing but a transition. Like crossing a field: you can take a minute or a whole month, but the end comes eventually, and there are shadows in the forest, beyond the field's edge.

It wasn't hard to make the journey. It wasn't always easy, but I've been lucky, Barone'. Truly lucky. I've loved wholeheartedly, more than a mother can love her son, listening to his breathing while he sleeps, gazing into his eyes. I didn't understand him, Barone'. And I didn't understand you either, when you stopped in the middle of your embroidery and sat there, in silence, staring into the empty air.

But it's not as if you necessarily have to understand, in order to love. Loving isn't something you do because you want something in return, for compensation. Loving is loving, period.

I'm not afraid, Barone'. If there's a place where you are now, we'll see each other and we'll have a nice long chat the way we used to on the patio by the garden. And if there isn't a place, then there's no reason to be afraid, because we just won't be there, and that's that. Inferno? And what did we do wrong, you and I? People like us, Barone', don't have it in us to do wrong.

I feel it in the air, the breath of death. I have to hurry. There are lots of things to take care of. Lots of things to set right.

The breath of death. A cold breath.

It may seem like a gust of wind, perhaps you'll think that you merely imagined it. But it's not a gust of wind, it's a *rèfola*.

And a *rèfola* can bring with it all the good and all the ill in the world, because it provides you with a dream in the inferno of heat in which you're sunk. A single dream, the length of a sigh.

So take it from me: close that window. The heat is better.

Better the inferno than a single despairing dream.

XXIV

Ricciardi found Maione catnapping on the wooden bench in the hallway outside his office.

As always, Ricciardi had come in very early, and as always there was almost no one else at police headquarters. Spotting the brigadier's large silhouette in the half light while he was thinking about Professor Iovine's case made him jump. He felt as if he were witnessing what Coviello, the goldsmith, had seen on his way out of the victim's study: a great big man waiting to go in.

"Raffaele? What are you doing here at this hour? I mean, have you decided you just don't want to go home anymore?"

Maione started.

"Nossir, Commissa'. It's just that in this heat I can't get to sleep so I came in early. But then, since it's actually relatively cool in here, I fell asleep. Forgive me."

"No apologies needed, as far as I'm concerned, you're welcome to move in here. I'm just sorry for you, spending more time at work than with your family. Come on, let's go into the office and try to figure out what our next step is in this investigation."

The early morning hour, the fact that schools were closed, and the massive heat meant the piazza was deserted; Ricciardi's open window let in only the lazy sound of a vendor's cart.

The commissario motioned at Maione to sit: "All right, this is how things stand: we are certain that we're looking at a murder, so our approach has to change. Now we're looking for the person who did it. The person who murdered the professor. What do we know about this person?"

Maione scratched his forehead and concentrated. He counted on his fingers: "First: it's someone very strong, because he tossed him out the window like a twig, picking him up by his shirt collar and his trousers. Second: for that reason, we can assume he's a man. Third: if we give credence to the goldsmith, who was the last to see the professor alive, he's big and tall, which fits with the fact that he tossed the man out the window without even letting him brush against the windowsill."

Ricciardi nodded: "Exactly. And what we know about the professor, on the other hand, is that he was someone who was hiding a few flaws in a life that was apparently respectable and honorable. First and foremost Sisinella, the name engraved inside the ring found in the drawer. What's more, there must be something to the hesitations we heard in the voices of Nurse Zupo and the director's head assistant, Rispoli.

"And I'd talk to them again, Commissa', if for no other reason than to understand clearly what happened when Peppino the Wolf swore he'd kill the professor."

"Sure, but first we need to learn where the Wolf was at that time of night, otherwise we might start digging where we don't need to. And let's not forget the letter from the owner of that clinic, which was pretty threatening too. In other words, we have plenty of work ahead of us. Like I told you yesterday evening, I'd start by gathering information about Sisinella and this *guappo*, the Wolf. And for information, as you know . . ."

Maione threw his arms wide, disconsolately: "I know. I have a long climb ahead of me. All right, Commissa', I'll go, give Bambinella her assignment, and then come back."

"Perfect. I'll wait for you here, then we'll go to the clinic together. Enjoy your walk."

After Maione left, Ricciardi concentrated on what he'd heard at the site of the professor's death. The feeling that had flooded his skin and soul, the victim's final dying sorrow, had been focused entirely on the mysterious Sisinella.

It was the commissario's theory that behind every murder was either hunger or love, the two eternal forces that ensured the survival of the human race. And so, each time he was confronted with a case, he did his best to figure out which of the two was directly responsible for the crime he was investigating. He'd never been wrong yet: one of these two faces of passion had always been at the root of the motive.

True, Iovine's last thought had been of love, but he had been a man of power, and the hunger for power is one of the most devastating emotions that can shake a heart, can even turn the power gained perverse, as the letter that the professor had received at home suggested might have happened in this case. On the other hand, the fury propelling the Wolf, who had sworn vengeance in front of witnesses, was the fury of love amputated. Who could say what the Deed would have said to him, if he had been present at the site of the *guappo*'s wife's death; who knows what thoughts of extreme love and extreme pain would have been left behind by a young woman facing the miracle of motherhood.

His mind turned to Rosa. Rosa who had been his mother in every way, shape, and form, Rosa who had tended to his skinned knees a hundred times, Rosa who cooked those terrible Cilento specialties that only his trained stomach could digest. Rosa, who wasn't doing well at all.

Once again, the night before, he'd found her asleep in the easy chair where she liked to sit and sew. Dinner was ready, made by Nelide, who was standing in a corner, arms folded across her chest. He'd asked the young woman how long her aunt had been sleeping, and Nelide had replied that Rosa had closed her eyes half an hour ago, and that she'd just tried calling her to see if she was still alive. The commissario realized that he was not alone in his concern for his *tata*'s state of health.

He'd put her to bed, overcoming her objections; with all the times you've put me to bed, he'd told her, for once I can return the favor.

After dinner, he'd gone into his bedroom, turned out the light, and looked out at the windows of the Colombo family's apartment. But again that night there was no trace of Enrica.

Where are you, he'd asked the darkness. Where are you. For months now, in the building across the street, he'd seen on the floor above Enrica's the ghost of a woman who'd killed herself for love. At last the image upstairs had dissolved and the sentiment of grief no longer filled the air, but the figure he so loved to watch on the floor below had vanished as well. Perhaps it had all been a dream, and Enrica had never really existed at all. Perhaps she was just yet another figment of his diseased imagination.

A middle-aged man with glasses and a mustache had come to the window. Ricciardi was certain that, with the light turned off, he wasn't visible from outside, but still he'd had the distinct impression that the man was looking in his direction. That must be Enrica's father, because he too was tall, and he had the same way of tilting his head to one side. After a few seconds he turned and left, and it seemed to Ricciardi that he had shaken his head with some sadness.

He wished he had the courage to push his head out into the scorching hot evening air and to shout, just like that, from one building to the other: Signore, Signore . . . *buonasera*, we don't know each other, my name is Ricciardi, Luigi Alfredo Ricciardi. I'm in love with your daughter and I was just wondering if you might be so kind as to tell me where she's gone, because I don't see her around anymore.

Sure, he said to himself, as the piazza below began filling up with women on their way to the market and workers heading to their jobs on bicycles, that sounds like an excellent way to be found insane or catch a few well-chosen insults. And perhaps

Enrica's father, if that's who he really was, might say to him: My dear sir, if you're in love with my daughter, why haven't you said anything? Why haven't you come here, to my home, and asked me for permission to see her? That's the way civilized people behave, don't you know that? That's the normal way.

And he, Ricciardi, would reply just as courteously: No, sir, I can't. Because, you see, it just so happens that I'm insane. Yes, insane like my poor late mother. Just think, I'm convinced I see dead people, and they tell me their last thoughts. Strange, no? You have to agree, it's a bizarre situation, and I'm sure that a man like you, a man who seems to love his daughter deeply, would never want a man like me for a son-in-law, not if the father knew that such a man might well hand down the same defect to his grandchildren. Do tell me what you think, good sir.

Ricciardi moved away from the window and sat down at his desk, his head in his hands. Yes, I'm crazy. And I'm inconsistent, too, he thought, because I ought to be happy that you've gone away, I ought to hope that, for your sake, you meet someone who can make you as happy as you deserve, and instead here I sit, wallowing in despair at the thought that I can't see you again, at the fact that I don't know where you are, terrified that I'm about to lose my Rosa and so will be crushed by an eternal loneliness.

Perhaps the smart thing was to spend time with Livia. Dull his senses with laughter, shows, and spumante, convince himself that superficial conversations could keep the suffering of others, which so haunted him, at bay. The widow wouldn't want a family and children of her own, she'd be satisfied with someone incomprehensible, someone with the unfamiliar allure of distance, of distraction. Seeing him with Livia, Enrica would abandon him once and for all. And perhaps Rosa would be persuaded that he was about to settle down at last, and she'd be happy.

His heart shrank as if it were clutched in an iron fist. No, he couldn't do that. Livia had a right to sincerity, to the honesty of true love. She'd already had enough pain in her life. Including the unnatural sorrow of losing a child.

The thought of that lost child took his thoughts to Maione and Lucia. Together, they'd managed to overcome a tragedy and rebuild their wonderful family on a foundation of love. He remembered the money worries that were tormenting the brigadier, and wondered how he could help him without wounding his pride. Still, money problems or not, he said to himself, Maione was a lucky man: his soul mate trusted him, and he trusted her.

And when you have trust, he reflected, picking up the autopsy report that had just arrived from the hospital, you don't need anything else.

XXV

Maione didn't trust his wife.

He felt guilty about it. In nearly twenty-five years of marriage, he'd never found himself doubting her word, and he'd never lied to her. They'd had their period of distance, from Luca's tragic death until roughly a year ago when, convinced that her silence was irreversible, he'd started to think he had feelings for another woman. Luckily, though, that spring had awakened Lucia from the apathy of her grief, and they'd rediscovered each other, more united and in love than ever.

Almost without being aware of it, he'd strayed from the route that led to Bambinella's apartment, and now he found himself standing outside the entrance to the apartment building he'd seen his wife emerge from the day before. Via Roma according to the official city registry of street names, Via Toledo to the populace at large; number 270. A building like many others: a tall, arched front entrance, topped by the carved stone coat of arms of who knows what long extinct family line; a dark red façade, which badly needed restoration; an atrium with a wooden concierge's booth, behind which were the small rooms occupied by the doorman; a broad flight of stairs leading up to the second floor, and a narrower flight from there up to the higher stories; an interior courtyard with a flower bed in the middle and a tall shade tree.

Maione didn't know what to do. On the one hand, he would have liked to overcome his doubts and convince himself that the woman he'd seen hastily leaving the apartment house and turning into the nearby *vicolo* hadn't been Lucia at all, as she had assured him; on the other hand, he thought, he was a policeman. And a policeman, by his very nature, investigates and goes in search of evidence.

An irritating part of his brain commanded him not to kid himself, his profession had nothing to do with any of this: he was a jealous husband who wanted to find out why his wife had lied to him. Whatever the case, his feet had brought him here, and he might as well take one more step in that direction.

In the atrium the air was cool and damp. The doorman was dousing a hydrangea bush with pails full of water; it was a laborious job, because it meant shuttling between a spigot in the far corner and the flower bed at the center of the courtyard, and the man was rather elderly.

Maione walked over to him. The awareness that he was using his police uniform to further a private investigation, combined with a sense of defeat over the fact that he'd been unable to trust Lucia, made his manner fairly abrupt.

"Listen, you. What's your name?"

The man stopped midway, holding the pail full of water with both hands.

"Oh, *buongiorno*. I'm the building's doorman."

"I didn't ask you what job you do. I asked you your name."

The man blinked, as if he'd been slapped in the face. He set down the pail and stood up, fearful: "Fanelli, Giovambattista Fanelli. At your orders, Brigadier . . ."

Maione chose not to introduce himself. The uniform alone authorized him to ask questions. And after all, he didn't want to leave any trace of his identity in that interview. He coughed sharply. He should never have started this, but now here he was.

"This is a police investigation. I need to ask you some questions about the residents of this building."

"But why, Brigadie', what's happened? There's no trouble here, all the tenants are respectable citizens, and I . . ."

Maione grabbed him by the arm and dragged him toward his little booth.

"You have nothing to worry about. I just want to ask you a couple of questions, but it's important, extremely important, that no one knows we've spoken. No one, understood?"

The man, slight and fearful, docilely followed the brigadier, stammering all the while: "But . . . but I don't know anything, Brigadie'. I assure you that, whatever it is that's happened, I know nothing."

Maione cocked his head: "Let's step into your place."

Inside the glass door there was a tiny apartment consisting of a room with a table and two chairs and an even smaller bedroom with a bed pushed against the wall and a twin-door armoire.

In a conspiratorial tone, Maione whispered: "Are you all alone here? Is this where you live?"

Fanelli nodded, eyes wide with fright. The fact that Maione had lowered his voice had terrified him.

"Yes, Brigadie'. I've been a widower for many years now, and my children are married and live on their own. But can you tell me what's happened? Something political, perhaps?"

Maione seized the opportunity.

"That's right. Something political, you understood right off the bat. You're an intelligent man. And seeing that you're intelligent, you understand that these are highly confidential matters, things that must be kept secret. If someone, anyone, learns that you and I have had this conversation, then we'd be forced to arrest you and send you . . . send you somewhere far away, and who knows when you'd ever be able to see your children again."

Fanelli's lower lip began to tremble. Sweat streamed off his forehead.

"But why, Brigadie'? I haven't done anything, I've never had the slightest interest in politics, which is why I never bothered to join the Fascist Party. But I'll take care of that immediately,

I'll do it today, I swear. I've always been a loyal Fascist, right from the start, and . . ."

Maione raised his hand: "That's enough. We know that you're a respectable citizen, we have our sources. But we need information about the people who live in this building, and you're going to have to give it to us . . ." The longer this thing dragged out, the more the policemen felt like a dirty impostor. He decided to cut things short: "So tell me: who lives in this building?"

Fanelli wet his lips and lowered his voice.

"Well, you see, Brigadie', this whole building is the property of Count Morrone di Visaglia, who keeps the top floor for himself."

"Describe this count for me."

"He's old, he's sick, he's pushing ninety, and he lives with two housekeepers who tend to him. He never gets out of bed and he no longer receives visitors. I doubt he's the person you're looking for."

By now Fanelli had entered fully into his role as political informant. Maione wanted to get out of there as quick as he could.

"Who else lives here?"

"Well, let's see: on the second floor is Signora Clelia's dressmaker's shop. She's a renowned seamstress, and customers come from all over."

Maione dismissed the information with a brusque gesture: "I don't care about that. I'm only interested in the people who live in the building. People who'd be at home around seven in the evening."

A cunning expression came over the doorman's face: "Oh, I see what you mean. This is something that happens in the evening, is it? Maybe some exchange of information. Now, there are two families that live on the third floor: the Frezzas— the husband, who's a clerk at city hall, his wife, and their eight children who make a tremendous ruckus from morning till night—and then a young married couple, the Marontis; he works in a factory, she stays home, and they have two children."

Maione scratched his chin, listening intently. Two families with lots of small children. He was beginning to feel reassured.

"What about the fourth floor?"

"On the fourth floor are two unoccupied apartments, and on the fifth floor lives Dottor Pianese."

Maione was suddenly alert: "Dottor Pianese? Does he live alone?"

"That's right, Brigadie'. The man's about forty; he's a lawyer, but he must have plenty of money because I never see any clients. On the other hand, there are always plenty of friends who come and go, and every so often even a lovely lady."

Maione felt his heart stop.

"What do you mean, a lovely lady? What lovely ladies? Why on earth would lovely ladies come call on him?"

The sudden change in the policeman's complexion and expression frightened the doorman, who took a step back: "Are you all right, Brigadie'? Can I get you a glass of water? Can I make you a cup of ersatz coffee?"

"Fane', talk! I asked you for information about this Pianese, now answer my questions, damn it! What's his first name? And what does he do?"

Fanelli was terrified. He backed up until he was against the wall and said: "For the love of God, Brigadie', I haven't done a thing, remember? Don't get mad at me! Pianese lives alone; he has a housekeeper, but at night she goes home. His name is Ferdinando. Everyone addresses him as Dottore and like I told you, he's a lawyer, but I don't know how he makes a living. He's rich, he has a good time, and I couldn't tell you whether there are foreign spies among the people who come to call on him. I can keep a close eye on him, if you like."

Maione took a step forward and grabbed the doorman by

both arms, practically lifting him off the floor. The man squeaked in fear.

"Fane', I'll tell you one last time: we never had this conversation, understood? Never! Keep an eye on Pianese; and in particular I want you to let me know if a blonde lady comes to call on him, very pretty, about forty years old. Blonde, you understand? Blonde hair, blue eyes. I'll come back when you least expect me to get your report. And you'll need to be ready when I come."

Fanelli nodded vigorously, doing his best to break free of the policeman's grip, and intoned dramatically: "At your orders, Brigadie'. If this is for the fatherland, never fear, I won't let anything escape me."

Maione gave him one last furious glare and then dropped him, letting him sag against a wall as if somebody had let all the air out of him. Then he left, but only after checking to make sure that there was no one in the atrium.

Outside, the city resounded with the cries of its thousands of busy inhabitants.

XXVI

K eeping an eye on the girls to make sure they were walking in line, Enrica thought to herself just how green that island was. She had occasionally gone to the woods around the Palace of Capodimonte and sat embroidering on one of the benches, especially in late spring or summer, but she'd never felt so completely immersed in nature as she did on Ischia.

Of course, at Capodimonte there was a constant awareness of the endlessly teeming city just outside the walls, while here what lay close at hand was the beach and a calm blue sea awaiting the children's cheerful shouts, but Enrica was inclined to believe that the earth itself was somehow different, more innocent and authentic, less a product of happenstance: even the countryside must have a vocation, must not be limited to a scattering of green between buildings.

Green were the grapevines, stretching out over acres and acres of land, heavy with bunches of still-ripening grapes and broad velvety leaves. Green were the broom plants and the tamarisks, growing thickly even along the sides of the roads. Green were the leaves of the geraniums on the balconies, and green were the hydrangeas in the gardens of the villas inhabited by vacationing aristocrats. Even the small, new oranges and lemons tangled among the leaves were green, still waiting to assume their bright colors, and yet sweeter smelling now than they would be once they ripened.

The birds sang free in the sky, the canaries sang back from their cages on terraces and balconies; the air was rife with the smell of sulfur and powdered copper scattered by the peasants to ward off pests.

The summer colony where Enrica was working was housed in a large aristocratic villa not far from Casamicciola. Like many other buildings in the area, it wasn't very old. In July 1883 an earthquake had razed nearly all the houses on the island, killing more than two thousand; it had been such an overwhelming catastrophe that it had become proverbial as a point of reference for unprecedented disasters. The memory of the earthquake, as Enrica had had an opportunity to learn for herself in the few conversations she'd had with locals, was vivid and painful. There was no one on the island who hadn't lost a relative or a friend.

The villa belonged to an old woman who'd been widowed many years ago and was lonely in a home that was far too big for her. She had been favorably impressed by the directives issued by the Fascist Party concerning temporary stays in summer resorts, especially as a means of preventing tuberculosis. She had therefore decided to make the building available, and had even paid for the necessary renovations out of her own pocket. She had given herself the title of director of the summer colony, but she mostly kept to herself: she spent her days on the terrace, lying on a beautiful chaise longue, reading under a sunshade that billowed and fluttered in the sea breeze, while her housekeeper brought her endless cups of tea.

The rest of the colony's staff consisted of two female teachers, one for the twenty-five boys and the other for the twenty-five girls; a rosy-cheeked Franciscan tertiary nun with enormous arms and an explosive laugh who served as the cook; a young and tireless female nurse; and two male attendants. Except for Enrica, who was in charge of the girls, they were all locals.

Since the little girls were easier to control than the boys, Enrica had some time to herself to read and tend to her two-sided correspondence: her official letters home, to satisfy her mother's ravenous curiosity, and the other, secret letters that she sent to her father, confiding her actual thoughts.

By now she'd been on the island for almost twenty days and she'd become used to the rhythms of work: awake at seven, ablutions and, if necessary, medical examinations for the girls with serious health problems; breakfast, and then down to the beach. The walk to the water, with the little ones in their white caps chattering away, was one of the nicest parts of the day. Enrica's heart seemed to be finding peace. At least as much as was possible, she thought to herself that morning, because that heart was nevertheless still wounded.

Her father had written to tell her to not think about it, to throw herself heart and soul into what she was doing; he urged her to focus only on the present day, then on the coming night and the next morning, without looking any further into the future; he had written her that time is the best medicine for all troubles, and time will pass if we let it. All very true, my dear *papà*, Enrica had written back, but every time I hope my heart is healed, it starts bleeding again.

In the meantime they'd reached the beach where the most daring boys, indifferent to the shouts of their elders, had already leapt into the waves that lazily slapped the sand. Enrica got the girls situated, warning the frailest ones to say in the shade of the rock cliff.

She looked up and noticed that not far off, on the nearby carriage road, someone was sitting on a stool and painting. Her nearsightedness, not entirely corrected by her spectacles, kept her from making out his features, but there was no mistaking the fact that he was a man. He wore a white, broad-brimmed hat from which his blond hair peeked, and a white jacket over an open-necked shirt. He seemed to be wearing a dark-red silk scarf around his neck. There was a canvas on the easel in front of him, and he was painting with rapid brushstrokes, dabbing pigments from a palette he held in his other hand.

Enrica studied the landscape and tried to imagine exactly what the man might be painting: the view really was magnificent here, with the pine grove sloping down to the sea, here and there white houses with red roofs punctuating the greenery, and the clean white sails of pleasure boats standing out against the pristine blue sky. She turned again toward the painter, and he stood up and tipped his hat in greeting. A blast of heat shot up to her face as she blushed for being caught in such an open display of indiscretion; instead of waving back, she pretended to be busy fastening one of the little girls' outfits. Disappointed, the man went back to his painting.

The morning progressed. The sun grew hotter and hotter and the children began to show signs of weariness. The other schoolteacher, a dark-haired sociable young woman named Carla, did her best to keep the boys in line by shouting louder than they; Enrica turned her attention to her little girls, and her heart skipped a beat when she noticed that one was missing. She turned to look out to sea and saw a tiny head bobbing in the water. How could she have failed to notice that Bettina, the biggest troublemaker of the group, hadn't come back from her swim?

She called her at the top of her lungs, but all Bettina did was wave back. Enrica waved for her to come to shore, backed up by her colleague Carla, who had come over; once again, Bettina waved back. Enrica begged her and threatened her, but to no avail. She was about to resign herself to the necessity of swimming out to get her when a white shape shot past her, dove in, and, with just a few powerful strokes, swam out to the little girl.

A short time later a colossus clad in shirt and trousers emerged from the water, with a laughing Bettina in his arms. It was the painter who had waved at Enrica from the road.

The little girl leapt down onto the beach, took a few steps, and then, as if she'd forgotten something important, turned around and went back to plant a kiss on her rescuer's cheek. Then she scurried away, easily dodging the backhanded smacks that both Enrica and Carla sent in her direction.

The man said: "Please, please, don't scold the child. After all, with this heat, there's nothing wrong with wanting to stay in the water, is there?"

He spoke a perfect Italian, but the harshness of his consonants betrayed his foreign origins.

Enrica replied brusquely: "I certainly can't allow them to do what they want, endangering their own personal safety, Signor . . ."

The man smiled as he did his best to dry his hands. His eyes, just barely irritated by the brine, were as blue as the water behind him, and his teeth were even and dazzling white. He was tall and well built, and he was eyeing Enrica with curiosity. He performed a very understated bow which led the two schoolmistresses to assume that they were in the presence of a soldier, an impression confirmed by the man's next words: "Major Manfred von Brauchitsch, cavalry of the Reichswehr, Signora. Or should I say Signorina?"

Enrica stood openmouthed. An officer in the German army. A cavalry officer, no less.

Carla, who looked as if she'd been struck by an apparition, was the first to recover: "*Signorina*, *signorina*, Major, she's a *signorina*. And I'm a *signorina* too: my name is Carla Di Meglio. *Grazie*, you were a hero!"

Manfred bowed his head slightly in her direction, but he never took his eyes off Enrica; then he cocked an eyebrow inquisitively.

The young woman finally heaved a sigh and said, still harshly: "Maestra Colombo. Thank you for bringing Bettina back to us, but it's our job to take care of the children so, in future, I must ask you not to involve yourself unless you're asked."

Carla shot her the look she usually gave ill-mannered children, but Enrica had no intention of melting into a puddle at the sight of the first pair of blue eyes to come along. Even if she had to admit that there was something exotic and alluring about that fair-haired athletic giant, all wet from the sea.

"I understand, and I beg your pardon," he said. "It's just that from a distance I couldn't tell for sure whether you were waving or asking for help."

Enrica nodded in some embarrassment. She regretted her words, but didn't want to let it show. She turned to look at the girls, who were lining up two by two to head back to the colony.

She heard a faint cough behind her; she turned around. The man asked: "Do you have a first name too, Signorina Maestra Colombo? Just to complete our introductions. I never like to leave anything half finished."

"Enrica, Major. My name is Enrica. And thank you for . . . thank you. Forgive me if I was curt. I was just frightened."

"I come here every morning to paint, until it's time for my mud bath at the spa. I generally sit in the shade of the pines, and no doubt that's why you didn't notice me until this morning. But I've been watching you for days now, you know; you're part of the landscape that I've been capturing on canvas. I beg your pardon for doing so in secret, and I hope that you'll allow me to continue. You don't mind, do you?"

Enrica was stunned, speechless; Carla prodded her in the ribs with her elbow, pretending to adjust a cap on one of the children's heads. The girl recovered: "No, no. I don't mind. Are you painting the little girls, too?"

The man burst out laughing: "No, not yet. But it will be a great pleasure to make up for that shortcoming."

Carla allowed herself to join in the infectious laughter, and even Enrica, blushing, ventured a smile. Then, with a courteous nod of the head, she summoned the girls and headed back toward the villa.

It was almost lunchtime.

XXVII

U sually Maione took the long way round when he went to see Bambinella.

It demanded a lot more effort, entailing a few extra uphill climbs, but such discretion was necessary to ensure that prying eyes didn't notice the brigadier's suspiciously frequent visits to the *femminiello*. Not that there would have been any reason for surprise, after all, policemen were men too, and a foible could be tolerated; if anything, a sign of weakness was welcomed in the *vicoli* and backstreets of that city, making the enforcers of the law a little more human, a little closer to the common folk. Nonetheless, Maione didn't want to give anyone a chance to guess at the real reason he went to call on the *femminiello*.

This time, though, he was too angry to worry about anyone else's safety. The idea that his Lucia might be secretly making her way to an apartment house that numbered among its tenants an unrepentant bachelor who lived on a private income and whiled away the hours doing nothing but enjoying himself, had a series of effects on him that he was having difficulty controlling. His stomach had shriveled to the size of a prune, and his heart insisted on imitating the beat of a furiously shaken tambourine in the midst of a tarantella.

Where could Lucia have met this Pianese? She never left their neighborhood, except to go to the market. Maybe that's where they'd first come into contact. He could just see Pianese strolling among the vendors' stalls, whistling, in search of other people's wives to importune. He pictured him handsome, young, and well-dressed, with a fashionably narrow mustache, an immaculate white suit, and a red carnation in his buttonhole; then he pictured himself, old, hirsute, out for a stroll down Via Toledo on Sunday morning with his family, wearing a suit that looked as if it had been worn for two weeks straight, even though he'd just put it on a few minutes ago, freshly ironed.

Lucia, on the other hand, was breathtakingly beautiful. Always, even after a hellish day of heat and hard work, even with six children to look after, even first thing in the morning. And she was dazzling and golden even dressed in the house-coat she wore at home to do her chores.

Without even realizing it, the policeman was walking along emitting a dull roar. The inhabitants of the *vicoli* were already naturally inclined to avoid the police, and his snarling expression only reinforced that impulse; even the *scugnizzi*, who would normally tag along after him in small knots, calling out insults and mockery, now pretended they hadn't seen him. It looked like stormy weather in the two square yards surrounding the brigadier: best to steer clear of him.

Reaching his informant's apartment was no easy matter even by the most direct route, since Bambinella lived at the high end of a steep *vicolo*, at the very top of an uphill network of alleys and lanes, and at the summit of a staircase that was, obviously, yet another climb. The perfect route to leave you panting, drenched with sweat, and even more irritated than before, if you were irritated to start with.

Bambinella was waiting for him at the door. Looking up at her from below as he labored up the steps, Maione decided that there was something unsettling about her: her masculine features and her feminine ones overlapped, creating an inevitable sense of disorientation in anyone who looked at her. Bambinella was tall and bony, broad-shouldered, with big hands and a dark five o'clock shadow perennially visible on her fair white skin that seemed unaccustomed to sunlight. But the heavy makeup, the red polish on the well-tended finger-nails, the perfectly shaved body, the long black lashes flutter-ing on the large, liquid eyes, gave a sharp jerk to the initial impression one might gather from a superficial glance.

In a heartfelt voice, the *femminiello* said: "*Madonna santa*, Brigadie', why what's wrong? Why are you here at this hour? You worry me, just look, I'm all sweaty I'm so upset!"

Maione replied, heaving like a pair of bellows: "Of course, it goes without saying that you already knew I was on my way. Probably someone galloped up here to tell you the minute the thought occurred to me this morning. Some little bird must have whispered to you: listen up, Bambine', if you ask me Brigadier Maione is going to come see you any minute now. I guessed it from the expression on his face when he got out of bed. Because in this filthy city no one can do anything without everyone else knowing about it before it even happens."

Bambinella held her hand over her mouth as she laughed: "Why, no, of course not. It's just that the *vicolo* gets organized, when we see someone like you go by. If you keep an ear to the ground, you hear it. It's like a wave in the sea, if you see what I mean. And then there's the smuggler down on the corner, that is, you wouldn't see him now because as soon as you showed up, he took his stall and left: but anyway, he's the one who sells cigarettes and matches. A series of little kids who take up posts at every corner warn him when the police are arriving, so if you take the main street, I know you're coming more or less fifteen minutes before you get here. Come on, come in and I'll make you a cup of ersatz coffee. Why is it you didn't come the back way like usual?"

Maione closed the door behind him, turned down the ersatz coffee with a grimace, and let himself collapse into the wicker chair, which moaned in despair beneath his weight.

"I'm glad you told me about him," he panted, "this smug-gler on the corner. I'll slap them all in jail, him and his lookout kids, so we can finally start cleaning this city up a little bit. Let's see if we can turn it back into a normal city, where a miserable cop can try and do his job with a little discretion."

Bambinella, sitting in a Chinese chair, fanned herself with a large oriental fan; she looked like a parody of Madame Butterfly.

"Oooh, *mamma mia*, Brigadie', how irritable we are, and first thing in the morning too. In any case, don't you worry, no one bothers about who comes to see me and why, or anyway they can guess for themselves. I have a very select, top-flight clientele, if I do say so myself. Only now, for example, the man who just left—he's the son of the owner of at least four shoe stores in Chiaia, I'm proud to say. He's the nicest boy you'd ever care to meet, I could even fall in love with him if he weren't a shade perverse. Just think, he likes it when I dress up in a pair of . . ."

"Bambine', take it from me: today of all days, I'm in no mood to sit here listening to you describe your profession. I'm going through a very difficult time, and I wouldn't mind having a chance to let off a little steam by strangling you. In fact, as soon as I catch my breath, I might just choke you to pass the time. After all, with the gang of crooks that come through here, I wouldn't have any trouble finding a stooge to set up for the crime."

Bambinella emitted a sound very much like a horse whinnying, which was how she laughed.

"Why, what a sweetheart you are, Brigadie'. But I know that you have a soft spot for me and you do your best to fight it: still, it's only a matter of time before you give in to my charms. I'm used to it: the men's men, they fall passionately in love with me. It's my cross to bear, what can I do, it's the way I was born: fascinating."

Maione put his hand on the pistol he wore on his belt.

"No, I'm not going to choke you. Too much work. I'll just

shoot you from over here, straightaway, not as much fun and not as clean, but at least I won't break into a sweat again."

"No, no, Brigadie', you know that dingus scares the wits out of me. What's more, the day you decide to assult me with something you carry in your pocket, I hope it won't be a pistol. But get down to business, to what do I owe the honor?"

Maione decided to ignore the ribald double entendre; he knew very well that Bambinella's propensity for digressions, if given free rein, could make a conversation last for hours.

"The only reason I don't shoot you is that I need you alive, remember that. The day I decide I no longer need you, I'll scratch that off my list, trust me. Now then, I'm here because . . ."

Bambinella lifted one hand to interrupt: "By the way, Brigadie', before I forget: so someone threw the professor out the window at the polyclinic, isn't that right? He didn't jump. What an odd turn of events though."

Maione gaped in surprise: "No, now I have to ask you to explain this to me! Who told you that someone threw Iovine out the window? Absolutely no one knows about that, not yet, anyway, so how could you possibly have found out? Tell me the truth, Bambine', are you somehow implicated in this thing? Because this time there's nothing I can do to help you, after all, this is murder, and . . ."

Bambinella whinnied again: "No, what are you talking about, Brigadie'! I learned about it completely by accident. There's a sweet young friend of mine who hooks it in a house at the corner by the Pellegrini Hospital, and she has a number of customers who are nurses and doctors. Yesterday she noticed you walking with the handsome commissario, the one with the green eyes who's jinxed. You went into the morgue with Dr. Modo, the nice doctor who frequents all the finest bordellos in the city. My little girlfriend asked one of her customers, who works as a morgue attendant, such a good boy but he has a teeny-weeny little thingie so he's embarrassed to go with whores, and so this boy made friends with her because she's so tolerant and understanding. He told her that the only fresh corpse they had at the moment belonged to the professor."

"I don't understand why the Fascists waste all that time and money assembling a network of confidential informants that reports to the secret police: they'd only really need to pay a little attention to you and they'd know everything they want to know and a good deal more in the bargain."

The *femminiello* made a delicate gesture, as if shooing away a fly: "You're too kind, as always, Brigadie'. Anyway, the professor's death has been the talk of the town, you can just imagine, he was a prominent figure in this city. Some have only good things to say about him, others have only bad, but everyone has something to say. And so when they saw you and the commissario heading for the morgue, it didn't take long to put two and two together. So someone pushed him out that window, didn't they?"

"I don't even want to answer you. I'm exhausted, believe me. Exhausted. In any case, let's just say for argument's sake that someone did throw him out the window, in your opinion who could it have been?"

Bambinella lifted her enameled forefinger to her chin and rolled her mascaraed eyes to the ceiling.

"Well, now, Brigadie', the only real problem is to narrow down the field of candidates. A physician like him may bring babies into the world, but he kills a lot of people, too. For instance, a month ago there was that thing with the Wolf, you heard about that?"

Maione nodded: "Something, yes, we've heard about him. He seems to be a dangerous type, isn't that right?"

Bambinella adopted a sorrowful expression. She was impressively skilled at accompanying her stories with vivid expressions, almost as if she were performing a skit.

"He's a beautiful young man, all the girls in the quarter were mooning after him, but he, poor thing, only had eyes for his wife, Rosinella. They'd been together since they were kids. He's a tough guy, Brigadie', strong and decisive, and he may have stabbed one or two men in his time, and he may even have a few men on his consience, but he's a man of honor, and the poor of this city, when they've been done wrong, turn to men like him."

Maione snapped in irritation: "Bambine', you shouldn't talk like that! Don't you understand that we're in this mess precisely because when people are in trouble, instead of turning to us, whose job it is to make sure the laws are obeyed, they go to the people who obey only the law of the knife and enrich themselves at the expense of others? That's the curse afflicting this city: that instead of coming to us, people in need of justice go to your men of honor."

"Don't you ever wonder why people do that? Well, in any case, the Wolf is a talented young man. And this professor was responsible for his wife's death in childbirth: when they brought the woman to the hospital that night, because she was giving birth prematurely, he was nowhere to be found."

"What do you mean, he was nowhere to be found?"

Bambinella put both hands together, impatiently: "Jesus, Brigadie', it means that instead of being at the hospital, he wasn't there."

"Well, who said he always had to be at the hospital? Maybe he was at home, asleep."

Bambinella snickered: "Oh, no, he wasn't. They combed the whole city looking for him. The Wolf has a network of men. His line of business is transport, and what with the horsecarts, the carriages, and the trucks, he has a whole army of drivers. You'd say it was the middle of the day from the noise of wheels turning on the cobblestones in *vicoli*, *vicarielli*, alleys, lanes, streets, and piazzas. Wherever you turned, there was someone looking for the professor."

"And did they ever find him?"

"Of course they found him. But it was too late. If they'd only thought to ask me, I could have told them right away where he was. Instead, by the time he got to the operating room there was nothing he could do for poor Rosinella; she never even lived to see her baby."

Empathizing, with a spectacular immediacy, with the suffering of the dead mother, Bambinella suddenly turned on the waterworks, sobbing and weeping like a fountain. Maione, accustomed to her emotional outbursts, waited irritably for her to stop: he knew there was no way to interrupt.

"I can't even think about that poor baby girl born without her mother . . . I'm a little orphan girl myself . . . and Rosinella, so pretty and so in love with her husband . . . who knows how badly she wanted that little girl . . . she'd even prepared a layette, she had . . ."

Bambinella went on crying for several minutes, her sobs punctuated by heartrending wails. Then the *femminiello* blew her nose into an enormous red handkerchief, producing a sound like a trombone's, and got a grip on herself.

Maione asked: "You said that if they'd bothered to ask you, you could have told them where the professor was . . ."

Bambinella dabbed at her face, twisting her mouth to protect her makeup.

"The professor had a *commarella*. That is to say, he had an understanding with a young woman. It was a serious thing, practically out in the light of day."

The brigadier threw both arms wide: "Well, tell me all about it, this light of day. That way we'll both know what you're talking about."

Bambinella once again put her hands together.

"Well then, Brigadie', a few years ago, maybe it was two, the professor happened to be examining a girl who was working in the Speranzella bordello. You know the place, it's on the cheap side: students, soldiers, sailors, that kind of clientele; a line stretching down the stairs, the madam at the cash register, and four or five rooms for the whores. This one was very young, not even eighteen, and she came from a neighboring town; she'd been a maid, then she'd been fired because the master of the house had lost his head for her and his wife had figured it out. In short, a girl has to eat, she wasn't welcome back home, and so she found a position at the bordello."

Maione laughed: "Sure she did, she found a position, as if they'd hired her at city hall. Well, all right, go on."

"As you know, in our line of work we run certain health risks, so to speak; in a luxury bordello they provide medical care, in second-rate bordellos, that's more rare. To make a long story short, she caught an unpleasant disease and went to the hospital. The professor, as I heard from a girlfriend of mine who'd been at boarding school with the girl, noticed her as she was being examined by one of his assistants, and was struck dumb. He insisted on taking over her case and they began seeing each other. Then he took her out of the bordello and set her up in a little apartment all her own in Vomero. He bought an exclusive on her, in other words."

Maione sighed: it wasn't an uncommon thing for wealthy men to indulge in that pastime: purchasing the lives of very young girls.

"I want the girl's given name, surname, and address."

"Don't you even want to hear how the story ends? Anyway, the *guagliona*'s name is Teresa Luongo, but everyone knows her as Sisinella. She lives in Vomero, on a street that crosses Corso Scarlatti, which I happen to know because a customer of mine who sells vegetables in that neighborhood sees her come and go. But now she'll have to find another special client."

"You said that there's more to the story?"

"For the past few months, there's been a rumor going around that Sisinella has a sweetheart. Another one, that is, aside from the professor. A musician who plays the *pianino*, you know, the ones who go around town selling sheet music."

Maione narrowed his eyes: "Were they seen together?"

"No, no, a girl who's lucky enough to be kept by a rich man doesn't gamble that away for love, Brigadie'. No one saw them. Still, the young man buzzes around her relentlessly, and he sighs and sings. When someone looks up at a window, sighs, and sings, there's usually a good reason for it."

"I see. And what's the singer's name?"

"Now let me think . . . his name is Tore. Salvatore Cortese. A handsome young man, from what I hear."

Maione got to his feet: "All right, you've told me enough. But don't be surprised if I drop by again, because it strikes me that this is one of those cases where you open one door and you find two more." As he was about to leave, he stopped for a moment and turned around: "One last thing, Bambine'. Do you know a certain Pianese, Ferdinando Pianese, Via Toledo, no. 270?"

Bambinella furrowed her brow: "Why, what does he have to with what happened to the professor? What has Fefè done?"

Maione pulled out his handkerchief and dabbed at his forehead: "Nothing, he has nothing to do with it. It's a completely different matter. So, you know him?"

"Why, who doesn't know Fefè? He's a mouthpiece, a two-bit lawyer who never has work. He lets himself be kept by a couple of old biddies he flatters, and spends all his money on cards and women. Every once in a while he comes to pay a call on one of us, too, or he invites us out to one of his parties that go on all night long. A guy who likes to have a good time, in other words. But why do you ask, Brigadie'?"

"Nothing, no reason. It's just a name that came up in another investigation, money that was involved in the numbers racket."

"Typical of Fefè, some little old lady must have died and until he finds a replacement he's trying his luck. He's not a bad-hearted boy, but he does have his weaknesses, and he's no match for temptation."

Maione feigned nonchalance: "Weaknesses? What weaknesses?"

"Oh, he likes to drink, for one thing, and he likes to go to the racetrack. But I'm surprised to hear that he might be involved in the numbers racket, it must mean he finally figured out that you can't get rich betting on the ponies. But his biggest weakness, the one he spends most of his money on, is clothing: he's a dandy, he certainly doesn't skimp on fine fabrics. And then there's his other weakness, the reason he dresses so elegantly in the first place."

"What reason is that?" Maione asked, immediately regretting the question.

Bambinella replied: "Blonde women. He's just crazy about blondes."

And she burst out laughing.

XXVIII

Mastro Nicola Coviello finished polishing the brooch with a rag and then laid it on the workbench beneath a ray of light that angled in through the low open door. And he sighed.

He always sighed, when he finished a project. It was a form of detachment, an instant of relaxation after the pangs of birth. He imagined that women must do just what he did, he who kept inside him, sometimes for a long time, something that was at first only an idea, an image, until he started working on it, shaping the cold, inert, soulless material. And little by little, something began to emerge, something perhaps even more beautiful than the vague idea he'd had in the beginning; finally he polished it, worked away all the sharp edges, eliminated the imperfections, until he found himself holding a piece of jewelry that was complete unto itself, with an aesthetic autonomy that transcended the heart and soul of whoever had commissioned it.

Obviously Mastro Nicola didn't think of it in these exact words: in his life, he'd only worked, he'd never had the chance to cultivate an emotional vocabulary with books and music. Still, he had a strong aesthetic sense, and he knew when the time had come for an object he'd made with his able hands to begin its own life. But he couldn't ward off a hint of sadness when that time came.

Mastro Nicola liked his profession. He'd always liked it, ever since he was a child and would spend hours playing at the foot of the bench on which a distant cousin worked; that cousin had imparted to him the rudiments of the art. His father was a fisherman, but the proximity of the goldsmiths' *borgo* to the port had created an incongruous contiguity between those two very different activities, and as a result both professions were practiced in many families.

Nicola didn't like fishing, and even though the sea appealed to him, it frightened him too; the sea had swallowed up his father. One day, after a terrible storm, the boat his father had sailed out in with three other fishermen was found drifting, empty. That was not the life for him.

Far easier and safer to craft precious metals, the profession that constituted the other pillar of the *borgo*. And since the son of Gaetano the fisherman showed enormous talent and applied himself assiduously, it wasn't hard for him to wangle an apprenticeship.

Nicola himself, however, didn't especially like apprentices; they were generally careless and lazy, they failed to reserve for their work that sense of the sacred that he demanded. But they were a necessary evil: the unwritten code of the goldsmiths demanded that the profession and the skills that went with it be handed down and kept within the bounds of their guild. Every workshop passed from one generation to the next, following a line of descent not always governed by ties of blood.

An apprentice necessarily ought to be involved with what his master is doing, but Nicola liked to have his little secrets. He worked on different objects in different moods, and he transfused his hidden temperament into whatever he was shaping.

To see him from without, his body deformed by constant work, he gave the impression of a sad man, introverted, taciturn to the point almost of mutism, but from his large, skilled hands came veritable masterpieces of the goldsmith's art, jewelry that never failed to elicit marvel and admiration in the salons where it was worn.

Nothing, thought Nicola as he looked at the brooch. Almost

always, those who received one of his creations as a gift understood nothing. Rich, spoiled women, illicit lovers, proud kept women who showed off his creations as if they were trophies, investitures, symbols of the role each played alongside wealthy, coarse men. Money. These jewels—fragments of the sky and the stars, the results of subtle, delicate invention and technique—were only as valuable as the money that had been paid for them. How squalid.

The brooch multiplied the shaft of sunlight it captured into a thousand glinting rays, illuminating Nicola's gloomy workshop like some tiny star.

Sergio, the apprentice, let out a soft whistle. He alone among the apprentices had been able to keep up with the incredible pace demanded by Coviello. He'd been working with him for almost a year, but he still couldn't help being surprised whenever he witnessed the ritual first display of a finished piece of jewelry. He murmured: "*Mamma mia*, Mastro Nico', it's so beautiful! Look at it, it seems to be made of light!

Nicola continued his critical inspection of the object: a fleur-de-lis reversed; flat, antique cut diamonds, gold-filled or *doublé d'or*, in a collet setting; fine sheet fretwork, welded and engraved in a detailed pebbling. Springing from the lily petals, each of which housed a series of diamonds decreasing in size toward the center, were gold stalks, each in turn supporting a natural pearl. On the reverse, a gold pin with an ornate fastener. Not bad, thought Nicola. Not bad.

Then, the face of the man who had commissioned that piece of work appeared in his mind, a fat, ignorant shipowner who had grown wealthy on the backs of hundreds of longshoremen, and who would be pinning that tiny masterpiece on the chest of the equally oafish peasant woman he'd married. Nicola's brooch would end up being gazed upon by dozens of half-wits, who would only have one question: how much had it cost?

As always, the thought put him in a foul mood. He gestured

to Sergio to take over the polishing and then to put the brooch away in its case; he'd already lost interest in it. Once again, the battle against the inert resistance of matter had been won.

He shoved the heavy workbench into the best light, then went over to the monumental gray safe that took up a substantial portion of the room. He pulled out the key, turned it in the lock, rotated the burnished metal handle, and extracted a package from the interior. The young man handed him the brooch in its case and Nicola put it back on one of the shelves, closing the door; he turned to Sergio and told him he could go. His apprentice had seen enough for one day.

Once the young man had respectfully ducked his head and left the shop, Nicola unwrapped the package on the workbench. The dark wood welcomed the black velvet at the center of which lay the piece on which Mastro Nicola had been working, always alone, for months.

His mind went to Professor Iovine del Castello, to his face, and to the expression he'd glimpsed behind the gold-rimmed spectacles when he'd delivered the two rings to him. Had he told the whole story to that commissario with his strange eyes that looked like a pair of flawless emeralds, and to the oversized brigadier? No, perhaps he hadn't.

Maybe he should have told them about the chilly glance with which the professor had opened the case meant for his wife and the loving tenderness with which he'd peered into the case for the other woman. The way he'd extracted this second ring, with the bigger stone, from its case and had held it up into the light, so he could make sure the name engraved on the interior had been spelled correctly. How those hands, with their soft manicured fingers, like a woman's, had hefted the weight and tested the surface of the stone's setting.

Maybe he should have told them how much love went into the second gift, and how little—none at all, really—went into the first.

It would be pointless to try to explain to the policemen the differences that can be detected in people who commission a piece of jewelry, he mused as he stared at the tools lined up on the workbench: it's a matter of gazes, of tones of voice, not money. He who puts his meager funds into the hands of the goldsmith might be making a greater sacrifice than the man who lavishes a vast sum, but perhaps only to assuage a dirty conscience. Pointless to explain to a pair of policemen, their hearts hardened by the violence they encounter and the violence they're obliged to inflict, just how much love it take to extract emotions from metal.

He stroked the tools that were extensions of his hands, that made his every gesture delicate and soft. The knurl, the perloir, the flat chisel, the gemstone-setting tools, the graving tools, the burins with oval-section wooden handles.

The sun was setting; he'd work deep into the night by the light of a gas lamp. In the end, he'd lose his eyesight just as he'd lost his stature, the shape of his spinal cord, plenty of friends, and any chance of a woman in his life. But the beauty that sprang from his fingertips was more than adequate compensation.

He brushed his fingers over the object to which he'd devoted so much attention. A goldsmith, my dear professor, is very different from a surgeon, even if both work with their hands, and with an intense focus, even if the mistakes of both are irreversible, and the outcomes both produce are unmistakable. You surgeons, professor, are required to try equally hard no matter what part of the body you're operating on, whoever that body part may belong to. A goldsmith, on the other hand, can devote lesser or greater consideration to a job, depending on how much he cares about it. You all are doctors, professor. We are artists.

He picked up his long graver. He slid his finger along the blade, he tested the tip. No sharpening required. He heard his cousin's voice echoing down from three decades ago: take care of your tools, *guaglio'*; your tools are the first thing. And the light. The right light.

It depends on who hires you, professor. Your work was brought to you: they'd summon you urgently and either you fixed the broken machinery or else you watched it grind to a halt. Not me. I can decide whether or not I like the piece of jewelry I'm called upon to make, whether I like the person who gives me the material, or the money.

He looked down at the object lying before him, and it gleamed back at him, a cautious golden glow. Its beauty was absolute: but it failed to extract so much as a smile from him.

It won't be long, he said to himself. It won't be long now till it's finished.

He spared a thought for the person for whom the piece was meant, a thought of distant tenderness.

And he started filing away again at the fluting of the golden flame, working with fine, patient gestures.

XXIX

My dear *papà*,

what a magnificent place this island is! How green, how blue, and what wonderful smiles I receive from everyone when they see me in the road, leading my line of little girls!

If it weren't for how much I miss you all, and you especially, my sweet *papà*, I'd certainly say that as the days pass and I become more accustomed to the courtesy of the inhabitants, I'm beginning to think that this really is heaven on earth.

People like us, dear *papà*, are far better suited to life in a place like this than in the big city. Here people talk in low voices and when there's a lull in conversation, they listen to nature, which never stops singing its song; in the city, people never stop running around, morning, noon, and night, and whether they shout or sit silent, they never find a good middle ground. You'd really like it here, believe me. It would be worth considering a vacation: perhaps even *mamma* might calm down in a place like this.

Life flows like always, here in the summer colony, punctuated by the day's schedules and by whatever might come up. We've started a new project for the celebration of the Festival of St. Anne: the girls, under my supervision, will embroider a panel depicting the saint in conversation with her daughter, Mary. The boys, with their teacher, Maestra Carla, will build the wooden frame to hold the embroidered panel. We will donate the resulting creation, if we finish it all in time, to the little church of the bay of Cartaromana. If you could only see how hard the little scamps work, dear *papà*! And the girls, even the naughtiest ones, are doing their best. At night, after they go to sleep, I work on it a little myself, helping the embroidery along, but without overdoing it: I don't want them to realize it, that would undermine the satisfaction of doing it themselves.

I try to stay as busy as I can to keep from thinking about you know what. I want the sacrifice of this distance to be justified by the remastering of my heart. The girls help me a great deal, and Maestra Carla, with whom I've established a genuine friendship, keeps me good company.

The one source of disagreement with her is our differing opinions concerning an officer in the German army, a certain Manfred, who is here for the mud baths. He comes every morning to the beach where we take the children, because he paints landscapes (though I've never been able to see them, since he always keeps the canvas turned toward himself). We met him under strange circumstances: he dove in and pulled one of the little girls out of the water, not because she was in any danger, but simply because she refused to come out. Since that day, for one reason or another, this gentleman insists on greeting us and speaking to us. I think Carla flirts with him a little, and he is always courteous and never more than that, but I find him somewhat annoying and, according to Carla, I show my irritation with unnecessary harshness.

I have to admit that he is one of those men that girls tend to like: blond hair, tall, with a nice smile and all the rest. But I don't know how to further my friend Carla's hopes, except by keeping to myself as much as possible.

This morning he came to offer us some chocolate that he had brought with him as a snack. I said no, but the little girls, dear *papà*, you should have seen them! They swarmed like bees attacking the leftovers from a picnic lunch, and, laughing, he broke the chocolate bar into little pieces and made sure that every girl got some. It happened just when Carla was away, because she had taken the boys for an outing. I thought it decent, just good manners, to ask after his health, and dear *papà*, what a story he told me!

He's a cavalry officer, and he was in the war, but the treatments he's taking here on Ischia with the mud baths are not the result of any battle wounds, but an ordinary fall from a horse while training. You might not believe it, but he actually blushed when he said it: as if he were mortified at some confession.

He has a special love for this island because a great-aunt of his, who owned a house here, was killed during the earthquake of 1883. He says that when a member of your family is buried somewhere, you have a duty to go back there from time to time.

He's thirty-eight years old, and he lives in a small Bavarian town called Prien, if I understood him correctly, on the shore of a lake. Since he's an amateur painter, he described it to me as if it were a picture: slate roofs, balconies full of flowers, artisans in their workshops, bicycles, women in their traditional garb. I admit that it was fun to hear him talking about his people in that strange accent.

He hinted that this stay in Italy was turning out far better than he'd expected: he likes the excitement he senses, the yearning for a better future that the people display by working hard. He made me proud of my own country, for once.

Then Carla returned, and it seemed to me that she was unhappy to find me conversing with Signor Manfred; but after he left, I explained to her that I certainly hadn't encouraged that meeting. Quite the contrary. I told her everything that had happened and fortunately, in the end, we were better friends than ever. The last thing I want is to fight with Carla, especially over a man who doesn't interest me in the slightest.

From here, my bedroom seems so small, and the window across the street so distant. At night, though, before I fall asleep, my mind always flies to him and to those sad green eyes that look at me from the darkness as if crying out for help, and a kind of weakness presses hard in my chest. Enchantment and desire.

I still don't see a future for myself, at least not an emotional one. But here at least I can live each day to the fullest without the anxiety of time passing while I build nothing.

I love you dearly, my beloved *papà*, and the idea of being able to hug you again helps me to think of my return without fear.

Yours,
Enrica

XXX

Ricciardi listened carefully to the information that the brigadier had collected from Bambinella, but he continued to wonder just what might be bothering Maione. The twist in Raffaele's mouth, the crease at the center of his forehead, his veiled gaze, all spoke of some very serious worry.

"Well, now we have a name, Commissa': Teresa Luongo, also known as Sisinella. She lives on a cross street of Corso Scarlatti, in Vomero. It shouldn't be difficult to track her down. I think it's worth going to talk to her, because among other things the fact that she seems to have a secret boyfriend might lead to interesting possibilities."

Ricciardi thought it over, his fingers knit together, his chin resting atop them.

"Yes. And whatever the case, Sisinella might be able to tell us about anything that was worrying the professor: threats he'd received, or even if someone had attacked him. Men will tell their lovers things they'd never confess to their wives."

Maione, stung to the quick, blurted out: "Don't get me started, Commissa'. Maybe wives tell lies, too. And maybe the husbands, fools that they are, fall for them."

The commissario detected the bitterness, but he preferred to pretend he hadn't. If Maione chose to open up to him, he'd certainly listen, but he didn't intend to force his hand.

"Certainly. But it's the professor we're interested in now, right? So let's go meet her, this Sisinella. Then we'll go look into the Wolf and the doctor from Mergellina."

184 · MAURIZIO DE GIOVANNI

"Sure we will, Commissa'. But I wouldn't overlook the *pianino* player, either, the lover's lover, in other words. Someone who's capable of betrayal is capable of anything."

The words resounded in a silence that lasted several seconds. Then Ricciardi said: "Raffaele, if you need to take a day off, go ahead. I can go on my own to question this Sisinella. You go home and spend some time with your children, your wi—"

Maione interrupted him: "Commissa', just drop it: right now, the way I feel, the less time I spend at home, the better, trust me. And after all, work helps take my mind off things, you know it. Let's head off to Vomero, maybe it'll be a little cooler there."

They took the Central Funicular. The inhabitants of the city looked on this remarkable rail system as a novelty, even though it had been up and running for four years. It was that screeching and rattling railroad, shuttling incessantly up and down the hill, that had made it conceivable for the city to grow upward, onto the hillsides that had long been good only for summer vacationers and vast broccoli plantations. Now the new hillside quarter was synonymous with modernity and cool air, concepts that the Fascist regime imposed on the country's culture, art, and general mind-set. Theaters, movie houses, and cafés were opening at a furious pace, and a number of prominent but less well-to-do families had moved to higher elevations using the abundant fresh air as an excuse.

Ricciardi and Maione chose to purchase round-trip tickets for one lira each. They took a seat on the wooden benches and noticed that, even though it was not the hour when people came back from shopping or from their offices, and even though the fare wasn't cheap, the funicular cars were packed.

As they emerged from the station at the top of the hill they immediately breathed in cleaner, sweeter-smelling air; the vegetation of the park of Villa Floridiana, the fact that there were fewer engines and factories, and the absence of crowds made for immediate relief. Newly built apartment houses alternated with older ones, erected in a late-nineteenth-century style, as well as with construction sites for buildings that would soon be rising. Work hummed in all directions, and many young couples smiled in greeting as they crossed paths.

Ricciardi thought to himself that it was logical to expect a man like Iovine to put up his lover in a place like that. It was close enough to reach in short order both by funicular and by car, thanks to the roads that had been improved to encourage the growth of the new sections of the city, but also distant enough to forestall undesirable encounters. The elegance of the shops and the gardens had no doubt played a crucial role in persuading the girl to move.

Maione asked around a bit; as was sometimes the case, luck would have it that his uniform functioned as a kind of pass, allowing him access to the information he needed. Signorina Luongo, according to the proprietor of a water and lemon kiosk, lived just a few dozen yards away, in a brand new apartment building on Via Kerbaker. From the sly expression on the man's face, it was clear that Sisinella's profession was an open secret among the locals.

They were greeted by a very skinny, argumentative doorman whose dark eyes were continually darting about. Maione inquired whether Signornia Luongo were home, and the doorman replied in a scratchy voice: "How am I supposed to know? Who do you take me for, the lady's butler?"

The brigadier was in no mood for smart answers: "Listen, friend: I asked you a question politely, and now I'm going to ask you again. Is Signorina Luongo at home by any chance? Now, either you respond appropriately and tell me your name and what I want to know, or first I'll kick your ass downhill, and second I'll throw you in jail for failure to cooperate with an officer of the law. Is that clear?"

Ricciardi scrutinized him uneasily; it was very rare for Maione to behave like that. In any case, his harsh tone had the desired effect. The man took a step backward, as if expecting a smack in the face, and said: "Forgive me, Brigadie'. It's just that with this signorina it's a constant procession. Don't take it the wrong way. My name is Firmino. Yes, the signorina is in, the man just left . . . in other words, she just had some visitor. Go on up: she's on the second floor."

The apartment building's staircase was brightly lit by large windows and gave a sense of freshness and coolness unknown to the austere buildings in the center of the city. A goldfinch was trilling from a terrace nearby and children could be heard playing in the courtyard. There were two doors on the landing, one of which bore a plaque that read "Luongo." Maione rang the bell.

After a moment, a voice asked from inside: "Who is it?"

"Police."

The door swung open, but only a crack. They could make out one wide eye and a long lock of curly black hair.

"And what do you want here? I haven't called anyone, and no one has done anything wrong."

Maione leaned forward and stared straight into that one eye: "Signorina Teresa Luongo, I would recommend you let us in, and right away. It's not in your best interests for us to get into a shouting match out here on the landing, is it? Or do you really want us to announce, at the top of our lungs, why we're here and what we want to know?"

The young woman unhooked the chain.

They were ushered into a luminous parlor which opened out beyond the small front hall. Signorina Luongo really was pretty, and was maybe a couple of years older than twenty. She was rather tall, well built in a simple but tasteful dress, with fashionable shoes and heavy makeup. The colors she chose and her facial features denoted a strong and unmistakable personality: her black hair, dangled curly around her neck and on either side of her forehead; her eyes were a deep blue, and her lips were full, painted dark red and twisted in a mistrustful grimace, doing their best to conceal her youth.

So this is the famous Sisinella, thought Ricciardi. No question about it, she's someone a man could lose his head over, the professor just like anyone else. He spoke to the woman: "*Buongiorno*, Signorina. I'm Commissario Ricciardi, and this is Brigadier Maione. You are Teresa Luongo, correct?"

The alleged Signorina Luongo had not invited them to take a seat or shown them any courtesy whatsoever. She watched them with a level, insolent gaze, practically a look of defiance. This is someone accustomed to dealing with the police, Maione told himself.

"Yes, that's me. And I ask you once again: what are you doing here? And what do you want from me?"

The brigadier decided to make things clear from the start: "Listen, gorgeous, you're in no position to play the indignant mistress of the house, believe me. You know perfectly well why we're here. So stop trying to get in our way and let us do our jobs."

In the small room Maione's thunderous voice rang out like a gunshot. The girl's eyes opened wide in a surprised expression that, in spite of the makeup, made her look her true age. Ricciardi didn't much like these methods, but he had to admit that they were effective. Teresa raised a trembling hand to her chest, then waved them toward the sofas: "Yes. Please, have a seat. Do you want . . . may I make you some coffee?"

Ricciardi raised one hand: "*Grazie*, no. Do you know Professor Tullio Iovine del Castello?"

"Of course I do. And I also know . . . I know what happened. If you're here, that means you know all about me . . . about us. This apartment, the furniture . . . in other words, yes, I knew him. We knew each other very well."

Maione continued staring at her with hostility: "When did you last see each other?"

Teresa returned his level gaze: "He came here Wednesday night."

"At what time?"

"Just after midnight. And he left around six in the morning."

The two men sat in silence. Then Ricciardi asked: "Did he call you before he came? Or did you have an appointment?"

"He was . . . he always did the same things. He came here three or four times a week, at night, if there were no emergencies at the hospital; and if he could get free during the day, he'd call me on the phone. He never showed up without advance notice."

Maione asked: "And was he supposed to come Thursday night?"

"No. Thursday nights he stays at the hospital . . . or he stayed. He spent the night with me on Fridays, and on Saturdays and Sundays we never saw each other."

Ricciardi tried to read the emotions on the young woman's face, but she was impenetrable, cautious, perhaps frightened by Maione's aggressiveness; she was probably afraid of contradicting herself, because she chose her words haltingly. Still, whatever emotions she might have felt toward Iovine, she didn't let them show.

"How did you meet the professor? How long had you been seeing each other?"

Maione shot a glance at Ricciardi. Why waste time asking things they already knew?

The girl stared into the empty air, then turned and addressed the commissario.

"I used to be a working girl, Commissa'. I imagine you already know that, and if you don't I'm telling you now. I wasn't even seventeen years old and I was already working in a bordello. I was pretty, and my mother told me: get out of here, out of this town. There's nothing here but hunger. Some guy will come along, get you pregnant, and ruin your life. That's what happened to her. I got sick, it was nothing serious, but if I couldn't work I wouldn't eat, so I went to the hospital for a cure. And I met Tullio."

Outside, the children all burst into shouting laughter together. I wonder what game they're playing, Maione thought to himself, and he felt a sudden groundless burst of sadness: he missed his children and his wife.

Teresa went on: "He was kind and gentle. Maybe that's because he'd never seen me up in the bordello. Up there, Commissa', we all look the same: young, old, pretty or ugly. People come up, do what they need to do, pay, and leave. In the hospital he saw me as pretty as I was back in my home-town. And he wanted to see me again. I don't know why, but I waited to tell him that I was in a bordello. I'd see him some-where else: in a café, in a bar. I really liked the way he treated me. He'd hold the door for me, he'd pull back my chair for me to sit down. Who'd ever been given this kind of attention?"

The cries of the children and the goldfinch's song formed a background to the young woman's words.

"It was strange for me, and it was strange for him. I wasn't Sisinella the whore, he wasn't a gentleman and a professor. It was like being in another world, you understand, Commissa'? Another world. He was a genie who granted wishes, you know the fairy tale? We spent five months like that, seeing each other out on the street. Sometimes he'd take me to a hotel and . . . and we'd make love. But that wasn't the most important thing. The most important thing, with Tullio, was that he wanted to take care of me, and that I wanted to be taken care of. If you ask me, it was a need we both felt."

She sat in silence, lost in her recollections. A vague smile played over her face, but her eyes were veiled. Like a father, thought Ricciardi.

"Like a father. A sort of father, at least, I think so," she said. "One time I saw a convertible, with a lady inside who laughed and laughed. He noticed that I was looking at her, and the next

week he came to see me with a car just like it. That's the way
Tullio was."

Maione coughed, then he spoke. And his voice was kinder
this time.

"Then he took this apartment and set you up here."

Sisinella nodded: "That's right, after Christmas. He liked
the neighborhood, and he said it would be a good investment.
He bought it and moved me in."

"And you accepted in a hurry, didn't you?"

"What else was I going to do? Should I have told him no and
stayed where I was? Brigadie', with all my respect, you have no
idea what it's like to have all those people on top of you, from
dawn to dusk: men who are filthy, or stinking, or drunk, or violent, disgusting old men, crazed little boys; their dirty hands on
your flesh and . . . and everything else. It ages you early. It ages
you fast. If I'd stayed there another year, I wouldn't even have
recognized myself in the mirror. Tullio saved my life."

Ricciardi shot a glance at Maione, who had been profoundly struck by Sisinella's speech. Then he asked the girl:
"Do you have any idea of who might have had it in for the professor? Did he tell you about any quarrels, any threats, or anything of the sort?"

Sisinella calmly gazed at the commissario, her blue eyes
focused on his green ones. Ricciardi thought about love, and
the thousand rivulets in which it runs.

"No, Commissa'. When he was with me, he left ugly
thoughts outside the door, that's what Tullio used to say. I
remember him happy and smiling, that's how I remember
Tullio, and that's how I want to remember him. I know that it's
all over, that I'm going to have to move out of this apartment,
sell my jewelry and clothing and shoes and all, but I don't
regret a thing: I always knew it wouldn't last forever. And the
finest gift he ever gave me is that I'll never go back to the bordello. No way, nohow, I'll never go back there."

They remained silent, for a while. Then Maione said, in a subdued voice that differed sharply from the tone he'd used until then: "Signori', do you have someone? Another man, in other words?"

Ricciardi noticed that Maione had gone back to the more respectful plural form of address. Sisinella seemed oblivious to the fact.

"Yes, Brigadie'. I was waiting for the right time to tell Tullio about him. A good boy, he works as a strolling vendor. He's more or less the same age as me. We're in love."

Maione sighed. "We're in love." As if that's all it took.

"So the professor didn't know about the existence of this gentleman, who I'm guessing is from the neighborhood, am I right?"

"Yes, he lives nearby. His name is Salvatore Cortese, and he sells *copielle*, sheet music for songs, and he travels around the city with his *pianino*. But he wants to be a singer, he has a beautiful voice."

"And do you know where this friend of yours was, on Thursday night?"

Sisinella didn't answer for a long time. She stared at Maione, as if trying to read his mind. Her lips were pressed together, and her hands tormented her rings. Then, in a firm voice, she replied: "He was here, Brigadie'. He was here with me, that night."

XXXI

The funicular that carried them back down toward the center of town was populated by a different crowd than the one that had taken them up into the hills. Now, for the most part, the passengers consisted of well dressed young men out to have themselves a good time in fashionable bars and clubs.

Maione turned to Ricciardi, pensively: "Well, then, Commissa', now we have another hypothetical tosser of professors out of windows: the secret boyfriend of the lovely Sisinella."

Ricciardi looked out at the darkness of the tunnel through the carriage window.

"I don't know. I wonder what interest the young man might have. After all, Luongo's economic welfare came in handy for him too."

Maione replied, somberly: "What about jealousy, Commissa'? Can you imagine the thought of your woman with another man? Someone else's hands on her skin, someone else's eyes seeing her . . . the way that they shouldn't, someone else's ears hearing certain words? Jealousy's a nasty beast, Commissa'. A big nasty beast."

Maione's tone of voice, more than his actual words, made Ricciardi turn to look at the brigadier.

"Certainly, I can imagine it. But jealousy, my dear Raffaele, needs to have some basis in reality. There should be evidence, the same as in the work we do. This Cortese met Sisinella after the professor, not before him. Now, let's go ahead and imagine that he had decided to get rid of him, that he wanted to put an end to the girl's relationship with Iovine, benefits or no benefits. All they'd have needed to say to the professor was that he could have his apartment, his furniture, and his jewelry back, and they could have gone on their merry way, couldn't they? What could the professor have said to them? They even had the tools to blackmail him by telling his wife and everyone at the university that the professor had such a young lover. They could have ruined him. Why kill him? It doesn't make sense."

Maione insisted: "What about a burst of rage, Commissa'? Maybe Cortese had gone to tell the professor exactly that, and the other man insulted him or refused to let the girl go; so he threw him out the window."

"Certainly, it's possible. But given the condition of the room and the marks on Iovine's body, that doesn't add up to me. If you have a fight like that, you raise your voice, you break things: you don't just grab someone and throw him straight out the window. No one heard a thing, we didn't find anything out of place, the victim had no marks on his body, aside from the scratches on his back and the marks on his neck where the murderer grabbed him. Does it strike you that there could have been a struggle?"

Maione shrugged his shoulders: "There are still too many things we don't know. But what fits best with the picture you're painting, Commissa', is someone who went there expressly to kill him, someone like the Wolf, who'd sworn he would, or the guy from the clinic, who wrote that letter. The sad thing is that, as usual, the deeper you dig the more people you find with a good reason to want someone dead. What a mess humanity is."

It was dark by the time they got back to headquarters. The next day was Sunday, their day off. Maione offered to continue questioning witnesses but Ricciardi said no: "I don't think that's necessary, Raffaele. Neither one, the Wolf nor the doctor, has any interest in running away, it would amount to a confession.

Let's start up again Monday; maybe we can meet and talk it over first. I'm going by the office now to organize some papers and then I'll head home. You go ahead, and put your mind at rest."

The brigadier headed off reluctantly. Ricciardi was thinking about his strange demeanor when the policeman standing watch at the front entrance came over to him, agitatedly: "*Buonasera*, Commissa'. You need to head over urgently to Pellegrini Hospital. They've already called three times."

XXXII

Maione was dragging his feet.

There was no respite from the heat, even after sunset. In fact, it got worse.

If by day you could blame the sunlight, that terrible pitiless light that showed no mercy, that wounded eyes and skin and made you wish you could just soak in a basin full of ice water, or made you dream of the worst possible winter, with downpours and windstorms, anything rather than that inferno without peace; if by day you could put the blame on the damned cowardly sun, which extended its fiery fingers down into even the hidden spots where you might hope to find a hint of cool shade; if by day you could complain and hope to find some reciprocal understanding in cafés and in the atriums of the apartment buildings; by night, when the light, the sun, and the scorching heat might all have been expected to retreat, then the suffering was simply too much to bear.

So just think, the brigadier said to himself, how it is if the soul is torn with grief.

Maione was worried. Worried that his anxiety would be visible, that his sadness would show to the outside world. He expected the women who put their chairs outside, in the street, seeking respite from the muggy heat of the *bassi* and launching into the endless conversations with their neighbors that would last until dawn, to say to him: *Buonasera*, Brigadie', what happened? You have an expression on your face that's too terrible to even look at.

Instead, no one noticed a thing. Everything seemed perfectly normal.

At last he arrived, after beating every record for slowness. The stairs, the children staging the usual ambush; the hello, the girls kneading dough, Lucia at the stove. Everything as it always was. He went into the bedroom to take off his uniform and his sweat-soaked shirt, and his gaze fell on Lucia's purse, which wasn't in its usual place. I don't want to see it, thought Maione. I don't want to notice that her purse is on the chair instead of in the armoire.

In the kitchen the usual cheerful atmosphere prevailed. Lucia said to him: "Hey, how did your day go? Are you tired?"

Impossible that they can't see it on my face, thought Maione.

"A little, yes. We went to Vomero to question someone, and we took the funicular. How about you?"

A moment's hesitation. Just an instant, or had it been an illusion?

"Me? Yes, I went out, this afternoon. I went to buy a couple pairs of shoes, for Maria and Benedetta, the old ones were falling apart."

Really? With what money?

"And right nearby, I found a great deal on shirts for you, Raffae'. You need lighter fabric, in this heat. Maybe I'll buy you some tomorrow."

Was this just a way of assuaging her conscience? In Maione's mind, through a link that was at first wholly subconscious but which then caused a sharp pang in his stomach, he saw Sisinella in her nice apartment, with all her dresses and jewelry. Money. Money, comfort. *I knew it wouldn't last forever*.

"No, thanks. I don't need them, I'm happy with the ones I have, if you have time to iron them."

"What's that supposed to mean? When have you ever found your shirts left unironed?"

Little Immacolata whined: "*Papà*, you know that *mammà* goes out and won't take me with her?"

Maria mocked her: "*Mammà* goes out . . . and why should she always take you with her? You're a big girl now. You see that you aren't even ticklish anymore?"

And she scratched her on the belly; the little one laughed and spat out some of her pasta.

Maione slammed his fist violently down on the table, making all the plates bounce and knocking over a couple of glasses: "That's enough! That's enough, I said! How on earth were you raised, in this house? Can't a poor man get some peace and quiet the one time all day he sits down to eat at his own table like a civilized human being? All of you, go to your rooms. On an empty stomach, without dinner! And I don't want to hear a fly buzz!"

Around the table, seven pairs of eyes as large as saucers stared at him. The littlest one started to cry and Maria took her in her arms, continuing to stare at her father with a frightened gaze shot through with reproach. The six children left the room, heads bowed, leaving six plates full of food.

Lucia's blue eyes were wide open in astonishment, and her lips were pressed tight. Their economic situation must truly be dire if it led her husband to an outburst like that, something that he had never done in all their years together, not even in the terrible days following Luca's death.

Maione stood up. His chin was quivering with rage; a muscle was twitching uncontrollably on his jaw.

He opened his mouth to speak, staring dementedly at his wife. Then he turned on his heel and went to get his jacket.

He'd better go out.

XXXIII

Ricciardi was out of breath when he arrived at Pellegrini Hospital. He'd tried to call back, but the switchboard operator had told him that Dr. Modo was in the midst of an urgent procedure and couldn't come to the phone; would the commissario care to try again later?

No, the commissario chose to hurry over to the large gray building at the center of the Pignasecca quarter. Along the way, he did his best to imagine what could have happened. An urgent procedure? Could someone be operating on him right now? What kind of trouble had Bruno gotten himself into this time? He was well aware of how his friend, especially after a glass or two, tended to uninhibitedly express his political opinions, which in that period could easily be branded "subversive," to use the usual euphemism. The Fascists must finally have beaten him bloody. This time there was no way around it.

When Ricciardi entered the ward, he was tremendously surprised to see the doctor walking toward him, without a scratch on him.

"Bruno? But what . . . they told me that . . ."

His friend took him by the arm: "Ricciardi, at last. I've been trying to find you since this afternoon. Where were you?"

The commissario was bewildered.

"I was in Vomero, on a case. What's going on. Are you all right?"

Modo had taken him into a corner; the eyes of the patients and a few visitors were fixed on them.

"Listen, Ricciardi. Today, around three, from what I've been able to gather, your *tata* had a stroke."

Ricciardi felt as if he'd just been plunged into the worst possible nightmare.

"A stroke? Rosa? What kind of a stroke? Where is she now? I have to hurry home and see her!"

Bruno restrained him: "She's not there. We've hospitalized her here."

The commissario, who in the past several days had been seriously worrying over Rosa's state of health, discovered to his horror that he was completely unprepared to lose her. Rosa was strong. Rosa was an oak tree. Rosa was indestructible. This must be somebody's idea of a joke.

He clutched the doctor's arm in a convulsive grip: "What are you saying, Bruno? Now . . . now . . . you can save her, you can save her, can't you? Because you're a good doctor, you're the best there is, and you'll save her, I know you will . . ."

Modo's face was twisted with sorrow for his friend. Ricciardi the perennially understated one, Ricciardi who never wept or laughed, Ricciardi so bitterly ironic before all human misery, now here he was sniffling like a terrified child, clutching him as if Modo were his last hope, no different from any of the other family members who came to him every day to ask him to work miracles.

"I'm not God, Ricciardi. I'm just a poor army doctor who's seen plenty and does his best with what little he knows. Now calm down and come outside, so I can explain."

Ricciardi followed him out into the courtyard. Modo lit a cigarette and ran his hand through his hair. They were immediately joined by the spotted stray that had been the doctor's constant companion ever since last November, when the dog had lost the boy it had belonged to. The doctor squatted down and scratched the dog behind its ear.

"Lucky you, dog. Lucky you, that you aren't human."

Ricciardi took a deep breath: "Tell me now, Bruno tell. Tell me everything. I'm ready."

Modo stood up, staring at his friend: "No, Ricciardi. No, you aren't. No one ever really is. Rosa has had an apoplectic fit. In practical terms, a serious problem with her blood pressure. While she was talking, she turned pale and walked over to the armchair and collapsed into it. Then she said she felt weak and it was as if she fell asleep. Her niece was with her, this Nelide, who looks like a younger Rosa, a girl, if you don't mind my saying so, of a remarkable homeliness, but one you can rely upon. If it hadn't been for her, Rosa would be dead right now."

"Then she's alive! She's alive, right, Bruno?"

Modo continued speaking as if he hadn't been interrupted: "Nelide—from what she told me, and getting words out of her was as hard as performing surgery—has already witnessed events of this kind, back in their hometown, which leads me to believe that there's a family predisposition to this kind of disease. So she recognized the labored breathing, what we doctors call stertorous respiration, and the chilly face and arms in spite of the heat. She tried to wake her up, and once she realized that Rosa had slipped into a coma, she went downstairs to the grocery store and phoned the hospital."

Ricciardi was confused: "Nelide did that? But who gave her your name?"

"Rosa herself, who may have feared the onset of a stroke from one moment to the next. In case of necessity, she'd told the girl to ask for me. An unfortunate habit that you seem to have passed on to her, I'm afraid. Luckily, I was at home: they called me and I came running. Good news for you and bad news for me, because an hour or so later and I would have been comfortably ensconsed at Madame Gilda's bordello, and no one would have known where to find me."

Ricciardi couldn't shake the feeling that he was caught in a nightmare.

"How is she now? Can I see her?"

"No, Ricciardi, better that you don't. She's fast asleep, and I don't think she's going to wake up anytime soon. Honestly, I'm very concerned; her face was cold and reddened, which leads me to fear a cerebral hemorrhage. I had cold cloths put on her head. A short while ago I measured her arterial blood pressure and found it elevated, which unfortunately only reinforces my diagnosis."

"What can we do now?"

"Very little. We've given her camphorated oil and caffeine to improve her breathing and support her heart, which sounded very weak. I've given her a subcutaneous injection of digitalin. I used Knoll Digipuratum, a pharmaceutical I tend to avoid because it's German, given the political drift I'm seeing among the Krauts once again, but unfortunately it's the best preparation available. Let's wait to see if her heartbeat stabilizes, otherwise we'll have to try something stronger, but not before tomorrow morning."

Ricciardi stared at the walls of the hospital; his gaze seemed to penetrate them.

"But I can't go visit her for even a minute?"

"Again, it's better if you don't. She's in a female ward now and if I let you go in there, I'll never hear the end of it. Also, Nelide, who's a genuine mastiff, is with her. She never says a word and just stares fiercely at her aunt. Listen, do they just cast them all from a single mold, where you come from? If so, I'll buy a dozen of them and take care of all my problems with female nurses."

"But if she were to wake up tonight . . ."

Modo laid a hand on his shoulder: "Ricciardi, don't hold out a lot of hope of that happening. I don't think she can wake up, and if it's true that she's had a cerebral hemorrhage, that might even be preferable. There's a real danger that she'll be left a vegetable for the rest of her life. It all depends on how much damage she's suffered. She's being well cared for, believe me. I asked the nun to keep her covered up and, if her temperature remains low, to put warm cloths on her legs. The important thing is that she be kept in as close to an erect posture as possible, so that the blood will ebb. And early tomorrow morning we can decide what to do next."

The dog walked over to Ricciardi, as if it sensed his sorrow, and yelped briefly. The commissario ran a hand over his face. He felt hopeless. He looked up at his friend.

"All right. If there's nothing else to be done, do you have any objection to my staying here in the waiting room? I don't want to be far away from her. And could she be moved into a single room tomorrow? I'll pay, of course. I'd like to stay close to her, hold her hand. You know, when I was little, sometimes . . . if I was frightened about something, I wouldn't even tell her why, and she wouldn't ask, she'd just sit down next to me and hold my hand. Just like that, without a word. And she'd wait for me to fall asleep. I want to hold her hand, Bruno. Just hold her hand."

Modo had seen a lot of things in his time, but he never remembered feeling his heart throb in his chest the way it did as he listened to his friend, there in the hospital courtyard on that scorching hot July evening. With a lump in his throat, he nodded yes.

Ricciardi went on, staring out at nothing: "You know, Bruno, she loves me so much, in spite of how I am. I am . . . I'm a man of many silences. That's how I was when I was little, too, I had no friends, I played alone. And she followed me everywhere; I knew she was there, I didn't even need to turn and look. And even later, when I grew up and I continued being . . . I continued being a loner, there was a part of me that knew I could turn around at any time and there she'd be, my Rosa, a warm statue, motionless, following what I was doing with her eyes. You know her, you know what she's like. She's stubborn, she's a complainer, she nags. But she's all I have. She's my family, my home, my everything."

The dog yelped again and looked up at the doctor.

Ricciardi whispered into the night: "Save her, if you can. If you can, keep her here, don't take her away from me too. Because without her I really don't know how to go on."

In the silence of the courtyard and the heat of the falling night, Modo realized with a shiver that his friend wasn't speaking to him.

Ricciardi was praying.

XXXIV

H ot night.
Night when you can't breathe. Night that tastes of
dust and rot, the market rubbish slowly decomposing
in the piazza.

Night when you'd like to be anywhere but where you are.
And you walk, and you toss and turn in bed, and you go out
onto the balcony in search of air, but there is no air, and no one
can say if there ever will be.

Night of still air, air that you struggle to pull into your lungs.
Night.

Maione arrived about an hour later, out of breath.

He found Ricciardi sitting, alone, on the outside steps leading into the waiting room. Not far from him, seated on its
haunches and still as a statue, was the doctor's dog.

"Commissa', what's happened? I went by headquarters, just
to see if there was any news, and they told me that you'd
rushed over here to the hospital, that it was an emergency. Are
you all right?"

Ricciardi raised his head and looked at him with bland
curiosity. He looked terrible. He summarized the situation for
his friend, then asked him: "But you, why didn't you stay at
home?"

Maione looked away, embarrassed.

"No, Commissa', it's just that . . . it was so hot, and instead
of tossing and turning in bed and keeping Lucia and the kids

up, I thought it best to get out and see if I could get some air. And my feet only know one route, so they took me straight to police headquarters. That's all. If you have no objections, I'll sit with you and keep you company for a while."

Night without respite.
Night when sleep brings no rest, when it's wearying to lie flat on your bed, eyes wide open, in the darkness.
Night without a future.

Nelide didn't take her eyes off Rosa.
She looked like a cardboard silhouette, the ones they put next to stacks of merchandise, depicting a housewife in the process of making a purchase. But unlike an advertising silhouette, Nelide wasn't smiling, nor could she be described as decorative.
Her solid, stout body was immobile, her arms folded across her chest, her jaws clenched, her forehead furrowed. At the doctor's suggestion, the nurses had placed a chair next to the bed, but she hadn't sat down for so much as a second. She was there for a specific reason, and it wasn't to rest her feet.
She'd immediately realized what was happening to her aunt. She'd already been through similar experiences with her grandfather and another relative. Both of them had died soon after.
Her mind, practical and rigorous, was devoid of imagination, and therefore of any false hopes and illusions. Rosa, too, would die, in spite of the speed with which she had acted, despite the apparent skill of this doctor, whose name had wisely been given to her in advance.
And she, Nelide, what would she do?
When her aunt had arranged for Nelide to come stay in the city, she hadn't told her parents, or Nelide herself for that matter, much. But everyone had taken for granted that the plan was for her to take Rosa's place as Ricciardi's governess. Rosa's enviable economic condition, and the fact that practically every member

206 · MAURIZIO DE GIOVANNI

of the Vaglio family was working in some capacity on the estate
of the Baron of Malomonte, placed Rosa at the summit of society
in that town and therefore, as far as Nelide was concerned, in the
whole world. For years everyone had speculated as to who would
take the *tata*'s place; the *tata* managed Ricciardi's entire patri-
mony, given the young master's utter indifference to his considerable worldly wealth.

For years, Nelide knew, the *tata* had studied all the family's
young women. And she knew that many of her countless
female cousins would have had a greater claim, by age and by
training, to that position.

But she possessed something that all the other young
women lacked: a perfect affinity with Rosa. Just like her aunt,
she was determined, loyal, and capable of rapidly adjusting to
any and all situations. In just a few days, confirming the sound-
ness of Rosa's choice, she'd learned all that she needed to keep
the Ricciardi household humming along.

But she knew very well that she was still quite young.
Would the farmers, the sharecroppers, and the peasants who
rented shares of the estate's farmland recognize the authority
of a little girl? Of course, she could count on help from her
father and her uncles, who constituted the network that Rosa
had relied on over the years, allowing her to build up the
Malomonte family estate, instead of presiding over its disper-
sal; but would that be enough?

Her eyes monitored the slow, regular rise and fall of the
sheets over Rosa's chest. The woman was breathing deeply, as
if she were asleep. And yet Nelide knew that that was no normal sleep.

Beneath Nelide's grim expression was a frightened little
girl. It wasn't Ricciardi who frightened her; in part because
she wasn't thinking about how to understand him, was limit-
ing herself to anticipating his needs. She would look after him
because she had been instructed to do so, and she would do

as she had been taught. Ricciardi was a task she'd been assigned, and she would perform that task scrupulously and with devotion, as was her nature. What worried her was something very different.

The fact was that Nelide really did love her aunt. She was bound to her by an animal love, without nuance, without selfishness. And when faced with difficulties she'd become accustomed to taking refuge in thoughts of her aunt.

How would she manage, without her? Without a chance to ask her for advice, to rely upon her?

In the darkened hospital ward, the tightly pressed lips of that homely, powerfully built young woman, standing erect in the shadows, quivered slightly.

But no one noticed.

Night of rage and fear.

Night without light, without hope.

Night that seems to possess all things and all thoughts. Night like a lake, that engulfs the city and its thousands of activities.

Night that fears to breathe, night without love.

Night that changes, that leaves no smiles.

Night without caresses.

Lucia was sitting up, eyes wide.

When Raffaele had stormed out of the apartment, slamming the door behind him, Giovanni, the eldest son now that Luca was gone, had emerged from his bedroom and asked why his father was angry. She had explained to him that *papà* had been right, that children should be careful of their table manners, and that they should show him respect.

Then she'd added that Raffaele was tired, that it was hard work to support a big family like theirs, and now that he was a big boy, he needed to understand his father and help him.

208 · MAURIZIO DE GIOVANNI

Giovanni had replied that he was hungry, and he'd asked if he could finish his dinner now, with his brothers and sisters. But Lucia had replied that if *papà* had given an order, that order was to be obeyed, even if *papà* wasn't there right now. *Especially* if he wasn't. So no dinner for anyone, not even for her.

It hardly mattered, her stomach was tied in knots anyway, she mused as she stared at the ceiling.

Lucia was worried. She couldn't figure out what was going through her husband's mind. Could their economic situation really be so serious? What if there was a debt, an obligation that Raffaele had preferred to keep to himself so as not to worry his wife?

Lucia could do no more than she already was doing. Walking miles and miles to shop in the cheapest stores and markets. Stitching and mending with her own hands until articles of clothing were completely worn out. Turning the children's overcoats inside out a hundred times, painstakingly laundering outfits and rubbing out sweat stains with ammonia or vinegar, and then washing them again in cold water to make them last.

And now she was doing even more, to try to add a little extra to the family budget, making good use of the gifts that nature had given her. She thought he'd be happy to see the girls in their new shoes, to know that she'd buy new shirts for him. And instead that violent reaction, which had frightened her even more than it had frightened the children, because she, his wife, knew very well how unlike him it was.

Sunk in the scalding air of an infernal night, Lucia wondered where Raffaele was at that moment.

And she prayed that he was all right.

Night of ghosts.
Night of voices and whispers from out of the darkness.

Night of visions, of movements glimpsed out of the corner of the eye. Night of sudden tremors, night of high fever.

Night of ancient words, of lifeless sighs. Night of the world beyond.

Night of spirits of the past, night of memories long thought to be buried.

As she slept a sleep that was not really sleep, Rosa saw that, right near her, sitting lightly at the foot of her bed, was Marta di Malomonte, the young master's mother.

Dreamily, she wondered to herself what the baroness might be doing there. It wasn't customary for the baroness to sit on her bed; nor, for that matter, to enter her bedroom. The baroness was very respectful of the domestic help's personal space: she knocked, she asked permission before entering. Her manners, so different from her mother's imperious and intrusive ways, had come as a pleasant surprise to everyone. If you added to all that the fact that Marta di Malomonte had been dead for more than fifteen years now, it all seemed pretty strange.

Rosa tried to get up, as she had always done in her mistress's presence, but she was unable to do so. She lacked the strength; she couldn't so much as lift a finger. And so she spoke to her instead: "Barone', what are you doing here? It's been quite a while since I last saw you."

Marta was holding her embroidery basket. She placed it on the bed, pulled out needle and thread, and started embroidering what looked to Rosa like an outfit for a newborn.

"Ciao, Rosa. You see? I came to visit you. I'll keep you company for a while."

Rosa considered the matter, then asked: "Does that mean I'm dead, Barone'?"

"No, you're not dead. You're not well. And you'll die, like everyone. But you're not dead. How do you feel, right now?"

Rosa tried in vain to move her hand.

"Well, Barone', I'm in no pain, but I just can't seem to move. If I can't move, as you know, I don't know what to do with myself."

The baroness nodded.

"I know, I know. You've always been highly judicious and energetic. That's why we chose you as Luigi Alfredo's *tata*, my husband and I. But now, you see, you're obliged to stay still. And you can rest."

"Barone', in that case you'll forgive me not getting to my feet. It strikes me as such a strange thing to lie here on my back, me, a servant, while you're sitting there uncomfortably on the edge of the bed."

Marta smiled at her, with a little smirk of the lips identical to the young master's.

"Don't worry. I know you aren't well, like I told you. What I'm wondering, though, is who's looking after Luigi Alfredo while you're here?"

Rosa thought it over for a moment.

"There's Nelide, my niece, the daughter of my brother Andrea, do you remember him? He's the one who keeps sheep and farms your land down by Sanza; your ladyship always said he was a good man. When your ladyship . . . when you passed away she was just a little girl, but she's grown up to become a strong, healthy young woman. She's got a good head on her shoulders."

Marta nodded and went on sewing.

"Nelide, yes, I remember her. So it was Nelide you've been training these last few days. You're quite right, she's a capable girl, trustworthy. Do you think she's ready to take your place?"

"Well, she's certainly young, Barone'. But we're an unusual clan, young and old we're all the same. She might make mistakes, after all, who doesn't? Still, she's honest and strong, bursting with health and with no foolish ideas in her head. Her one fault is that she doesn't talk much, and when she does she speaks only in proverbs: maybe she does it to seem wise."

Marta sighed. Rosa interpreted that as a sign of fear.

"Barone', understand me. I didn't have any time left, I had to act quickly. If I'd had, I don't know, maybe another couple of years, I'd have educated her properly, I'd have kept her with me for longer periods of time, I'd have made her to go over the renters' accounts to see if she knew how to do it on her own. Forgive me, Barone'. I thought I could get it all done in time."

Marta caressed her cheek.

"Don't you worry, Rosa. She'll do fine, she'll figure it out. Now you get some rest. I'll stay here and sit with you. When you like, we can talk again."

Rosa smiled and fell asleep for a while.

Nelide, who was studying her face, saw her lips wrinkle in a sort of smile. Her respiration was deep and regular.

The girl checked the warm cloths on her aunt's legs. How long this night was.

Night.
Endless night. Night without light.
Night for the dead, night for the ghosts.
Night without life.

XXXV

M ajor Manfred von Brauchitsch had awakened very early, even though life on the island moved even more slowly on Sunday than on the other days of the week. The problem of different speeds had always been an issue during his stays in Italy. It was as if Manfred was a cog in a gear that was spinning very fast, and that was then inserted into a weaker engine. For that matter, he was German: his people were typically a little frantic and maniacally devoted.

He stepped out onto the balcony of his room. Dawn, from the pensione where he usually stayed, imbued the sea and the spit of land that jutted out into it with indescribable hues, colors that he would be incapable of extracting from his palette even in a thousand years. Perhaps, he thought, that's what makes the people here so slow: how could you stop, even after centuries of being accustomed to it, from pausing to admire such a wonderful landscape? How could you keep from taking it easy, breathing this blossom-scented air, listening to the music that saturates it?

He went back in to do some calisthenics. He was determined to keep in shape: the years passed and his profession demanded absolute efficiency. He had to admit to himself that he was gratified by the frank appreciation he seemed to receive from the island's women, whenever he crossed paths with them during his evening walks.

While he was doing his second round of deep knee bends, he found himself thinking about that girl, the schoolteacher at the summer colony whom he'd run into for the past several days out at the beach where he went to paint.

There was no doubt that he'd made quite an impression on the other schoolteacher, Carla, that was clear from her attitude and the glances she shot him; but the one he liked was Enrica, who was in charge of the little girls. She offered him no encouragement, which only stimulated his natural competitive spirit.

She wasn't especially beautiful; at first glance she might in fact appear insignificant. Her legs and arms were too long, she wore eyeglasses and her clothes were mousy. But deep inside, Manfred was first and foremost a painter, and he'd recognized her remarkable figure, lithe and firm, her handsome bosom and her swan's neck. And the smile that she beamed so frequently at the little girls, luminous and full of tenderness.

Perhaps it was because he was accustomed to capturing particular appearances and intense expressions that he'd been so taken by Enrica. The measured gentleness with which she moved, the womanly way she had of sitting on the beach, with her white skirt gathered beneath her legs and her chin resting on her hands as she gazed out at who knows what, in the distance.

He wiped away the sweat with a hand towel and headed off toward the bathroom.

This wasn't something that happened often, he mused. Since Elsa had died, more than ten years ago, he'd had only a few fleeting affairs, and each woman had been gone from his mind as soon as the moment of their physical intimacy was over. But this time, he found himself counting the hours that separated him from his next painting session on the beach.

Enrica, he understood, was shy and reserved, a delicate blossom, a butterfly; if he moved too quickly he ran the risk of ruining everything. He also sensed a certain insecurity on that woman's part, or even fear: perhaps there was some sadness or grief in Enrica's past, as there was in his own, for that matter.

In their infrequent conversations, he'd preferred to stick to

214 · MAURIZIO DE GIOVANNI

unremarkable topics. He'd told her about his hometown, the land he hailed from and where now, perhaps, one of those terrible summer rainstorms was coming down, auguring the onset of autumn. It was too early to tell her about Elsa, of the way he used to be, of how he had changed and why. Of war and serving under arms. Of the fact that he was a soldier.

Times were changing. The aftermath of the postwar sanctions and the burning sense of defeat were gradually being overcome; in Germany there was a new spirit in the air. Alsace and Lorraine had been lost, the German empire's colonial possessions were lost, most of the army, now shrunk to a hundred thousand men, was lost, the navy, which had preferred to sink the fleet rather than hand it over to England, was lost; nonetheless, the sense of honor, the belief in the nation's own grandeur, the urge to rise again, were more alive than ever. Nationalism, fomented by the harsh terms of the peace treaty, had engendered a political party that had sunk its roots deep into the populace, and the preceding April it had come tantalizingly close to sweeping the elections, gathering over thirteen million votes. This in spite of the fact that the movement's leader was a man who nine years earlier had been in prison for spearheading an unsuccessful coup attempt right in his own home state of Bavaria.

When Manfred had left for Italy, there had already been talk of new elections to right the political imbalance. He personally favored the leader of the National Socialist Party. Though he didn't care for the excessive fury and bullying methods the man used to put his ideas across, he had to admit that the pride and patriotism that quivered in the words of that excellent orator moved and enflamed him. Deep down, he was a soldier: his love for his homeland, his desire to defend it from foreigners and expand its borders, formed part of his nature.

Moreover, he liked the fact that the man took his inspiration, more or less explicitly, from the Fascist regime. In Italy, he sensed a liveliness, an optimism, and a confidence in contrast with the difficult conditions in which most of the people seemed to be living. He wished he could see the same attitude spreading through Germany, among the elderly in particular, wearied by the war and the economic collapse. If the two countries, brothers deep down in their souls, were to share certain values, nothing and no one could ever stop them. That's what he thought.

In the meantime, he told himself as he splashed cold water on his arms and back, he'd establish a nice strong alliance with the girl on the beach.

It was nice to feel that sensation again. It was nice to feel he was still alive. At the end of July he'd return home to vote in the federal elections, and to see if he could be useful in the reconstruction of German military might, which had until then been progressing slowly and discreetly. A couple of days ago he'd received a letter from a veteran, a onetime fellow soldier, asking if he was done with his life of leisure and was ready to venture once more into the breach. He'd written back, informing his old friend that nothing on earth could make him miss the opportunity to let him eat the dust of his charging steed.

The thought of his horse reminded him of the treatments he was taking on this island. Daily training and mineral water mud packs, that volcanic mud that so many doctors had described as miraculous, were having their beneficial effects. The pain in his shoulder was almost gone.

Manfred brushed his thick blond hair and looked up at the blue sky. He suspected that there was also another reason for his renewed sense of vigor.

Good officer that he was, he wondered exactly what strategy he should employ to outflank the barriers that Enrica had erected to protect herself. He was sure that if the girl could be persuaded that he would never do her any harm, she'd lower her defenses and soon let herself be lulled by her feelings.

As he was biting into one of the biscotti that the elderly proprietress of the pensione had given him, he caught himself fantasizing about the expressions on his parents' faces if he returned home with a new wife, and an Italian one to boot. His mother had told him over and over again that Elsa was gone, that he needed to make a new life for himself, and that before she died, the one thing she wanted was to cradle in her arms a grandchild, to be certain that the family name would not die out with Manfred.

Enrica was young and self-assured, and she had beautiful hips. All the right features.

The major flashed a smile at the sea. After taking the mud, he would go back to the beach.

He had a painting to complete.

XXXVI

As soon as he was allowed, Ricciardi had run to Rosa's bedside, taking the stairs two at a time.

He'd finally managed to send Maione home late into the night, convincing the brigadier that sleepy as he was, he was of no use to him: he could come back to work the next morning. Modo, as was so often the case, had stayed the night in the hospital's internal quarters, and had gotten up twice to update Riccardi on his *tata*'s condition, which remained stable.

As for Ricciardi, he hadn't slept a wink. He couldn't manage to get used to the idea that he might be about to lose the woman who had always been his entire family.

He found her complexion pale, her breathing labored; she was sitting practically straight up, her body propped on four pillows. Standing in front of the bed, erect and motionless, was Nelide. Ricciardi greeted her fondly: it touched his heart to see her pure and silent love, and he was impressed by the fact that she showed no signs of weariness. And yet she must have stood there all night long.

He sat down, took Rosa's hand in his, and his heart sank: the hand was icy cold. To look at her face, though, she appeared untroubled, and even faintly alert, as if she were listening to something. Ricciardi didn't know what to make of it. He turned to Nelide.

"She didn't ever wake up? Not even once?"

The girl shook her head. Then she spoke: *"Cchiú scura d'a mezanotta nu' ppò vveni'."*

It can't get any darker than the middle of the night, the commissario translated mentally. He knew the young woman's habit of speaking in proverbs; once or twice he and Rosa had even joked about it. Now, looking down at his old *tata*, he wondered if he would ever again hear that off-kilter, contagious laugh that had formed the background of so many moments of his life.

He missed Enrica—powerfully, sharply. He would have liked to let her know that Rosa—the woman who had become her friend, the woman who had talked endlessly to him about the shy, sweet girl who lived across the street from them—was ill, gravely ill. And that his heart was in tatters, and that a major part of his desolation was due to Enrica's absence.

He rested his head against the bed and fell asleep.

After an amount of time he couldn't have quantified, he felt a hand on shoulder. He woke up with a jerk and found Modo next to him.

"You didn't go home, did you? Stubborn hardheaded man, I told you there was no point in staying."

Ricciardi looked at Rosa; she hadn't moved a millimeter.

"I can't bring myself to leave her. And after all, today is Sunday, I don't even have to work. I might as well stay here, don't you think? If she happened to wake up . . ."

"Ricciardi, I'll tell you again: she's very unlikely to wake up. It's practically impossible. We'll transfer her to a single room and we can try some therapy, but there isn't much we can do."

The commissario turned to look at Nelide; she was still on her feet, motionless like her aunt, but from her lively intelligent eyes, it was clear that she wasn't missing a word.

Modo resumed, more or less talking to himself: "I'll see if I can lower the blood pressure from the hemorrhage. If she were younger, I'd try a decompressive skull trepanation, but a woman of her age, in her condition, would almost certainly die. I'm afraid even to attempt a phlebotomy, that is, cutting a vein in her arm. I'm going to have come up with something else." He turned to Ricciardi: "Now get out of here, and this time I'm serious. You're harmful, not just useless. You distract me and you worry me. Go home. And take the young lady with you, because she's starting to scare me, standing there at the foot of the bed."

Nelide gave him a long, hard look: *"'Ntiempo re tempesta, ogni pertuso è casa."*

Modo turned to look at Ricciardi: "What?"

Ricciardi made a face: "In stormy weather, any hole in the wall becomes a home. I think it means she doesn't intend to budge."

The doctor stared at Nelide, eyes wide, as if he'd suddenly noticed that one of the metal lockers against the wall were actually alive.

"What are you saying, that she speaks in proverbs like an Indian chief? Fantastic. Well, if she wants to stay, I'm certainly not going to kick her out: just look at the muscles she has, I wouldn't dream of trying to outwrestle her. But, please, you go. In addition to everything else, out in the hall there's a sad brigadier turning his hat in his hands, and his mere presence is terrorizing the entire hospital. You know that a majority of my clientele is quite allergic to policemen."

Ricciardi planted a kiss on Rosa's forehead and bade farewell to Nelide with a nod. The girl, to his surprise, whispered: "Signori', don't worry. I'm in charge here. And anyway I'll come home tonight and take care of your things."

The similarity to his *tata*'s way of speaking tugged at his heart.

In the hallway, Maione came up to him immediately, asking for an update on the situation. Ricciardi ran his hand through his hair: "For now she's in stable condition, but Modo is pessimistic."

"Commissa', of course he is, that doctor is pessimistic on general principle. You'll see, everything will turn out fine. You're tired, that's understandable. You want me to walk you home?"

Ricciardi thought of Rosa's absence and Enrica's empty window, and he shook his head: "No, no. I don't want to go home. I'm too tense to sleep. I'll drop by the office to kill some time."

The brigadier gingerly patted his uniform: "I arranged to trade shifts with Cozzolino, who couldn't quite believe he was getting a Sunday off, and is planning on taking one of his bimbos to the beach for a swim. I preferred to come in to work, too. At this point, Commissa', why don't we just get caught up on our work for next week and head over to the nursing home in Mergellina? That way we can look the man who sent the letter to the professor in the face."

"Look at what's become of us, eh, Raffaele? We're diving into work on a Sunday in July, when everyone else is heading for the beach."

XXXVII

After a short huddle, they decided to head over to Mergellina on foot. The endless night they'd just spent had left deep marks on both their moods, and the idea of subjecting themselves to a ride in a trolley full of beachgoers didn't fit with their need for a breath of fresh air. So instead they would take Via Toledo, cross Piazza del Plebiscito, and follow Via Cesario Console to the water, then stay close to the waterfront, following Via Partenope and Via Caracciolo. An hour's walk under the hot sun of the second Sunday in July.

Maione had gone home to change into a fresh uniform, and managed to take a short nap, but that had certainly done nothing to improve his state of mind; Ricciardi hadn't had any chance at all to recharge, as could be seen from the stubble on his face and the marked unruliness of the lock of hair dangling over his forehead. They both felt out of place in the midst of the stream of people pouring out of both working-class neighborhoods and the posher streets of the city, and heading town toward the waterfront in search of coolness.

The city was dying of heat. And since it was July, the city wanted to have fun. And since the city wanted fun, it was willing to spend a little money, thus attracting a swarm of characters determined to take advantage of that willingness, whether by selling, bartering, or pilfering. This led to the creation of two opposing armies, Customers and Strolling Vendors, the latter more or less equipped with official permits, their ranks more or less battling to win the best spots.

From one end to the other, the city's beaches had assumed the aspect of a long trench in which a bloodless war was being waged, where the phrase *no thanks, I don't need anything* only marked the beginning of a skirmish. The fastest and most insistent vendors, who traveled with wooden crates hung over their necks on a leather strap, or else pushing ramshackle old perambulators repurposed for the occasion, were only encouraged by a rejection, which was after all a reply, and were capable of pestering a potential customer for hundreds of yards, repeatedly and irritatingly touching his or her arm to attract attention, until the exasperated victim shelled out a few cents in exchange for a useless packet of *semenzelle* or a flavorless *spassatiempo*, a mixture of pistachios, toasted chickpeas, and various seeds and nuts, wrapped in a conical sheet of newsprint. After eating whatever he'd been forced to buy, the hapless customer would toss the rinds to the ground, to the delight of the pigeons.

Far different was the attitude of those vendors who enjoyed the enviable advantage of a fixed location, foremost among them the fresh water sellers, the most beloved vendors on those sweltering days, with their circular kiosks topped with handsome round roofs reminiscent of cool Chinese pagodas, adorned with cascades of lemons and oranges, the mere sight of which offered relief from the heat. The water vendor would shoot an inviting wink, his big face red beneath the broad brim of his straw hat, his clean white smock reminiscent of the ice he scraped with a trowel to add to the *limonata a cosce aperte* ("spread-eagled lemonade," so called because when the vendor added a teaspoon of bicarbonate of soda, the glass always overflowed, obliging the customer to gulp it down hastily, legs spread wide to keep from staining his trousers). Moreover, there was mineral water for sale, the iron-rich *acqua ferrata* of Beverello or the sulphureous *acqua zuffregna* of Chiatamone, which was kept in *mummare,* or amphorae, had a faint whiff of rotten eggs, and was beloved for the fundamental aid it provided in digestion. That aid came in especially handy because, if there was one desire that assailed visitors to the waterfront, it was for food, a temptation second only to that prompted by the naked legs of girls in swimsuits, the sight of which attracted more men than any burlesque show. Everywhere you turned, people were eating or trying to sell something to eat.

The air was full of calls. *Jamm', 'nu sordo: magne, bive e te lave 'a faccia!* shouted the *mellonaro*, or melon man, displaying his multipurpose watermelons for just a penny; as his call in dialect explained, you could eat them, drink them, and even wash your face in them; and to emphasize how ripe and bright red they were, he added that they were full of fire, containing a veritable inferno: *è chino 'e fuoco, tene ll'infierno dinto.*

Currite, currite, 'e ppullanchelle! came the call-and-response from the opposite side of the street, as the *spigaiola* advertised her roasted corncobs, emphasizing their savory similarity to fat hens piping hot from the oven.

And it was virtually impossible to remain indifferent to the wares of the *tarallaro*, the vendor touting little salty doughnuts made of stale bread, pepper, pork lard, and almonds. *Taralle, taralle frische, taralle càvere,* he shouted, advertising a remarkable contradiction of temperatures, good for whatever a customer might prefer, cool or hot. Maione was a glutton for *taralli*, but he didn't so much as deign to glance in any of the vendors' direction.

Another summer delicacy were the prickly pears, sold from small stands. In this case the transformation of commerce into spectacle was even more interesting; not only did the vendors show off their skill at freeing the fruit of its thorny rind in less than two seconds with an incredible display of dexterity and the simultaneous use of two knives, they had also come up with a sort of *riffa*, or contest, known in dialect as the *appizzata*, that attracted throngs of customers. For just a few cents, a contestant could toss a long knife, tied to a length of twine, into a sack full of peeled prickly pears in the hopes of piercing one, which was then fished out of the bag, the winner's property. Unfortunately, the vendors invariably placed the softest, ripest fruit at the top of the heap, and these of course always slipped off the knife.

Then there were the barbers, musicians, and shoeshine boys, the vendors of cigars, fried foods, goldfish, lottery tickets, bananas, gelato and candy, wine, oysters and seafood of all kinds, octopus, and ricotta, all of these entrepreneurs boasting in a magnificent cacophony the freshness, the quality, the unparalleled specialness of their goods to the throngs willing to subject themselves to an unspeakable ordeal in order to obtain just a moment's cool respite from the heat at the beach.

The street urchins, naked or clad in nothing more than a rag, tied around the waist, chased after each other, laughing and playing pranks on the passersby, knocking off hats or hiking skirts, adding even more chaos to the general state of confusion. Off the piers and the boulders of the breakwaters, boys and girls showed off their dives in a roughly competitive style, lifting geysers of water and provoking all sorts of insults from the elderly gentlemen trying to read their newspapers while soaking their feet in the lapping water. Mixed teams challenged each other to games of tug-of-war after recruiting the fattest men on the beach, who competed clad in full-body bathing suits that stretched tight over their prominent bellies.

Just inland from the waterfront ran the Villa Nazionale, every bit as crowded but at least free of the automobiles, carriages, bicycles, and motorcycles with sidecars that struggled to push their way through the traffic on the main thoroughfare. There the population was different: sweaty nannies, in black domestic uniforms with lace headpieces, pushed monumental perambulators, struggling to keep the older children from breaking away to play soccer with their lower-class contemporaries; ladies on their husbands' arms, shielding themselves from the sun with silk parasols; well-dressed young men with well-tended mustaches strolling two by two in search of pretty girls willing to accept offers of a cool beverage in a café.

The latter dandies reminded Maione of the notorious Fefè and the mystery of Lucia's afternoon outings, putting him in an even worse mood than ever. But he wasn't the only one walking through a forest of phantoms. Ricciardi practically hadn't uttered a word the whole way, his heart ravaged by the thought of Rosa and her dark sleep.

Neither alive nor dead, he thought, as anguish darkened his soul, in sharp contrast to the explosion of summer joy surrounding him. In the midst of so many young people smiling at life, so many men and women enjoying the summer Sunday as if there were no such thing as tomorrow, the Deed showed him the lingering traces of madness, violence, and tragedy. A half-naked boy with a broken neck called to his mother from the cliffs onto which he'd slammed down; two fishermen prayed and cursed, face-to-face, their lips blue from the icy water in which they'd drowned; in the shade of one of the holm oaks of the Villa Nazionale, a man was gushing blood in spurts from his belly, sliced open by a knife blade, as he muttered about the money that had been taken from him.

Stories, thought Ricciardi. Stories of the living, stories of the dead. And you, my sweet tender *tata*, hovering between the two worlds, just like me. You don't know it and you never will, but we've never been so close.

Maione said, grimly: "There it is now, Commissa'. We've arrived."

XXXVIII

The Villa Santa Maria Francesca nursing home was a small building, sand-yellow, on Via Tommaso Campanella, at the corner of Viale Principessa Elena; a quiet place, the last stretch of city before the pristine greenery of the Posillipo hill. At the entrance, in a cool, private front room, sat a young woman in a nurse's uniform. When she saw Ricciardi and Maione come in, she furrowed her brow, probably because these weren't the kind of clients she was accustomed to greeting. Then, however, she put a smile on her face and asked what she could do for them.

The two policemen introduced themselves and asked to see Dr. Ruspo di Roccasole. The young woman replied hesitantly: "Perhaps you're looking for his son, Guido. I don't believe Dr. Francesco can see you right now."

Maione was in no psychological state to engage in any skirmishes: "Signori', maybe we didn't make ourselves clear: we're the police. We're not asking to be seen, we're demanding to be seen. So when we say . . ."

Ricciardi laid a hand on his arm: "Let it go, Raffaele. We're happy to talk to the son, too, thank you, Signorina. We might ask him whether it will be possible to talk to the doctor."

The nurse lifted the receiver of a thoroughly up-to-date telephone switchboard that loomed, enormous, black, and riddled with cables and jacks, on the counter in front of her, waited a few seconds, and then whispered something.

After a few minutes, during which Maione scowled at the woman, the young Ruspo di Roccasole came in and filled the room to bursting.

He was little more than a boy; his childish features betrayed his youth, but his physique was gigantic. Not only was he practically six-and-a-half feet tall, he was extremely overweight: a veritable colossus. He approached the two policemen and, with a surprisingly querulous voice, introduced himself: "I'm Guido Ruspo. What can I do for you?"

Both Maione and Ricciardi immediately thought of what the jeweler Coviello had told them, namely that on the night of the murder he'd glimpsed a person with a huge frame waiting outside the professor's office.

Ricciardi said: "We need to speak with your father, Dr. Francesco. But actually we need to speak with you, too."

"I'm at your service, Commissario. My father, though . . . my father is sick. Very sick. He's here, in a room upstairs, but I doubt that he's well enough to talk to you."

Maione snorted: "Here's someone else who thinks it's up to him who we can talk to. Take us to your father, and if he can't talk to us, we'll decide what to do next."

Though he towered over Maione by a good four inches, confronted with the brigadier's aggression, the young man blinked and, after a moment's hesitation, nodded: "As you like. Please, come with me."

He led the way up a flight of stairs and down a hallway that he nearly filled with his bulk, until they arrived at a closed door which he opened without knocking.

Inside was a bed shrouded in dim light and shadows, with a male nurse sitting in a small armchair against the wall. The young man nodded a greeting: "Lui', you can go, just wait in the hall outside. I'll call you when we're done. And close the door behind you."

There was a sharp tang of disinfectants and medicines in

the air, mixed with an acidic aftertaste that could have been either urine or sweat. The smell of death, thought Maione.

Guido went over to the bed and delicately laid a hand on the sheets.

"*Papà? Papà*, are you awake? Do you think you have the strength to talk to these gentlemen?"

A faint moan rose from the bed, followed by a cough. At last, a rough voice said: "Yes, I'm awake now. Before long, I'll be sleeping all too much, as you know. Who are these gentlemen? Let in a little light, Guido. Maybe even a little fresh air."

The young man went over to the window, opening the shutters so as to let a shaft of sunlight filter in without flooding the bed itself. Then Maione and Ricciardi were able to see the room's occupant.

The man was at death's door, no doubt about that. The skin on his face was dark, as if it had been treated in a tannery, and it was stretched across his bones; practically no flesh was left, suggesting the appearance of a mummified corpse. A few hairs clung stubbornly to the cranium, dangling from his temples in grayish shocks. The lips were chapped and, here and there, cracked. The sheets covered a body so rail-thin it could hardly be seen. Only the eyes, black and bright, still betrayed curiosity and intelligence.

"So it's daytime, then. In that case, *buongiorno*, gentlemen. If I had to guess, I'd say you're from the police."

Maione and Ricciardi exchanged a look of surprise. Then the commissario spoke: "*Buongiorno*, Dottore. Yes, I'm Commissario Ricciardi and this is Brigadier Maione. May I ask why you were expecting our visit?"

The doctor let out a sharp laugh that ended in a burst of coughing. The son moved toward the bed with a gesture of concern, but his father waved him away.

"Because I may look dead but I'm not quite dead yet, that's why. And since I'm not dead yet, I have my nurse, Luigi, whom you met earlier and who isn't as ignorant as he seems, read me the evening paper. I'd have read it myself, because believe it or not my eyesight is still good, but I don't have the strength to hold anything in my hands. Interesting, no?"

Ricciardi stared at him, expressionless: "The fact that you read the newspaper by proxy, Doctor, still doesn't explain why you were expecting us."

The man cracked a smile which, on that devastated face, made for a horrifying effect.

"It's obvious. Our good friend Tullio Iovine, in defiance of the odds, has shuffled off this mortal coil before me. And you must have gone to his residence, where you no doubt found my letter. The letter I sent him a couple of months ago, the best I can remember."

Guido looked startled: "A letter? What letter, *papà*? You promised you wouldn't interfere! You promised . . ."

The man pulled a bony hand out from under the sheets. Like his face, the hand was dark, almost black, and like the arm it bore multiple puncture marks.

"Please. Hush. It was the only way."

Maione shot a glance at Ricciardi: he doubted that Guido had been kept in the dark about the letter, and he was inclined to think that it was all just put on for show.

"So you, Guido, are telling us you knew nothing about it. And you want us to believe that your father wrote the letter on his own."

The young man stared at him with hostility: "My father's condition, Brigadier, has deteriorated sharply in the past few weeks. Two months ago, he was perfectly capable of writing. Unfortunately."

Ruspo coughed and said: "That's right. I was even capable of getting out of bed. Then things took the turn you see now. It's called cancer, Brigadier. It attacks the organs one by one, and eats you up from within until you die."

Maione nodded.

"I know what cancer is, Dotto'. It took my mother. And I can assure you that at least it's natural; Professor Iovine del Castello, on the other hand, didn't die of natural causes, and that's why, as you said yourself, he shuffled off before you."

Ruspo burst out laughing, as if regaining strength.

"Del Castello. Incredible, with that cheap trick he fooled everyone right up to the end. That wasn't his real name at all, Brigadier. His name is Iovine, just plain Iovine."

Maione was baffled: "Then why did he tack on the second name?"

"Because he was a buffoon and an impostor, that's why. That's what he was as a student, that's what he was as an assistant, and that's what he was as a professor. Since he was convinced that the halls of medicine were too aristocratic to accept some commoner, he decided that a double-barreled surname would open a few doors. And maybe he was right."

Ricciardi made an effort to steer the conversation back to more relevant matters. Seeing that man in a terminal condition took his heart back to Rosa; he was in a hurry to return to her side.

"What reason did you have for writing that letter, Doctor?"

The man in the bed gave him a malevolent stare: "And why do you think I did it, Commissario? You read the letter, didn't you? That bastard flunked my son here, three separate times, keeping him from taking his degree in medicine, and therefore, my place here at the helm of the nursing home. I decided to warn him that I wouldn't tolerate the situation any longer."

Maione said: "Actually, if we want to be accurate, you blackmailed him, Dotto'. You threatened to produce documents concerning medical errors that . . ."

Guido looked at his father, clearly upset: "But *papà*, what have you done? Why . . ."

Ruspo waved his hand in the air: "I tried to do what I had to. In any case, it was only a threat, those corrupt officials at the physicians' guild would never have undertaken proceedings, it was my word against the university. Still, as you can see, I've run out of time, and it was my one chance. I had to give it a try. That bastard would never have let my son pass that exam."

Ricciardi leaned forward: "What reason would Iovine have had for trying to keep your son from graduating?"

Guido mopped his father's brow with a cloth. He said: "Commissario, I don't think it's wise to continue. My father . . ."

Ruspo interrupted him: "No. I don't want to take this thing into the grave with me. Let me speak."

"*Papà*, I'm begging you . . ."

"That's all you know how to say: Papà, *I'm begging you.* Shut up and get me some water . . ." Once he'd swallowed a gulp from the glass his son had brought him, the man resumed: "We were in the same year at medical school, Iovine and I. We were even friends; he chose whoever he thought could help him in his climb to the top: he was smart that way. I belonged to the upper crust, and I had a distinguished name. And I liked him. He was intelligent, cheerful, and brilliant. We had fun. After we got our degrees, we both began our university careers, he out of ambition, me because I wasn't the type to start my own business, too much work. We were volunteer assistants. We were the youngest ones there, but by far the best."

Ricciardi asked: "And how long did it last?"

"The director was too smart to keep the two of us in a subordinate position. After a year, when a couple of chairs opened up elsewhere and someone went into retirement, he took us on as paid assistants. And before long he'd stopped talking to anyone but us; he'd call us whenever there was something interesting to see. We grew to love the field thanks to him. We worked day and night, there was nothing else in our lives."

"What about relations between the two of you?"

"As far as I was concerned, they had never changed. But that was only true for me, I realized later."

232 - MAURIZIO DE GIOVANNI

Ricciardi was very interested.

"And then what happened?"

"First I should tell you something about the professor. A genius, a wonderful man, never again in my life did I find myself speaking the same language with anyone the way I did with him. He became director at a very young age; he wasn't much older than us, but he was gifted like no one else, a true luminary. People came from all four corners of the earth to get him to treat their wives, mothers, daughters. And he never thought of money or of advancing his career: he fought. He was a man who fought against suffering, in whatever form it might take. He could only imagine that other people thought as he did."

"What about the two of you?"

"We had different motivations. Iovine wanted to establish himself, become respected and rich. He came from a small town, and he suffered from an inferiority complex. He was angry and envious, that was the source of the energy that drove him. I, on the other hand, wanted to become like the professor."

Ricciardi was fascinated in spite of himself.

"And then?"

Ruspo had a coughing attack. His son, worried, supported his head and gave him another sip of water. Maione noticed a slight reddening on the handkerchief Guido used to dry his mouth.

When the coughing fit subsided, the man went on in a softer voice: "And then. And then we came to the point that was inevitable. The obstetric and gynecological clinic has one director and two aides, five assistants, plus a variable number of volunteers. One of the aides went abroad and a position opened up. Just one."

Maione nodded: "And there were two of you."

Ruspo gazed into the empty air.

"That's right. There were two of us. Equals in every way: in terms of dedication, surgical skill, diagnostic intuition. It was all up to the professor's judgment, which was not subject to appeal."

"And who did he choose?"

Lost in his memories, the man paid no attention to Maione and went on with his story: "His name was Rosario Albese. He was about forty. He was tireless, courteous, hardworking. I told you: a genius. For Iovine, Albese had become an obsession: he watched him from afar, he studied his every gesture. He wanted to be him. To take his life: his university chair, his shoes and his pen, his desk, his tie. He wanted his job."

Ricciardi asked: "Where is Albese now?"

"He died a few years later. He had heart problems. He suffered a heart attack on the job, as could be expected."

Maione drove in: "But who did he prefer, between the two of you?"

Ruspo placed a trembling hand on his forehead: "He preferred me. All three of us knew it. He preferred me because I had none of Iovine's rage and viciousness. He never said so, but he would have chosen me, without a doubt."

Ricciardi wanted to know more: "He never said so? Why not?"

"Because Iovine ruined me. He ruined his friend, the friend who had helped him so many times by introducing him to wealthy and important men, the men who allowed him to create the network that supported him until the day that, thank God, he was killed."

"How did he ruin you?"

"It was simple. I was having an affair with the wife of a count, a very prominent man. He wrote an anonymous letter, stating where and when the woman and I were planning to meet. It was a scandal, and the university takes these things very seriously."

Maione asked: "Are you sure that it was Iovine who wrote the anonymous letter?"

"A scandal three days before the appointment of the new aide? Of course I'm sure. For that matter, he admitted it himself, by choosing never to see me again."

There was a long silence. Then Ricciardi said: "And you really never spoke again after that?"

"I set up shop on my own, and before long I had a huge clientele in my own social sphere, the sphere of the very wealthy. Then, when my wife died, leaving Guido to me at a very young age, I wanted to have more free time for myself, time to spend with him, and I formed a partnership with two investors to start this nursing home. I was in charge of running the place, and I was able to do it until six months ago, when the disease forced me to stop working."

Maione was unwilling to leave any area unexplored: "This problem of your son's degree . . . why? After all, he was the one who had done harm to you."

Ruspo didn't answer right away. He seemed to be sleeping. Then he answered, in a faint voice: "I've wondered the same thing, and I've never managed to come up with a satisfactory answer. Perhaps he wanted to prove to himself that he was right to ruin me, that I wasn't even capable of teaching my own son. Or else the mere fact of seeing the boy reminded him of what he'd done, and he didn't like the feeling. Or maybe he thought that Guido, sooner or later, if he remained in the profession, would find a way of exacting vengeance on my behalf. I don't know. Better to eliminate your enemies' progeny, no? He used to say it, when he was a boy, and I thought he was kidding . . ."

There was another silence. The man gasped out a breath. Ricciardi and Maione stood up; Guido walked them out.

The brigadier said to him: "Before leaving, we have to ask: where were you on the night between Thursday and Friday?"

The young man met the brigadier's eyes: "I was with my father. The way I have been every night since he's been like this. I don't like to leave him alone. He's always taken care of me, as far back as I can remember. It seems to me that the very least I can do is take care of him now."

Ricciardi understood him well. He understood him, and how.

"Tell me one last thing: what will happen, if you don't take your degree? If your father dies before you take your degree?"

Guido shrugged his shoulders. The commissario noticed that the left shoulder hung lower than the right; a slight curvature, a minor deformation he hadn't noticed at first.

"He was the director of the clinic, so he kept our shares constant even though the chief investments came from the other two partners. In other words, everyone was happy with this split. But if I can't replace him, they'll have to hire an outside medical director, and pay him a salary. At that point . . ."

Ricciardi finished for him: "At that point it will be easy to push you aside, won't it? They need only demand a new investment and you'll be unable to do anything."

Guido looked away and out to sea, to the blue water glittering in the noonday sun behind a line of buildings.

"Yes. I imagine that could happen. But I will succeed, Commissario. I'll pass that damned exam, I'll get my degree, and I'll take my father's place."

Maione murmured: "I'd bet on it. Now, of course you'll pass the exam."

XXXIX

On the way back, they chose to cut inland; the route was a little longer but less packed with people, horses, and wheeled carts. Maione was the first to speak: "Commissa', if you ask me, these two aren't telling it straight. In practical terms they'd have been ruined, if the boy hadn't had this stroke of good luck, so to speak, with the professor's death. Because the professor, if I'm understanding this correctly, would have gone on flunking him, now and forever."

Ricciardi agreed: "Right. If he couldn't pass that exam, he'd never have gotten his degree, he'd never have been able to take the place of his dying father, and the partners would have forced him out of the clinic."

Maione wasn't done: "Apart from the exam, it seems to me that the dying doctor had other motives for wanting his old colleague dead. The man had ruined his life by writing that anonymous letter."

The commissario wasn't entirely convinced.

"All quite true. And what's more the sheer bulk of the son lines up with the size of the man that the goldsmith told us about. Still, I have to wonder: what sense does it make to send a threatening letter and then proceed to do something like that? It amounts to a confession before the fact. What's more, why take revenge after more than twenty years? It doesn't add up. It's one thing to die and leave your son unemployed, it's another to send him to prison for the rest of his life."

The brigadier wasn't willing to dismiss his theory: "Maybe

it just wasn't premeditated, Commissa'. Maybe the son just went to have a talk with the professor, and since he showed no signs of changing his mind, he picked him up and threw him out the window. And the father, lying on his sickbed, found himself with a murder to cover up."

"That could be. Anything could be. Did you notice that one of the son's shoulders is lower than the other? The jeweler might have noticed that detail. It's worth having another talk with him. In any case, first I want to meet Peppino the Wolf, and go see the professor's widow again; I'd like to figure out whether she knew about little Sisinella."

Maione mulled over the idea. Then he said: "That's a possible lead, too, Commissa'. If a guy finds out that his wife . . . No, sorry, if a wife finds out that her husband is cheating on her, who can say what she might be capable of doing. But the lady was over at her cousins' place in the same apartment building, with her son, and I doubt she has the strength to throw anyone out a window."

"No, I wasn't thinking about it that way. It wasn't the wife, that's for sure; I was thinking about Sisinella and her new boyfriend. I want to understand whether she might have taken any initiative on her own, such as going to call on the professor. As for Signora Iovine, I wonder if she might have noticed some change in her husband's mood."

Maione murmured grimly: "Sure, of course. When a husband's being cheated on, or a wife for that matter, he's always the last to know."

They reached the corner of Via Toledo and parted ways: Ricciardi continued toward the hospital, and Maione headed home. The brigadier said that he'd swing by later to see how Rosa was doing, but the commissario replied: "No, Raffaele; stay with your family today. I'll see you tomorrow in the office, we have a lot to get done."

And he headed off, with a dagger in his heart.

Nelide stared at her aunt's placid face. The doctor had told her it wasn't possible, but she sensed that something was happening inside that head: she could spot almost imperceptible movements of the facial muscles, as if the old woman were dreaming.

The young woman's practical mind kept chugging away. What was she supposed to do now? Of course, she could go back to her village. It would be more appropriate for one of Rosa's sisters to be at her deathbed. That, however, would mean that for a period of at least two days, there would be no one tending to the sick woman but the young master.

Ah, yes, the young master. Another problem. Rosa had explained to her how incapable the man was when it came to running a house and taking care of himself. And she'd assigned to Nelide the task of looking after him: the young woman would inherit Rosa's responsibility to care for him.

Her first duty was to obey the instructions that her aunt had left her. Yes, she was sure of that. This is what she was born for. Once the thing that she felt was inevitable had happened, all obligations concerning Ricciardi would rest on her shoulders, and she would assume those tasks without doubts or hesitations.

No other woman in the family, Nelide decided, had a greater right than she did to run the household of Luigi Alfredo Ricciardi. Her own aunt had conferred that enormous charge upon her, and she would rise to the responsibility unless Ricciardi himself sent her away.

She turned her attention back to Rosa. Her aunt had taught her everything she could, and her example had formed the basis of Nelide's entire education. She loved her Aunt Rosa, and she felt ready to inherit her position. She only wished, though, that Rosa had been able to stay on a little longer with her and the young master, even bedridden; so that she could talk with her, confide in her, ask her advice.

In silence, without even mouthing the words with her lips,

she said a prayer to the Madonna del Carmine—Our Lady of Mount Carmel—whose feast day would soon be here. *Madonnina*, she asked, won't you leave her here with me a little longer? If you don't need her up there right away, to tidy up heaven, maybe you could let her stay on a little longer here with me. Just so she could tell me one more time how to make the *teneredda*, or the *pizza roce*; or what I should do if the sharecroppers fall behind in their payments for more than a season; of if one of the plants out on the balcony starts to wither.

She wasn't afraid, Nelide. She didn't consider the task overwhelmingly challenging, nor did she think of herself as a girl who was still too young. She'd battled against drought, against two floods, against the epidemic that had ravaged the livestock. You're ready for anything once you've survived a winter during which hail has destroyed the harvest or the wolves have devoured eight sheep out of fourteen, if you've survived temperatures of 15 degrees with almost no firewood, when you've been forced to cut up the table and three chairs just to heat the house, and if the fever has carried off two baby brothers in a single autumn. Whatever happens, her aunt used to tell her, gives you a gift: the good things and the bad things. And the finest gifts come from the worst things, because they teach you what to do to keep from having it happen again. The good things leave you nothing but a pleasant memory, and that's not very helpful.

One time Rosa had taken her by the hand and led her to the window. 'Look, Ne'," she'd told her. "You see those two young ladies shielding themselves from the sunlight with that white silk parasol? You see them? Well, that little umbrella is just stuff and nonsense. You have to carry it in your hand and it has the same weight and bulk as an ordinary umbrella, but it shelters you from neither the sun nor the rain. It's good for nothing. You, Ne', should only load yourself down with the things that you need. You shouldn't carry anything useless. I will teach you the things that are necessary, and those are the only things you need to carry with you."

Nelide had thought it over. Then she'd turned to look at Rosa and had said to her: '*Sí, 'a zi'*. I understand. Only the things that are necessary."

'*Nu sacco vaco nun se regge all'erta*, she thought to herself. And it was true: a empty sack can't stand up. An empty sack flops over onto the ground. And she, Nelide Vaglio, wasn't an empty sack. Aunt Rosa had filled this sack to the brim.

Madonni', just a little longer, if it's possible, she thought, addressing the Virgin Mary. Just a little longer.

With a quick swipe, she brushed away a tear.

XL

D r. Modo walked into Rosa's bedroom and found Ricciardi sitting beside the bed, holding his *tata*'s hand. Just beyond them stood Nelide, in the shadows.

"It seems to me that you're worse off than she is, you know that? Take a look at yourself: your hair isn't combed, you need a shave, your shirt wants buttoning. You're losing all your charm. Your legendary success with women is in danger, and the ladies of this city will notice that there's a magnificent physician, no longer so young, but still perfectly fit."

"The clock has run out as far as you're concerned, Bruno. Your only hope of winning women's hearts these days is with cold hard cash."

"Money well spent, *caro*. And after all, those women are the best: professional, kindhearted, good listeners, and they don't care about being taken to dinner. It's a choice, not a necessity, remember that."

Ricciardi looked at Rosa.

"I came back and found her unchanged. Aren't there any signs of improvement?"

"Perhaps I didn't make myself clear, or more likely you're refusing to listen. She could remain in this condition for a long time. I can't rule out the chance of her waking up, I've seen it happen: once a soldier was hit by a shell fragment and he slept for nearly two months; we'd even thought of finishing him off ourselves so we could use the cot, and it looked like he didn't have a chance. Then he opened his eyes and asked for something

242 · MAURIZIO DE GIOVANNI

to eat. But he was twenty years old. Rosa, on the other hand, I don't know . . . a day, a month. She's an old woman. Strong, but old."

Ricciardi rubbed his eyes.

"Then what can we do? I . . . I can't just stand here and do nothing."

The doctor leaned back against the wall and hugged his arms to his chest.

"No, in fact. And if you did, it wouldn't do a bit of good. You need to go home, wash up, put on some clean clothes. Get something to eat, go to your office. If anything does happens, and I don't expect it to be anytime soon, I'll call for you. The staff has been alerted: they'll let me know the instant there are any new developments. For that matter, it's thanks to you, you and people like you, that I sleep here in the hospital as often as I do, and that poor dog has gotten used to sitting around waiting in the courtyard; the nurses feed him scraps every day."

"Please, Bruno, do whatever you can. If there are special treatments, however expensive, I'd . . ."

"Sure, as if it was a matter of money. I know that you're rich, you think I don't? I'd have told you. And after all," he added, lowering his voice, "if there had been anything we could do, I'd have already done it, in part because the young lady over there scares me silly, and has no intention of leaving this room. A couple of hours ago, when you weren't here, I told her that she could go home, because Rosa was being given excellent care."

"What did she say?"

"She glared at me and said something in that Cilento language of yours whose meaning remains obscure to me: three dentals, four gutturals, a couple of aspirates, and vowels as tight as any dipthong. Then she swiveled her eyes back to Rosa's face, and that's where they stayed. I don't know if the girl has had a chance to pee since yesterday, I certainly haven't seen her budge. Can you ask here whether she'd be willing, anytime in the next hundred years, to donate her body to science? I'd love to study her."

In spite of himself, an amused expression appeared on Ricciardi's face.

"The women of Cilento are indestructible, Doctor. By the time Nelide will be available for scientific study, you'll be a plaster bust on a plinth in the atrium of this hospital."

The doctor gave him a worried look.

"Seriously, though, Ricciardi: go home. Get some sleep. You're no help to Rosa in this state."

The commissario turned his eyes back to his *tata*: "I'll just hold her hand until this evening. Then I'll go home. But right now, just let me stay with her a little longer. Maybe she can feel my hand, who knows?"

Rosa felt a caress on her hand and opened her eyes. She felt fine, well rested. She tried to get up but couldn't.

The baroness smiled at her, while still focusing on her stitching: "Calm down, *tata*. Don't make any unnecessary effort, you can't move, I already told you that."

"Barone', then who is it that just caressed my hand? I could feel someone touching my hand."

Marta shrugged her shoulders.

"Maybe a sigh, or a gust of wind. Or perhaps the kind thoughts of someone who loves you. It must have been Luigi Alfredo."

"What, the young master? Where is he?"

The baroness sighed.

"Who can say. It's not as if we can see them. Maybe he's here, by your side, right this second."

"But I can't see anyone, Barone' . . . there's no one here but you and me."

Marta laughed softly: "No, we're not alone. See?"

And she cocked her head toward the far side of the room,

where there was a tall old man, standing straight as a rod and dressed to the nines.

"Oooh, the baron!" said Rosa, her heart pounding in her chest. She'd always been in awe of that frosty, silent man.

Marta lowered her voice, as if to avoid being overheard: "Yes, that's him. He's over there because he's ashamed, but he still wants to see what happens. It matters to him, too, you know?"

"It matters to him about who, Barone'?"

Marta held up the newborn baby outfit against the light and scrutinized her work.

"About his son, of course. This is the only way we have, after all."

Rosa was baffled: "What way, Barone'? To do what?"

"To find out about him. To let him know that we love him. You're our only contact."

Rosa didn't understand.

"What do you mean, your only contact? What are you talking about?"

Marta stopped stitching and looked at her: "Because he loves you dearly, *tata*. And he's suffering the pains of damnation right now, sitting next to you. He's afraid. He, a man who feels the pain of others, a man who thinks he's insane, is suffering as he's never suffered before. That's why we're here, his father and I. To see if we can comfort him just a little."

Rosa considered the matter.

"I'm so sorry, Barone'. I never managed to find him a wife, help him start a family. I knew that I wouldn't live forever, that my time would come. But in the end all I could do was set Nelide up here at home, at least in time to teach her how to cook. I failed. Forgive me, Barone'. Forgive me."

"What on earth are you taking about? Utter nonsense. You were a marvelous *tata*, and you did everything within your power, and then some. You see this little romper for a newborn baby girl? It's for you, for when you're here with us. I'm stitching ever so slowly, because when it's finished, you'll be reborn. And then Luigi Alfredo will be left all alone. Let's hope that by then, he'll be ready."

Rosa asked: "Ready to do what?"

Marta stared at a point in the middle distance.

"Ready to share his life. To understand that it's still possible to love, even when you're bearing the burden that we carry."

"What burden, Barone'? What burden does the young master carry, what burden did you two bear? Will you tell me?"

"And why should I, poor *tata*? You wouldn't understand. You just need to get a little sleep now. Don't worry: I'm a slow stitcher."

XLI

L ivia reached Gambrinus right on time.

The driver pulled up in Piazza Trieste e Trento and walked around the car to open the door for her on the side facing the café. She stepped out, provoking a couple of shrill wolf whistles of approbation as she did so—whistles that she more or less ignored. It was the driver—also as a way of establishing his own presence—who shot an angry glare at the idlers sprawled at the outdoor café tables, fanning themselves with their straw boaters and twirling their mustaches as they waited for pretty girls to go by, maybe those leaving evening services at the nearby church of San Ferdinando.

Stepping briskly, Livia walked into the café. Two young men lept to their feet: such a woman, alone in a café, was rare catnip for them. They hurried after her into an interior space, but a human colossus sitting at a table rose to his feet and barred the way, crossing his arms and blocking the threshold. The two men exchanged a glance of surprise, then one adjusted the knot of his tie, the other smoothed the crease of his jacket, and, crestfallen, both returned to their lookout posts.

Livia looked down at a sheet of paper she held in one hand and crossed the empty room to take a seat by the plate glass window overlooking Via Chiaia. She caught a faint whiff of lavender and looked up from the list of drinks, locking eyes with a distinguished, middle-aged man of average height standing not far away.

"*Buonasera*, Falco," Livia said.

The man bowed his head in a respectful greeting. He held a leather briefcase in one hand, just as he had every other time that Livia had seen him.

"*Buonasera*, Signora. May I sit with you?"

"You summoned me to an urgent meeting, you offered to send a car and driver to bring me here, from what I can see you've reserved the entire interior dining room at Gambrinus, so I'd have to say that, yes, you're free to take a seat."

As if Livia's irony had gone clear over his head, Falco executed a second small bow, and sat down across from her. A moment later, the waiter arrived with a tray.

"I took the liberty of ordering you a vermouth. Perhaps at this time of the day you'll enjoy it."

Livia shot him a look.

"You know where to find me. You know what I do, how I dress, and where I shop, the places and people I visit. I'm hardly surprised to learn that you also know what I like to drink, or even that you decide for me what I'm going to drink, which amounts to the same thing. So vermouth will be fine, *grazie*."

The man returned the look, unblinking: "Believe me, Signora, the last thing I want to do is inconvenience you. And I'm sorry to hear that you've come to think of my presence as a nuisance. We do our best to be discreet, that's in the nature of the . . . work that we do. But when we are forced to intervene, we intervene. Though we try to do it cautiously, we have no choice."

"Oh, really? So tell me, why have you been forced to intervene this time? And then, answer me this: why on earth have you chosen to summon me here with a written note? You've always simply materialized as if by some magic spell in my living room, without even being announced. This time, instead, you've actually written to make a date."

"A date, you say? Far too bold for my style, I'm afraid. The loveliest and most alluring woman in the city is far above

248 · MAURIZIO DE GIOVANNI

anything I could hope for. I've told you before, just think of me as a sort of guardian angel. If I reach out, it's only to help you."

Livia leaned forward and spoke harshly: "Falco, let's not kid each other. Guardian angel, my foot. What I am for you, and for your governmental structure, or section, or department, or whatever the devil you choose to call it, is a tremendous pain in the neck. That's what I've been for you since the day I decided to move down here. May I ask why you insist on taking such good care of me even though I never asked you to? Would you please just let me live my life in peace?"

The man sipped his espresso, gazing lazily out at the people strolling past in the street outside, though the intense heat had winnowed down the usual crowds. Then he set down his demitasse and spoke.

"That's very good. The coffee is one of the best things about this city. I've been around and believe me, if there's one thing I always miss when I travel it's the coffee here at Gambrinus. I believe that its distinctive aroma was the deciding factor in my choice of this café as our meeting place. A pity you don't drink espresso."

Livia had no intention of going along with that digression.

"I'll drink what I please, Falco. And I don't have to account for my tastes to you. Now, if you'd be so good, will you answer my question? Why won't you stop spying on me?"

"I'm sorry. I'm sorry to hear you use this tone with me, and most of all I'm sorry that I must be the target of your ill will. You want to know why we keep spying on you? I'll answer your question." He took a drink of water. "You, see, we do surveillance on a great many people. You'd be surprised to know the number. These aren't always prominent individuals, they aren't necessarily troublemakers or subversives. There are a variety of reasons we might decide to put someone under surveillance. And believe me, my dear lady, it's not an easy task or a particularly enjoyable one. We make use of a network of informants who do not belong directly to my . . . structure, in fact, I'd say that in our surveillance we rely for the most part on ordinary people. Tradesmen, strolling vendors, even priests. Everyone spies on everyone else. And they report back to us. The most complex part of the work we do, Signora, has to do with separating the chaff from the wheat in these reports, lest we take seriously warnings that are actually just people settling scores, avenging old grudges, working out their envy or jealousy, or simply slandering their fellow men."

Livia recoiled in disgust: "My God, what a filthy mess this country's become. I'm almost ashamed to belong to . . ."

Falco raised a hand: "Please, Signora. Don't say things that I'd be forced to remember from this day forth. Please. It's hard enough already."

The man at the entrance was leaning against the doorjamb, making a great show of indifference. Falco went on: "In any case, with you it's different, and you know that. We don't watch over you, to use the terminology we prefer, because we suspect you of any significant activity, though I have to say that some of your indirect acqaintances, as you well know, are of some concern to us. Our care as far as you're concerned . . ."

Livia snapped: "Your care, is that what you call it?"

". . . stems from other issues. You, Signora, are very, very dear to someone in Rome who is very, very important. This matter was communicated to us the day you arrived in this city, and we are still held responsible for anything that happens to you or even anything that might happen to you."

"Which means that if I want to rid myself of this obsessive surveillance all I need to do is make a phone call to . . . to some girlfriend of mine? Would it really be that simple?"

"No, Signora. It wouldn't be that simple. Certainly, you'd never see me again; and you'd hear nothing more from me, or from my . . . colleagues. But if anything, our observation would become even more strict. For example, you rightly asked why we're meeting here and not in your home."

"Well, why are we?"

"I thought it best in order to protect you from the person whose job it is to keep an eye on your apartment, a person who doesn't know me and might well take me for someone else entirely."

Livia restrained an impulse to laugh: "Really? You're telling me that you don't even know each other? Incredible, quite a show of efficiency . . ."

"No, Signora. You're wrong. Our decision not to introduce those performing surveillance to each other makes it possible to cross-check the honesty and accuracy of their reports."

At this point she really did laugh out loud: "Honesty, you say! What an interesting choice of language, my compliments. Let's get to the point, Falco, why did you want to see me?"

"As you wish. Now, then, you've decided to host a party, am I right? Quite a party indeed, with a great many guests. So . . ."

Livia interrupted him, aghast: "But . . . but how could you know that? I've hardly mentioned it to anyone! Then that means my housekeeper, Clara . . ."

Falco shook his head: "No, no. The domestic servant Clara Fenizia, twenty-two years of age, is not in contact with us. Let's just say that the orders you placed with your suppliers, as well as a few phone calls and one or two meetings, are what alerted us. I must ask you for your guest list, Signora. We need it so we can deploy the appropriate security measures."

Livia shot to her feet, her lips white with fury: "I won't give you a single thing, Falco. Not a thing! I'm a free woman, until proven otherwise, and in my own home I'll do as I please with anyone I like."

She'd raised her voice; a few people outside turned their heads to look. The man at the threshold took a step in their direction, clearly worried, but Falco stopped him with a wave of his hand, without bothering to look up.

"You know, Signora, like all truly beautiful women you

become even lovelier when you're angry. Please, sit down, and listen to what I have to say."

Livia sat back down, reluctantly, her hands, clad in black gloves, clenched into fists.

"We'd get that list in any case, you realize that, don't you? Only it would cost us more effort and we'd run the risk of leaving off a few names. We are quite sure that you plan to invite people who are very important to us. And I'd never dream of trying to cause you any difficulties. It's just that there might be some . . . incompatibilities among your guests. What we'd like to do is spare you any potential awkwardness that might result from unwished-for meetings. That is the reason for my request."

Falco's heartfelt tone made it clear to Livia that she'd been needlessly rude and excessively aggressive. That was the political situation: what was the point of taking it out on someone who had only tried to be kind, however odd a form that kindness might take? Perhaps even at his own risk and peril.

"Please forgive me, Falco. I went too far. You understand, I'd given up on this idea of a party, then things changed and now it seems like it would be a nice thing to introduce myself, and introduce someone I care about, to the better sort of people in this city. And on that occasion, I'd like to do something that I haven't done in too long. Far too long."

Falco had never betrayed any signs of emotion in any of their intermittent meetings. He resembled one of those butlers you see in movies and novels from across the Channel, unfailingly phlegmatic, never batting an eye. He was always obsessively neat in his old-fashioned, nondescript gray suits, his thinning hair neatly combed, his hat in his hands. That was why the sudden change of expression and the powerful burst of emotion that showed on his face were such a stunning surprise for Livia.

Falco's eyes were glistening like those of a child who'd just been promised a longed-for gift. He extended his hand across the table and laid it on Livia's begloved one: "Don't toy with me, Signora! You're going to sing! You're going to sing again, at long last!"

Livia stared at him in astonishment: "Yes . . . I thought . . . but what . . . why are looking at me like that, Falco? I don't understand."

Falco shook himself, as if emerging from a brief trance. He pulled back his hand, leaned against the backrest, and looked around, confused. The man at the door put on a show of indifference, but his ears were bright red.

"Please excuse me. I beg of you, Signora, excuse me. You see, I . . . that is to say, singing, opera, it's a weakness of mine. I had the fortune, as I've told you, to hear you sing once, at the opera house, and since then I've followed your career with great interest. I own your five recordings, various magazines . . . and so, when we learned that you would be coming to this city, I asked to be assigned to you. And I couldn't resist the temptation to meet you in person, even though that's something that's frowned upon in my organization's tradecraft. I've always regretted your decision to retire, an overhasty one if you'll forgive my boldness. You have a gift, you know. An important gift."

Livia didn't know what to think.

"You know, my husband, while he was still alive . . . the fact is, he didn't much care for my singing."

Falco nodded seriously.

"Yes, naturally. Perhaps, if I were in his place, I'd have been jealous of your bravura. Even if he was a genius himself."

"Yes, well . . . in short, I've decided to sing again, at least among friends. Perhaps a song, just one. Written by a composer from this city. It only seems right."

"You'll be magnificent, Signora. Magnificent. I've been assigned to dissuade you from hosting this party. It's not a simple moment, as I'm sure you'll understand, with the upcoming elections in Germany . . . We'll have extra work on our hands.

But if you're going to sing, that changes everything. I'll make sure to be there, and I assure you that you won't see me. But I'll be there. The chance to hear you sing again is an experience that I wouldn't miss for the world."

Livia couldn't help but be flattered by such intense admiration on the part of a man who, she suspected, wasn't much given to expressing it.

"I thank you, Falco. It will be a pleasure for me to know that you're out there, somewhere. It will be a fancy dress party, with a maritime theme. I'll let you have the guest list, of course. You'll have no difficulty guessing most of the names in advance, for that matter: clubbable society in this city is a fairly restricted circle. I'll add a few other names, just to repay debts of courtesy. For instance, I was thinking of Garzo, the deputy police chief, who's always been so nice to me and who has on several occasions agreed to let Ricciardi take me out to the theater, in spite of the fact that the commissario ought to have been on duty instead."

"Certainly, I understand. And let me take this opportunity to tell you how sorry I am to hear about the lady, the commissario's governess. It's not easy when someone you're so fond of . . ."

Livia stood up abruptly: "Are you talking about Rosa? What's happened to her? I haven't heard anything!"

Falco stood up in his turn: "What do you mean? He hasn't told you? Why, I thought . . . The governess didn't feel well yesterday and was taken to Pellegrini Hospital, where she was put under the care of Dr. Modo, whom you, unfortunately, know all too well. She's in fairly grave condition, from what I've been able to learn."

"What about him? He must be with her, at the hospital. She's the only person that he's close to. I must go to him, I need . . . I need to be with him, right away!"

The man's face took on a look of consternation: "Signora, please. It's not necessary. I've already told you on more than one occasion that the doctor . . . oh, no question about it, a good man and an extraordinary physician, but his political views . . . could cause you some serious problems, both you and your commissario. I really have to urge you . . ."

Livia had already grabbed her handbag. She spoke to him in a chilly voice: "Falco, do me a favor, don't waste my time telling me the usual things. You'll forgive me, I'm sure, but right now I have somewhere to be. *Buonasera.*"

And she left, striding briskly.

XLII

At midnight Ricciardi went to listen to the Deed.

It was something he hadn't done in years. There was a time, when he first decided to become a policeman, that he considered it important. At the time of day or night at which the death had occurred, the Deed was strongest and most direct. It clearly narrated the emotions of the victim, almost amplified them.

Then he had realized that all too often the thought that reached him, slicing into the spine of his soul like a whip, was merely empty pain and sorrow; that if anything it distracted him more than it helped him to untangle the mystery.

It was the Deed that first drove him toward his chosen profession. Perceiving the suffering that went along with a violent departure from this life, the awareness of the absurdity of a non-natural death, these factors had been crucial elements of the process, had made it impossible for him to abandon the urge to try to put things back in order, if only after the fact. Moreover Ricciardi had neither the personality nor the disposition to loll about in cafés, theaters, and opera houses, squandering the family fortune, with a university degree hanging on the wall.

This time, though, he felt called upon to listen to the professor on the cobblestones of the polyclinic's lane, on the spot where he landed three days earlier, at the same time of night when the murder had presumably taken place.

After Nelide had returned to the hospital from a trip home, where she had changed into clean clothes, Modo had evicted

Ricciardi from Rosa's hospital room. Livia, breathless, her face twisted with heartfelt grief, had also come by in the late afternoon. Ricciardi had asked her how she'd known, but the woman had been vague, mentioning a visit she'd made to police headquarters. Ricciardi had reassured her and convinced her to leave quickly: for some odd reason, she'd seemed incongruous to him there, in a hospital room with Rosa in the bed. He'd even wondered, with a twinge of sadness, how he would have felt if it had been Enrica. But she hadn't come. Who knew where she was.

Instead of taking him home, his feet had taken him to the general hospital, as if of their own accord. He was tired, and he knew it; but weariness was fertile ground for the Deed. When he was tired, his instinctive defenses tended to come down, and his special inner ear, the one that heard the dead, grew more attentive.

He spoke to the night watchman, who let him in without a second thought and without even getting up from the chair in which he'd been nodding off. He walked the length of the lane, lined by the menacingly dark silhouettes of trees, until he reached the point that was still marked by a dark stain on the ground. The professor's blood.

Even if he hadn't remembered the exact spot, he'd have found it all the same. The figure of Iovine, his spine shattered, his cranium fractured, the small red cascade oozing from his face like lava from an erupting volcano, stood grimly before him, translucent in the darkness, visible to his heart as if illuminated by a spotlight.

Sisinella and love, love and Sisinella, Sisinella and love, love and Sisinella. A murmured litany. He remembered the words, but now he wanted to capture their shadings, their nuances.

He looked up at the office window. It was dark and very high, more than sixty-five feet above him. How long did you take, Professor? He made a quick calculation: at least a couple of seconds. Time enough to shift his thoughts from one subject to another.

He stared at the image. Love. What came to your mind was love. It was love that bobbed to the surface. It's not necessarily linked to whoever threw you out that window, in revenge, for self-interest, out of cold calculation, or out of regret. But it was love that shut your eyes once and for all. Love for a girl who was young enough to be your daughter, a girl who gifted you moments of illusory happiness.

He stood there a while longer, observing the phantom, and then turned to head home. He'd try to get a few hours of sleep now, then he'd swing by the hospital to see Rosa, and after that he'd do his best to put things right. Because death comes far too soon, even left to its own devices. It's not right to wake it up so far before its time.

It's not right.

Dear *Papà*,

The festival of Our Lady of Mount Carmel is drawing near and my thoughts go to you with even greater tenderness. Every year you took us to see the burning of the bell tower, and before that the release of the balloons, the fireworks, the decorated balconies. I can still taste the hazelnuts, the ice cream you bought for us, and I can still hear the shrieks of joy of my siblings. I think back to it with happiness and a twist of homesickness.

Here at the summer colony life goes on as usual. The girls have wholeheartedly embraced the task of making the embroidered panel for the festival of St. Anne (do you remember, dear *papà*? I wrote you about it in one of my previous letters), and we have sound hopes of finishing it in time. The little boys are busy making the wooden structure to support it, though from what I can see, they're behind schedule. My colleague Carla is certain they'll make it. Let's hope so.

I ought to tell you, dear *papà*, that my relations with Carla have suffered recently, and not due to any fault of mine. We've never discussed the matter, but I suspect that the root cause is the fact that Manfred, the German officer I wrote you about, has shown an unmistakable preference for me. I couldn't tell you the reason why, since Carla flirts quite openly with him while I, in contrast, am even harsher and more unpleasant than necessary, precisely because I wouldn't want my colleague to accuse me of being interested in him; still, Manfred keeps after me quite insistently, he never misses an opportunity to speak to me, and I even have the sneaking suspicion that he arranges situations in which he can just happen to run into me. Yesterday, for instance, I found him right in front of me when I went out before dinner to get a little fresh air in the pine forest.

Never fear, dear *papà*, he is respectful and well mannered. He has the savoir faire of a soldier and a German, and I'm certain that he'd never behave offensively toward me; but I find it embarrassing, terribly embarrassing, to see the gleam in his eyes when he speaks to me.

In a conversation we had on the beach, during a break in his work as a painter (he won't let me see the canvas he's painting!), he told me something about his life. The poor thing was widowed years ago when his wife suddenly fell ill; I haven't even managed to get him to tell me exactly what it was that killed her. Her name was Elsa. His face took on an expression of profound sadness when he uttered her name; it's clear that his heart was marked by the loss. He told me that since then he has been incapable of imagining himself as the father of a family, and that he was convinced that he would remain alone for the rest of his life. Then, looking straight at me, he added that at least that's what he thought before coming to stay on this island.

I found an excuse and hurried away, dear *papà*. You know how badly my own heart has been wounded and how I still, at night, glimpse the gaze of the man about whom I told you. I'm not ready, and I won't be for quite some time to come, to talk about certain topics with other people.

Still, there's something I should tell you, and only you, *papà*. Do you remember when, a year ago, *mamma* got it into her head to try to arrange an engagement with that horrible Sebastiano, the son of Signore and Signora Fiore? Do you remember how she contrived to leave us alone at every opportunity, whenever he came calling at our home in the evening? And do you remember how I asked for your help in avoiding him? It was torture just to have him near me.

Well, this time, my dear *papà*, I will confess that a part of me is flattered by Manfred's attention; and it's certainly not a burden to spend time alone with him, even if I do feel sorry for Carla. All the same, no one can say that I've encouraged him or am encouraging him.

My heart belongs to someone else, though. And perhaps it's wrong to force myself to think about someone else to try to forget about him. I don't know much about love, in fact, practically nothing, but I believe that in matters of the heart the saying that one problem replaces another doesn't apply.

Before I was able to make an excuse and hurry away, Manfred asked me if I'd give him a chance to speak to me more formally. He has something he wants to tell me. I didn't reply and I'm terrified at the thought that he might ask me the same thing again.

At night, after dinner, I look out to sea. And beyond the sea, in the trembling lights of the distant city, I see two green eyes staring right at me. If only my heart, my cursed little heart, weren't so keenly aware that he is still thinking about me, perhaps I'd feel free to look ahead to the future.

I send you my fondest love, dear *papà*. You can't imagine how comforting it is to be able to write you about my troubles.

Yours,
Enrica

XLIII

This time they weren't at all surprised to find themselves together so early in the morning. By now it was clear to both Ricciardi and Maione that in this strange, uncomfortable period they were more at ease at work than at home, even though the commissario couldn't figure out why the brigadier had had such a sudden change in mood.

They planned out their day: Ricciardi wanted to make sure that police headquarters would be able to track them down precisely in case word came in from the hospital. They'd go talk to Giuseppe Graziani, aka Peppino the Wolf; then, if their schedule allowed it, they'd go by and talk to the professor's widow.

They had no need to say anything about the challenges attendant upon their first appointment; the Wolf, young though he might be, was a powerful man who acted in accordance with a code that was hard for those outside of his world to understand. They'd need to be cautious but determined, they'd need to move along a very fine borderline: too far to this side and they'd be unable to learn anything, too far to the other and they'd be putting their own lives in danger. Many were the acts of violence that had been committed against policemen who ventured to set foot in territory ruled by forces other than those of the state.

As they were getting ready to head out, Garzo himself stuck his head into Ricciardi's office.

It was uncommon for the deputy police chief to come into the offices of his subordinates. He considered it a prerogative of his high position to receive subordinates in his own office, while he waited behind his monumental mahogany desk as they were ushered in by Ponte, the onetime concierge who Garzo had transformed into his personal assistant, even though the official personnel structure didn't call for such a position.

Ricciardi and Maione, therefore, were enormously surprised to see Garzo's broad, beaming face, with his well-tended mustachio, his perfectly shaven cheeks, his neatly brushed dark brown hair, and his long salt-and-pepper sideburns, loom into the doorway. Just as surprising was the time of day: Garzo never showed up in police headquarters this early in the morning, faithful as he was to the principle that important people can afford to come in late.

The commissario and the brigadier shared the same opinion of the deputy police chief: a dimwitted, social-climbing bureaucrat, incapable of even the faintest flash of insight, but an adroit diplomat, kind to the strong and cruel to the weak, terrified at the thought of appearing to his superiors in any but the most favorable light. And since it was often the case that police work wound up treading on the feet of the high and mighty, more than once there had been friction between these two and the deputy.

But that day Garzo was all smiles, and the sight gave Maione the willies. Always fear the devil, especially when he pats you on the head, the brigadier thought to himself.

"Ah, *caro* Ricciardi, I knew I'd find you already here at work. Tireless and devoted to your duties, aren't you? And stalwart Maione's here too, excellent, excellent. How is it going? What's the word from the criminal underworld?"

Ricciardi and Maione exchanged a look. The situation, whatever it was, must be pretty serious.

"*Buongiorno*, Dottore. We're working on the case of Professor Iovine del Castello, you must have heard, he was thrown out a window over at the general hospital . . ."

Garzo waved a hand in the air.

"Yes, yes, I know. The poor man. Then again, he was a par-
venu, never invited to truly join the upper crust because it wasn't
clear just who his people were. Politically, too, he seemed to lurk
in the shadows, without ever taking a clear position. But now, my
dear Ricciardi, is the time to come out into the open, to look the
future in the eye. The Duce says so, and so does History."

Maione coughed softly: "Commissa', may I remind you that
we need to go if we hope to track down that suspect and question him."

Garzo took a seat at Ricciardi's desk: "Ah, excellent! We
already have suspects! It's magnificent to be able to rely upon
people like you, so diligent and conscientious, to keep the city
clean and running smoothly as it is and does, and as it will be
and will do. It's no accident that we receive a steady stream of
recognition and praise from Rome."

The commissario had had only a few hours of sleep and was
shouldering an enormous concern. He wasn't in any kind of
shape to carry on polite chitchat with Garzo, nor to withstand
his political proclamations.

"Dottore, what can we do for you? We have a pretty busy
schedule this morning and . . ."

"Of course, of course. Work before all else. And we, who
have our daily war to wage, we who are on the front line, we
must never forget it: I always say the same thing to my wife, who
doesn't seem to want to understand. Certainly, then, Ricciardi,
let's get straight to the point. A confidential report arrives on
my desk. From this report it is possible to deduce that preparations are underway for a soirée at which, among the guests who
will be attending, we expect not only the leading municipal
authorities, but also certain personalities from Rome. When I
say personalities, you follow me, Ricciardi? That's exactly
what's written in the report: 'personalities.'"

Garzo fell silent, his eyes gleaming as if he expected some

reaction, but Ricciardi sat impassive, waiting for the rest. Maione coughed again, dragging his heavy boot across the floor; he didn't know whether to burst out laughing or crying.

"I beg your pardon, Dottore," said the commissario, "but I really don't understand how I can help you out in this matter. I don't . . ."

Garzo burst out: "Ricciardi, don't you see? Among those attending this soirée there might even be . . . I hardly dare to say it . . . a member of the Duce's family! The language of certain reports, you understand, becomes comprehensible only if you read between the lines: if someone writes 'personalities,' rather than, for example, 'authorities' or 'institutional figures,' it means individuals of the highest stature. There's nothing more important than 'personalities.' Do you understand?"

"Yes, Dottore, I understand. Personalities. I'm certain that we won't have any trouble providing the required security, I'll make arrangements with my colleagues who . . ."

An overexcited Garzo leapt to his feet: "No, no, what are you talking about? You're not going to be put in charge of security. Good lord, perish the thought! That night you'll be perfectly free. You'll be able to devote yourself wholeheartedly to welcoming those 'personalities,' and that's not all. Because the party, my good Ricciardi, is going to be held at the home of your friend Livia Lucani, the widow Vezzi. Don't tell me that you weren't aware of it already!"

Ricciardi furrowed his brow, remembering what Livia had told him three days earlier. It seemed a lifetime since that conversation.

"Yes, yes, I believe I remember that she mentioned it to me. But I . . ."

Garzo laughed, disjointedly: "He believes he remembers, the man says! Why, this is going to be the most important social event of the summer! Ricciardi, let's talk straight here: we all know how much the widow Vezzi cares about you . . . and by the way, I have to say I can't imagine why, she's a woman who could have anyone she wants with a crook of her finger; if you only knew how green my wife and her girlfriends turn whenever they gossip about her. In any case, I demand, and let me underscore that one word, *demand* an invitation. I'm counting on you. This is an opportunity that I simply cannot miss. And given the relationship that unites us, bonds, if I may venture to say, of profound friendship and mutual esteem, I believe that I have the right to expect you to put in a good word on my behalf."

Ricciardi would have been willing to say anything, so long as it allowed him to put an end to that conversation.

"Dottore, I promise you that I will lobby on your behalf with Livia the minute I have a chance to see her again. Right now I'm completely absorbed in this investigation and certain other matters of a personal nature, and therefore . . ."

Garzo headed for the door, satisfied: "I understand, I understand. Well then, listen carefully, Ricciardi: I expect an invitation from the lady. And I assure you that my esteem for you can only rise, given your marvelous social connections. Ah, youth! If I only had your freedom! Get going, get going. And keep me posted on the investigation, naturally. Work, before all else!"

And he walked out, humming a tune.

XLIV

From the archives of Antonelli's memory an address had surfaced: Vicolo Santa Croce al Purgatorio. It was a narrow lane just off Piazza del Mercato, a short walk from Piazza del Carmine, named after Our Lady of Mount Carmel.

As they moved down cramped alleys that suddenly widened into broad stretches, Ricciardi and Maione had the impression they were moving, step by step, deeper and deeper into a living organism, driving straight toward the heart. The Pendino quarter had in fact just begun to experience the most important week in its whole year, the week that culminated with the festival of the Madonna Bruna—the Black Madonna.

This wasn't just another of the countless neighborhood festivals, and it wasn't limited to the locals: Our Lady of Mount Carmel was a central figure in the city's traditions, and she was invoked constantly by the faithful, whether in requests for divine assistance or as a lively conversational interjection. When confronted with a tragic or terrible event, or some collective emotion, men, women, and children would cross themselves as they murmured the name of the Signora Bruna—the Dark Lady, Our Lady of Mount Carmel.

The icon took its name from the dark-hued complexions of the Virgin Mary and the Christ Child, clasped tenderly in her arms. On His face, tinged with just a hint of sadness, there is a foreshadowing of the pain to come; cheeks and lips brush together. A mother, a child. A perfect and eternal union that always called the people of that wonderful and unfortunate city to express their love.

The festival began with the procession on the last Sunday in May, in which Mamma Schiavona, as the common folk called her, was carried through the neighborhood, escorted by the highest officials. After that, preparations began for the events that would take place on the 15th and 16th of July.

The frenzy of anticipation was obvious even to passing pedestrians. Pagan and religious aspects were intertwined even more than usual, drawing in everyone who lived in the quarter or happened to be passing through it. People stitched outfits and made panels bearing the image of the Black Madonna with a golden star on Her shoulder, balloons were inflated to be released into the sky on each of the three nights of the festival, lights were arched over the streets that led to the church; the balconies, terraces, windows, and even the simplest apertures giving onto the piazza, were decorated, a blaze of flowers and festoons; and then there were the countless stalls and stands where tons of goods of every description would be on offer to the whole city when it poured into this piazza.

Maione noticed that their presence had not passed unremarked. His trained eye had picked out glances that lasted just a second too long, an old woman who moved a chair, making a loud scraping sound, a little boy who suddenly broke into a run, a man who emitted a shrill whistle. Moving along with the two policemen was an invisible wave made up of ostensible indifference and intense alertness.

Ricciardi showed no indication that he had noticed a thing. He kept his hands in his pockets and his eyes on the ground. All around him, the living and the dead whirled in their two separate worlds, distinct and unaware of each other, murmuring, speaking, and shouting their sufferings and their joys. The commissario did his best to keep his mind off this, and off Rosa as well, tried to keep from thinking about her unnatural sleep, wondering to himself what he could do, and forever coming to the same answer: nothing. And he tried to focus on the murder he was investigating, because the professor had a right to his full devotion to the case; whoever had cut his life short ought to pay for that crime. Because the professor should have been able to die in his bed. Like Dr. Ruspo. And like his Rosa.

They realized that they had reached their destination when an empty alley appeared before them, an oasis of silence in the tempest-tossed sea that was the rest of the neighborhood.

A young man, leaning against the wall and smoking, tossed his cigarette, gave Maione a bold stare, and ambled off. Two floors up, a pair of shutters slammed shut, while a woman began singing from a balcony.

On the pavement in front of a ground-floor hovel, a *basso,* an old woman sat peeling potatoes. She looked up at the two policemen and asked, in thick dialect, whether they were looking for someone. From her expression, Maione understood that his answer would be virtually useless.

"*Buongiorno*, Signo'. Yes, we're looking for a certain Graziani, Giuseppe Graziani. Do you know him?"

The old woman stared at him, as if she didn't understand the language the brigadier was speaking. Then she shouted loudly: "Tanino!"

A half-naked boy came running out of a doorway. He couldn't have been any older than seven or eight. He was barefoot, his arms and legs, stick-thin, dotted with scrapes and scabs. He came to a halt next to the two men, turned his back to them, and returned to the building he'd just emerged from. At the threshold he turned to see if they were following him. Then he jutted his chin in the direction of a staircase. Ricciardi and Maione started upstairs.

On the second floor, in front of a door, two young men dressed in work shirts and caps gave them an unfriendly stare, without so much as a hint of greeting. Maione met their hostile gazes and asked: "Is he in there?"

The elder of the pair nodded yes.

Maione turned to Ricciardi: "After you, Commissa'. Apparently we're expected."

They stepped into a clean and tidy apartment, furnished in a sober style. Daylight filtered through the half-open shutters. The heat was suffocating. An elderly woman in black came to meet them: "Who are you looking for? No one here has done anything wrong, we're honest folk."

Maione faced her sternly: "Excuse me, Signo', but did anyone here say that we'd come because you weren't honest folk? This damned bad habit of thinking of the police as an enemy—when is this city going to get over it?"

A deep voice boomed out from behind them: "Evidently, Brigadie', if people behave that way there must be a reason. Or maybe we're all just crazy, is that what you think?"

They turned around and found themselves face-to-face with a very tall man, with an athletic physique, dressed in a white shirt, a waistcoat, and a pair of dark trousers. On his arm he wore a black band, a mark of mourning. His hair was tousled and he hadn't shaved, he had bags under his eyes and his face wore a harsh expression that made him look old: but he couldn't have been even thirty.

Maione touched his fingertips to the brim of his hat and, without changing his tone of voice, asked: "You're Giuseppe Graziani, isn't that right?"

The man, leaning against the doorframe, his arms crossed on his chest, nodded. He really was huge, his powerful forearms made muscular by hard work. He seemed indifferent to the presence of the two policemen in his home. He told the woman: "Don't worry yourself, Mammà. Go see if the baby has woken up. Earlier I thought she sounded a little restless."

The old woman reluctantly moved away.

Graziani gestured with his head, inviting them to follow him into a room that was furnished with a table and chairs; against one wall hung a mirror covered by a black cloth. On a low credenza there was a framed photograph of the same man, standing, clearly ill at ease, in a jacket and tie; sitting in front of him was a beautiful girl in a wedding dress. Both of them had solemn expressions, as was customary when people posed for a portrait; but she was holding his hand, their fingers intertwined in a gesture of great tenderness.

Maione said: "I'm Brigadier Maione, and he is . . ."

The man interrupted him: "Yeah, yeah. I know who you are, and you know who I am. And I know why you're here, too. The answer is: no, I didn't kill that piece of shit, Professor Iovine. I didn't get to him fast enough, because someone else took care of it before I could."

Maione laughed: "Congratulations, Signor Peppino the Wolf. That's what they call you, isn't it? Bravo. Since you're so clever and you're willing to tell us what we need to know, excuse us for barging in on you like this, we'll be on our way. If you'd just sent us a note, informing us that you hadn't committed the murder, we could have even spared ourselves the walk over in this heat."

"I'm telling it to you straight. But if you want to waste your time and shoe leather, there's nothing I can do about it."

Maione roared: "Grazia', you're just a little too much of a comedian. You make me want to take you into police headquarters and start asking you questions there. What do you say, do you feel like taking a walk? That way, you can stroll in the midst of your own people and show off a nice pair of steel bracelets."

Ricciardi knew that this wasn't going to get them anywhere. He decided it was time to intervene: "Listen here, Graziani: I'm sorry about your loss. We heard how it went, and I understand the kind of grief that . . ."

Peppino hissed back: "You don't understand a thing,

Commissa'. You don't know how it went, you don't understand the grief. You don't know anything and you can't know anything."

Maione said: "Now, Grazia', I'm warning you: unless you start speaking respectfully to the commissario, I'll . . ."

"What are you doing, Brigadie'? What are you doing? You do understand, don't you, that if I'd wanted to make sure you never got this far, you never would have? That you could have disappeared a hundred times along the way here, you and your commissario, and no one would ever have known what had become of you? So do me a favor and do yourself a favor while you're at it: don't threaten me. Not here, not in my home. All right? Are we understood?" Then he turned to Ricciardi: "Commissa', I wasn't trying to get a rise out of you. I was telling the truth. You can't possibly know, because no one's told you the way things really went."

Ricciardi said: "Well then, why don't you tell me yourself how they really went?"

"Then who would you believe, Commissa'?"

"Graziani, you strike me as an intelligent young man. If we'd already decided not to believe you, would we have come down here into your lair to talk to you? Wouldn't it have been much easer to have you come down to police headquarters for a deposition or, easier still, simply put you on trial straightaway?"

Peppino looked amused: "The Wolf's lair. Very nice, Commissa'. You've convinced me. What do you want to know?"

"Everything, that's what we want to know. Your relations with Professor Iovine. Why and where you swore to kill him. And why you say you weren't fast enough to do it yourself."

XLV

I wonder if you love anyone, Commissa'. If you can only be happy when a certain person is close to you and you breathe the same air that she breathes. I wonder if you've ever felt your heart bursting in your chest with joy, and whether you know the color of despair, the misery that makes you think you're already dead and cast down into hell, but all the while you're still here on earth.

I lost my father when I was still just a little boy, you know. My father was taken by the sea. So then it was just me and my *mammà*, you saw her, she's a tigress who defends her cub, even though now I'm three times her size. She was no different when I was a child, she raised me with her claws and her teeth. Our streets around here are like the jungle, Commissa'. The weak don't survive, only the strong. *Mammà* and I were strong, and we survived.

If you have nothing to eat, if you don't have clothes to wear, and you have to fight the dogs for a crust of stale bread, you sure don't have time for happiness. You don't even know that happiness exists. Until I was twelve, the only thing I thought about was making it to tomorrow. That's when I met my little Rosinella.

Are you married, Commissa'? No? What about you, Brigadie'? Then you, yes, you must know what I'm talking about. Everything changes. When I met my Rosinella, I realized that I wanted to live. Not survive: live. I wanted a home, children, a future. My little Rosinella changed my soul. I met her and I understood what sunshine was, what it meant to laugh, and why it was worth opening your eyes in the morning.

She was my woman, Commissa'. Even when we were just children, she was my woman. We were born together, so it made sense for us to die together, don't you think?

I know that it's not possible to decide how many years a life should last, I'm not crazy. I know that. And I understand that you can die before your time. I live on the street, I'm a businessman: a stabbing, a gunshot, a wagon wheel—any one of them could come around the corner any second. So I get myself organized. That's the whole story, Brigadie', I get myself organized. The only difference between me and these kids you see outside, or the ones you met on your way over here, is that I've gotten myself organized. I think about the things that can happen, and I prepare myself. I examine the hypotheses, the possibilities. And I get myself organized.

That's why they call me the Wolf. Because I do fine on my own, I don't need to hang out on a street corner and play cards, waste time and get drunk with my friends. I'm a man who thinks and thinks. That's the way I was when I was little, too. I was a kid who thought.

The Wolf, you know, remains alone until he finds a companion. And Rosinella was the companion of my life. Someone like me can only have one companion, and if he loses her then he won't go looking for another.

When she started to suffer strange pains I thought through all the various possibilities. *Mammà*, her mother, and the other women in the neighborhood all told me not to worry, that this was normal, that it happens with the first baby. But I get myself organized, like I told you. So I asked around for the name of the very best doctor there was for women who are going to give birth. The very best one.

Take a look at me, I'm a big man. I've always been big: my father was too. People think that big men are stupid, who knows why. But I made good use of the fact that I'm big, at the beginning. Then I started using my head. I help people, Commissa'; hurting people is pointless. If people only respect you out of fear, sooner or later you're bound to run into someone who's not afraid, and the next thing you know there's a knife in your back. On the other hand, if people respect you because you're fair, and if you help others without asking anything in exchange, then people will stick by you.

In the past few years, since the day Rosinella and I decided to get married and have children, I got things ready, I put together a business. We got rich and everyone who worked with me got rich too. Certainly, every now and then, we ran into an obstacle or two and we had to take care of it; as the saying goes, these are the risks that go with the territory. But now we could afford a good doctor, the very best one.

At first he didn't want any part of it, he said that he didn't have time. Maybe he thought that we couldn't pay him. So I showed him my cash, I gave him a nice fat retainer, and he immediately changed his tune. He said that my little Rosinella had some health problem; he used long words that we couldn't really understand. But I paid him and he put on a smile and told me: don't you worry about a thing, Grazia', everything will be fine.

Everything will be fine.

It's just a matter of money, you know that, Commissa'? The difference, when it comes right down to it, is money. I'm a young man, but I figured it out early. I asked around before I put my Rosinella in that doctor's hands. He's good, they assured me; for that matter, if someone teaches at the university, he has to be good, right? The professor who teaches other doctors. The most educated one, the best one. Only he was expensive, very expensive. It was a matter of money, and I was willing to give him as much as he wanted.

He'd told his colleagues, he'd said it in our presence: Signora Graziani is one of my patients. I'm to see her, and no one else. Because I was giving him the money, and he couldn't let me think that it would be the same if some other doctor, an ordinary doctor, tended to her. So if he wasn't there when we came in, and this happened once or twice, they'd ask us to wait: the professor gave instructions that your wife is to be examined by him and nobody else.

The night that Rosinella began to bleed even though she hadn't yet reached her due date, we rushed to the hospital. The nurses exchanged glances and kept silent. He was on duty but he wasn't there, and no one knew where he might be. The custodian told us that his car wasn't there, either. I asked the other doctor, a kid who knew nothing, and he told me: only the professor can examine his patients. That's when I grabbed him by the lapels, lifted him into the air until we were eye to eye, and explained to him: well, right now, you're the professor. And you're going to examine my wife.

Meanwhile I'd sent my men all over the city, to find out where that piece of shit was hiding out. They went to his apartment, they woke up his wife who was fast asleep, but he wasn't there. They went looking everywhere for him, but he was nowhere to be found. And the minutes were passing, and the minutes turned into hours. At last, word came down from Vomero that his car was parked outside one of the new apartment buildings. He had an unusual car, beautiful and expensive. Like I said, it's a matter of money.

By the time they brought him in, with his shirt buttoned all wrong, his tie undone, two of my men holding him by the arm, Rosinella was white as a sheet and no longer answered when I called her. The young doctor didn't know what he was doing, he was crying; Professor, Professor, the hemorrhage was just too vast, he kept saying. The man went and closed the door behind him, shutting himself up with Rosinella. Then we heard a noise.

It was the baby girl, and she was crying.

He came out with a nurse: she was holding the baby in her

arms, hiding behind her as if she were a shield. He didn't have the courage to look me in the eye. He was trembling.

My mother took the baby. It took seven people, between hospital staff and my own men, to pull me off him. Seven.

I swore an oath, that's right. I swore an oath that I'd see the color of his blood, that I'd kill him with these hands of mine, the way he'd killed me, because instead of being where he was supposed to be, he'd been up in Vomero with his whore. While Rosinella was dying.

I swore it on Mamma Schiavona, our Madonna. You know her, Commissa'? She's the patron saint of souls in purgatory, the souls that have to try to save themselves from damnation. And just as it's true that Saturday is her feast day, it's true that my soul was the most damned of them all.

For two days, I didn't want to even look at the little girl. I thought that in the end she was the one who'd killed my Rosinella. And I locked myself in my room. That's what a Wolf does, you know, when it's fatally wounded, it hides. It stays out of sight, when it's dying.

Then I came out of my room, and she was in my mother's arms and she was crying and crying. She wouldn't stop crying. I went over to her, I touched her, and she didn't cry again. Since that moment, whenever I come near her, she stops crying.

And she's the spitting image of her *mamma*, you know, Commissa'. The absolute spitting image.

But I'd sworn an oath. And when someone like me swears an oath, Commissa', he has to keep it.

I thought to myself: I'll wait a few days. Better not to go out, otherwise the baby girl will start crying again, and then she'll never stop.

Then, a week or two later, one of my men came to see me. Peppi', he said, have you heard the news? That piece of shit fell and was killed, he fell out his own window. You need to run, everyone will assume it was you, because of that oath you swore.

Maybe, Commissa', maybe I should have been happy to hear he was dead. Or maybe I really should have run away: no one believes people like us, the souls in purgatory. We alone believe each other. But there was the baby girl, Commissa'. You know, the minute I move away from her, she starts crying again.

No, it wasn't me. Men like me, if they're going to do something like that, they do it in broad daylight, not by night, not in secret.

And I wouldn't have thrown him out of a window down onto the pavement. No, I wanted to look him in the eyes while I gutted him like a fish, making sure that it took him an hour to die, drop after drop of blood, just as my little Rosinella died at his hands. I wouldn't have killed him like that, with one quick shove.

Someone killed him, no doubt about it. Men like him don't kill themselves, because they possess neither honor nor conscience. To kill yourself takes pride, or despair. And he had neither.

That's right, Commissa', I should have killed him myself. I'd sworn an oath. And maybe I would have done it, as soon as I was done with this baby girl who starts crying as soon as I step away. Or maybe I wouldn't, because in the past few days I've started to wonder if it's Rosinella making her do it, just to keep me at home. And I was at home, that night, with my mother and the baby girl. All the family that's left to me.

I should have killed him myself.

But I didn't.

XLVI

Maione glared grimly at the young man leaning against the wall at the mouth of the *vicolo*.

"It's like an army, just think about it, Commissa'. Look over there, a sentinel standing guard on the road that leads to headquarters. I'd arrest them for that fact alone."

"Yes, but the fact that they're criminals doesn't necessarily mean that we have to assume they're guilty of everything. Graziani struck me as a young man in the throes of an enormous personal loss."

"Sure, Commissa', whatever you say, but he had sworn in front of a crowd of eyewitnesses to murder the professor. And a few weeks later, the professor was murdered, and he has no alibi."

Ricciardi corrected him: "He was home with his family. The same alibi as the professor's son and hundreds of thousands of other people who live in this city, including you and me. And it was nighttime. We can't base things merely on the existence or absence of an alibi."

Maione defended his thesis: "Commissa', if a criminal swears that he's going to murder someone and that someone is murdered, I'm inclined to believe that the criminal kept his vow, and that's that. And don't let's forget that I can always have one of my men do the deed while I stay at home, nice and comfortable, don't you think?"

"No, in that case, I'd go out and mingle with the crowds, make sure everybody saw me, and then I'd have a real alibi, don't you think?"

Maione shook his head: "Well, this isn't getting us any-where. How are we going to proceed now?"

"The way we always do: we'll keep asking questions and hope either that we can figure something out, or that someone says something unintentionally revealing. We just have to grope in the dark, Raffaele, and wait for something we don't know to stick in our minds."

They'd reached the apartment house where Iovine had lived. Ines, the concierge, was delivering a speech to a smaller crowd than she'd had the first time: two housekeepers and a tradesman who were listening to her, mouths agape: ". . . and that means someone pushed him for sure, he didn't jump the way they thought at first. I hear that the police . . ."

Maione came up behind her and coughed. The woman started and her audience scattered, only to stop to peer from behind the corner at the epic unfolding of events, an appro-priately exaggerated account of which would later be spread around the neighborhood.

"Oh, Brigadie', you gave me a fright. *Buongiorno*."

"So tell us, Signo', now you're certain someone pushed him? And just what are the police doing now? Tell us about it too, maybe we'll learn something."

"No, Brigadie', what are you trying to say? I'd never dare to say such a thing! It's just that the general hospital's charge nurse, who I've known for many years, came to see the poor widow, and the charge nurse confided in me that she had learned from the assistant the same thing that you found out from the doctor at Pellegrini Hospital, namely that maybe, and I repeat, just maybe, someone threw the professor out the win-dow. And this was confirmed by the custodian of the general hospital, who saw one of you—now, I couldn't say which because he didn't tell me—even go to the scene of the crime late at night, at the same hour it happened, to see, and . . ."

Maione turned to Ricciardi, with some exasperation: "I

wonder why we bother to go to all the trouble. We might as well just come to see Signora Ines here, and let her tell us the whole story. Just think how much walking we'd spare ourselves, how much less sweating we'd do in this heat."

The concierge put on a contrite expression: "Sorry, Brigadie', but we have to talk about something, no? The days are long, and a major event like the professor falling out a window isn't something that happens all the time. We'll be arguing about it for years."

Ricciardi decided it was time to break up the cheery conversation.

"Is Signora Iovine home?"

The woman looked around, prudently.

"I wouldn't really know . . ."

Maione was furious now: "Ah, so you're familiar with every nook and cranny of our investigation, but you don't know whether a person who lives in the apartment building where you work as a concierge is home or not? Now you're going to come straight upstairs with us, or I swear to God I'll arrest you!"

Ines shot off up the stairs, motioning for the policemen to wait. Soon she was back: "If you please, Brigadie', come right on up. The Signora will see you."

A housekeeper in a black dress with a white apron ushered them into the same parlor where they'd spoken to the woman on their first visit. The pitiless noonday sun filtered through the shutters, but the air remained reasonably cool thanks to a pleasant breeze, possibly produced by a clever combination of open windows and doors. Everything was clean and tidy, and there was a faint odor that Maione was unable to identify.

Maria Carmela Iovine came in a few minutes later. She was dressed in black, with a string of pearls around her neck and her hair gathered in a bun. Her face was serene and her wrinkles, so unmistakable the first time, were less marked now. Only her dark eyes spoke of an intractable grief.

"*Buongiorno*, gentlemen. Forgive me, I wasn't expecting visitors and the housekeeper just cleaned the silver with ammonia. The last few days have been challenging, as you can imagine, and we'd neglected the apartment. Make yourselves comfortable."

Maione put a name to the odor he'd noticed and hearing talk of caring for apartments gave him a stab of discomfort; it seemed to him that lately his wife had been paying less attention to her domestic duties.

Ricciardi looked at the woman: "Forgive our intrusion, Signora, we should have called ahead, but we're working the entire city trying to figure out just what happened. First things first: I must inform you that the findings of the autopsy might lead us to conclude that . . . that it was not the professor himself, of his own free will, who caused his own death."

She nodded, her long slender fingers interlaced.

"Yes, Commissario, I knew that already. My husband's charge nurse told me, when she came to keep me company after the funeral. You know, rumors spread from one hospital to another, and my husband was quite well known."

"May I ask what you think of this news? If it's confirmed, naturally."

"What can I tell you, Commissario? It would have caused me more grief to learn that he'd taken his own life. I'm religious, and an act of that sort would have sent him into eternal damnation. What's more, the scandal would have affected my son: a father who killed himself, can you imagine? And what's more, for a woman, it would be terribly sad not to have realized that the man she lived with had been brooding over such a decision."

Ricciardi went on: "I understand . . . Signora, the last time we were here we asked you whether for any reason your husband might have been so desperate or upset that he might have been pushed to commit an extreme act. Now, however, we must focus on the hypothesis that there was someone who greatly resented him."

Maria Carmela thought it over: "Commissario, I already gave you that letter from Ruspo, and the charge nurse, Ada Coppola, told me about a man, someone whose wife died in childbirth, who had made threats. I don't know anything else."

"Did this sort of thing happen frequently? That the husband of one of his patients talked about taking revenge?"

"You see, Tullio was one of the best known physicians in the country. He was constantly being asked to consult on cases; he was truly gifted, but that hardly means he was infallible. It could happen that, in one of the vast number of procedures performed under his supervision, something went wrong. But there were very few patients that he took under his direct care. He never mentioned that episode to me, presumably because he didn't want to worry me. All the same, I doubt that anyone would kill a doctor for a tragic event that was hardly his fault, wouldn't you say?"

Maione and Ricciardi remained in silence. Then the commissario said: "Are you by any chance aware of . . . other situations outside of work that might have created problems or conflicts for your husband?"

The woman remained silent for a few seconds, her eyes calmly fixed on Ricciardi; from the piazza came the rumble of traffic. Then she said: "Let me see if I understand, Commissario: are you asking me whether my husband was leading a double life, and if I was aware of the fact?"

Ricciardi exchanged a glance with Maione. They had reached the crucial point.

Signora Iovine stood up and went to the window. She spoke without turning around: "Tullio wasn't my first husband. I was a widow. I'm a widow now, too, of course, but I'd already been widowed once. However, I had no children. My only child is my son Federico. He's eight years old, I think I told you that the last time you were here. Every love is different from all the others, in my opinion. Love is like an article of clothing. You choose a certain size and you wear it, maybe even for many years. Then one day you look at it and you wonder why you ever put it on. It doesn't suit you anymore. Your first love, the love you first feel when you're young, is made of flesh and blood. You can't conceive of anything else, you're jealous, you even suffer. But when you're an adult, on the other hand, you reason. Above all, you reason."

She turned halfway round. Looking at her profile, Ricciardi noticed the long, narrow nose, the willful chin. A woman who might not be beautiful, but who was strong and intelligent.

"Children are a different matter. Children split your life in two. When you have a child, you must protect him against everything and everyone. You carry a child in your womb forever: a parent is responsible for anything that happens to him. And also anything that doesn't happen." She came back over to them: "No, Commissario. I imagine, certainly, I have my ideas. Let's say that I wouldn't be surprised to learn that he had another woman, or even that he had two other women. And I couldn't swear that Tullio didn't have other vices. When a man has a job that keeps him out of the house most of the time, a wife can't have too many certainties. He was a good husband, and a good father. He took care of us, he made sure we never wanted for anything. That's what I know and that's what I can tell you."

Ricciardi nodded: "I understand. I beg your pardon for having to ask these questions, but I hope you'll understand that everything we're doing is meant to clarify the facts of the event, as I'm sure you want, too. One last thing: are you aware that the professor had purchased a gift for your upcoming name day?"

The woman smiled: "Every year he bought me something more expensive. I believe it was his way of proving to me how successful he was."

"Do you have any idea of what it might be?"

"A ring? I'd told him I wanted a new one. A girlfriend of mine, I can't remember which, told me about an artisan with a workshop down in the goldsmiths' *borgo* who makes especially beautiful rings, and I remember that Tullio wanted to know the man's name. He was so transparent when he thought he was planning a surprise. You men can be so naïve sometimes."

Before Ricciardi had a chance to reply, a little boy dressed in a sailor suit ran into the room. The resemblance to his mother was extraordinary.

He threw his arms around her neck. Tenderly, she asked him: "Federico, have you said hello to the nice men?"

The little one turned around, his expression serious: "*Buongiorno*, Signori. Did you know that my *papà* is dead? Now when we go on vacation, we'll have to hire a chauffeur."

Maione felt a knot in his throat. He said: "Why, what a brave little man. Listen to me, now you have to take care of your *mamma* . . ."

The little boy looked the brigadier up and down. Then he said: "But if bad men come I'll call you, because you have a pistol."

Ricciardi saw Maria Carmela Iovine's eyes glisten.

The woman kissed her son and whispered in his ear: "My little man will take care of me. And I'll take care of him. For the rest of my life, I'll take care of him."

XLVII

Livia told her driver to take her to Pellegrini Hospital to see whether the condition of Ricciardi's governess had improved.

Actually, she was hoping to run into the commissario there and persuade him to go out for a bite to eat; he'd looked pretty rough the night before when she'd hurried over after her meeting with Falco. She'd realized immediately that Ricciardi wasn't especially pleased to have her at his side, but she hadn't taken that personally. She understood that this was a very private matter, and it was quite understandable that he would prefer to be left alone at his *tata*'s sickbed.

She knew how close he was to the woman who, according to what little he had told her about himself, had been a second mother to him and was the only family he had left. She had hurried to the hospital, obeying a blind impulse and the urge to be close to him at a difficult moment. Unfortunately, Rosa's condition had seemed hopeless. The doctor had already gone home, and so she'd been unable to get a specific diagnosis firsthand. Ricciardi had been vague, but Livia had seen other cases of apoplectic fits and she could see how serious the situation was.

The image of the man she loved holding the old woman's hands in his own in a nondescript hospital room, while that unsettling young woman—so similar to her aunt that they seemed to be the same person at two different stages of life—lurked in the shadows, had upset her. She didn't like to be in the presence of pain; perhaps that made her a coward, but she felt she was justified by what she'd already been through.

On her way home, she'd wondered whether it was a good idea to continue preparing for the party, and she told herself she'd have to speak with Modo and ask him for some advice.

The doctor came to greet her, beaming with delight: "Well, look who we have here, Signora Livia. And yet my horoscope didn't tell me that this would be one of the happiest days of my life."

Livia found the man, with his ribald, explicit gallantry, extremely likeable, even though Falco always spoke of him as a serious danger to Ricciardi and even to her.

"Doctor, whenever I feel ugly all I have to do is come see you, and you immediately make me change my mind."

"For that, Signora, all you need is a mirror. Believe me, you are a ray of sunshine in the life of this poor old combat physician. To what do I owe the pleasure of this benediction? I ask, even though I fear I know the answer already."

Livia locked arms with him and led him into the courtyard. The dog came closer, tucking itself into a seated position a few feet away from them. The woman looked down at it.

"That dog hasn't left you yet, has he? And yet you've shared some decidedly unpleasant adventures."

Livia was referring to the previous Easter, when she, Ricciardi, and Maione had rescued the doctor from a nasty political situation.

Modo leaned down to pet the dog, who, perhaps sensing that he was the topic of discussion, had begun to wag his tail.

"Dogs aren't like women, my lovely lady. They bestow their hearts and never take them back.

Livia laughed: "Women, as you well know, my good doctor, don't have hearts at all."

"True," Modo admitted, "but it's so much fun to go on looking for one. Tell me everything, Signora."

Livia turned serious: "Yesteday I saw Ricciardi's *tata*. She seemed to me to be in truly critical condition. Do you think that we could do anything for her somewhere else? I don't know, in Rome. I . . . well, as you know, I have many friends."

"I know, and I always wonder how a woman like you can stand to frequent certain people. No, I appreciate your concern, but unfortunately our dear Rosa's situation wouldn't improve even with the intervention of the finest doctor on earth. What's happened has happened, and it's practically impossible to repair it without surgery, and that unfortunately would be far too risky. Cranial trephination, for a person of that age, is fatal in virtually 100 percent of cases."

"Poor Ricciardi. He loves that woman so much. But tell me, doctor, what's the prognosis? That is, when . . . when might the final crisis come?"

"No one can say. Rosa has a very strong constitution, and if you ask me the cerebral damage is relatively circumscribed. As long as we're able to feed her and her internal organs don't collapse, she'll survive. I believe that she could last a couple of weeks, barring a sudden and unexpected deterioration."

Livia nodded.

"Then you're saying that this week, she still ought to . . ."

"Certainly, I would say so. Can I know the reason for your question?"

The woman looked at him like a little girl hoping not to be scolded for a bit of mischief: "You see, Doctor, I'm afraid that it's something rather frivolous. I had decided to throw a party, next Friday. Just to introduce myself to the city, and to return the many invitations that have been extended to me over the past few months. I wanted . . . you see . . . it's important to me that Ricciardi be there. You know, you must certainly have guessed, and for that matter you are practically the only friend he has . . . in short, I'd really like him to come. And if his *tata*'s condition were to worsen, I doubt that he'd be willing to be away from her even for as much as a few hours."

"It's just too easy for you to strike tenderness into this rumpled old heart, Signora. I'll make sure to kick him out of here by reshuffling my shifts and staying with Rosa in his place. It will be up to you, though, to persuade him, and I don't doubt that you possess the tools to do so successfully."

"But that would mean not having you at the party, Doctor."

The doctor laughed: "I'm afraid that's our only option; Ricciardi wouldn't give up his post to anyone other than yours truly: also, I'm the only person who has the power to kick him out of the room. And let me add, Signora, that I'm pretty sure that many of your guests would be delighted not to see me there and, if I may, I would be just as delighted not to see them, either. It means that, if the plan works, you'll owe me a meal together, just four old friends: you, me, old Brigadier Maione, and the prince of darkness himself, our man Ricciardi. With a bowl of scraps for my hairy little friend here."

Having cleared things up with the doctor, Livia gave her driver an address on Via Duomo. The knottiest detail in her preparations for the party still had to be taken care of.

She stepped out of the car and strode confidently through the atrium of an apartment house, politely greeting the doorman, who responded with a bow. Everything suggested the woman had a certain familiarity with the place. After climbing two flights of stairs, she rang a doorbell.

"Is he in?" she asked the housekeeper who came to the door.

"Of course, Signo'. Let me go tell him that you're here."

After a few moments, a middle-aged man came trotting to the door. He was on the short side and overweight. His double chin was tucked into an over-tight collar, and his white smoking jacket, dotted with a light-blue geometric motif, was wrapped around his jutting belly with a broad red sash, creating an unusual chromatic effect.

"Donna Livia, what a pleasure! To what do we owe this visit? Have you come to announce that you've conquered your last lingering reservations and have made up your mind to elope with me this very day?"

Livia let the little man kiss her on both cheeks.

"Don Libero, what woman on earth would be capable of resisting the allure of the greatest living poet in the most beautiful language on earth? Certainly not me, your most fervent admirer. But as for eloping . . . How would you live without your Maria?"

The man waved a hand in the air, as if shooing away some annoying idea: "Maria? Who's Maria? Ah, you must be referring to my wife. Oh, of course, you have a point, unfortunately. I can't live without her, largely because she's constantly underfoot. You'll see her for yourself when she gets back from her grocery shopping; she insists on buying our food in person, otherwise she claims that both our housekeeper and the shopkeepers will rob her blind. Please, come right this way. What can I do for you?"

Livia entered a living room at the center of which stood a concert piano, like some kind of pagan altar. Seated at the keyboard was a man in shirtsleeves; he had a mustache and a pair of thick-lensed reading glasses, and he was jotting down something on a sheet of paper. Other sheets of paper partly covered with notes and lyrics were scattered all over the room: on the carpet, on the piano, on armchairs and sofas.

The man at the keyboard stood up and made a bow: "Donna Livia, what a pleasure! Have you come to rescue me from the talons of this lunatic?"

Livia extended her hand for a gallant kiss from the pianist: "Don Ernesto, your prison cell is the forbidden dream of every singer and musician in this city. And I consider myself lucky to be allowed entrance to the workshop where so many marvelous masterpieces are brought into being. How have you been?"

"How do you think I've been, Signo'? It's a tragedy. We'll be doing one thing and *that* one comes up with something entirely different. We skip around from a Neapolitan canzone to a poem, from a poem to a romanza from a romanza back to a canzone. I'm going out of my mind trying to keep up with him."

From the far end of the room, Don Libero, standing with a page from a musical score in one hand, called loudly: "Pay him no mind, Signo'. He just likes to mock me behind my back. If he were anything less than the finest composer in this town, do you think I'd keep his ugly mug around? And after all, when inspiration strikes, who am I to ignore it? We try to describe human passions in the simplest possible terms. It's what I've always said, isn't it? It's so simple to write difficult, it's so difficult to write simple! But enough trivial chitchat: how can I repay you for having brought such a ray of loveliness into this vale of tears?"

"I've come to ask a favor. To ask a favor of you both."

She explained what she wanted. When she was done, Don Libero and Don Ernesto looked at each other. Then the little fat man excitedly threw his arms out wide.

"Donna Livia, what you say is wonderful. When a singer rediscovers her will to sing, after so many years and so much grief, it means that she's rediscovered her will to live. For me, and I feel safe in speaking for our friend Ernesto, too, it's an immense joy and a great honor to know that you chose to come here to us in search of the right words and music. Tell me: what sentiment do you wish to sing? Jealousy? Regret? Sorrow? Love?"

"I couldn't say, exactly, Don Libero. But I think passion. Simply passion."

The man's face lit up: "Passion. Of course, passion! What else, if not passion?" He wandered the room, murmuring under his breath and digging through the mess until, triumphant, he seized a couple of sheets and cried: "Here it is!" He went over to the piano and placed the pages on the music rack. "Now then, Donna Livia, listen carefully. You said that you're looking for a canzone that has never been sung, and you wanted us to write it especially for you. But now I want to ask a favor of you. This is a song that our friend Ernesto and our beloved Nicola, whom you know, have stitched together. We were planning to debut it at the Piedigrotta festival, though not this year's, because we've already got too many projects underway. Still, we believe that this song could truly go down in our city's musical history, if we do say so ourselves. And so, what better challenge for your enchanting voice?"

"Don Libero, perhaps this isn't the right occasion for such an important canzone. Perhaps something more modest . . ."

The little man raised one hand: "No, I've made up my mind. You're the one to sing it, you must."

Livia was frightened.

"I beg of you, not something like this. It's been such a long time since . . . I'm not sure if I'm up to it."

The pianist took the sheet music and said: "At least listen to it. Then you can decide."

After Ernesto finished playing, Livia, with tears in her eyes and her heart racing wildly, decided that she would sing that song or no other.

If it was the last performance of her life, she was determined to sing that canzone.

XLVIII

It was too late to head back to police headquarters. Ricciardi and Maione opted instead for a pizza cart that stood at the corner of Piazza Quattro Palazzi, on the harbor side. The plume of smoke rising from the large kettle of hot, bubbling oil and the unmistakable, heavenly aroma were better than a neon sign.

Maione's police uniform ensured that the line of famished citizens ahead of them quickly grew noticeably shorter. From time to time, the sidewalk chef, wearing his grease-stained white smock, shouted: *Pizze càvere, oggi a otto!* The phrase in dialect announced hot pizza you could eat today and pay for eight days hence. This cunning and traditional term of sale made for a grateful and loyal clientele, with only a limited risk of an unpaid pizza every now and then.

Maione opted for *cicinielli e pummarola*, tiny fried fish and tomato, while Ricciardi went for garlic, oil, and oregano. The commissario realized, from his stomach's angry rumbling, that he hadn't had a bite to eat in the past twenty-four hours, and his thoughts went sadly to Rosa.

As he sank his teeth into the pizza, precariously perched forward to keep from dripping onto his uniform, the brigadier said: "All things considered, Commissa', it just doesn't add up. It seems to me that the widow must have had her suspicions about the professor's affair, but didn't really give a damn."

Ricciardi swallowed: "Yes, I had the same impression. One

292 · MAURIZIO DE GIOVANNI

of those marriages that turn into something like a business partnership: each looks to his or her own best interests."

With an exchange of hand gestures, Maione ordered a second round from the fry cook.

"I can't understand it, Commissa'. If two people are married they're married, and they should be husband and wife. Otherwise, they should just break up."

Ricciardi looked at his watch: "We have another hour or so, then I want to go to the hospital to see if there's any news."

Maione nodded as he chomped.

"Well then, we'd better swing by and see Coviello the goldsmith, Commissa'. He's close by, at the *borgo*. We can be there in ten minutes. There's something I want to do, too, before going home."

It was in fact a short walk from there to the *borgo degli orefici*—the goldsmiths' district—but the distance between those two worlds, the world of Corso Umberto, a busy, crowded thoroughfare overrun by carriages and automobiles, lined with gleaming shopwindows, and the world dominated by a tangled grid of narrow, identical alleys and lanes that hadn't changed an iota in more than a century, seemed enormous.

Over time, though, the work done by those extraordinary artisans, who belonged to a school of craftsmanship as good as that of any of their rivals anywhere on earth, had altered with the shift in demand from their clientele. The imitation of antique jewelry, which had been so popular sixty years earlier, had been replaced at the turn of the century by a more international taste. Certain trades, such as wire-drawing and crucible-handling, had gradually disappeared, giving way to cloisonné enameling and engraving. And many artisans had opened shops on Via Toledo, featuring glittering window displays that attracted women's eyes and intimidated men's wallets.

The craftsmen who had remained in the *borgo* were the

ones who tended to cleave to tradition. Nearly all of them had kept their workshops, but now they sold directly to a retail clientele; only a very few persisted in remaining strictly creators of custom-made jewelry. The age-old vocation of making objects of sacred art had declined with the waning of demand, but it survived in the hands of a few authentic artists who created the images displayed in the family chapels of noble houses or that decorated monumental tombs at the cemetery.

The impression that Ricciardi gathered, as Maione inquired as to the whereabouts of the workshop of Nicola Coviello, was one of a general decline. The poverty that had insinuated itself everywhere, however loudly the state-controlled press proclaimed the opposite, was having its effect on trade. If I can barely afford to eat, the people reasoned, then I certainly can't spend money on gold and coral.

The workshop they were seeking was tucked away in a dead-end *vicolo* far from the main piazza. A few hens pecked away at the cobblestones, while two women sitting on rickety chairs in the shadows repaired a fishing net. One of the women, noticing the policemen, gestured to the other, and both women stared, though without pausing in their work, running the mesh through their fingers in search of rips and tears that might need to be reknotted, as if telling a rosary. At the far end of the *vicolo* stood a low door, without a sign; Coviello, clearly, had no interest in attracting the attention of walk-in customers.

They stepped in and stopped, waiting for their eyes to become accustomed to the difference in light. The heat in the *vicolo*, where the air stagnated, was bad enough, but it was even more intense in the workshop, where a small furnace to melt metals increased the temperature. The lighting, which came from an oil lamp, was focused on a heavy, rough-hewn block of wood that was being used as a workbench, its surface worn smooth with use and marked by hammer blows, its massive legs spaced widely enough to leave room for at least four workers to sit around it. At the moment, though, only Coviello was working at it; when Maione's imposing silhouette darkened the door to the street, the goldsmith looked up, his eyelids blinking rapidly behind the thick lenses of old spectacle frames.

"*Buonasera*, Coviello. We've come, Commissario Ricciardi and I, to ask you a few questions, if we're not intruding on your work."

The goldsmith wrapped the object he'd been working on in a dark cloth. He stood up, walked over to the safe, and opened it, depositing the bundle inside. After closing the safe, he turned to Maione: "Come right in, Brigadie'. I'm sorry, but I have no place for you to sit, unless you come join me at the workbench."

Ricciardi stepped in and took a look around. He'd expected something else: so renowned a craftsman, someone whose skills were so widely acknowledged that he was given commissions by clients like Iovine, ought by rights to have had a proper atelier. Instead, the workshop was bare, with no goods on display, no decorations, no furnishings to speak of. Aside from the workbench and two low stools, there was a tool rack with instruments of various shapes and sizes, the furnace, and a safe. Hanging over the stool where Coviello sat was the oil lamp.

The walls were spotted with damp patches. Occupying the center of one wall hung a faded print of the Madonna del Carmine and a bunch of fresh flowers slipped into an iron ring fixed into the masonry. On the facing wall was a calendar from ten years earlier decorated by an equally faded drawing of a steamship departing, and then a hand-colored photograph of a young man with a spectacular mustache and a cap on his head; beneath the picture stood a lit candle on a small shelf. Against the third wall was a cabinet and on the fourth, next to the door to the street, were pages torn out of a magazine depicting female models wearing complicated-looking jewelry. Bare rafters crossed the ceiling.

It could have been a cobbler's shop, or a blacksmith's forge. And Coviello himself could have been a very different kind of artisan, with those huge hands and long arms and his stout, bent body. His eyes, behind the thick lenses, were enormous and expressionless.

"What can I do for you?"

Ricciardi said: "We'd like to ask you a few more questions about the night you took the two rings to the professor. Could you tell us anything else about the silhouette you glimpsed as you were leaving?"

Just as Coviello was about to reply, a young girl hurried in: "Mastro Nico', excuse me, *mammà* told me that she has to go down to our apartment for a moment to do something, can you come look after your mother?"

The goldsmith gazed at Ricciardi and Maione, then spoke to the young girl: "All right, I'm coming." He got to his feet and addressed the policemen: "Forgive me. My mother . . . my mother isn't well, and a woman who lives in the same apartment house does me a favor and stays with her. But right now she has an errand to run, so I have to head home. You could either wait for me here, though I'm not sure how long it will take, or come along."

Ricciardi exchanged a glance with Maione, who said: "We'd prefer to come with you, if you don't mind. It's just a matter of five minutes, it's not worth the bother of making you come back here."

Coviello locked the workshop door by sliding an iron bar into two runners and then set off down the *vicolo*. Observing his back, Ricciardi noticed again how the man's spine reminded him of a question mark, and wondered how he managed to move with such agility.

The man's home wasn't far away, just around the corner from the dead-end *vicolo*. Coviello climbed a narrow staircase, at the top of which a door stood open. A young woman wearing a grim expression, came toward him: "Mastro Nico', forgive me, I have to go out because my sister-in-law is here and . . ."

She saw the policemen and fell suddenly silent, shutting her mouth with an odd sound.

"Don't think twice, Donna Conce', take your time. The gentlemen here haven't come to arrest me, don't worry, they're just interested in asking a few questions about a customer of mine. When you can get back, I'll head back to my shop."

The woman slipped away, not without one last unfriendly sidelong glance at Maione, who once again reflected bitterly on how his uniform was far from a ticket to the hearts of his fellow Neapolitans, whatever the neighborhood.

The apartment was dark, the heat was suffocating, and there was a strange smell, the sickly sweet scent of mold mingled with the acid scent of cooking and a deeply unpleasant lingering whiff of urine. A very old person lived there, you could sense it in the air.

Coviello called out in a loud voice: "*Mammà! Mammà*, where are you?"

A woman appeared. In the dim light of late afternoon, she was a frightening vision; Maione felt a shiver run down his spine.

Her thinning white hair stuck straight up from her skull, forming a sort of cloud around her head. Her nose, with a large mole in the middle of it, had a hump in the center that turned the tip downward, until it practically touched her jutting jaw. Her toothless mouth hung open in a ghoulish grin that had something of a leer about it. But most shocking of all were the eyes, veiled with cataracts, in which a glitter of youthful folly played.

"Oooh, Nicolino's home. *Mamma d'o Carmene*, Nicoli', how ugly you've become! And just who are these gentlemen who've come with you? Look how handsome the one in uniform is; who is he, a soldier? Does he want to be my boyfriend?"

Coviello replied brusquely: "*Mammà*, these gentlemen need to talk with me. Go in the other room, please. Do me a favor. Afterwards, I'll bring you a candy, all right?"

The old woman stepped closer still, staring at Maione. She ran a huge black tongue over her lips and said: "Listen, soldier, did you know that Nicolino is engaged? His fiancée has come back, and now he's going to get married. I want to get married too. Do you want to marry me?"

She reached out her hand toward the crotch of Maione's trousers, and the policeman leapt backwards. Coviello, more annoyed than embarrassed, grabbed the old woman by both arms, dragged her into the adjoining room, and closed the door on her.

"I'm sorry, my mother is terribly old and doesn't under-stand a thing anymore. She thinks she's a young woman again. Now then, down in the shop you were asking me about that night. I can't see very well, the work I do has hurt my eyesight. Also, it was dark out. But anyway, there was someone sitting on the bench. He was a very big man, no doubt about that, or I wouldn't have been able to see him at all. He looked like a mountain, that's how big he was."

Ricciardi insisted: "But was there anything unusual about him? Try to think. Was he bent over to one side? Was he young, old . . . Even the slightest detail might prove useful."

The jeweler stopped to think, one hand under his chin, his myopic eyes staring into space.

"Commissa', perhaps, but just perhaps, he might have seemed . . . young, I suppose. I couldn't say why, but now that I think back I did have the impression that he was just a boy."

Ricciardi nodded.

"And the professor didn't seem particularly worried, did he? When you went to deliver the two rings to him, I mean."

"No, Commissa'. He was the same as he'd always been. For that matter, I didn't really bother to notice his mood; all I wanted was to deliver the jewelry and get paid. He was a brisk, practical man, and so am I."

Maione decided to insist on the topic, to see if he could extract any evidence at all.

"And the other times, when he came to see you, did he stay? Did he tell you anything, for instance, about why he wanted two rings that were identical? And why he picked that particular style of ring?"

"Brigadie', I really couldn't tell you. He was no different from all the other clients who come to the workshop. I never ask questions and I keep my mouth shut. I mind my own business. My line of work, believe me, is one where it's best to be discreet: if you only knew how many people commission fine objects that aren't for their wives. The style, however, was something I'd recommended for the first ring, and like I told you before, when he came back for the second ring, he wanted it to be identical, only with a larger stone. It's a piece of jewelry in the latest fashion; I told him that it was ideal for slender fingers, and he seemed happy about that. I delivered both to him as soon as I was done with them, as agreed; he paid me and that was the end of it."

Ricciardi sighed in disappointment: "And you don't remember anything else: a phrase, a reference . . ."

The goldsmith held out his long arms: "Commissa', I'm sorry."

The policemen said goodbye to Coviello and left.

That was the last time they saw him alive.

XLIX

M aione's feet, indifferent to the aches and the heat that still persisted in the late afternoon, refused to take him back home or to police headquarters, and the brigadier found himself wandering down Via Toledo.

The Iovine case was weighing on him. He didn't feel any particular compassion for the doctor, who was leading a double life and had something of a shadowy past. Nor had the widow seemed particularly crushed by her grief: if anything, the woman seemed to possess abundant resources, both emotional and economic, that would allow her to bounce back; and to be rather cynical, this was hardly the most cold-blooded of murders. After all, when you throw someone out a window, you don't even see him die. No, what was making Maione uneasy was his own state of mind during this investigation.

Usually it was Ricciardi who tended to split hairs, to keep pressing during questioning, to mistrust anything a suspect or a witness had to say. Maione was usually the one who started with the assumption that everyone was innocent, that everyone was telling the truth. Hatred, envy, and a desire for vengeance were strangers to him, and it struck him as absurd that anyone could be pushed to commit a murder by those emotions.

But this time it was Maione who was seeing guilty parties everywhere. He saw Dr. Ruspo, lying at death's door, as guilty by proxy, thanks to his gargantuan son. He saw the Wolf as guilty, either directly or thanks to any one of the numerous members of his small criminal army. He even assigned guilt, before ever meeting and questioning him, to the mythical fiancé of Sisinella, the young prostitute whom Iovine had transformed into a wealthy signorina in Vomero. In fact, Maione and Ricciardi had agreed to return to Vomero the following day to learn more about Signor Salvatore Cortese, aka Tore 'o Pianino.

That case had turned him glum. Or maybe it was him, not the murder. He was transferring his uneasiness into his work.

Walking along, grim and grumpy, his hands in his pockets and his eyes on the pavement, indifferent to all those who called out greetings or doffed their caps and then turned away, puzzled by his failure to reply, Maione thought to himself: it must be the heat. All big men suffer from the heat, right? They sweat, they snort, they pant. And big men who are policemen, men who have to walk the city in uniforms that become as heavy as suits of armor, suffer even worse. That must be what's putting me in this bad mood, he told himself.

Or not.

Perhaps it's this thought of Lucia that's poisoning my soul and making me see evil everywhere.

Maione was torn. One part of his soul rejected the thought that his wife might betray him; after so many years of living together, after so many moments of happiness and terrible despair, after the challenges they'd faced and overcome together, he couldn't bring himself to imagine her in the arms of another man.

With a smaller—and more treacherous—part of his soul, though, he had no difficulty imagining it at all. Lucia was so pretty, and still so young in spite of the children, the hard work, the grief, and the worry; no one who met her could help but desire her, he told himself. That same treacherous part of his soul chimed in: now take a look at yourself and compare. You're fat, old, covered with hair everywhere except where it ought to be, that is, on the top of your head; you're awkward and never well dressed, not even when you're wearing your

Sunday best; uncouth and a bit of an oaf, constantly worrying about your job, which you can't seem to forget even when you're home; and you can never manage to make conversation about anything but your children and how to make ends meet. What's more, you're poor, and no matter how hard you work, you can't seem to come up with enough money for a bigger apartment. Why would a woman like Lucia, who could have any man she wants, whose smile outshines the sun, who has the sky and the sea in her eyes, who seems to dance even when she just walks, why should a woman like that want to stay with you?

That's what the smaller, more treacherous part of his soul had been murmuring into Maione's ear since the day he'd seen Lucia emerge from that damned building on Via Toledo. The same building he was standing in front of right now, concealed in the half-light of an atrium, after silencing and waving away with sharp and imperious gestures the doorman who had approached him to ask what it was he wanted.

Maione had a gift which had helped him immensely in his profession. He blended in. Like that species of lizard he could never remember the name of and that he'd seen in one of his children's schoolbooks, he took on the color of his background and turned invisible. He was the first to realize how strange it was: a big strapping man who stood six feet three inches tall and weighed in at over 240 pounds, with hands like spades and enormous feet, to say nothing of the fact he was in police uniform. And yet, whenever the brigadier wanted, people paid no more attention to him than they did to a vendor's stall, the vendor himself, a beggar, or the statue of a king on horseback. When he followed a person, that person remained unaware of him, even if the two of them were otherwise alone on the street—and this was certainly not the case today, since Via Toledo was bustling.

Maione boasted proudly of that skill. He attributed it to the fact that he was perfectly in tune with his city, as if the city were a concert and he a note played by a musical instrument. He believed that he was so highly adaptable to his surroundings that he stood out no more than the flaking building fronts or the bollards blocking the sidewalks. And it seemed almost a violation of professional ethics to use such a skill for his own personal ends—on the order of pulling his regulation pistol during a fight in a tavern. But the small, treacherous part of him whispered that this ability could come in handy in eliminating any last lingering doubt, in convincing himself that his eyes, quite simply, had deceived him.

Lucia stepped out of the entrance of the building across the way. This time, there could be no doubt about it. That was her, just a few yards away from Maione, in her black dress, as beautiful as ever; the brigadier could see her face was lined with weariness, but her eyes sparkled with all the mischievous glee of a little girl who's stolen the jam jar. The expression she always had right after making love.

The thought hit him like a carriage pulled by a runaway horse. Where the devil was Lucia going, his Lucia? In what damned apartment in that damned building?

His masculine instinct tempted him to leap out of the shadows and demand an explanation. But Maione also possessed a policeman's instincts. He let her walk past him. He could have reached out his hand and grabbed her by the arm, made her turn around and look him in the eye; he could have fleetingly caressed the hair stuck to the sweaty back of her neck, under the scarf covering her head.

He stayed where he was, gray and motionless as a pillar. He watched her stride past briskly and vanish into the *vicolo*. Every so often the doorman shot him a worried glance as he swept the courtyard. He was sweating and didn't bother to wipe away the drops that slowly oozed down from his cap, streaked his face, and leaked into his collar.

He waited.

After ten minutes or so, there *he* was.

Elegant, fresh as a rose, and intolerably slender, a man emerged from the same front door through which Lucia had just left. He was wearing a bow tie and a white straw hat with a black satin band; his handlebar mustache was impeccably groomed, and he wore an off-white linen suit and a pair of two-tone shoes. He carried a slim walking stick whose golden handgrip reflected the rays of the setting sun.

Ferdinando Pianese, aka Fefè, thought Maione. And if a thought could ever have blasted anyone off the face of the earth, he was the ideal candidate. A useless dandy with a passion for blondes.

The man waved a hand nonchalantly in the direction of Fanelli the doorman who, in his new role as a secret police informant, studied him with malevolent interest. Then Pianese lit a cigarette and with a smile strolled off on his walk. Maione had to stifle the savage impulse to lunge at his neck, rip the flesh off him with his teeth, and feast on his innards.

The appearance of Lucia followed by that damned Pianese gave Maione's heart an unwished-for confirmation. The small, perfidious part of him that argued for Lucia's treachery was dancing gleefully, delighted to have been proved right. Still, the remaining rationality imposed upon him by his investigator's mind—and his desperate desire to be proved wrong—demanded further digging.

He decided that he would say nothing to his wife. That he'd withstand the temptation to question her, to delve into any contradictions he might uncover. He would wait and let her give herself away. In the meantime, he'd do his best to carry on as if nothing at all were out of the ordinary.

It would take a great effort of will, so he decided to spend the next hour trying to force it upon himself, and headed off for the tavern. A cold glass of white wine would help.

L

The second trip up to Vomero, the following morning, took place in silence.

Ricciardi had just had a sleepless night, half of it spent at Rosa's bedside, replacing Nelide, whom he'd grimly ordered to go get some rest, and half back home, in a wakeful sleep infested by the phantoms of the future.

Modo was really outdoing himself. Ricciardi would never be able to thank him enough. The doctor was worried about the onset of pulmonary complications and cardiac arrhythmias; he checked on Rosa practically every hour, and the expression on his face was increasingly tense, no matter how hard he tried to conceal it. He'd explained that feeding was being done by enema rather than intravenously, because he wanted to avoid subjecting her circulatory system to undue strain.

When he arrived at the hospital, the commissario was told that a woman had come to visit Rosa. In his heart, Ricciardi had secretly hoped that it had been Enrica and that she had learned, through some obscure channels, from a tradesman, from the apartment house's custodian, from anyone, in other words, about what had happened to his *tata*. It would have warmed his heart to know that the two women were together, and he would have been relieved and happy to see Enrica again.

But Livia had been the visitor; Ricciardi had figured that out from the description given by Nelide: *Bella 'nchiazza e 'ncasa sciazza*, beautiful on the street and sloppy at home, she'd murmured with a smirk. Rosa must have had time to express her opinion of the widow Vezzi, who had brought a useless and decorative bouquet of flowers that the young woman, the minute Livia left, had put in a vase at the foot of the statue of the Madonna, out in the corridor.

Enrica wasn't there. Enrica had left. He'd never see her again.

These absences—his mother, Rosa, Enrica—had populated the remainder of Ricciardi's night; never had dawn been more welcome.

Maione hadn't gotten a wink of sleep all night either, though he had put on a passable imitation of a slumbering brigadier. His mind roamed rapidly through images he never would have wanted to entertain, bedrooms and boudoirs of unknown apartment houses, expensive restaurants and deluxe cafés that he could never afford to enter. When he finally did manage to drop off for a few seconds, he immediately jerked back awake, convinced that he'd heard his wife talking in her sleep, and he had lain there in that terrible state of doubt for the rest of the time to which the night condemned him.

And so a grim-faced brigadier and an introspective commissario were ready to launch themselves with relief into the distraction of their investigation. They reached Vomero early in the morning and went straight to the address they knew well by now. This time the doorman greeted them with proper deference and went on watering the plants in the courtyard, leaving them free to walk up to the second floor and knock on the door.

Teresa Luongo, aka Sisinella, came to the door in a nightgown, with the face of someone who'd been rousted out of a deep sleep. Ricciardi had to admit that, if it's true that the one sure way to judge a woman's beauty is to see her when she's just woken up, no makeup on, her hair unbrushed, well, then, this was a genuinely pretty girl. She looked even younger than her age, her cheeks reddened from sleep, her lips pouty, one hand holding her nightgown closed over her firm, ample bosom, her black hair crowning her broad forehead and her sleepy blue eyes.

"But . . . what do you want? What time is it?"

Maione reacted as if the girl had just personally insulted him: "Girlie, it's the time of day when people with honest jobs have already been at work for quite a while. Let us in, because we have more questions to ask you."

From the outset, the relationship between Sisinella and Maione had been steeped in hostility. The girl had worked in a nonregulation brothel, and she'd learned at her own expense just how cruel policemen could be and how frequently she and her fellow working girls were forced to ply their trade free of charge in order to be left alone. The brigadier, on the other hand, thought that selling one's body was an immoral shortcut to a prosperity that was otherwise unattainable, and that the dignified thing to do was to work as a housekeeper or scullery maid, doing backbreaking labor for a relative pittance. The two were born enemies, they knew it and they recognized each other at first sight. They displayed their rancor in two different ways: the policeman by using the disrespectful informal form of address, the girl with her insolent defiance.

The young woman turned and went back inside, leaving the door open behind her but without bothering to ask them in. Ricciardi followed her, ignoring Maione's guttural muttering. They found her sitting in an armchair, legs crossed and bare, lighting a cigarette.

The brigadier spoke to her in a sarcastic tone: "Are we done playing the great lady leading the life of leisure, eh? I hope so. But everyone according to his nature."

Sisinella insolently blew a column of cigarette smoke in his direction: "Don't start crowing victory, Brigadie'. I'm not going back to being a whore. If I have to starve to death, I'm not going back to that bordello."

Maione wasn't willing to go easy on her: "Oh, no? So where are you going to go live? In your opinion, when the professor's widow learns about this little love nest, you think she's going to let you keep it?"

"Oh, sure, because a poor girl, if she's even a bit pretty, can't be anything but a whore. But that's not how it is. I have a man, understood? A man. And he loves me, and he'll support me with the work that he does. I knew that all this wasn't going to last. I knew that and I put a little something aside for when it ended. I'll sell all the gifts Tullio gave me. By the way, Commissa'," she said to Ricciardi, addressing him in a way that made clear she had misgivings about his underling but trusted the commissario, "Tullio mentioned a surprise that was going to leave me breathless. You haven't found anything, have you? He kept the gifts he had for me in his office, so his wife wouldn't stumble upon them."

Ricciardi nodded: "Maybe so, Signorina, but they're items that have to do with the investigation, and we can't dispose of them freely."

"But once the investigation is finished, can I have my gift?"

Maione shook his head decisively: "No, you can't have it. The victim's personal effects will all go to the family, as is only fair. Because the family has a right to them, and an illicit lover doesn't."

Ricciardi shot the brigadier a disapproving glare. He couldn't understand such hostility toward a young woman who, apart from this illicit relationship, had done nothing wrong; what's worse, that attitude might easily push Sisinella to shut down, which would only undermine their investigation. Maione's personal issues were starting to affect his work, and that was serious.

"The brigadier has a point, Signorina. Even if the victim's intention had been to give you a gift, it's quite unlikely that you'll ever lay hands on it. Still, we need to get some other information from you. Are you willing to answer our questions?"

Sisinella seemed touched by Ricciardi's courtesy and nodded, though not without giving Maione an angry sidelong glare.

The commissario went on: "The professor spent his free time with you; as much as he was able, anyway. He was with you, we believe, roughly a month ago, when some men came to get him for . . ."

"Of course he was, Commissa', I remember that night. We were . . . we were fast asleep, when we heard a car braking and right after that the sound of shouting in the courtyard. They'd woken up Firmino, the doorman, and were asking him where Tullio was. Not even a minute later, just enough time to throw something on, they started pounding on my door: *open up!* they were shouting, *open up!* I unlocked the door and they knocked me aside; two of them, ugly, dirty hooligans, grabbed poor Tullio by the shoulders and marched him off."

Maione broke in: "Do you remember if they explained who they were and on whose behalf they had come?"

"No, no. They kept insulting him, they told him that if anything happened it would go all the worse for him, that kind of thing. He told me over and over to stay calm, not to get upset. Two or three days later he came back, relaxed, as if nothing had happened, and that was the end of that."

Ricciardi asked: "And you didn't ask him what had happened?"

"Of course I asked him, but he just told me: one of my patients wasn't well, nothing important. Then, ten days or so later, he wanted to know whether anyone had come around bothering me, but no one had."

The details matched up with what the Wolf had told them; and the professor's display of nonchalance might have just been because he wanted to keep the girl from worrying.

Ricciardi said: "Signorina, I know that you're not going to be happy about this, but we also need to talk to your boyfriend: it's crucial to our investigation."

Sisinella looked startled: "But why? What has he done? Commissa', he has nothing to do with all this. And after all, he never even met Tullio or saw him, I don't see what . . ."

Maione took a step forward, menacingly: "Hey, sweetheart, watch out how you talk, understood? We can toss you into jail, you and him both, and keep you there as long as we like. Don't you dare try to interfere with who we choose to talk to!"

Ricciardi grabbed his arm gently: "Raffaele, calm down now. Let me do the talking, please."

He'd used a gentle tone of voice, but it had the desired effect. Maione quieted down, sighed, and said to him, without once taking his eyes off Sisinella: "Sorry, Commissa'. You're right. I let my anger get the better of me. But you, girlie, watch your step!"

The girl hissed defiantly: "You don't scare me, Brigadie'. You don't scare me. I've known people who would gut you like a fish for the fun of the thing, so just imagine how scared I am of you."

Ricciardi felt he needed to intervene again.

"Signorina, if we have made up our minds to track down a person—whose first and last name we know, by the way—we can look for him by questioning people on the street. That would do your sweetheart far more damage than if you helped us to get in touch with him directly. We only want to talk to him, that's all. It's up to you: all you can do is cause us some minor inconvenience and a slight waste of our time."

The girl considered Ricciardi's words. She was young, but life had already taught her to evaluate the pros and cons of every situation in the most objective way. In a voice so low that it was barely audible, she said: "He has a *pianino*. He strolls through the city, but he keeps to a specific route. Usually, around noon, you can find him at the Belvedere di San Martino, because that's where people from out of town come to see the museum and the view. Today is a beautiful day, that's where you're likely to find him."

Ricciardi bowed slightly: "*Grazie*, Signorina. May I ask what you plan to do with this apartment?"

"What can I say, Commissa'? I'll wait for them to evict me."

Ricciardi left, followed by Maione. The brigadier shot one last grim glare at Sisinella, who responded ironically by blowing him a kiss.

LI

Ricciardi and Maione were ahead of schedule and the walk to Piazzale di San Martino was a short one, so they took their time, and even stopped off at a café with a terrace that overlooked the city's rooftops.

The volcano was silhouetted against the blue sky and together they looked like a painted backdrop, the kind you could see in the stage sets at the Salone Margherita music hall. From above, the streets and buildings of the center of town resembled a manger scene, wood and terra-cotta models built for children, with tiny automobiles and carriages moving along silently. The air was steeped in the pungent odor of horse manure and sunbaked vegetation.

Ricciardi sat waiting for Maione to say something, hoping he might reveal the reason for his jangled nerves, but the brigadier did not seem inclined to confide his thoughts; he just pushed the tiny spoon around in his demitasse and looked out at the panorama.

At that point, the commissario tried coming at it in a roundabout way: "I feel sorry for that girl, you know? She was confident that she'd closed the door on her previous life, and now she's in danger of slipping back into it. Unless it turns out that this Cortese actually has honorable intentions."

Maione replied without taking his eyes off the gridwork of tiny buildings: "You really think so, Commissa'? Women like her have only one thing in mind: their own self-interest. They're like animals, like dogs and cats, eager to eat, and once they have, off they go, with not another thought about you."

"Are you sure that's the way things work? Just think about the doctor's little dog, the one we found with the little boy up at Capodimonte. That child certainly can't have been giving him much food, but the dog never left his side, even after he was dead."

The brigadier shrugged his shoulders: "There are always exceptions. But believe me, Commissa', that's how women are. They look for economic security, for comfort. And if you can't give it to them anymore, they'll go looking somewhere else."

"What are you talking about? That's something you of all people can't say. You've shared your whole life—its pains and its joys—with Lucia. By supporting each other you've survived despair, you've overcome a tragedy that would have destroyed almost anyone else I know."

Maione spoke in a broken voice.

"Things change, Commissa'. Things change. Well, we'd better get going, it's practically noon."

And he got brusquely to his feet.

The large piazza in front of the Charterhouse of San Martino was broad, practically circular, its surface almost entirely covered with packed earth. One reached it by climbing a handsome, not especially steep road, which was busy with carriages that took visitors up to one of the most enchanting overlooks in the city. The contrast between the peaceful hilltop hermitage and the frenzy that reigned at the foot of the hill was accentuated by the presence of a herd of goats, whose tinkling bells contributed to the bucolic atmosphere.

A number of street vendors had taken up positions with their merchandise; at a certain distance, as if to emphasize the difference in what was on offer, stood a *pianino* drawn by a mule that had seen better days. Turning the handle, surrounded by an audience of a dozen or so people, mostly women, was a young man who accompanied the music in a tenor voice. As he sang, he stared at a young foreign female tourist who was dressed in white and carried a fetching parasol. The young woman, who had a horsey face, listened with a look of enchantment, her eyes sparkling, her mouth half open, revealing a set of buckteeth.

> *Chisto è 'o paese d'o sole,*
> *chisto è 'o paese d'o mare,*
> *chisto è 'o paese addò tutt'e pparole*
> *so' doce e so' amare,*
> *so' sempe parole d'ammore!*

> *This is the land of sun,*
> *this is the land of the sea.*
> *It's the land where words,*
> *whether sweet or bitter,*
> *are always words of love.*

To give further emphasis to his performance, the musician underscored his lyrics with his free hand. Ricciardi studied him: not particularly tall, skinny and lithe, wearing a shirt under his waistcoat, the collar buttons unfastened, his cap pushed back on his forehead, curly black locks poking out from beneath it, gleaming white teeth, a cleft in his chin, and a bronzed neck. The classical Neapolitan type who always manages to insinuate himself into women's hearts.

The young tourist turned to speak to an older woman, whom Maione identified with some confidence as her mother, given the similarity in dental configuration: "Wasn't he wonderful, Mother? Did you hear him? Such a fantastic voice, and he's so gorgeous . . ."

The young man smiled at her, oozing connivance from every

pore: "Do you like, madame? I'll be happy to sing again, don't you worry."

Maione coughed meaningfully: "Maybe in a little while. Right now the commissario and I want to talk to you."

The other man grimaced in disappointment: "Can't it wait, Brigadie'? You're going to make me miss my opportunity with the signorina, here."

"No, it can't. And don't worry, even if chipmunk girl leaves, there'll be plenty more later. But perhaps you'd rather come have our little conversation at police headquarters. Your choice."

The young man sent a morose sigh in the direction of the young Englishwoman, made a smiling apology, and blew her a kiss. The young woman blushed as her mother grabbed her arm and dragged her off.

While the audience that had been listening to the *pianino* drifted away, the three men moved off to the side.

"At your orders, Brigadie'. What can I do for you?"

"Are you Salvatore Cortese, also known as Tore 'o Pianino?

"Yessir, Brigadie'. But what have I done wrong?"

Maione snorted: "I don't get it: every time I speak with someone, they always think they must necessarily have done something wrong. Nothing, you haven't done anything wrong. At least I hope that's true, for your sake. I'm only interested in getting some information. Do you know a certain Luongo, Teresa Luongo?"

"Who, Sisinella? Of course I know her. Why?"

Ricciardi took over from Maione: "Where were you on the night between last Thursday and Friday? It was the 7th, to be exact."

Cortese narrowed his eyes: "Commissa', what are you trying to say? Is that when the guy died, the one who was with Sisinella, the one who gave her money? You wouldn't by some chance be thinking that . . ."

Maione interrupted sternly: "Just answer the commissario's question."

Cortese remained cautious: "I . . . Commissa', I don't really remember. I think that . . . I believe that I was in Vomero, anyway. I live in Arenella, not far away, I was on the street, or else maybe . . ."

Ricciardi stepped in quickly, forestalling Maione's furious reaction: "Cortese, listen to me, this is a serious matter and we can't stand around here wasting time. Either you tell us or we're taking you with us."

"No, no, now I remember. I was with Sisinella, in her apartment. I spent the night there, like I frequently do when . . . when we're certain that no one else is going to be coming, in other words."

Maione nodded: "Got it. So Sisinella is covering for you. She's your alibi."

Tore began whining, on the verge of tears: "But Brigadie', what on earth are you talking about? What alibi? I don't need any alibi, I never even met this professor, I've only seen him once, and that was from a distance, because he showed up one day when he wasn't expected and I had to escape over the balcony, half naked, with my clothes clutched under my arm; it's a good thing it was at night, or they would have arrested me. What do I know about what happened? Take pity on me, I'm just an honest, hardworking . . ."

Ricciardi cut him off: "So you never met the professor. But weren't you jealous of him?"

The young man seemed sincerely surprised: "What? Why on earth should I have been jealous of him?"

Maione glared at him angrily: "And why do you think? The man was spending time with your sweetheart, he came to see her whenever he wanted, and when he did you had to scurry out the window, he'd lie down in your bed, and you weren't jealous of him?"

Tore darted his eyes a couple of times from Maione to Ricciardi and back again.

"My sweetheart? . . . No, no, no, Brigadie', you've got it all mixed up. Or else someone told you everything backwards, completely backwards. I don't have a sweetheart, and I don't plan to get one! Sisinella is a pretty girl, I'm very fond of her, and we have plenty of fun together, but come on, Sisinella is a whore. Do you think that a young man like me, an upright, hardworking Christian would get serious with a whore?"

Ricciardi said: "As far as I know, she's no longer a prostitute. She even left the bordello."

The other man burst out laughing uncontrollably: "What does that have to do with it, Commissa'? Once a whore, always a whore. I go to see her, I have myself a good time . . . And after all, as long as she had that fool paying for everything, lavishing gifts on her and even giving her hundred-lire banknotes, it was worth my while. Where do you think I got the money to buy this mule? Before I got the mule, I had to drag the *pianino* all the way up here myself. But I'm planning to spend the rest of my life with something better, not some whore."

Maione and Ricciardi fell silent. Then Maione said: "So you weren't jealous."

"On the contrary, Brigadie', he was a source of income! When we heard he was dead, we thought it was the end for us, damn him to hell. Why on earth would I kill the goose that laid the golden eggs?"

The brigadier eyed him with revulsion: "Believe me, Corte', you truly disgust me. You're telling me that when another man comes and takes your girl to bed, instead of going crazy what you do is take his money and consider yourself lucky?"

The young man was exasperated: "Brigadie', you're not listening to a word I've said: Sisinella isn't my girl!"

Ricciardi said, in a low voice: "But that's what she thinks.

And she hopes to stay with you, now that she's about to lose everything."

Cortese broke out laughing.

"Oh, right . . . I'm going to have a whore for a sweetheart, and support her in the bargain. Me, supporting her! Seriously—and now they're going to kick her out of her apartment; what do you think, should I bring her home to live with my mother? The idea of bringing a whore into a respectable household. In fact, I haven't been to see her in three days, not since I heard about what happened to the professor. No question about it, she's pretty and . . . well, let's just say that she's experienced. But I need to get to work. Maybe some girl like the one over there with the buckteeth, you saw her: they have plenty of money, these Englishwomen . . . a girl like that, if she falls head over heels, might even take you back home with her by steamship."

Maione grabbed him by the lapels and hoisted him off the ground. Cortese squeaked in fear, kicking his feet in the empty air.

"Let me look a miserable good-for-nothing like you right in the eye," said the brigadier. "Who knows when I'll find another specimen like this one." He suddenly released his grip, and the frightened young man fell to the ground. And Maione continued: "Let me tell you something, Corte': I've got my eye on you. I've got my eye on you. If you stray over the line by so much as an inch, even a hair, first I'll kick your ass black and blue till you can't sit down, and then I'll throw you in prison. I can just imagine how happy they'll be to see you, the lifers, with your pretty smile and your beautiful operatic tenor voice."

Cortese got back to his feet briskly, brushing off his hindquarters: "Don't give it a second thought, Brigadie', I never do anything wrong. Anything you need, just send for me and I'm entirely at your disposal. Thanks, Brigadie'; thanks, Commissa'; at your service. Can I go now?"

As they were riding the funicular back down to the center of town, Ricciardi commented bitterly: "Poor girl. In just a couple of days she's lost both the man who was supporting her and her sweetheart. Life can be cruel."

Maione sat in the wooden seat with his arms crossed.

"Yes, Commissa'. And I'm sorry now that I treated her so roughly. She's more honest, with the work she's done and where she's done it, than this human sewer Cortese, who was exploiting her while she actually cared for him. It certainly is true that there are a thousand ways to betray. And a thousand reasons to do so."

LII

This time, it was cold. There was a wind slicing the harbor in two, a wind that wouldn't stop blowing. He could have taken shelter behind a warehouse wall, or a boat in dry dock, but he didn't want to.

Plenty of steamships had set sail since she'd left, and he had come back every time, rain or shine, and he'd sat in their old spot even though he knew she wasn't coming. Not for now.

What must it be like, to set sail in stormy weather? Maybe the sea was scarier, chilly and black, tossing and noisy, but then again, maybe without the scent of flowers in the air, without melodious strains of music, without the sun shining to catch all the colors out of the houses along the waterfront, vanishing slowly into the distance, maybe then the departure weighed less on you.

The emigrants hugged each other close to keep warm. He scrutinized their faces, but he saw no trace of the fear that had once been there. Things had changed. They'd changed for everyone: for him too.

The departure of the steamship: that had always been their place and their time. For the two of them. Ever since, all those many years ago, they were little more than children. She'd followed him here, without asking a thing: she'd understood intuitively. Because they understood each other.

Both of them silent, both of them determined, both of them poor, both of them convinced that they wouldn't always be.

But he wondered now, as the sailor lowered the gangway

with the passenger list in one hand, what did they want from the future? Did they really want the same things?

He pulled his collar tight, lowered his cap over his ears. America. What he wanted was America.

So many people had told him that, with his skills, he could make plenty of money. In America, there was no tradition, nor was there imagination. His ambition would know no bounds.

Because yes, he was ambitious. No one had ever understood just how ambitious he really was. He was good at what he did, and he was going to get even better. But what good is it to have a skill, what good are success, money, reputation, except to make the person you love happy? What good is all that, if it doesn't bring a smile to anyone's lips?

He would have liked America, but with her. Without her, America was empty. It meant nothing.

For so long now, one steamship after another, he'd hoped that she would fall in love with the idea: him and her together, across the sea, far away from those who didn't understand, far away from those who let life roll over them. Him and her together in a new world, part of a people who were capable of looking the future in the eye and changing it.

He'd been told that across the ocean, there were no aristocrats. That what you were was what you were, and that you could build something without anyone asking your name or who your parents had been. He'd been told that you could even become president, which was something like being king, even if you came from the manure of the stables.

Here, on the other hand, if you were you, you remained you, even if you were a genius capable of working miracles with your hands.

But she didn't want to leave. She was captivated, he could sense it, and she cared for him; maybe not as much he cared for her, but enough to accept as a given that they were going to spend their lives together. That's the way things were, where they lived. Two people would meet, and they'd stay together for the rest of their lives. They wouldn't part ways, they wouldn't take different paths. Together for the rest of their lives. The two of them had met and they were never to part, just like their parents before them, and their grandparents before them, and so on, back into the dark night of time.

This is what he couldn't seem to figure out, as he watched the weary line of emigrants wend its way up the gangway, lashed by the gusts of chilly wind. If he wanted to leave, why hadn't she just accepted that? Why hadn't she said yes, like women were supposed to, and then set about helping him scrape together the money for the tickets?

He'd understood that she didn't want to go, and he'd stopped talking about it. He'd hidden his dream from everyone. That had been their secret, the reason they sat in silence, among the hawsers and the nets: they watched the departures that would always be for others, never for them.

She was different. That was the truth. Her eyes were different, her hands were different, her mouth was different. Different. She didn't belong to their world, even though she was born there just as he had been, even though she had breathed the same air and eaten the same bread, even though when it was a feast day she put on her Sunday best and linked arms with him so that he felt like the king of the world. She was different.

When she had told him, right on that spot, as they were watching a steamship depart, that she was going to be leaving, but leaving *him*, he had died. He'd felt the blood stop in his veins, and if he hadn't spoken, if he hadn't shouted out his despair, it was only because he didn't want to sever the thread that still held them together.

Because love—he thought to himself as he watched a woman pick up her toddler, who was unable to climb up the gangway on his own—love is a germ. A disease that springs from a tiny seed and takes root in a specific spot. At the bottom of your heart.

She had promised that she'd come back. That it was just a matter of time, the time needed to gather the strength, the money, and the prosperity so they could stay together for good.

She had promised that they'd never be apart again and that, however long it took, sooner or later their paths would converge again.

She had promised.

But she was different. She belonged to another world, not to his. And he, who was of that place, of that neighborhood, would never have another woman, because she was his companion, and she had been on his arm the night of the festival, when they set fire to the bell tower and made a wish.

He had her. He had no one but her.

At the bottom of his heart.

LIII

That evening, Maione's feet were not really what carried him to no. 270, Via Toledo. His encounters with Sisinella and Cortese, Vomero with its heady romantic atmosphere, the heat he'd suffered on the funicular, a vivid image of a descent into an inferno of despair: all these things had conspired to sow in his tormented soul an irresistible desire to gaze into the eyes of the man who was pitching woo with his wife.

He posted himself in the atrium as he had the day before. The doorman pretended not to see him and went straight into the inner courtyard with a chair, the evening paper, and half a cigar. The brigadier prepared for a wait that he expected would be short: this was the right time of day.

And in fact, after no more than half an hour, Lucia emerged, tucking her hair under her scarf. Just like the night before, she shot a quick glance around her and then headed for home. Maione wondered where she'd gathered such confidence, this stranger who had been at his side for so many years. How had she learned so well to master the arts of dissimulation and untruth?

No more than ten minutes, not even the time to sink into a state of bitter rancor, and out came the damned Ferdinando Pianese, the horrible Fefè that Bambinella had told him about, the debauched useless creature capable of poisoning even his troubled sleep in those nightmarish days.

He gave him a few yards' head start and then set off after him. There weren't many people out on the street; the heat discouraged strollers, and a number of shops had closed early. The two men, Maione and Fefè, couldn't have looked any more different. The brigadier's pace was that of a policeman hard at work: hands in his pockets, cap pushed back on his head, eyes darting from a shopwindow to a beggar, from a newsstand to a married couple out with their children; Fefè, on the other hand, ambled along like a dandy waiting for dinnertime and in the meanwhile calmly mulling over the various possible places to enjoy an aperitif, smiling at life and at a bright future. To all appearances, two characters among so many in the city; not a ravenous predator stalking his unsuspecting prey.

The brigadier's brain was scheming, planning out the instant in which he'd face his rival head-on. There, he thought, now he's turning the corner of Via Chiaia . . . there are still too many people out walking in the street . . . then he'll head downhill toward Piazza dei Martiri, and he'll stop at the café with all the other good-for-nothings to pester other people's women.

I have to stop him before that.

Just a few yards short of the last stretch of street before the piazza so popular with the city's high society—an ideal hunting ground for people like Fefè—Maione lengthened his stride and caught up with him at the mouth of a narrow *vicolo*, a broad, dead-end flight of steps; he grabbed the man by one arm and dragged him into the shadows.

The man seemed more surprised than frightened: an enormous policeman, grim-faced and sweaty, in uniform and with a pistol on his belt, was gripping the immaculate white sleeve of his summer jacket with huge fingers; that sleeve would most likely never be the same again. No doubt, a case of mistaken identity, Fefè reassured himself. The policeman need only take a close look at my face.

Instead the brigadier slammed him carelessly against a wall. Two young men who had been completing some transaction that required a certain degree of privacy decided that it was probably wise to take to their heels. Now Maione and Fefè were all alone.

The slim dandy opened his eyes wide: "But . . . but what do you want from me, Brigadie'? There must be some mistake, I've done nothing."

"Nothing, Piane'? Nothing? There's been no mistake, it was you I was looking for. And if you examine your conscience, that is, if you still possess such a thing, then I think you'll have no doubt about what I want from you."

Pianese did his best to think quick, but he was finding that easier said than done, because now Maione had released his grip on his sleeve and had grabbed him by the neck; he clutched in his enormous fist collar, bowtie, and jacket lapel, all scrunched up together and pressed so forcefully on the lawyer's throat that he couldn't take a breath. In a glimmer of lucidity, it dawned on the policeman that the man was suffocating, and he loosened his grip ever so slightly.

Fefè took a deep, sharp breath, and moaned: "Brigadie', you must have taken me for some other person, I can assure you that I've done nothing, I . . ."

Maione's hissed whisper turned bitter: "Nothing. Sure. It's nothing to wreck a family, introduce a serpent into an honest household, take a mother away from her children. It's nothing to destroy a life, shatter the heart of a man who thought that the woman beside him was a faithful loving wife. It's nothing to take someone's sunlight and fresh air away. You're a bastard, Piane'. You're a rotten bastard."

The other man looked wildly around him, hoping in vain that someone might come to his aid. He was afraid to shout for help, fearing that if he did, that uniformed lunatic would simply snap his neck by squeezing his hand shut.

He tried to think. If the man hadn't already killed him, if he was talking to him, he might still have a chance. This had to be about Lucrezia.

After a courtship that had lasted months, he'd only recently managed to work his way into the good graces of the Marchesa

Lucrezia Carrara di Morsano, one of the city's most prominent matrons. The woman was hardly delightful to behold, with her big bug eyes, her long skinny legs, and the frizzy yellow hair that did its best to escape the confines of every little hat, forming a sort of cloud around her forehead; still, the money that her husband possessed—an elderly landowner with vast holdings whose only real interest was in food—more than made up for it, and she, in exchange for his sexual favors, was happy to disburse considerable sums on a regular basis.

Lucrezia, who was sailing blithely toward her sixtieth birthday, had two children, a son and a daughter, but thirty-six and thirty-four years of age respectively, both married and with children of their own: to talk about taking a mother away from her children struck Fefè as something of an exaggeration. Also, Fefè had to wonder why the elderly and gluttonous Marchese di Morsano should have requested and obtained no less than the violent intervention of the legal authorities to settle a matter that could have been handled with a gentlemen's agreement, the dispute placed in the wise hands of some common friend, as was generally the procedure.

Hoarse from the choking, he coughed out: "Brigadie', calm down, for the love of all that's holy. Tell the marchese that I understand and I'll act according to his wishes. Just reassure him that the marchesa . . ."

Maione paid no attention to the man's stammered words, having decided in advance that he'd ignore all excuses: "Now listen to me, and listen good, you cowardly bastard: if you see her again, even once, just once, I'll kill you, you get it? I'll kill you. And when I'm done with you, your own mother won't be able to identify the corpse, do you understand me? Not even your own mother. Say yes. Say it now, and say it loud."

If it meant escaping alive from that situation, Pianese would gladly have admitted to being the star ballerina of the dance troupe at the San Carlo opera house, proving his claim with a few demonstrative demi-pliés right there on the uneven cobblestones of the *vicolo*.

"Yes, yes, Brigadie', don't worry, never fear. And tell the marchese that he can be sure that I'll never, never see the marchesa again as long as I live."

Maione roared. That man was intolerable, and now he was mocking him, too.

He felt disgusted with the man, with the *vicolo*, with Lucia, and even with himself. He dropped Fefè and the man fell to the ground, panting; then he got to his feet and broke into a shambling run.

In the shadows of the evening now falling, the brigadier covered his face with his hands and wept.

LIV

On his way back, he felt at peace.

This was the first time that he'd felt that way in as long as he could remember. His soul had been in a state of tumult for so many years now that he'd become accustomed to that basso continuo of pain, regret, remorse, and incompleteness that had given his life the color that it now possessed.

Preparations for the festival were reaching their feverish finale. The quarter was teeming with frantic activity, everyone seemed to be carrying something from one place to another, hanging up festoons, applying ornaments.

Along the way he'd looked around him with the greatest possible watchfulness: it would have been a terrible twist of fate to be robbed now of all times. But everything had gone perfectly, according to plan. It had taken three extra days, that was all. To complete his masterpiece. But everything had worked out perfectly.

As he walked his usual route, one step after the other, he breathed deeply. He took the baking hot air, freighted with odors, into his lungs. He felt no sadness whatsoever, none of the sadness he'd expected; he'd preferred not to think about it, choosing instead to remain focused on the work he was completing, in accordance with the plan he'd sketched out first in his soul, and then in his brain.

Readying, completing, and fine-tuning every detail—it was the first thing he had done for himself in too long. Now that he was walking, avoiding the busy pedestrians, now that he was striding past places he'd known since his childhood, he didn't regret a thing. Not even the words he hadn't spoken—he didn't regret them either. They wouldn't have done a bit of good. They wouldn't have changed the course of his life, they wouldn't have added or subtracted a thing. Better to remain silent, then.

The thought formed before his eyes. The usual face. Like every other time, every single time, a hundred times a day for years and years. He walked along the wall, and instead of tasting the air, instead of looking out at the sea or climbing the hill to admire yet again the silhouette of the mountain against the blue of the sky, he reconstructed her face. Not the way she was now, her features marked with hardness and sorrow. No, her face the way it had been then. The way it had been the night of the festival, years ago: when he'd walked with her on his arm, fiercely proud of her smile, of her white dress.

They'd been beautiful together. The rest of his life wasn't long enough to remember her light pressure on his arm, her hand, the hand that was like a light-winged butterfly.

Someone called out to him, from a stand on the street. In this moment of peace he'd now attained, he thought about his people, about the struggle against hunger and privation. He thought of the faces of those who had stayed; he'd never thought about those who had left in these terms, and there had always been a light in his eyes, even in the midst of the blackest sorrow. Those who had stayed behind, on the other hand, no: that light, many of them had never had it.

He caught a few surprised glances from the women seated in the strip of shadow from the apartment building. After years of precision, of absolute predictability, here he was overturning all his routines. But it was necessary to complete that last step. Without the delivery, you couldn't say that a job was finished.

He opened the door and went in. He pulled the heavy door partially shut and allowed a shaft of morning sunlight to filter through. Not that he'd need it: in that cramped space which he knew so well, he could move around in pitch darkness without even brushing against furniture and objects; still, he decided to light the lamp. Its warm golden light had kept him company so often: it seemed right to him that it should illuminate this as well.

He went back to the door and locked it from inside. He looked around, the way he did every night before leaving.

Before leaving.

Everything was in order. He felt serene, contented. Full of hope, absurdly enough. He felt like those about to embark and leave. As if he too, now, were one of them. The sea, then America.

He went over to the workbench. He took the strongest of all his tools and made the last engraving. Then he picked up the rope he'd had ready for the past two days, stepped up onto the wooden surface, and ran it over the rafter.

He was at peace. His eyes went to the steamship on the wall.

He put his head in the noose and hauled himself up with both hands. He thought about her the way she had been, seated amidst the ropes and hawsers, watching the ship and the sea. There you are, at the bottom of my heart. There you are. I just wonder if I'm there too, at the bottom of your heart.

And at last he set off on his voyage.

LV

E nrica would never have admitted it to herself, but by now she expected him.

She was shooting covert glances from the beach up to the ridge where Manfred set up his easel; she was awaiting the arrival of that courteous man, the sunlight glinting off his blond hair, the wave of his hand in her direction before he sat down on the stool overlooking the water.

It had become a morning ritual of sorts, and an agreeable one. By now Carla, the other teacher, had given up in the face of the German officer's clear preference for Enrica. Carla had even started giving her advice on how best to rope him in, offering to take her evening shifts watching over the children so Enrica could go out with him.

Deep down, Enrica split the day into two parts. Daytime, when there was sunshine and the shouts of playing children and the cries of seagulls, the smiling greetings of the island's inhabitants and the gentle sea breeze; and nighttime, when the scent of flowers and the chirping of crickets filled the air and the soul, when the mind wandered in search of something to caress. Daytime housed Manfred's spiky accent, the stories of his far-off land, snack time with the children, at which the German was a regular guest; nighttime housed the thought of Ricciardi, his green, feverish gaze, the passion that quivered beneath the surface of a placid pool of water, apparently so tranquil.

At night, Enrica understood how deeply in love with him she still was. At night, when her brain ceased building castles

of rationality, when she could no longer battle against the facts
of a situation built out of silence and solitude. At night, when
she felt his eyes upon her and inside her, across the sea that
separated them.

And yet, she welcomed Manfred's company. She liked his
witty conversation, his keen sensibilities; he wasn't entirely without an inner gentleness, even though he practiced a harsh and
violent profession: it was a contrast that made her shiver, but
which bespoke a complex and intriguing personality. The stories
he told her took her to other worlds, made up of country celebrations and battlefields, deeds of honor and bitter defeats.

She liked Manfred's stubborn confidence in the future, too,
a confidence that hadn't been dulled by the harsh experiences
of a brutal past. When the figure of his dead wife emerged
from his recollections, Enrica never sensed regret or suffering:
only a hint of melancholy for a time gone by. Greater sorrow,
and a hint of rage, came with his memories of the war and the
harsh sanctions that had subsequently been levied on his
nation, a nation he loved passionately, and to which the officer
was sworn with an absolute devotion.

Even with regard to that topic, though, what prevailed was
optimism. The upcoming elections, he had said to her while looking out to sea, would once again make people aware of German
might, and of the country's desire to raise its head, to reaffirm the
role that Germany must play in the international panorama.

Enrica wasn't especially interested in politics and ferocious
and irreconcilable disputes seemed to her a particularly fruitless way of passing the hours. But she certainly understood
enthusiasm, the desire for a better future; and weighing the
gleam of optimism that she could glimpse in Manfred's blue
eyes against the hopeless sorrow that lurked in Ricciardi's was
a new feeling, and it bewildered her.

From the wave that Carla had given her, she knew that he
had arrived. She turned toward the ridge and he, blond hair

tossed by the sea breeze, raised his hand in her direction. Enrica responded without displaying anything more than a faint smile.

Who knows why, but she felt sad. As if she were leaving home.

Ricciardi shook off sleep and sat up straight. The hospital room, the lights of dawn filtering through the drawn curtains. It was already hot.

He looked at Rosa's serene profile, her faintly furrowed brow; he listened to her profound, regular respiration; he stared at the sheets that rose and sank over her body. He checked his watch: it was 5:40 A.M. He'd slept for two hours. In the shadows, Nelide sat in a chair, wide-awake, arms crossed, her eyes on him. That girl never sleeps, thought Ricciardi.

"Signori', are you hungry? I brought a bit of *pizza chiena*, shall I give you a slice?"

Ricciardi felt a pang in his heart as he recognized the very words and even the same tone of voice as Rosa. And the same heartfelt care for him, the same determination to stuff him with absurd delicacies. Just think: the *pizza chiena*. A confection of pork lard, eggs, and pepper. At five thirty in the morning.

"No, thanks. But what about you? Why don't you go home and get some rest?"

Nelide shook her head.

"'A cera se cunzuma, e 'a processione nú camina," she said in a mournful voice. The image of candles burning down in silence while the procession remained motionless emerged from the venerable folk wisdom of Cilento and plowed into Ricciardi like a speeding train. She was right. Rosa's flame was burning lower, and her life wasn't resuming.

For the first time since his *tata* had fallen asleep, Ricciardi emerged from the exclusive domain of his grief and realized that poor Nelide was bearing a heavy cross; she was young, fond of her aunt, and far from home. She had come to keep Rosa company, and now she found herself keeping vigil over her sickbed.

"Nelide, listen. You're free to go back to your village. I'm here, as you can see, and there's Dr. Modo, the other physicians, and all the nurses. You have nothing to worry about."

"Signori', Aunt Rosa called me. She chose me, she learned me everything. I'll stay. I want to stay. If you don't kick me out. I'm like Aunt Rosa, *comme 'a mamma vene 'a figliola*. If you want me."

Ricciardi felt a pang in his heart: she'd known. Rosa had known, that she would die soon. And she'd thought about who would stay with him, because he refused to make up his mind to start a family of his own. Stubborn old lunatic: instead of telling him that she wasn't well, instead of getting medical care, she'd arranged to train the niece that most resembled her.

Comme 'a mamma vene 'a figliola: like mother, like daughter. Stubborn Rosa, stubborn Nelide. Strong as a pair of oak trees.

"Yes, Nelide. Stay with me. And stay as long as you like. If you wish."

A rapid smile flashed across the girl's lips, so quickly that Ricciardi wondered if he'd really seen it at all.

His mind followed his heart toward Enrica. How he wished he could feel her close to him. It was absurd: he had written to her, he'd looked and looked at her, but they'd spoken very little. And only once, one unexpected time, in the street, under a strange drizzly snow one winter night, had he tasted the bittersweet flavor of her lips. And yet he felt a sharp painful pang: he missed her there, by Rosa's bedside, at dawn, as if that were where she belonged, alongside him.

How absurd love is, thought Ricciardi. Absurd in its acts, in its behaviors. Absurd in the wails of the ghosts on street corners, absurd in the sighs of those who died for love in the gardens where they'd slashed their wrists, beneath the windows they'd jumped out of, in the locked rooms where they'd drunk poison. And how absurd love was in this absence that weighed on him like a boulder, that crushed his heart as if it were made of tin.

There you are, he thought to himself. There you are.

Baroness Marta di Malomonte giggled and went on stitching. Rosa, curious, asked her: "Barone', why are you laughing?"

Marta turned toward her: "No, it's nothing. It's just Nelide and Luigi Alfredo. They're so strange: they think and they think. They don't talk much, but they think so much."

Rosa sighed: "It's because they're from Cilento, Barone'. You know what we're like, don't you? Don't you know us by now?"

"Sure, sure, of course I do. But the two of them are so afraid that they make me laugh."

The *tata* was bewildered: "What, they're afraid and that makes you laugh? And what are they afraid of?"

"They're afraid of being left without you, and each of them thinks that the other will suffer more, and each of them wonders if they'll be strong enough to help. That's what always happens. It's just something . . . human, I'd say. But you'll see, they'll survive. Because you really have been extraordinary."

"Me, Barone'? Me, extraordinary? At what? Nelide is just a girl from the country, and the young master can't even bring himself to talk with the woman he likes. Even I'm afraid for them."

Marta's expression turned reproving: "Now listen, Nelide has a good head on her shoulders, she'll do your job perfectly: you couldn't have left my son in better hands. And he, perhaps, will take from you and no one else the strength to emerge from his shell. Don't worry. People get used to the most difficult situations easily. But what about you, how do you feel?"

Rosa looked around. The room was growing brighter and brighter, and a pleasant cool breeze was coming in through the window.

"That's better, Barone'. That's better."

Marta held up the newborn's romper she was working on, in a delicate pink that in the light of the sun reminded Rosa of a Jordan almond.

"It's turning out very nicely. Before long, you'll look lovely in this romper."

"Me? But don't you see how big I am? How am I going to fit into that little romper of yours?"

"Oh, you'll see, you'll fit just fine. And I'll be so proud of my *tata*, you'll be the loveliest *tata* of them all."

"You think you can even make me lovely? Then it really is true, what they say about miracles. But tell me, what about the young master? What will become of him?"

Marta stopped. She laid her work in her lap and gazed out the window. Stretched out in the bed, Rosa couldn't share in the view.

"You know, Rosa, sometimes it seems as if the suffering will go on forever. It takes you, it envelops you, it seems as if it's never going to end. Like when there's a thunderstorm, you know what I mean? You feel overwhelmed, plunged into despair. And then you see it, the sun comes out. I didn't believe it, when . . . when I was with you, with all of you. It seemed to me that there couldn't be anything but the inferno. That pain, that terrible, constant pain . . . all those corpses talking, talking . . . I thought it would never come to an end. Instead, it does end. It ends."

Rosa listened, attentively. She thought she understood some of it, but not all.

"But the young master understands, doesn't he? He understands that the inferno will come to an end?"

Marta turned toward her again: "Maybe he does. And maybe he doesn't. It depends on so many things, you know that, *tata*? Not just on him. Now let me finish, there's not much time before dark."

And she started stitching again, smiling as if to some music that only she could hear.

LVI

Maione stayed overnight at police headquarters; he couldn't bear to look Lucia in the eye after his confrontation with Pianese.

He'd arranged for a phone call to be placed to Signora Ruggiero, the only tenant of the apartment house who had a telephone at home, and got word to his family that he'd have to stay overnight at the office. Not half an hour later Giovanni, his eldest son, arrived at headquarters: he was bringing his father a soup tureen wrapped in a carefully knotted cloth napkin, and inside was an abundant portion of pasta with chunks of tomato and *spollichini*, the fresh summer green beans that were one of Maione's favorite things to eat.

"*Papà*, here's what *mamma* told me to tell you: eat every bite of it, but slowly, otherwise it'll upset your tummy. And she also said: tomorrow, when you come home, don't forget to bring the soup tureen with you. And make sure you rinse it out, after you're done eating, or we'll never be able to get it clean."

He had responded by giving his son an offhand pat on the head, but the boy hadn't even noticed the pained expression on his father's face, intent as he was on taking in everything around him with greedy curiosity, the way he did every time he came to visit headquarters.

Maione didn't manage to eat at all, and there could be no more eloquent testimonial to his state of despondency. His stomach had simply closed up. He didn't know what to do, how to behave; with Fefè he'd acted on impulse, according to an instinctive drive, but with Lucia, who knew him well, he couldn't have successfully put on a show of indifference. Should he just leave, then? And where would he go? And was it right for him to resign himself to his loss like that, without fighting? And what about his children, what would become of them?

He was sitting there, assailed by countless anxieties, when the phone call came in.

The news caught Ricciardi and Maione off guard.

As they walked the short distance from police headquarters to the goldsmiths' *borgo*, they'd both been beset by the uncomfortable feeling that their minds had been taken off the investigation by the personal situation each was experiencing, and for policemen as conscientious as they were, that was a grave failing. The call that had come in, and whose contents had, in any case, been unclear, only heightened that perception, making the two policemen even gloomier than before, and during their walk over they were practically silent: Maione limited himself to asking how Rosa was, and Ricciardi said only that there was nothing new. Neither man commented on the tragic news that had summoned them, first thing in the morning, to a dead-end *vicolo* in the oldest part of town down by the harbor.

There was a crowd of rubberneckers standing outside the workshop. The wooden door stood half open, as if it were uncertain whether it should be thrown wide or remain shamefacedly shut to conceal the horror that lay within. The atmosphere, though, was different from the more customary one of morbid curiosity that the policemen were used to encountering. That sensation carried with it the witnesses' vague sense of relief that dire misfortune had befallen someone else; this time, there was a diffuse sadness, a sincere melancholy, if not outright grief.

An elderly woman dressed in black came toward them with a wobbly step, her legs stout and her voice hoarse: "Brigadie', I'd said that it was odd. Mastro Nicola arrived every morning at eight on the dot, you could set your clock by it. This morning it was seven when he showed up. I told my girlfriend Amalia that it was strange, and when I told her, she said the same thing. She told me: 'Really? That's strange.' And that's when I . . ."

Maione halted the flood of words by raising both hands: "Signo', Signo', do me a favor, stop talking for a moment. Who exactly are you? And what are you talking about?"

A second woman had come over, more or less the same age and similarly clad in black, but skinny as a rail and bug-eyed; she started talking as if everyone there were anxiously awaiting what she had to say: "When Enzina here told me, the first thing I thought was: something's happened. Mastro Nicola was always so punctual, he arrived every morning at 8 and you could set your watch by it, but instead this morning it was seven o'clock, and so I said: Enzi', why, what a curious thing this is, here's a man who always comes in at eight o'clock and . . ."

Maione exchanged a discouraged look with Ricciardi, then he turned to the woman who had piped up last: "Signo', you must be Donna Amalia, I'd imagine. And you," he said to the first woman, "will be Signora Enza."

The two women looked at each other in surprise: "Jesus above, Brigadie', how on earth would you know that? Then it must be true that the police have us all under surveillance and know all about us!"

Maione sighed.

"Well then, apart from the early arrival, will you tell us what happened next?"

It appeared however that both women had lost the urge to talk. They elbowed one another in the ribs, each inviting the other to answer, until Enza took for herself the role of spokeswoman: "We sit right there, you see? At the end of the *vicolo*. It's hot, and in the *bassi* it's impossible to breathe, we're old, and we've been friends forever. And so, while it's still night out, we sit down in our chairs and talk."

The other woman cut in: "Sometimes, if there's light, we do some knitting, or we stitch."

Enza shot her a glare, as if to say: are you going to talk or am I? Then she resumed: "Then we take a look around and see what's happening in the *vicolo*, and . . ."

". . . but not to stick our noses into other people's business, let's be clear. It's just because we sit down there and . . ."

Enza raised her voice, making it clear that she wouldn't put up with any further interruptions: ". . . and then we saw Mastro Nicola arrive. He told us good morning and then he shut himself in."

Ricciardi asked: "What do you mean, he shut himself in?"

"That's right, he shut himself in. He closed the door and we didn't hear anything more out of him."

Amalia couldn't resist: "Shut, locked."

Maione was perplexed: "In that case, who found . . . in other words, who called us?"

A young man stepped forward: "I did, Brigadie'. I'm the apprentice."

Ricciardi said: "Everyone wait out here. Raffaele, I'm going in."

Ricciardi waited for his eyesight to become accustomed to the partial darkness of the workshop. Everything was just as it had been on the occasion of the first and only visit he'd paid on the goldsmith, even the oil lamp on the workbench was still lit.

He turned his head, and saw what had changed.

The body of Nicola Coviello, renowned goldsmith and master jeweler, dangled from one of the ceiling rafters by a rope wrapped around his neck. Motionless, his outsized hands dangling at his sides, his legs aligned, his feet a good five inches off the floor.

The commissario concentrated on the spot toward which the hanged man's face was turned, a corner of the workshop shrouded in darkness; standing, in the same position as the hanging corpse, his simulacrum was revealed to Ricciardi, his tongue sticking out between his teeth, his spectacles askew, one eye half closed, the other staring wide.

Ricciardi could make out the mark left by the rope on his neck, a dark deep groove, and there was a line of reddish drool running down from the corner of his mouth. Ricciardi turned his eyes back to the rope hanging off the rafter, and saw that the slipknot had jammed before reaching the end of its run. So Coviello had died of suffocation. Not even the mercy of a broken neck.

The commissario focused on the image of the corpse in the shadowy corner. The head bent to one side, as unlovely as it had been in life, the short curved body, the long arms and legs. Dead, he looked younger.

Ricciardi listened.

And the corpse told him: *the bottom of your heart.*

LVII

O utside, Maione had managed to move almost everyone away. Only the apprentice and the two old women, Amalia and Enza, who had appointed themselves the brigadier's interlocutors, remained.

Maione spoke to Ricciardi: "Commissa', so this is Sergio, here, who found him. He's the young man who worked with Coviello. He shows up around nine, because the master always wants to be left alone for the first hour. Same thing for the last hour at night, when he closes up. That's what the boy told me."

Ricciardi questioned the young man, a terrified adolescent whose face was pocked with acne.

"Was there anything unusual about this morning?"

"The door, Commissa'. The door was shut from inside. I had to go back home, that's where I keep the other key that Mastro Nicola gave me for any emergency; his mother is sick, and a couple of times he couldn't leave his house and I had to open the workshop."

"And when you went in, what did you see?"

The boy was trembling, and he kept his gaze turned away from the shop's open door.

"I saw . . . I saw him right away, Commissa'. And I left, and called for help."

Enza stepped forward, proudly: "We were the only ones in the *vicolo*, Amalia and me, Commissa'. We saw *'o guaglione*, here, the boy, and heard him shouting, and we came hurrying. Then . . ."

Amalia interrupted her, earning herself a sour glare: ". . . then we went to see Signora Grimaldi, because she has a telephone, and we told the young lady at the switchboard: we want to talk to police headquarters!"

Ricciardi said: "All right. Let's go in now. No, ladies, not you: just the two of us with the boy. *Grazie*, if we need you we'll send for you."

The two women's disappointment was enormous. Defeated, they moved away, but not far: just to the threshold of a *basso* across the way, on the far side of the *vicolo*, and there they took up their positions on their chairs so they could be sure not to miss a single move the policemen made.

Maione murmured: "Nothing to be done. No one has any business of his own to mind, in this city."

The young man was reluctant to enter, and once he was inside he kept his eyes on the workbench, the wall, and the chair, making sure not to catch so much as a glimpse of the corpse hanging from the ceiling.

Maione said: "I had the photographer and the medical examiner summoned before we left headquarters, Commissa'. They should be on their way."

The bottom of your heart, Ricciardi sensed on the hair on the back of his neck, on the hairs standing erect on his fore-arms, and inside his chest. *The bottom of your heart*.

He asked the young man: "Did he say anything to you yesterday? Anything strange, I mean."

The young man shook his head no, eyes on the ground.

Ricciardi insisted: "But did you see him do anything unusual? What sort of mood was he in?"

Sergio shrugged his shoulders. Maione broke in harshly: "Sonny, you'd better answer, and answer fast, or it's going to go hard for you."

The boy started, then, in a low voice, he said: "He was . . . contented. Contented. He smiled. He never smiled, but for the past few days he'd been smiling a lot. He even whistled a little tune, and when had he ever done that before? It almost scared me."

Ricciardi and Maione exchanged a baffled glance. A man planning suicide who whistles a tune and smiles.

"And he didn't say anything to you? Not even, I don't know, something about work, or . . ."

The young man shrugged: "Work, I guess that was the one strange thing: he was turning down jobs."

Maione mopped his brow: "What do you mean?"

"That people would come to have jewelry made, or shopkeepers from Via Toledo, and he wouldn't even let them in the door. If they insisted, he'd say: no, I can't right now, I'm busy, come back next month. He'd never done that before; he was capable of staying all night to get more work. But now he was turning people away."

Ricciardi grew alert: "But what was he doing, instead of working? Did he receive visitors, or go out on calls, or . . ."

"No, no. He kept working, and how. He was making something. Something . . . something for himself. I wasn't even allowed to see it, he made me stand in the doorway, with my back to him. He paid me just the same, to stand there not doing anything, and to tell people not to come in."

The photographer arrived, almost at a run, dripping with sweat: "Excuse me . . . Is this the place? *Mamma mia*, it's so hot this morning, Brigadie'."

Maione pointed to the corpse, and the photographer, out of breath, arranged his equipment and set up the tripod.

"I'd like to know where people find the energy in this heat to murder each other."

Maione hushed him with a brusque gesture, and asked the young man: "And you, this thing he was working on, you have no idea what it was?"

"He kept it wrapped in a piece of dark cloth, in the safe.

Only once I was safely standing at the door to keep people out, would he go get it. I . . . I've never seen it."

Ricciardi picked up on the hesitation and swooped in: "And I think you *have* seen it. Be careful, this is a murder investigation: if you leave anything out you could wind up in some very hot water."

Sergio was a good boy trying to learn a trade; he was eager, and he'd succeeded in landing a berth with the best craftsman of them all, even if Mastro Nicola had a very particular personality. He didn't want to get in trouble, and that commissario with the strange eyes made him uneasy.

The photographer's flashes lit up the workshop at intervals.

The boy made up his mind to answer.

"Once, Donna Concetta, the lady who stays with Mastro Nicola's *mamma* . . . you know that the *mamma* isn't well, that she's not right in the head . . . came here to say that there were problems at home. Maestro Nicola was gone for five minutes. He told me: stay here and don't move, don't let anyone in. He wrapped his work in the cloth and placed it in the safe, but he was in such a hurry he forgot to lock it, Donna Concetta was yelling, the whole *vicolo* came out to see what has happening . . . and I . . ."

Maione finished his sentence: "And you went and took a look. Is that right?"

The boy looked at him with a guilty expression: "Yes, Brigadie'. I couldn't resist. I was too curious, he'd never hidden his work from me before. Never."

Ricciardi waited; then he asked: "Well? What was it?"

Sergio said, as if speaking to himself: "He was skillful, my old master. The most skillful man around. Sometimes goldsmiths who were more famous than him, late at night, when there was no one around to see, would come here and give him their commissions, and they'd pay him extra not to tell anyone. If you only knew how much of the jewelry now being worn by the finest ladies of the city—women convinced that they're wearing the handiwork of the grand jewelers of Via Toledo—was actually made right here, in this little workshop, by my master."

The photographer murmured that he was done, gathered up his equipment, and left. From the Incurabili Hospital a young physician and two morgue attendants arrived. Maione pointed to the corpse and told them to go ahead.

Ricciardi gestured for Sergio to go on.

"But the thing he was best at was traditional objects. They're done less nowadays, because people don't have the money, but there was a time, Commissa', when the *borgo* made its living from them. And that's when he learned the profession, when these things were still being made."

Ricciardi asked: "What do you mean by traditional objects? What sort of things was Coviello best at?"

The young man looked up and met Ricciardi's gaze; to his surprise, the commissario realized that the apprentice was weeping.

"At ex-votos, Commissa'. Mastro Nicola was making an ex-voto."

LVIII

D ear *Papà*,
the festival of Our Lady of Mount Carmel is drawing near. I can just imagine how busy it's getting in
the streets of the city, how everyone is preparing for the festival, both the strolling vendors and the men and women
who have to see to the various installations. Do you remember, dear *papà*, when I was just a little girl and you took me
to the festival? You'd let me ride on your shoulders, and I
felt like a queen being carried in triumph!

In the island's tranquility, where I can listen to the birds
singing during the day and the crickets chirping at night,
there are times when I miss the hubbub of the city; but I
know that once I return, once I'm back amidst the constant
noise that comes in from the street even with the windows
closed, the cries of the vendors, the screaming fights in
neighboring apartments, the singing, I'll look back on this
silence with nostalgia. We're never satisfied are we, dear
papà? We're always yearning for something else.

My heart is the same way. How can it be, dear *papà*, that
sorrow and suffering, in the end, keep us company? How
can it be that I even miss suffering, tears in my pillow at
night, loneliness and the fear of the future?

And how can it be, on the other hand, that the prospect
of a serene, ordinary life, with a home, children of my own,
and a loving man at my side can somehow frighten me so?

Manfred, the German officer I was telling you about, has

asked for a date. He wants to see me alone, at night, on Friday. He says that he knows a place, here on the island, where when the weather is fine you can see the fireworks as well as if you're sitting on a balcony on the piazza. And he says that he wants to show me the picture he's painting, because by Friday it will be done.

He says that he wants to talk to me. That there's something he must say.

You know, dear *papà*, this date fills me with anxiety. Manfred is a lovely person, sensitive, and I know that he'd never hurt me. He has told me many things about his homeland and his family; and he's told me that in the past few days, during the wonderful summer he's spent on this island, he has realized that life is too important, you can't let it flow past like this, empty and sad, you need to fill it with wonderful things, first and foremost, love. And family. And children.

He was talking about himself. But to my ears he was talking about me.

I'm afraid that I know exactly what he'll say to me, dear *papà*, and I'm terrified at the thought. Because I don't know what my poor heart will want to answer him. I want to live, dear *papà*; and I want to be happy. But I know what I have in my heart.

Yours,
Enrica

Giulio Colombo took off his eyeglasses and placed them on the café table in Gambrinus, next to his empty demitasse. He massaged his forehead with his fingers, in a gesture that came to him when he was concentrating or confused. Right now, he was both.

Enrica was a strong-minded girl. She always had been, since she was a child. Kind, quiet, she never raised her voice, she never objected, she stayed calm and never allowed herself to venture into drawn-out, fruitless arguments, but she never showed indecision. And yet what emerged from this last letter were worry and uncertainty.

Even though it was hard for a father to admit, by now his daughter was a grown woman and no longer a little girl, and he ought to rejoice in the fact that she was being courted; all the more so since the man courting her, as she made clear in her own descriptions, had every quality essential to capturing her interest: he was handsome, mature but not old, and had an important position. And, most of all, he showed genuine feelings for her, to the point that he spoke to her of an emptiness in his life to be filled, of family. What more could he ask for?

Instead—and this was the point, the reason for the headache that Giulio felt coming on—Enrica was worried and unhappy. As if she were being marched to her death.

He tried to put himself in his daughter's place. The similarity, the profound resemblance that had always tied them together allowed them to understand each other at a glance. He need only read between the lines.

He picked up Enrica's letter. What was really written in it? What had his daughter been trying to tell him, when she wrote him about that appointment?

Giulio knew that he belonged to another generation, and that he could not entirely understand the things that young people were experiencing these days. Politics and society were changing faster than he could imagine. He wasn't even sixty years old, and already he felt like an old man.

He worried about his children, his young grandchild, for the times he was afraid they were going to have to live in; he could hear once again the rattling of sabers, less than twenty years after the end of a war that had taken hundreds of thousands of lives and had brought an entire continent to its knees. It seemed as if all that had been forgotten, and once again he heard talk of grandeur and destiny, of a brilliant future and the coming struggle. Much of the happiness that young people would manage to win for themselves and, more importantly, much of the unhappiness that would befall them, was entirely out of their control; nor was it within the control of the generation that preceded them. It wouldn't, other words, be controlled by men like him.

He tried to imagine his Enrica married to a German; in a foreign land, perhaps safe from the terrible winds of war that he was reading about in the evening newspaper, or hearing about in the proclamations on the radio. Far from a place where all it took was the whisper of an informant, or an anonymous note, to send someone into internal exile or get them beaten bloody and thrown into prison. Far away, married to a well respected, beloved officer of the German army. Far away, and safe.

Or maybe not. Maybe in the elections that, he had read, would be held at the end of that sweltering July, Germany too would become an unsafe place. And Enrica would be trapped there, unable even to take refuge in the arms of her *papà*.

But he was certain, knowing her as he did, that Enrica didn't even consider the problem. He was certain that his little girl was strong enough to take on any challenge, once she'd made up her mind. And that was exactly the point: making up her mind. Choosing between love, the kind that grabs you by the guts whether or not it has a future, and reason, the faculty that helps you to distinguish between what's better and what's worse.

He had no doubts as to what his wife would say if he confided the question to her: she'd celebrate, delighted that finally her greatest source of concern, her eldest daughter, still unmarried at the age of twenty-five or close to it, had found an opportunity to settle down. That was why Enrica had said nothing about it in her official letters, those playful, cheerful letters that she sent home. That was why the tone of the letters that she sent to him at the shop was so very different.

Giulio Colombo ordered another espresso, even though he

was well aware that this was his third and that he ought to be heading back to the shop, at that hour probably packed with customers asking for him. He looked at the letter, a sheet of paper, harmless enough in appearance, on the café table in Gambrinus. What were you really trying to tell me, my darling? What's written between the lines of your letter?

Suddenly it was painfully clear to him what Enrica had been asking, when she wrote about that Friday appointment with Manfred.

It was a plea for help.

LIX

Ricciardi stared at Nicola Coviello's apprentice in surprise: "Ex-voto? What do you mean, an ex-voto?
"Yes, Commissa'. What do you call them? Those objects
that you donate to the church, dedicated to saints, for a grace
received or in order to ask for one."

Maione broke in: "The commissario knows perfectly well
what ex-votos are. He wants to know what kind of ex-voto."

Sergio lowered his voice, tense, as if anxious not to let his
boss overhear him. The morgue attendants had untied the
corpse from the rafter and laid it on the floor, where the physician was performing a rapid examination. The noises made the
boy jump, though he continued to obstinately face the wall, so
he wouldn't have to look.

"I saw that he'd just started working on the engravings,
Commissa'. But it was very beautiful. He . . . he had a kind of
magic in his hands. There was no one else like him."

Ricciardi was starting to run out of patience: "Yes, but what
was it? What did it depict, what was it shaped like?"

"A heart, Commissa'. It was a heart with a flame over it, big,
and all in solid gold. It must have been worth a lot of money."

An object of great value, and a man in a great mood who
had killed himself after being the last person to see a murder
victim alive. The picture was getting complicated.

Maione asked: "Who has the key to the safe now?"

"I don't know, now. He . . . he kept the keys to everything,
to the shop, the safe, and his apartment, in his pocket, hooked

with a fob chain to his waistcoat pocket. They were always on him. I didn't check to see if . . . if he still has them."

Maione and Ricciardi turned to look at the corpse, which the young physician was still examining. The brigadier went over to him: "Dotto', forgive me: can I ask if you're almost done?"

The young man got to his feet, adjusted the gold-rimmed spectacles on his nose, and cleared his throat. He was thin, looked younger than thirty, and the center part in his hair was so perfect it seemed it had been drawn with a ruler.

"It's certainly a suicide, Brigadie'. There are no signs of a fight, nor are there contusions of any kind. The rope seems to be the kind used to moor boats, it was neither greased nor soaped, so it jammed, and the poor man died of suffocation. Not a nice death. He hauled himself up by himself, using his own bare hands, which show marks from his grip on the rope: he must have had exceptionally powerful arms. Sure, he was light, skinny as he was, but still, it took considerable strength. In any case, based on the stiffness of the corpse and the hypostatic stains, I would say that death took place three or four hours ago, at most."

Ricciardi asked: "Doctor, do you see any signs of disease or illness? Anything that might have led him to . . ."

". . . to actually kill himself? No, Commissa', I really don't think so. Certainly a quick glance at these deformities, his kyphosis, suggests his life can't have been easy, but I don't think he was suffering from any extreme pain. He was healthy. I'll be able to tell you more after the autopsy, of course."

Maione had gone over to take a look at the clothing: "Ah, here they are, the keys. Just like the boy told us."

He picked them up and shook them so they jangled. The apprentice jumped and put both hands on his face. Ricciardi nodded, and Maione headed over to the heavy safe in the corner of the room. He opened the massive door and bent over to peer inside. Then he turned around: "Nothing, Commissa'.

There are just a couple of empty boxes, some notes with columns of numbers, and that's all."

Ricciardi looked at the boy: "When did you last see him working on that object?"

"Last night, when I left. I think he must have been putting the finishing touches on it: there were certain noises he made, clucking noises, whenever he was putting the finishing touches on something, Commissa'."

"And he was cheerful, you said."

"And how. I'd never seen him like that."

There was just no figuring it out. Who had ordered the object from Coviello? And when had Coviello delivered it? Was there a connection to Iovine's death? And most important of all, why did the goldsmith kill himself, taking all the answers with him to the grave?

The corpse was loaded into a wooden casket and then into the morgue's van, under the curious eyes of the many windows overlooking the *vicolo*, as well as of Donna Enza and Donna Amalia, those watchful sentinels. Ricciardi touched the apprentice's shoulder: "He's gone. You can turn around now. I'd like you to examine the workshop carefully and tell me if there's anything there now that wasn't there before, or if anything that should be there is missing, aside from the ex-voto we were discussing."

The young man slowly turned around. His eyes went immediately to the rafter at the center of the ceiling, from which his employer had hanged himself. Perhaps at that moment, thought Ricciardi, the boy was able to picture the man as, in the dim light, he grabbed the rope, hoisted himself up, and slipped his head through the noose, only to let himself drop; and perhaps he felt pity for that deformed body, those powerful, sensitive hands, that silent, grieving soul.

The apprentice began to cry. Maione coughed, touched. Ricciardi, saddened, allowed himself a glance at the shadow in

the corner that kept repeating, from the mouth with its
bulging black tongue and the rivulet of red drool: *the bottom
of your heart.*

But whose heart?

After blowing his nose on his sleeve, the boy began explor-
ing the workshop. He moved objects aside, lifted benches and
stools, checked racks on the wall.

Then he came to a stop behind the workbench, in the exact
spot where Coviello sat when he was working, in the cone of
light from the oil lamp. He reached out a hand, then drew it
back. Then, he pointed with a trembling finger: "Right here,
Commissa'. Here. This wasn't here, I'm sure of it."

Ricciardi drew closer. At the edge of the workbench, carved
with some pointed tool so masterfully that it appeared to have
been written with pen and ink, a few words stood out in all
capital letters:

AT LAST I CAN DEPART

The commissario raised his eyes and found himself staring
at the facing wall, at the old calendar with its faded drawing of
a steamship. Behind him, equally faded, Our Lady of Mount
Carmel was tenderly caressing Her child.

What could have made the goldsmith feel he was *finally*
free to make that last, definitive departure? Ricciardi turned to
the boy, the only person he knew of who had been in contact
with that shy, silent man, with the exception of the late professor: "Listen, Sergio. Do you remember Iovine, who commissioned the jewelry from Coviello?"

"Yessir, Commissa', I remember him. He's the one who
wanted the two identical rings. Those are major rings, they cost
as much as an apartment: the diamonds are large and pure,
especially the diamond on the second ring, the one that was
made afterward. He must have been very rich, that professor.

It was after he finished those rings that my master stopped taking on new work."

"And do you remember how many times he came, and what was said?"

Sergio concentrated: "Twice when I was here, Commissa'. He said that his wife had been given Mastro Nicola's name by some girlfriends of hers, and that was why he had come to ask him to do this work for him. Then, when he came back, he said that he needed another ring for another person, and that he was relying on my master's discretion."

That matched what they already knew. Ricciardi sighed, defeated.

Then Sergio said: "I remember it clearly, because the first time he came, it was the day after the lady with the veil."

Maione practically jumped into the air: "What lady with the veil?"

"She came here late one evening, Mastro Nicola was teaching me how to work with coral. She knocked on the door, she was wearing a hat with a dark veil, and I couldn't see her face. Mastro Nicola said: we're closed, come back tomorrow. And she said: tomorrow, there are no steamships departing. Then Mastro Nicola told me to leave immediately."

The brigadier asked: "What was this lady like? Tall, short, young, old? And what did Coviello do?"

The apprentice shifted uneasily.

"She was normal, neither young nor old, neither tall nor short. But Mastro Nicola turned white as a sheet, and his graver dropped out of his hand. I asked whether he felt all right: he looked as if he'd seen a ghost. But he just told me again to leave, and in a hurry."

Ricciardi pressed further: "And the next day, did he say anything?"

"Nothing. A few days later I asked him if the lady had commissioned some new work from him, and he raised his voice: what lady? There's no lady. You must have dreamed her. That's why I remember her: because of what Mastro Nicola said to me."

At last I can depart, Ricciardi read on the edge of the workbench in the silence that followed. *The bottom of your heart*, the image of the dead goldsmith murmured from the shadowy corner.

He felt exhausted. Maybe it was that heavy air. He needed to get out of the workshop.

Outside, in the heat of the rising sun, Ricciardi decided that at last he had a lead.

LX

On the way back to police headquarters, Ricciardi and Maione found themselves plunged back into the dark thoughts and glum moods that had oppressed them that morning. They were both wrapped up in the same fear. How little of themselves had they devoted to that investigation? How badly had they been distracted by their personal problems?

Ricciardi had the impression he now possessed all the elements he needed to arrive at the solution, but he couldn't find the thread, the connection between the individual fragments that would allow him to put together the picture.

Maione said: "I can't imagine why Coviello killed himself. He was untroubled, in fact he was downright cheerful, according to what the boy told us. He was completing a major project, so major he was even keeping it a secret from his own apprentice, then he finished it and killed himself. But why?"

Ricciardi was walking with his head down, his hands stuffed in his pockets. An unruly lock of hair dangled over his forehead.

"I don't know, Raffaele. I wonder whether there could be some connection between the veiled woman and this ex-voto. Whether the secret client was her. But if she was the one who commissioned such a significant project, why didn't she go to Coviello's workshop more than once, to see how the work was coming along?"

Maione mopped the sweat from his brow every three paces or so. The sun beat down mercilessly.

"And another thing, Commissa', is there some connection

between Coviello's suicide and the professor's murder? There's no suicide note, and he didn't say anything to anyone. Maybe they're two unrelated incidents."

Ricciardi made a face: "One man delivers jewelry to another, who is tossed out a window a few minutes later; the first man is the last person to see the other man alive, and he has probably met or glimpsed the murderer who was waiting outside the office, and then he kills himself. I don't believe in coincidences, Raffaele. Two fatal events just a few days apart and a single person as the common denominator: Coviello. It seems unlikely to me that there are no correlations. We just need to identify them."

They'd reached the door to Ricciardi's office. As he opened it, the commissario perceived a vague, spicy scent of perfume and the thought of Livia was promptly confirmed by her physical presence. She was sitting in front of his desk.

He felt annoyed at that invasion of his personal space: how dare she enter his office in his absence?

"What are you doing here? Who let you in?"

Livia turned a hesitant smile in Riccardi's direction, but the spoken answer came from the occupant of the other chair, concealed behind the coat rack: "Oh, here he is, our man Ricciardi, at last! It's a good thing I happened to meet the lovely lady, who was wandering the halls; while you, Ricciardi, spend your time pursuing yet another criminal, such an important visitor—and let me repeat: *important*—is forced to wait for you here. What on earth were you thinking?"

At the sound of Garzo's voice, Maione, behind Ricciardi's back, emitted a dull snarl, like a dog would, sighting a cat.

The commissario replied, courteous and cold: "*Buongiorno*, Dottore. Yes, in fact we were out on duty. I don't know if you've heard about the suicide of the prime witness in the Iovine case, but we'd been to examine the scene and . . ."

Garzo waved one hand in the air, as if he were shooing away a fly: "Yes, yes, I know. Work. But it's also your job to look out for the safety of the important individuals who live in our city. And to ensure that the events, let me repeat, the events that are being held here go off without a hitch, so that they can bask in the prominence they deserve. That's why Signora Livia came to visit us—to come to an understanding about these security measures."

Ricciardi's tone remained dry: "With all due respect, Dottore, I believe that a murder and a suicide are slightly more urgent than a masquerade ball that . . ."

He was interrupted by a falsetto shriek: "What? A masquerade ball? But . . . but you never told me *that*, my dear lady! What a wonderful idea, this party will go down in city history! I would imagine that even in Rome the personalities—and let me repeat: the *personalities*—that you've invited will be over the moon with delight! I have to tell you that when I received the invitation, for which I must thank you again, I felt honored and happy, and I felt even more keenly than before a responsibility to ensure the highest possible level of security by means of a surveillance plan that I worked on myself and which I will submit for your perusal."

Livia was ill at ease; she sensed Ricciardi and Maione's hostility and kept her eyes glued to the commissario's expressionless face as she replied to Garzo: "I certainly would have told you, Dottore, but it's still two days away. I didn't want to interfere with your work, and . . ."

Garzo laughed noisily: "But my *cara, cara* Signora, this is work too, you know! I always tell my wife: work, before all else. But a party, and a masquerade party to boot! Our man Ricciardi lets himself get carried away with investigations into street crime, and that's very much to his credit, but your party is also a matter of public security, given the prominent personalities—and let me repeat: the *personalities*—that will be attending!"

Ricciardi felt he had to say something: "Dottore, please forgive me, but we can't stop our work on this investigation: as you know very well, time is a crucial factor."

Livia started to stand up.

"Certainly, Dottore, Ricciardi has a point. For that matter, the only reason I came by was to inquire after the health of Signora Rosa, and . . ."

Garzo interrupted: "Ah, right, yes, Ricciardi, I heard that your servant had an apoplectic fit. How is she?"

Maione took a step forward and blurted out in an exceptionally harsh voice: "Signora Rosa is no servant, Dotto'. Signora Rosa is a family member to the commissario—and let me repeat myself: a *family member*—and she alone is more important than all of police headquarters including the top brass,—and let me repeat: the top brass."

In the awkward silence that ensued, Garzo, as he always did when he was irritated, sat with his mouth partly open; he blinked repeatedly and his throat turned red in patches. He was about to deliver a stinging retort to Maione, who was staring at him grimly, but Livia didn't give him the opportunity: "The brigadier is quite right, Dottore: Signora Rosa is an exceptional woman, and I'm very fond of her. One of those rare people who have the privilege of winning the affection of everyone they meet. I would take any offense paid to her just as if it were directed at me."

Garzo had all the shortcomings in the world, but he was also exceptionally quick on his feet, able to adopt with extraordinary rapidity whatever position best served his own self-interest.

"Why, of course, Signora. And we at police headquarters care very much about the family members of the men who work with us. Why, I'd venture to say that we're all just one great big family. Well, Ricciardi, and how is this dear lady doing?"

The commissario whispered a reply: "These aren't matters that can be solved easily, Dottore. I'm glad to be able to say that she's in excellent hands, perhaps the best: Dr. Modo, at Pellegrini Hospital."

Garzo made a face: "Ah, yes, Modo. A singular individual, from what I've heard. I believe I've seen a confidential report or two . . . but we'll drop that. All right then, shall we talk about the security plans for our—and I venture to call it: *our*—party, my dear lady?"

Livia, unlike Garzo, was capable of taking the room's temperature. She looked Ricciardi in the eye and said, in her deep, unflustered voice: "Dottor Garzo, I believe that the commissario and the brigadier really have very different matters on their minds just now. But I'd consider myself truly fortunate to have a chance to discuss it with you . . . Perhaps you could invite me to your office so we could talk about it more freely, don't you think?"

Garzo happily leapt to his feet: "Why, certainly, Signora, what an honor. Please, come right this way: I'll ask my assistant Ponte to arrange for an excellent espresso to be brought up, and you can tell me all about the party. A masquerade party, we were saying? And with what theme? I hope my wife doesn't kill me when she finds out that she'll have to find herself a costume on such short notice. In fact," he said, laughing jovially, "she's sure to kill me!"

Maione, under his breath but within Ricciardi's hearing, said: "And she'll be doing us all a favor, your wife will."

Livia smiled at Garzo: "Lead the way, Dottore. I'll catch up with you right away, let me just say goodbye to these two gentlemen."

"Don't make me wait too long, though. As I always say: work before all else!"

Maione nodded to Ricciardi and headed in the opposite direction: "Commissa', I'll see you later."

Once they were alone, Livia laid a gloved hand on Ricciardi's arm: "I'm so sorry, *caro*. I happened to run into him outside your office, I asked him whether you were here, and I was turning to leave, but he insisted on letting me in. I never would have dared do such a thing."

The commissario nearly exploded: "Livia, I've told you before: you come here to police headquarters too often. You know that when I'm working, I . . ."

She interrupted him with a bitter laugh: "Work before all else, of course. Listen to me, Ricciardi, let's not mince words here: I'm a woman, and I have feelings. And I'm actually not stupid. You're having a terrible time, I know how dear Rosa is to you: you're not sleeping, you're not eating, look at the state you're in, you haven't even shaved. You must, you absolutely must let me love you and take care of you."

Ricciardi ran a hand over his face, realizing that the woman had a point.

"Livia, there's a time and a place for everything. If we're going to talk about this sort of thing, I need to have a clear head, and I . . ."

"You can't choose to remain alone. Whatever secret sorrow you have, you have to share it with someone. No one can live alone, remember that. That's the real inferno, the only hell that exists here on earth: solitude. Take it from me, I've experienced it even when I was surrounded by crowds of people. You need to throw open this damned locked door that you have in your chest. You have to, do you understand me?"

Ricciardi stared blankly. Loneliness is hell on earth. A hell, he thought, to which I've condemned myself since I was a child. The hell of my madness. *The bottom of your heart*, the memory of Coviello's phantom told him. The bottom of your heart.

He looked at the woman, who still had her hand on his arm. Her eyes were black as night, her mouth was partly open, her cheeks were red from her impassioned speech. What did she lack? What was it she didn't have?

"Livia, dear, it's just a difficult, complicated moment. We can talk about it some other time, if you like. But first let me get through this."

She stared at him in silence. Then she said: "I'm . . . I'm going to do something, at this party. Something I care very much about, and I'm going to do it for you. Whether or not you're there."

She brushed his lips with a kiss and left.

LXI

Maione was furious. With Garzo, who was an idiot, an uncouth imbecile; but also with Lucia, Pianese, and even Coviello, who had killed himself for no conceivable reason.

But most of all he was angry with himself. He'd been a bad husband, if Lucia was cheating on him; a bad father, who had by his own stupid example induced poor Luca to follow in his footsteps and get himself killed; a bad policeman, who instead of focusing on an investigation was using valuable time when he was on duty to assault some guy on the street. He could sense the opinion he had of himself crumbling, along with the life he'd built for himself through hard work and pain. And he was afraid.

His shirt unbuttoned, his face cradled in his hands, he sat alone behind a closed door in the room where he had a desk, a chair, and a cot where he slept when he was working the graveyard shift. This heat, he thought to himself. This terrible, miserable heat, that kills all desire to move around, to live, that shatters your thoughts into pointless jagged shards. It's no accident that the inferno is hot.

Someone knocked at the door. Maione called out, brusquely: "Come in!"

Camarda appeared at the door, gripping a struggling child by the scruff of the neck: "Brigadie', forgive me, I didn't want to bother you, but this kid here says that he has something he needs to tell you."

Maione's terrible mood was the talk of the day among the

rank and file at police headquarters, and before Camarda decided to bring the boy into the brigadier's presence, he'd thought long and hard; then the fear that it might be something important had outweighed the fear of earning a kick in the ass, and now here he was. Stepping cautiously, though.

Maione observed the boy. He didn't know him: just one more *scugnizzo* of the thousands that infested the city's streets, playing pranks on passersby and hitching rides on the city buses by grabbing onto the overhead electric trolley poles. "What are you doing in here?" he asked.

The boy looked at him with defiance in his eyes: "Unless you let me go right now, I won't tell you anything."

Maione gestured to Camarda, who released him. The boy, who couldn't have been older than seven or eight, shot the police officer a vicious glare as he rubbed his neck. Then he turned to look at Maione: "I can't speak unless it's you and me and no one else."

Amused in spite of himself by the boy's formal tone, the brigadier nodded in Camarda's direction, who reluctantly left the room, closing the door behind him and leaving the two alone. Maione said: "Well? Who are you, what's your name?"

The boy cleared his throat and intoned in a stentorian voice: "Do you confirm that you are Brigadier Raffaele Maione?"

"Yes, that's me, but . . ."

"Then I've been sent to tell you that there's a lady at the Café Caflisch, in the inside salon, waiting to speak to you. You must come alone, make sure that no one sees you arrive, and give me a tip for my service."

The brigadier had listened openmouthed.

"How about if, instead of giving you a tip, I give you a good hard kick in the ass and just stay right here, what do you say to that?"

The boy didn't bat an eye.

"The lady said that it would be all the worse for you. That's what she said. And anyway, Brigadie', no disrespect, but by the time you get around this desk I'll be halfway up the hill to Capodimonte."

Maione would gladly have burst out laughing, but he didn't want to set a bad example. He dug in his pocket for a coin and tossed it in the boy's direction; the kid snatched it out of the air, snapped a passable military salute, opened the door, and shot out at top speed through the legs of the astonished Camarda.

"Brigadie', forgive me, but the kid, that *guaglione*, told me that he knew you and . . ."

Maione looked at him disgustedly as he donned his uniform cap: "You're useless creatures, that's all you are. A person could walk in here, stab someone to death, and leave, and you'd never even notice. Get out of my way, go on, I've got work to do."

The Café Caflisch was one of the most elegant places in the city. Maione made his way through the crowded mass of customers who were sipping tea and slurping espresso and eating *sfogliatella* pastries and rum babas, then headed for the inside salon as the *scugnizzo* had told him to do.

He'd made quite sure no one had followed him, by taking a series of narrow *vicoli*. He didn't like secret meetings, but he wasn't about to ignore an opportunity that might prove helpful to the challenging investigation that lay before them. Perhaps he ought to have alerted the commissario, but he thought there was a chance Ricciardi might still be busy with the widow Vezzi, a woman who, by the way, Maione would have been happy to see at his superior's side, especially now that Signora Rosa's condition seemed to promise nothing good.

A uniformed waiter blocked his way.

"Sorry, the salon is reserved."

Maione looked him sternly in the eye: "I know. Apparently I'm expected."

The man shot a suspicious glance around him, making certain that no one was listening, then asked in a low voice: "Then, you would be Brigadier Raffaele Maione?"

Maione was starting to lose his patience. He pushed his face close to the waiter's and hissed: "Listen, youngster, I am who I am, and that's all you need to know. Either you let me in, or I'll kick your ass sideways and then I'll shut down this café for the next month, what do you say?"

The waiter stepped aside. Maione stepped in and shut the door behind him.

Seated facing the entrance was a tall woman in a flowered dress wearing long black gloves and a hat adorned with a thick veil that covered her face. Maione's mind immediately raced to the mysterious visitor that poor Coviello's apprentice had mentioned.

He went over to the table and introduced himself, raised his hand to the visor of his uniform cap, and asked: "You wished to see me?"

The woman laughed lightly and lifted her veil. A disconcerted Maione found himself face-to-face with the unmistakable features of Bambinella.

"Brigadie', *buongiorno*. You didn't recognize me at all, did you? Of course you didn't, when I decide to clean myself up, I'm the prettiest girl in this whole city."

"Bambine', give me one good reason, and it had better be a really good one, why I shouldn't strangle you right here with my own two hands. Have you gone stark raving mad? What is this playacting? What do you think, that I have nothing better to do? And all this secrecy . . . Do you mind telling me what on earth you were thinking?"

The *femminiello* snapped open a fan with an affected gesture and started fanning herself, batting her eyelashes as she did: "Oooh, *mamma mia*, Brigadie', how fiery you are! Don't you notice how hot it is out? Take a seat, now, come on, we need to have ourselves a talk. What will you have, an espresso? A pastry? Order, order, don't be shy: it's on me."

Maione felt as if he was trapped in a nightmare.

"Excuse me, but would you tell me what you're doing, dressed like this, in the private salon of one of the most exclusive cafés in this city? And why is it your treat, what, did you win the lottery or something?"

Bambinella laughed with her characteristic whinny, covering her mouth with the fan: "No, no, what lottery; it's just that the waiter you saw outside is a customer of mine, and when I ask him to do me a favor, he just can't say no. I ought to tell you that he likes it when I wait for him in my fishnet stockings and . . ."

Maione clapped his hands over his ears: "Stop! Tell me one more word about the things you do when you work and I'll absolutely have to take you in. But before I do, I'll smash your face in and claim that you were resisting arrest!"

Bambinella assumed a bitter look: "There. That's my reward for doing a favor for a friend. After all, I come all the way down here for your sake, at the risk of getting into serious trouble—because if anyone sees me talking to you they're likely to assume that I'm your informant—and that's the thanks I get."

Maione threw his arms out wide, disconsolately: "What do you mean, aren't you my informant? Sometimes I think that if someone murdered you, they'd be doing me a favor."

The *femminiello* replied, offended: "Why, what a thing to say! I tell you things because you're a friend, it's not as if I'm an informant! I'm a respectable girl, I am! Anyway, this time I had no choice but to run the risk, because it seems to me that the information I have for you is urgent, very urgent indeed: and I couldn't just wait for you to call on me. So I put on my nicest dress, I took care of these disgusting black hairs that just won't stop growing on my thighs—and if it weren't for the hair, let me tell you, I'd have the finest thighs in the city if I do say so myself—and I told Egisto, the waiter and a client of mine, to close off the salon just for me, and here I am. And after all, Brigadie', can you just imagine if someone did kill me? Just think of the newspaper headlines: *Bambinella, the City's Most Beautiful Woman, Murdered. Brigadier Maione, Who Was Secretly in Love with Her, Personally Conducting the Investigation.*"

Maione considered the matter and concluded: "No, I'm not going to wait for someone else to you kill you: I'll do it myself, right now, and rid myself of the bother. I don't want to let anyone else have the honor. I'll give you one minute, and I'm timing you, to tell me what you want, then I'll leave you all alone with your perverted waiter friend."

Bambinella made herself comfortable, put her gloved hands together, and raised her eyes to the ceiling: "Now then, Brigadie', the last time you came to see me you asked about a certain Ferdinando Pianese, known to his friends as Fefè, isn't that right?"

Hearing that name, and remembering, along with it, how he had made illicit use of a police informant for his own personal ends, Maione felt a further pang of annoyance.

"Yes, that's all right, Bambine', forget about it. I don't need to know anymore."

Bambinella's eyes opened wide: "Oh, you don't? Too bad, because I'd rounded up some interesting information. Actually, not interesting: fascinating."

"Well, then, tell me what you know. But be quick about it, I've got work to do."

"Well, the first thing you need to know is that in that apartment house there lives a girlfriend of mine, who used to work in a bordello that's in the Sanità district, but she didn't like working there: soldiers, students, some of them paid, others didn't bother, and even the madam was a filthy character who pretended to pick and choose her clientele but actually didn't give a damn, so finally she said, enough, what am I putting myself through this for, and since she was good at sewing—she tends to put on a few pounds now and then and constantly has to let out her dresses and so got quite good at it—well . . ."

Maione roared: "Bambine', I'll kill you right now and sneak out of here, that way they'll charge your waiter with the murder and I'll be rid of you both, once and for all! Just tell your story!"

"Hey, Brigadie', if you do like that you're going to make me lose the thread of my story! In any case, this girlfriend of mine found a job as a seamstress and the lady, her boss, is very happy with her work. They have plenty of business and . . . all *right*, Brigadie', why, what a grouch you are this morning! It can't be good for your health, with all this heat! Well, to make a long story short, she's on good terms with the doorman of the building, in fact, if you ask me she services him every once in a while, just to keep her hand in the game. Well, and do you know what she told me?"

Maione was suddenly alert: "No, what did she tell you?

"That Fefè is under surveillance by the Fascist police, that's what she told me. And that's nothing! Since yesterday, Fefè has locked himself in his apartment and won't open the door to anyone. It seems that he's scared of something, I hear that he told the doorman not to let anyone upstairs, to tell anyone who asks that Fefè left for America, that he's not home. Just think that he gave the doorman money to have his groceries delivered, even though everyone knows that he's a first-class penny-pincher."

Maione was crushed.

"So what? Why are you bothering to tell me this?"

"Listen closely, Brigadie', because the best is yet to come. Fefè told the doorman not to let anyone up, and especially not to let two people in under any circumstances, even if it costs him his life: one is a tall strapping policeman, very angry, whose name he didn't know but that the doorman would recognize because he's a kind of monster, violent and sweaty. Strange, eh?"

Maione mopped his brow.

"Strange, but I continue not to see why I should give a damn about this story."

"Fair enough, you shouldn't care at all, I was just telling you as a curiosity. The other person that Fefè has refused to see—well, that's something even more curious. The Marchesa di Morsano. Do you know who she is?"

"No. Who is she?"

"The Marchesa Lucrezia di Morsano is an aging harridan who only recently became Fefè's lover, but whom he'd been wooing for years, very rich and very generous. Blonde. Ugly as sin, but blonde. Isn't that strange?"

"Isn't what strange?"

"It's strange that, after all this time that he's been courting her, now he refuses to see her. Also because poor Fefè by now was seeing her exclusively. He'd decided to make an honest man of himself, in a certain sense. Evidently, his encounter with this policeman scared him so badly that he's more or less collapsed."

Maione said nothing. Bambinella smiled like a sphinx who had gone a little overboard putting on her makeup that morning.

"Then my girlfriend told me something else. Apparently no more than a week ago a lady came in to see her employer, and said that if there was any extra work for a seamstress she'd be eager to try her hand at it. This is a respected dressmaker's shop, you know, Brigadie', it's not as if they take in just anyone who shows up. There's more: this lady has children at home, and maybe there's a pigheaded husband to deal with, and she only wanted to work an hour or two a day, in the afternoon, who knows why. She just wanted to make a little extra money to help out her husband, since he seems to be having some financial problems."

Maione was struck dumb. Bambinella went on, unfazed: "And so my girlfriend's employer gave this lady a chance, and it turns out she's good, but really good. So she hired her, but

only for an hour or two a day, and this lady is coming in regularly. The dressmaker's shop, you know, is on the second floor
of the same apartment house that's under surveillance by the
Fascist police. Strange, no?"

The brigadier did his best not to smile, and the effect was
spectacular, his mouth spreading wide under a glare that
remained grim.

"Bambine', I continue not to understand the cause of the
absurd confidences you're imparting to me this morning.
Would you mind explaining why you're telling me all this?"

Bambinella slipped off a glove, uncovering her hairy fore-
arm, and began examining her lacquered fingernails with
ostentatious interest: "No, Brigadie', it's nothing, it's just that I
thought I might tell you that, if you ever happen to run into
this monstrous, strapping, angry, sweaty policeman, you might
want to tell him from me to stop being such an ass; that if he
has a wife—I mean, in the unlikely case that he still does have
one and she hasn't yet told him to go take a hike like he
deserves—that that wife is a veritable saint who not only puts
up with him but even tries to give him a hand in making ends
meet for their family. That he might consider leaving poor Fefè
in peace, since he wants nothing more than to support himself
by taking advantage of his ability to go to bed with a woman
who's ugly as sin, a woman who, poor thing, just wants a little
happiness in her life, homely as she is and married to a
Methuselah to boot. And also you can tell him from me that a
man as charming and handsome as he is, any woman that has
him isn't likely to cheat on him. There. Could you do me this
little favor, then?"

Maione got to his feet and looked long and hard at
Bambinella, who returned the gaze with her large dark eyes.
Then he said: "Bambine', I've never heard of this policeman
you're talking about, and that strikes me as odd, because we
policemen all know each other. But if I were ever to meet him

I'd have to tell him that he's one lucky cop to have the friends that he has, friends who are willing to remind him what an ass he is. I'd tell him: lucky you, that you have such friends. While I, on the other hand, am surrounded by people who never seem to be willing to mind their own damn business, and one of these days I'm probably going to wind up in jail because I'm going to have to slit their throats with my own two hands. That's what I'd tell him."

And, attempting to regain some shred of his lost dignity, he turned to go. Bambinella called after him: "Brigadie', if you slit my throat you'll miss my smile. Believe me, you're missing so much already: ask the waiter on your way out and he can tell you!"

And she laughed, with her usual horsey whinny.

LXII

Ricciardi was standing at his office window, which was thrown wide open to let in a little breeze. The afternoon wasn't bringing relief from the heat, quite the contrary, but the piazza below was bustling; the commissario watched the intersecting trajectories of cars, wagons, carts, trucks, trolleys, electric buses, mothers and nannies with strollers, in a general state of ungovernable and indecipherable chaos.

He would have been almost astonished not to see any collisions; still, he certainly would never have expected to see two fresh fatalities occur right before his eyes, practically simultaneously. He saw them, and he wondered bitterly what kind of a person he might have been without the unfortunate ability he possessed to make out quite distinctly the two new victims, far apart as they were—one at the corner of the entrance to the wharf, the other just a few yards away from the front door of police headquarters. They were victims of distraction, haste, and carelessness, Ricciardi saw. A little girl with a basket who was carrying fish from one of the boats that lay moored below, supplying the nearby market, had been sliced nearly in two by an automobile; and an aged businessman, perhaps a lawyer, had been clipped in the head by the ironshod hoof of a rearing horse.

From that distance, all Ricciardi could pick up from the two victims was a faint murmur. Still, the murmur reached him. The girl was singing the words to a popular song, *Tutta pe' mme*: *pe' dint' all'ombra va 'stu core, ca nun pò durmi'* . . . The man, in contrast, was running some numbers: *two hundred forty lire, less thirty-one makes two hundred and nine, plus twelve gives me . . .* They'd been hurrying. And now they'd never hurry again.

How many things, Ricciardi thought—his arms crossed on his chest, the city below him tossing like a stormy sea—are lost through haste. And if you die, how many more things you lose. Rosa, who was leaving this earth and who perhaps, though his conscious mind was unwilling to admit it, had already left; Enrica, whom he hadn't seen in a long while; Livia, forever awaiting a smile that he was incapable of bestowing. Leaving, waiting. Perhaps returning. Haste.

As usual, almost without realizing it, his thoughts went to the murder he was investigating; perhaps to take his mind off the dark musings that were piling up, Ricciardi began reflecting on Coviello, the goldsmith who had killed himself. Coviello had worked, day and night, on something that had been commissioned by a party who remained unknown. The young man, Sergio, had seen an ex-voto: a heart topped by a flame.

Ricciardi actually knew next to nothing about ex-votos; but he remembered the church in his hometown where his mother and Rosa would take him to Sunday services, and he recalled that on one wall adjoining the altar, topped by a cross and a Christ that was taken out for a procession twice a year, there were a number of strange objects. Once he'd asked his mother what they were, and she had uttered those words: those are ex-votos.

He had been particularly impressed by a small silver leg, rather crudely made, beneath which lay a sort of leather legging, rather timeworn. Rosa had told him the story of a farmer's son who couldn't walk because a horrible sore had formed on his leg, and how he had to wear a bandage and that legging to cover it until, through the direct intervention of the Christ on the cross, it had finally healed. The father, to thank Jesus, had ordered that silver leg and donated it to the church. Laughing, Rosa added that the cost of the ex-voto, however, had almost forced the family into starvation, so in the end the boy's miraculous cure had actually made things worse.

Ricciardi felt a pang in his heart. He didn't know how he'd survive without his *tata*; he missed her intrusiveness, her laugh, and the unconditional love that he'd never again feel on his very skin, the love he'd taken for granted for far too many years.

Haste. Distraction, eyes always trained straight ahead, so little looking back or to either side. What a mistake. You too, Coviello: why were you working with such haste, if you'd already decided to die? Or else, what happened to transport you from an unusually good mood, a newly attained tranquility, to a noose hanging from a ceiling rafter? What was it that made you so frenzied?

Some twenty yards below, a number of strolling vendors were all heading in the same direction, as in a secular variation on a religious procession; one of them, a gigantic man whose self-propelled stall was loaded down with walnuts, hazelnuts, and chestnuts piled high in a spectacular display, swayed under the burden of his merchandise, threatening to crash to the ground. His curses rose to Ricciardi's ears, muddled by the cacophony of the piazza. The commissario thought it was absurd to curse so furiously if the man was going, like the others, to set up his stall near the church of Our Lady of Mount Carmel—in haste, come to think of it—to find a good spot for the impending festival.

Haste, he thought.

Haste. Hurry. Festival, ex-voto, hurry.

With his heart in his throat, he yelled for Maione.

The brigadier's mood had undergone a change for the better so spectacular that even Ricciardi noticed it, though he was preoccupied by a complex set of wheels in his mind that had finally begun to grind and spin. Maione's face, which for the past several days had been furrowed by a network of wrinkles that made him seem much older, was now relaxed and serene; from time to time, he even broke into a cheerful little whistle, as if he were singing some ditty to himself.

As they walked along together, the commissario shot him baffled glances: he was almost more worried by that sudden change than he had been by the bad mood which had preceded it.

Maione burst out in a delighted voice: "Just look at all these people, Commissa'! The voices, the smells, the music. Don't you think they're just wonderful? They're like a symphony, like the band that plays at the Cassa Armonica, the bandstand at the Villa Nazionale: each with an instrument of his own, all of them together playing the music of the city!"

As they pushed their way with greater and greater difficulty through the increasingly packed crowd, Ricciardi shot back: "Raffaele, do you mind telling me what's going on? First all that anger, everything bothered you, everyone got on your nerves, and now you talk to me about the music of the city?"

And Maione replied contentedly: "No, Commissa', it's just that there are times when something opens your eyes. You know those investigations where you try to force evidence and clues to fit in with some preconceived idea you've come up with? And the evidence never really does fit together perfectly, but you never notice that because, by then, like an ass, you've made up your mind and nothing's going to change it. Then, in fact, someone comes along, a man, or maybe a woman, it doesn't matter, tells you something, and your whole view of things changes, and all the evidence and proof slides right into place and everything becomes clear. You know what I mean?"

"Certainly I know what you mean. It's the main risk of the work we do, isn't it? Prejudice. As well as how much time it makes you waste, the way it leads you to make a bunch of mistakes, possibly irreparable ones. Who can say how many innocent people are in prison because of it. And that is precisely why we must move quickly."

They reached their destination and strode through the large entrance.

The interior of the Basilica del Carmine Maggiore, the church of Our Lady of Mount Carmel, resembled a construction site more than a place of worship. The impending festival, an occasion that involved the entire city in an explosion of joy, fire, and dances that had clearly been influenced by pagan celebrations, was heralded by a frantic activity that was evident even along the nave of the beautiful old church.

A dozen or so men were clambering up precarious wooden ladders to hang draperies and festoons in silk and cotton, white and sky-blue, decorating the internal portal and the altars, the columns and the nave. A number of florists were busy replacing flowers that were beginning to wilt in arrangements already laid out for the initial services: green plants beneath the altar, ferns and boxwoods, sky-blue hydrangeas and calla lilies and gladioli in white, while hundreds of roses filled the hot air, along with incense and the melting wax of a thousand candles. The immense, monumental organ located, according to tradition, above the main portal, lowed melodiously in the rehearsals of sacred music that would be played on the day of the festival.

Adding to the confusion, thirty or so of the faithful were tending to candles and pews, trying to make sure that immense space would be able to accommodate all those who would be trying to crowd into it two days from now.

Drawn by the sight of Maione's police uniform, a young friar walked up to them.

"Peace be with you. Is there something I can do for you?"

Ricciardi looked at him. He might have been a little older than twenty-five, and his tonsure and eyeglasses weren't enough to make him seem much older; the brown cassock of the Carmelite order was a little large on him, and he kept his hands inside the sleeves, in the characteristic monkish posture.

Maione, who had removed his cap when he entered the

church, returned the greeting: "Peace be with you, Brother. This is Commissario Ricciardi and I'm Brigadier Maione, from police headquarters. We'd like to speak to whoever receives the ex-votos from the faithful."

The young man's eyes hardened. He strode silently to a recess off the side aisle, where there were no crowds of people engaged in preparations for the festival; still, a couple of men and a woman or two had turned to watch, their curiosity piqued. Tight-lipped, he said: "How dare you? The relations between the church and the faithful are private, top secret. What authorization brings you here?"

The two policemen were surprised by this reaction. Ricciardi said: "Excuse me, I'm not sure I caught your name."

The man held Ricciardi's gaze: "I'm Friar Simone. And let me reiterate, you have absolutely no right to investigate the ex-votos. Or even to see them without our permission."

Maione was disconcerted by the friar's categorical rejection.

"Excuse me, Brother, but aren't the ex-votos on display? Aren't they there for anyone to see?"

The friar shook his head no: "Only a very small portion of them are kept in the vitrines adjoining the altar. Those are on display. And they're all anonymous, except for the ones that bear the names of the faithful, either painted or engraved."

Ricciardi said: "Could you take us to see them, then? We only want to look, not investigate. Will you allow that much?"

The young man nodded mistrustfully, and walked away without inviting the two policemen to follow; they strode after him all the same.

Next to the main altar was a chapel that opened into a smallish room. Both the room and the chapel were lined with ex-votos. Maione, who had clearly been here before, smiled at Ricciardi's gasp of surprise.

There were objects in gold, silver, and painted wood, of all shapes and sizes, several of them quite old. Body parts alternated with hunting scenes, accidents, and shipwrecks depicted on panels; there was quite a lot of silver and gold, and Ricciardi wondered if these ex-votos were truly safe from burglars, even if they were in a sacred edifice.

As if sensing his thoughts, Maione whispered to him: "No one would ever dare to touch any of them, Commissa'. These things belong to Our Lady of Mount Carmel, no one would even think of it."

The most precious objects, especially the jewelry made of gold and precious stones that reflected and splintered the gleam of the candles, were contained in glass vitrines.

Ricciardi asked the friar: "Has one of these been put on display recently? In the last two days, I mean."

"No. The ex-votos are only put on display after an examination and an evaluation by the priory of this monastery. Let me repeat that these are matters over which you have no jurisdiction. Please, if you're not here to pray, I must beg you to leave immediately. And if . . ."

A deep voice from behind them broke in: "Friar Simone, since when do we kick people out of the church? I understand that we're busy preparing for the festival, but this seems a bit much, don't you think?"

They turned and found themselves before an elderly man, dressed exactly like his younger colleague; he was short and his cassock was clean, if obviously worn. But from his blue eyes emanated a liveliness and authority so strong they were almost palpable.

Simone bowed: "Father, I certainly had no intention of kicking anyone out of the church. The gentlemen here are from the . . ."

". . . from the police, I'd have to imagine. Unless the brigadier is an actor or has just left a masquerade party. *Buonasera*, gentlemen. What can we do for you?"

Ricciardi returned the greeting, introduced himself, then

said: "We've come because we need information concerning the ex-votos. One ex-voto in particular, actually. It's just that Friar Simone tells us that unfortunately we are forbidden from obtaining that information. We cannot even lay eyes on the ex-votos, from what we are told."

The old man nodded, pensively. Then he said: "I'm Friar Bartolomeo, the prior of this monastery, and therefore in charge of many things, far too many; the ex-votos among them. My young brother is quite right, the ex-votos are secret: they are inherent in the relationship between the church and the faithful, something that still remains, by God's grace, beyond the reach of human meddling."

Ricciardi replied in a conciliatory tone: "I understand, Father. And believe me when I say that the last thing I'd want is to interfere in such matters, our hands are already full with pain and grief. But this concerns a murder; and I'm determined to leave no stone unturned in my efforts to set things right, and especially to prevent an innocent man from being punished instead of the guilty party."

The prior looked hard at him. Then, as if he'd come to a decision, he said: "Well done, Friar Simone. Now I'll take over. Gentlemen, please come with me."

Going through a door and then down a hallway, they finally emerged in a marvelous cloister, a quadrilateral a good hundred feet on each side, with finely frescoed walls and a luxuriant garden in the center; from there they walked on into a low building with white walls. Friar Bartolomeo made his way up a steep flight of stairs, displaying a youthful agility, then he came to a stop before a heavy door made of dark wood. He pulled a large ring with many keys out of his cassock, opened the door, and invited them to enter.

The prior's office was cool thanks to the high ceiling and the thick walls that kept the temperature low. The few items of furniture were made of heavy, hand-carved wood. There were no concessions to luxury, nor were there decorations, but the impression that Ricciardi had was of a place where great power was administered.

Friar Bartolomeo walked around the desk and took a seat, gesturing to the policemen to do the same. Then he addressed Ricciardi: "Commissario, do go ahead. To take a human life is a mortal sin, an act of arrogance by a human being convinced he can act in God's stead. Not even we can allow such an act to go unpunished."

Ricciardi told the story of Iovine, from the moment the corpse was found at the polyclinic up to what had happened that very morning.

"According to what we've been told by his apprentice, the goldsmith, Nicola Coviello, had been working frantically over the past few days to complete a very valuable ex-voto, an engraved golden heart with a flame on top. I guessed that his haste might have been due to the approaching festival, in part because there's an image of Our Lady of Mount Carmel in his workshop, right above his workbench."

The friar listened attentively: "But couldn't you ask this Coviello?"

Maione and Ricciardi looked at each other, then the brigadier said: "Unfortunately, Father, Coviello took his life this morning. He hanged himself in his workshop."

The prior sat in silence; he joined his hands together and stared down at the top of his desk, and then he crossed himself. He had such a look of sorrow on his face that Ricciardi thought he might have known the goldsmith personally.

Bartolomeo asked: "Could you describe this man to me, Commissario?"

Ricciardi did so, as accurately as he could remember him; eyeglasses with very thick lenses, disproportionately long arms and legs, a figure made ridiculous by a hunchback; he even told him about the change in the man's mood the last time that he'd been seen alive. As he proceeded with the description, the look on the prior's face grew increasingly sorrowful. When he was done, he asked him: "You understand clearly, Father, just how important it is for us to understand the reason for this ex-voto. Who commissioned it, why Coviello's last act before his death was to work on it, and above all why he killed himself. Except for an engraving on his workbench, he didn't leave a word."

Bartolomeo sat for a long time without speaking. Then he stood up and went over to the window: "You know, Commissario, no one is brought face-to-face with the mysteries of the human mind like a priest. In confession, people throw open the door onto certain abysses they have within them, gulfs in which specters of every kind lie concealed. Sometimes a person may choose not to go to confession, to keep their distance from the sacrament. Still, we understand them; perhaps because we are used to looking into and through the eyes of others."

In the cloister, a bird cawed mournfully.

"The man you've described was here very early this morning, before dawn. The Lord willed that he should meet me while I was taking advantage of the early morning hours, after reading Matins with my brothers, to take some time to study before dawn. He appeared at my side, almost frightening me. I asked him what he wanted, and he spoke to me."

Ricciardi wanted the friar to tell him everything he could remember: "What was he like, Father? Did he seem upset, anxious, confused?"

The prior turned to look at him, his fingers clasped behind his back: "No, Commissario, quite the opposite. That was what I was trying to tell you, earlier. There was no anguish, fear, or despair in him; nor was there resignation or anger. He was a man at peace, tranquil and serene. That is why the news you've given me is so upsetting, and why I asked you to confirm with a description. After all these years I thought I could recognize a human being on the verge of an act as terrible as suicide, but instead, as you can see, I was wrong."

Ricciardi understood him perfectly.

"What did he tell you, Father?"

"He told me his name, and his profession. He had a bundle, which he gave to me. He told me that it was a gift from him to the Virgin Mary, and he asked me if I would display it on the day of the festival."

Maione asked: "Did he say if it was on the behalf of some other person? Did he say by chance whether it had been commissioned by a woman?"

"A woman? No, Brigadier. He told me that it was an object that he had made for the Madonna, to whom he was particularly devoted. For that matter, I remember that man very clearly because he attended all the services every Sunday, and often during the week as well. He really must have been very devoted to Our Lady."

Ricciardi said nothing. He had placed his hope in the mysterious female visitor's mission, and he'd thought he would be able to track her down to learn what bond linked her to Coviello, and what had caused him to kill himself. At last he said: "Can we see this object, Father? Perhaps it can help us to understand."

The prior said: "I can't see how it would. However exquisite the workmanship, the fact that it was donated by a man who then killed himself strips it of all value, and there is no way that I can comply with poor Coviello's request. The Virgin Mary, on the day of Her festival, certainly cannot wear a bloodstained jewel."

Ricciardi decided to insist: "Just one more reason, Father, not to conceal it from us. If it cannot be a venerated object because the man who made it and donated it died a suicide, and therefore its mere venal value can only serve to do some act of charity, perhaps in that case showing it to us would not violate your rules."

The prior sighed: "All right. You're probably correct."

He went over to a tall, deep cabinet. Once again, he pulled

out the ring with the many keys and opened it. The policemen glimpsed, beyond the friar's diminutive physique, a great many metallic objects that glittered in the light of the setting sun; the man picked up something and quickly shut the door, turning the key several times in the lock. Then he came back to the desk carrying a bundle wrapped in dark cloth that Ricciardi recognized as the one that Coviello had wrapped up hurriedly and stowed away in the safe the first time they had come to his workshop.

The friar stepped over to the desk and spread the cloth out on the surface. At the center, gleaming brightly like a small sun, was Coviello's heart.

It was the size of a clenched fist, and it was topped by a nine-pointed flame. It had been carefully polished, and the front, the part that was visible as it lay on the cloth, featured very fine arabesques that almost looked as if they'd been embroidered.

It was absolutely beautiful, Ricciardi thought; it had every right to serve as the artistic last will and testament of a great craftsman.

He asked the prior: "Does it have a meaning, Father? Does it mean something, in and of itself?"

The friar made a baffled face: "Hard to say. Votive offerings, you see, haven't always been the same throughout history: it's a testimonial, a sort of signature on the pact between man and God or His saints. Every object can have a different meaning, even if they have roughly the same shape: as you must know, ex-votos take the shape of diseased and cured organs, or the ones on behalf of which a grace is being asked. The material used symbolizes the seriousness of the disease or the importance of the grace that is being requested. Gold, obviously, means something of maximum gravity. The donor does what he can, and at times the funds at his disposal don't allow him to allocate large sums, but the faith that underlies the gift is almost always dictated by immense hope or true gratitude. A heart with a flame, like this one, can have an array of meanings. It's a burning heart, either burning with grief or pain or else with love, like the heart of Jesus: a flame that does not consume, and that is never consumed. An eternal love, like the love of the Savior for His children."

Ricciardi murmured: "An eternal love. A love that extends to death. A love that doesn't end with death, that turns death into a departure."

The friar and Maione looked at each other, perplexed.

The commissario seemed to be praying: "A love that is never consumed, you said. There is no point in fighting such love. Better to put an end to it." He turned toward the friar, pointing to the heart on the desk: "May I?'"

The friar nodded. Ricciardi reached out and carefully took the object.

It was massive, a single block of solid gold. It must be worth a fortune. Ricciardi thought about how many years of obscure and wonderful work Coviello must have done, losing his sight and his health by the faint light of the oil lamp, to piece together enough gold to complete that object of immense beauty.

He turned it in his hands, admiring the workmanship from up close. He tried to sense, from the smooth decorated surface, the emotion, the passion with which its maker had infused it; he tried to recognize, on the metal polished mirror-bright, Coviello's oblong irregular face, all his sorrow. A flame that is never consumed, that continues to burn.

The inferno. The inferno in a heart.

Ricciardi noticed an arabesque, at the top of the heart, offset slightly with respect to the rest of the design.

"Father, do you have a magnifying glass?"

The friar nodded, picked up a crystal circle with a silver handle, and extended it to Ricciardi.

The commissario held the lens close to the heart and peered through it.

Then he read the name that was at the bottom of the heart of Mastro Nicola Coviello.

LXIII

A cross from the front gate that constituted the entrance to the ancient convent that had become the general hospital's complex, there was a café: a place of refreshment for the family members of the sick in search of a break from their sorrow and worry, and for the physicians and nurses who felt the need to get a little time away from a workplace that could easily become oppressive and sad.

Ricciardi was sitting there, at a table from which he could clearly see the front door, that Thursday morning prior to the final celebrations of the festival of Our Lady of Mount Carmel.

He was waiting for someone.

After leaving the church and the prior, he'd spent all of Wednesday evening at Rosa's bedside. The old woman's breathing seemed rougher and more labored than ever. He'd asked for an explanation from Bruno, who'd stopped by more than once, and his friend had simply shrugged. At a certain point he'd placed a hand on Ricciardi's shoulder and uttered two words: brace yourself. As if it were possible to brace yourself for the loss of a loved one, he had thought to himself. As if it were possible to shake off, through sheer force of will, the dark louring mantle of loneliness.

Early that morning, after a few hours of troubled sleep, he'd set out for the general hospital, where he had his first interview of the day. The little pieces that together formed the overall picture of the investigation were starting to move into place, but there were still a number of gray areas that needed illumination.

The previous afternoon, upon their return from the church of
Our Lady of Mount Carmel, the commissario and Maione had
agreed they'd only rendezvous back at headquarters late the
next morning: Ricciardi would then fill the brigadier in on the
findings of that nonmedical visit he was making to the hospital. Maione, beaming and a bit absentminded for some secret
reason, hadn't insisted on accompanying him as he usually did,
nor had he detained him with questions. Strange. He'd seemed
to have decided to come live full-time at the office, but now he
was eager to head home. The commissario had deduced, therefore, that Raffaele had successfully settled some major conflict
with his wife. He was happy for him, knowing how important
domestic tranquility was for the brigadier. Seeing a smile again
on that great broad face was the only good thing that had happened in a long time.

Nonetheless, Ricciardi had asked Maione to drop by the
general hospital before dinner to ascertain in his discreet way
what time the person the commissario wished to see finished
his shift; not that they couldn't have relied on information
from the switchboard, but he'd given Raffaele a rough idea of
what he now believed had happened, and it was best to act
cautiously. The brigadier had returned in half an hour and told
Ricciardi he'd be able to see the person he was interested in
tomorrow morning, around seven, at the front gate. While at
the general hospital, Maione had gone upstairs and made sure
no one had been into Iovine's office, which remained off-limits
to the staff of the obstetric clinic.

"Everything's all right, Commissa'," he'd told Ricciardi.
"No one enters that room, it must strike them as creepy. I'll see
you tomorrow morning around eleven, and then we'll wrap
this case up."

As he sipped his coffee, Ricciardi wondered whether certain
matters were ever entirely wrapped up. Whether blood, once
shed, doesn't continue spilling forever, red and malignant,

defiling the lives of whoever came into contact with that murder for all time. As was true for him.

At last, the person he was waiting to see emerged from the gate. The man greeted the custodian with a nod of the head, then looked around, squinting into the morning light, and started walking directly toward the café. He didn't notice Ricciardi at first, and when he did recognize him he greeted him with surprise: "Oh, *buongiorno*, Commissario. What are you doing here?"

"*Buongiorno*, Dr. Rispoli. I was actually waiting for you. I wanted to buy you an espresso and have a chat. If you can spare five minutes."

The man took a seat across from the commissario. His curiosity was aroused, but he didn't seem nervous.

"Certainly, Commissario. When you get out of that place," and he jerked a thumb toward the polyclinic, "you never really feel like heading home, even if you're working double shifts as we have been lately. It's as if you needed to cleanse yourself . . ."

Ricciardi broke in: "Are you doing Iovine's work, or has someone else already been assigned to replace him?"

Rispoli lit a cigarette, with a sad grimace: "No such luck, Commissario. It will be months before they assign a new director to the professorship, and therefore the clinic. You can't imagine how slowly the bureaucracy moves, and a civil war is no doubt already underway throughout Italy over this post. I can assure you that poor Tullio's murder is being viewed as a winning lottery ticket for many doctors at various universities. Countless hands are outstretched to grab this brass ring; I can only imagine the phone calls that are being made in a quest for the right recommendation. And until that's settled, my colleagues and I will have to pick up the slack."

Ricciardi sipped his coffee.

"What about you? Don't you aspire to succeed Iovine? After all, you were his first assistant."

"No, Commissario. The university career path means that, at most, I can hope to take that job in a smaller teaching hospital somewhere else, and then, perhaps, come back: but I have no desire to do that. First of all I'm already too old to aspire to a university chair like this one; moreover, I don't have the academic credentials. I'm someone you might call a hands-on physician, good for the operating room and for rounds, certainly not the kind of doctor who does research or writes scientific papers. In fact, that's why Tullio picked me."

"What do you mean by that?"

Rispoli exhaled a puff of smoke: "He would never have taken someone ambitious to work alongside him, someone he would have had to watch out for. What he needed was someone reliable, someone who could run things when he was away."

Ricciardi shifted to a more comfortable position in his chair.

"Still, the night that Graziani's wife died, neither you nor Iovine were on duty."

"That's not unprecedented. In fact, though, since I wasn't working that night, he shouldn't have left. But then . . . well, but then you know what happened. He did leave, and the rest is history. I was summoned urgently, but I got there too late, after Tullio had already tried to do the impossible. Like I told you the other day, Commissario, in all likelihood the woman would have died in any case. These things do happen."

Ricciardi nodded.

"They do. A few minutes ago, you said that Iovine would never have taken on someone he'd have to watch out for. Why not?"

Rispoli crushed out the butt of his cigarette in the ashtray.

"Because he was determined to hang onto his position, Commissario. Like almost everyone who makes their career the central pillar of their existence. Tullio was like that, no one around him who might undermine his status: the great professor, the grand luminary. I was perfect; I was an assistant.

And an assistant I shall remain, although now to someone else."

Ricciardi strained to detect rancor or sarcasm in the doctor's words, but he sensed none.

"And what happens, when a person makes his career the central pillar of his existence? What might he be willing to do?"

The doctor stared long and hard at Ricciardi: "Commissario, I don't understand. Why have you come to see me this morning? What do you want me to tell you?"

Ricciardi waved his hand in the waiter's direction and called for another espresso.

"I need information about the past, Rispoli; about how Iovine became who he was, about how he attained his position. Information about a time, perhaps, before you knew him, but that you might have heard about from people in your line of work."

Rispoli was bewildered: "But . . . Commissario, I don't understand: what does the way Tullio advanced his career have to do with anything? He'd held the chair for a great many years, what . . ."

The commissario interrupted him with a sharp gesture: "I know that. And please, let me be the judge of what's useful and what's not. These are things that, if I took the time and dug through the archives, I could find out anyway: but it would take more time, and I want to resolve this case as quickly as possible, if for no other reason than to keep innocent people from winding up in serious trouble just because they happen to be unable to prove they weren't here that night. That's why I've come to see you, and why I'm trusting in your good sense. Otherwise, I'll say goodbye."

Rispoli said nothing. Ricciardi realized that he was mentally calculating what problems he might cause for himself if he gave the commissario the information he'd asked for, and what problems he might cause for himself if he didn't. Then he nodded, and he too ordered another espresso.

"I've worked with Tullio, I told you, for many years. I'm pretty good at what I do, and when he chose me I was honored—at least until it became clear to me how he wanted to use me and my professional skills; but since I was willing to accept even that, and there's plenty of work but also an excellent salary that always arrives on time, let's just say that we built a good partnership. And I should tell you that everything I'd heard about him was fully confirmed."

"And what had you heard about him?"

"I'd heard that he was determined and hardworking; but that he was unwilling to share what he knew, that he guarded his expertise jealously, and was even a bit of a money-grubber. In short, a perfect boss if you stayed in your place and made no mistakes. As far as I was concerned, there were no problems, because in the end he gave me free rein."

"What about in personal terms?"

"Well, he wasn't exactly effusive. We eventually were on a first-name basis, and sometimes we'd make small talk, but nothing more than that. Recently, he'd shown me his new car, which he was very proud of; but we didn't talk much about our lives outside of work."

Ricciardi wanted to know more: "What about the past? Did he tell you anything about that? I don't know, memories, references to his own time as an aide or an assistant . . ."

Rispoli smiled, with a gleam of malice: "No, I'd say not. And for that matter, from what I heard when I was still a student, there certainly wasn't anything he'd be eager to tell."

The commissario grew more alert: "Why not? Tell me everything."

The invitation was accepted with enthusiasm. In fact, it seemed that the doctor had just been waiting for the chance. Ricciardi settled in to hear a story he already knew full well, with who knows what variations: "Tullio was one of the two assistants to a famous professor, a real genius, a man who had become director of the chair at a very young age: Albese was his name. He was so good that—though he came from a small town and certainly had no noble ancestry which, believe me, should have disqualified him from pursuing this career—he was still a leading light in the academic community. Well, at a certain point, the other assistant, a certain Ruspo who now has a nursing home out Mergellina way, was knocked out of the running by an anonymous letter that accused him of carrying on an affair with a married woman. In medical school circles, the word was that Tullio himself wrote that letter, since he was the only one who could benefit from the ensuing scandal. Aside from the cuckolded husband, of course."

Rispoli snickered as he sipped his espresso.

Ricciardi asked: "And then what happened?"

"After that, luck played its part, as far as Tullio's career was concerned. Albese had a heart condition that got worse, and he died. And Tullio happened to be at the right place at the right time, more or less like I was, but with much greater support and far more determination: he had created such a powerful network of friendships and supporters that he was appointed director of the chair, and he remained in that position ever since. Until he fell out that window."

Every detail matched the information Ricciardi already possessed.

"And naturally in that period Iovine, in order to be able to take advantage of the opportunity when it presented itself, spent all his time at work. That must have been a sorry life for his young bride."

Rispoli shook his head: "Why, no, Commissario: at the time, Tullio was still unmarried. And he couldn't have been married, for that matter."

"Why not?"

"That's easy: because the woman he married was Albese's widow, Maria Carmela."

Ricciardi held his breath. That was the answer he'd been waiting for.

An old automobile went rattling past the café, pursued by a crowd of running, half-naked children.

"How long after Albese's death did Iovine and Albese's widow marry?"

Rispoli concentrated: "It seems to me it was exactly two years, once the widow's strict period of mourning was over. The story was pretty sad, in fact. She was pregnant, four or five months along I believe, when her first husband died. It was Tullio himself who took responsibility for looking after her pregnancy, but it ended badly, unfortunately; you know, primiparous pregnancies are always the riskiest, and the widow had a miscarriage. Tullio stayed by her side, kept her constant company, and in the end they were married. Some time later they had a child of their own, and the baby survived without problems."

Ricciardi observed the treetops inside the walls of the polyclinic, motionless in the still air of that infernal July morning. He thought of Iovine falling, in the midst of those trees, until he slammed into the walkway below. And he thought about the twisted paths of love and the lust for power, ambition, and tenderness, paths that intersected and split a thousand times as they headed down into the abyss.

He thought of Sisinella, who had been Iovine's last desperate link to life; the smidgeon of happiness that perhaps she had been able to give him, though in exchange for cash; he thought of a man whose entire life had been consecrated to self-interest and his career. And he thought of Enrica, now far away, perhaps following the path that would lead her to happiness.

He looked up at Rispoli.

"And what was their relationship like? Are you aware of any marital difficulties, any fighting between husband and wife?"

"I wouldn't know, Commissario; like I told you, Tullio wasn't particularly open. In the past ten years, I've met his wife no more than a couple of times: once at a retirement party for one of the general hospital's directors, and one summer when they were going on vacation and Tullio dropped by to make sure everything was running smoothly. More recently, she came by one day when her husband wasn't here; I only caught a glimpse of her because I was scheduled to perform an operation, but the staff gave her a warm welcome: I believe that when she was married to her first husband, she came into the clinic more frequently. But I have no idea what she was like with Tullio. I had the impression of a strong woman, perhaps a little hard; but once you've suffered certain losses, you probably become hard, don't you, Commissario?"

Ricciardi thought it over and then, in a voice so low that it seemed as if he were only speaking to himself, said: "Yes. You do. Suffering hardens you. Thanks, Doctor. You've been very helpful."

And he called the waiter for the check.

LXIV

I f any of the passengers had bothered to look around, on the funicular that wended its way up toward Vomero on the morning of that July 14, they would have caught sight—in that little knot of laborers, shop clerks, and civil servants, each on his way to give his personal daily contribution to the growth of the new quarter—the large head of a police brigadier, topped by his regulation cap and adorned with an ecstatic smile.

Life, thought Maione, indifferent to the terrible heat, the mosquitoes, and the sweat-drenched, intrusive, annoying crowd, is so beautiful. Especially when it gives you the rare opportunity to look down into the abyss of despair and then makes you see that it was all just a bad dream, and that upon your awakening, the sun is still shining.

His chat with Bambinella at the Café Caflisch had at first confused him, and then had made him incredibly happy. Lucia wasn't cheating on him. Lucia hadn't stopped thinking about him. Lucia was still the wonderful wife and mother she always had been. He, Maione, would no longer have to erase the most secret memories that constituted his past and his very essence; he no longer had to devise dark vendettas; he no longer had to retreat into bleak despair.

The first beneficiaries of the new Maione were the policemen at headquarters who had seen a tempestuous giant in uniform, quick to anger and violence, leave the building, only to witness the return of an indulgent, avuncular superior officer, inclined to praise and kindness. The suddenness of the change had thrown

them into a state of confusion, and for a while they had continued to steer clear of him, but before long they ventured closer
and took advantage of his new demeanor to ask for a more per-
missive drafting of the schedule for summer vacation time.

Then Maione had hurried to order a bouquet of wildflowers,
arranging for delivery before he arrived home. The gesture,
however, hadn't produce the hoped-for effect: a weary, overheated Lucia had received it shouting in exasperation that she
hardly saw the point of wasting money—hard-earned money
that their household barely had enough of to make ends meet
every month—for such frivolities as an oversized bouquet of
flowers that the girls could go and pick for themselves in the
neighboring countryside. Who knows how much that thief of a
florist had charged, taking advantage of her husband's credulity.

And by the way, now that Lucia stopped to think of it, did
this mean that he was asking forgiveness for something?
Because if a man decides to send his wife flowers, on no special
occasion and for no other conceivable reason, then the explanation can invariably be traced back to some unspeakable mis-
deed and the need to assuage his remorse-plagued conscience.

Fortunately for Maione, he had an excellent memory and a
lengthy string of special occasions and anniversaries, and he
promptly reminded his wife of their first kiss on a warm, hope-
ful July night, in the coolness of the forest of Capodimonte;
actually, the date was at least a couple of weeks away, but Lucia
didn't have his same steel-trap memory and she believed it,
replacing the rebukes with smiles, and rewarding the brigadier
with a night that was worth an entire grove of trees, forget
about a bouquet of wildflowers.

All the same, Maione had willingly sacrificed a few extra
hours with his family when he might have enjoyed his newfound domestic peace because he had an errand to run.

Who knows why he'd thought about it first thing after leaving that café in the possession of news that had restored his

equanimity. Over those last few days, the conviction that he'd lost the love of his life, and that he'd probably never even possessed her at all, had driven him to act in ways that were very distant from his true nature; at the same time it had made it clear to him how important that emotion was, and how terrible it must be to be forced to live without it.

For that reason, he'd come to a decision the night before. Taking advantage of Ricciardi's request that he go over to the general hospital and see what time Rispoli's shift ended, Maione had made his way into the office that had once belonged to Iovine. He'd looked around and wondered just how much of a role love had played in that ugly story. The commissario had confided the theory that he'd come up with, a theory that had been bolstered by their visit to the church of Our Lady of Mount Carmel, and Maione had been forced to admit that it all added up; but as a husband, a father, and a man, he still hoped that it wasn't true, that the commissario had misread a fact or made some other blunder.

And for the first time he had the sensation that his commissario, his friend and companion, had revealed himself—the truth, right down to the very bottom of his self—to him. It wasn't the pang in his heart that he always experienced when he thought of his solitary superior officer. The absence of love, hope, and family. No woman at his side, no children. To know everything that there can be in a man's life, and to go without. You have to love someone, Maione reflected in his unassuming way; otherwise, what are we here for? When poor Rosa was gone, who would the poor commissario have left in his daily life? Aside, of course, from Maione himself.

The funicular discharged its cargo onto a sun-drenched piazza. From the surrounding countryside came a faint breeze that improved the brigadier's already good mood as he headed off toward the apartment house on Via Kerbaker that he had already visited twice in the past few days. From a distance he thought he heard the notes of a *pianino*, and this made him furrow his brow for a moment: there are people, he mused, who were born to take advantage of others. They might not do so explicitly, they might conceal their cold calculation behind a warm smile or a seductive song, but they're much more dangerous than those who do it professionally, out in the light of day. Or under the light of a streetlamp, on a street corner.

The night before he had thought of Maria and Benedetta: the daughter born of his blood and his love, and the little orphan who had also become his daughter, even more so. He'd suddenly seen them, so grown-up now, capable of taking care of their younger siblings, better and better at imitating their mother as cooks and seamstresses; they were no longer playing, messing around with flour and water or poking holes in rags with a needle. Now they were completing tidy little pieces of work, competing to draw cries of pleasure from their *papà* when they brought him dishes of fritters that were identical in every detail to the ones produced by Lucia.

He'd imagined them fully grown, adult. The first coquettish glances at a boy, the first heartbreaks, the occasional tear. And then he himself in dress uniform, walking them, beautiful and flower-bedecked in their long white gowns, to the altar.

And then he'd imagined something happening to him: getting stabbed with a knife, like Luca; or being shot by some criminal he'd caught red-handed. Or some sudden disease. Poverty, despair, the demands of survival; and the grief, the grim sorrow of loss, which could push them toward who knows what, or into the arms of who knows who. His daughters, his sweet, beautiful daughters, condemned to who could say what fate.

That sudden thought, which came while Lucia and his girls were laughing happily at some clownishness he'd engaged in at dinner, hadn't been reflected on his face, and hadn't dulled his merry laughter; still, it had chilled his heart like a gust of icy wind from the north. Now that he had glimpsed the abyss, he was a hundred, a thousand times more terrified at the thought of losing his family, and that his family might be dispersed. And then his thoughts had gone to Sisinella, the young whore who had believed for a very short season that she was escaping from the inferno in which she had lived, and whom he, Maione, had treated unfairly, as if she were the worst of evildoers.

The image of the girl, fighting the tears in her eyes, had infested his night. And his ears echoed with the words she had spoken in response to his threats: *You don't scare me, Brigadie'. You don't scare me. I've known people who would gut you like a fish for the fun of the thing, so just imagine how scared I am of you.* What a life she must have lived, that woman who had grown old in her soul while she continued to live in such a young body. What a curse her beauty must have been to her.

That was why he now found himself in the lovely courtyard of the Vomero apartment house. The doorman, Firmino, came over to him with a smirk on his face: "Oh, Brigadie', good morning. So easy days are over for the signorina, eh? And about time. To see a penniless nobody giving herself airs like a lady, a whore being worshipped as a signora—it was simply too ridiculous, no?"

The man must have overheard the altercation between the brigadier and Sisinella, and he was clearly on Maione's side. A little camaraderie among real men, with real values. Maione felt like smashing his face in.

He stared at him coldly and said: "Don't you dare to presume we're friends, Firmi'. In fact, I've noticed at least a dozen irregularities in the maintenance of this apartment building and I'm inclined to slap you with a hefty fine; if you want to keep that from happening, then take care not to sling mud on people who live here. Slanderers go to prison too, and nothing would make me happier than to lock you up. So watch your step."

The man stepped back, blanching.

"Certainly, Brigadie'. Forgive me. It won't happen again.

Please, be my guest, go right ahead: take your time, I'll stay here, on lookout."

With a shudder of disgust, Maione realized that this individual had assumed he'd come around to take advantage of the girl. A rush of heat rose to his face and he grabbed Firmino by the throat, lifting him like a sprig of wheat, and jerked him close to his face. With a hiss, the doorman exhaled all the air in his lungs and turned purple.

"Firmi', another broad hint like the last one and you'll be a dead man. I swear on my children's heads: you say one more word about that poor girl and I'll murder you with my bare hands. Do you understand? Do you understand? Nod your head yes, if you do."

When the man repeatedly nodded his head in assent, Maione let him go. The man flopped to the ground like an empty suit, coughing and hungrily sucking air into his lungs. Maione shot him one last disgusted look and headed up the stairs.

The door to Sisinella's apartment stood ajar. Maione knocked and called out, asking if he could come in, but there was no answer. He stepped inside.

It was all very different from the first time he'd been there. The apartment was bare, stripped of life and cheer. The furniture was the same, the light was the same, the place was still clean and well kept, but now it lacked that giddy energy, that garish, coquettish harmony that had first struck the brigadier. Maione noticed that the curtains had been taken down, a carpet was missing, and a few embroidered antimacassars had been taken off the sofas.

In the kitchen there was large bundle wrapped in a sheet and containing some household furnishings; other items had been stowed in two pillowcases. Maione glimpsed Sisinella sitting with her back to him, out on the terrace: she was smoking a cigarette as she surveyed the trees and countryside behind the apartment building. He knocked lightly at the balcony door: "Excuse me? May I?"

The girl half-turned: "Ah, it's you. What else do you want? Have you come to gloat at my fall back to my old life?"

Maione stepped out onto the terrace. The air was hot but sweet-smelling, and the birds were singing.

"Nice place, this. Really pleasant. You're doing the right thing, Sisine': it makes a person want to sit down and just think."

The woman emitted a mocking laugh: "Think? Better not, Brigadie'. Better not to think. Because if I start to think then I realize what a stupid idiot I've been, and then I'd kill myself. Better not to think."

Maione took the other chair and sat down not far from the young woman.

"But why? What did you do wrong, Sisine'? Lots of people turn out to be different from how they seem, it's not like you can always know right away."

From this close vantage point, he realized that the girl was silently weeping. Tears were running slowly down her face, leaving behind them a black streak of makeup.

"I loved him. For the first time, I loved someone. I believed that he was going to marry me and change my life; what a fool I was. I was willing to work hard, to earn for him so I could have an honest life. But maybe girls like me aren't destined to have an honest life."

Maione said nothing. The girl turned and looked at him: "Happy now, eh, Brigadie'? You have your confirmation. A whore is nothing but a whore. That's what she does, and she'll do it for the rest of her life. You were right."

The brigadier tilted his head toward the kitchen.

"I see that you're packing your bags. Where are you going to go?"

Sisinella shrugged.

"I only took my own things, the things I bought with my own money. The things that Tullio bought me, I left them all here. You know, it was like a frenzy had come over him, he had fun, as if he were a little boy. For him, this apartment was just a game. He said that the other place, the apartment at Quattro Palazzi where his wife lived, with all the gold and silver and old paintings in it, seemed like a museum to him, but that here he felt at home. What a nut, eh?"

At the memory, she'd smiled through her tears, and just as Maione had imagined the women that his little girls would one day become, he now saw the little girl that woman had once been. The idea tugged at his heart.

"You know, Brigadie', I think that Tullio really did love me. Sometimes he didn't even want to do that thing, you know, he would just sit and gaze at me. I'd sew, cook, clean the floor, sing, and he'd watch me as if he were at the movies or the theater. I was all the show he wanted to watch. Poor Tullio."

She stood up, sniffing loudly and wiping her face with the sleeve of her nightgown.

"You asked me where I'll go. And all I can tell you is that I won't die, Brigadie'. Sisinella won't die, not even this time. Sisinella is leaving with her head up, with a few dresses and a couple of pairs of shoes, and she won't die. For now I've sold off the gifts Tullio gave me, a few little jewels that I kept for myself, and I've rented a little room in a tenement not all that far from here, in Arenella. A new quarter, people who don't know me. I want to try and see if, by some chance, I can find a place as a servant, or some business that needs a salesclerk. Because the news is this, Brigadie', I'm not going back up there, to the place you know. A whore isn't always a whore, you're wrong about that. She can change."

Maione stood up too.

"You're right, Sisine'. And I was wrong. I'm here to apologize for what I said to you the other time I was here, it wasn't what I really thought. I shouldn't have said those things to you. I was going through a period . . . whatever I was going through, I shouldn't have allowed myself to talk to you like that, and I shouldn't have judged you. I'm here to beg your pardon."

The girl stared at him, baffled: "But . . . no harm done, Brigadie'. Thank you, actually, for what you're saying to me now. And maybe you did some good, because you gave me the strength to act. It's just that . . . I'd set my heart on Tore. I gave him my heart. And now I've lost it."

"No, Sisine'. That's what I came to tell you. You never lose your heart. Your heart can be wounded, battered, but you get it back. Especially the young, beautiful heart of a girl like you."

The girl smiled at him, hesitantly.

"I'll try my best, Brigadie'. I promise you, I'll try my best."

Maione smiled then too. Then he slapped his forehead: "Ah, I practically forgot. Here, this belongs to you."

And he pulled a small jewelry case out of his pocket. Sisinella opened it, doubtful, and then sat there, slack-jawed.

"It's a gift that the professor commissioned for you, Sisine'. The artisan delivered it to him the same night he died, and he would have given it to you as soon as he came back here. I just thought that in the end it was only right for you to have it, no? Because that is what the professor would have wanted."

The girl pulled the ring out of the case. The enormous precious stone glittered in the light like a second sun.

"Brigadie', but I . . . how . . . how can you give me this? The widow . . . I have no right to this ring, Brigadie'."

"His widow already has plenty of money, don't worry about her. This apartment, whose existence she doesn't even suspect, is hers, with everything in it. But inside this ring, if you look, you can see your name, so it's yours and no one can deny it. It was just a matter of making up my mind to give it to you."

The girl couldn't tear her eyes away from the diamond set in gold. The craftsmanship was splendid.

"But this must be worth a fortune, Brigadie'."

"That's right, a fortune. I asked a friend of mine who's a

jeweler on Via Toledo, and he told me that with the money they'd give you for this ring, you could buy a little house and even start up a small business of your own here in Vomero, where the prices are low. Or, of course, you could run through it quickly and then go back to being a working girl. In other words, now you have that choice."

Sisinella pressed her lips together decisively: "Yes, Brigadie', now I can choose. For the first time in my life I can choose. And have no doubt, I'll make the right choice."

She walked over to Maione, stood on tiptoes, threw her arms around his neck, and planted a loud smacking kiss on his cheek. He smiled, lifted his hand to the visor of his cap, and turned to leave.

There was no trace of the doorman in the courtyard.

LXV

With the words of Iovine's assistant still ringing in his head, Ricciardi suddenly felt all the weight of weariness he'd built up in the past few days. He headed back to headquarters, in no hurry.

There was the usual frenzy in the streets, only slightly dampened by the muggy heat hanging in the air like a casting of molten metal. This would be no ordinary weekend: there was the feast of Our Lady of Mount Carmel, that week. There would be the festival, the festival of summer and heat, the festival of the Black Madonna and of the Graces requested and received, the festival of dancing in the piazza and the burning of the bell tower.

But Ricciardi, walking along slowly with his hands in his pockets and his eyes on the ground, hatless as usual, wasn't thinking about the festival at all. He was thinking about love, and about death.

What the doctor had told him was important. How could he have overlooked the fundamental clues to the solution of the case? Right from the first questions, from the first interviews; it was all there, it was all clear and understandable from the very beginning. And yet he'd had to run smack into it, face-first. Like someone walking in the dark.

Perhaps, he thought, as he stepped around a skinny peasant woman balancing an enormous basket of cheeses on her head, it had always been like that, his profession. A walk in the dark, banging one's face against evidence before recognizing it as such; and yet he wouldn't have known any other way of doing it.

The investigators who solved their cases by tracing the murderer thanks to infinitesimal details caught on the fly in a barren locked room lived in novels from across the Atlantic and across the English Channel; they wore funny hats, smoked pipes, and played the violin. The street, the smell of blood, the slimy swamp of twisted emotions—these were entirely another matter.

It was always so simple. So very simple. Too simple, at times, to see at first glance. Hatred, jealousy, and revenge were unsubtle actors in the daily performance of emotions, and before long you wound up not even noticing their presence. You got used to them, in the end.

Still, thought Ricciardi, there was a piece missing from the puzzle. The most important piece. Even though he knew the outline and the colors, even if he'd intuited its features, the general image remained incomplete. He needed to have one last, definitive conversation.

When he reached that point in any investigation, when the knot had been untangled and he clearly understood the motive for the murder and how it had been carried out, for a brief moment he grew shy. As if to stare with full awareness into the abyss of hatred, into the cold determination to kill or desire the death of another human being, was to glimpse a terrible and all-devouring panorama; a necessary act but one he would gladly have done without.

It was the same this time. The professor's murder had been a simple, brutal act, but it had deep roots. Roots that ran far back, in time and space.

He had almost reached police headquarters, and at the corner of the street he glimpsed a silhouette that struck him as familiar. A tall man, middle-aged, nicely dressed and standing stiffly. As he drew closer, Ricciardi was increasingly certain that he didn't know the man, yet there was something about him that rang a bell: he wore a pair of spectacles and carried a walking stick.

The man stood motionless, as if he were waiting for someone;

he too saw Ricciardi, and he tilted his head to one side in an instinctive gesture of recognition. His heart skipped a beat as the commissario realized that that man was Enrica's father.

How the man resembled Enrica, was the only thought he managed to formulate. He couldn't be certain that the man was actually looking for him, but how could it be a mere coincidence? He looked the other man in the face, as if requesting some new sign of acknowledgment. The man took half a step forward and, lifting his hand to his hat brim, asked in a barely audible voice: "Commissario Ricciardi, by any chance?"

Ricciardi stopped. His heart, for some reason, was pounding in his throat.

"Yes, Signore. With whom do I have the pleasure . . ."

The man was ill at ease. He doffed his cap with a bow and extracted a calling card from the breast pocket of his jacket.

"I am Cavalier Giulio Colombo, from Via Santa Teresa. We . . . I believe that we're neighbors, Commissario. We live directly across the street from each other, in fact."

I know that well, thought Ricciardi. Oh, how well I know that.

"Certainly, Cavalier. Certainly. Would you care . . ."

He looked around him, in search of the proper words. Invite him up to the office? But if the man had wished to meet him there, he would have found him seated on the bench in the hall, waiting for him. Ask him what he wanted, right there in the street? Or else . . .

The cavalier saved him from his quandary: "May I be so bold as to invite you to take an espresso with me, Commissario? That is, of course, if you have nothing urgent to attend to. I only want five minutes of your time."

"Don't think twice, Cavalier. No problem, not at all. Where . . ."

"Is Gambrinus all right with you? I usually . . . That is, the coffee is very good there."

Ricciardi nodded: "It would be a real pleasure. I go there frequently myself."

They headed off. It was no more than a hundred yards to the café, but both men felt as if they were scaling the Himalayas. They walked side by side, without glancing at each other, at a brisk pace. They exchanged the occasional laconic comment on the heat, and they crossed paths with a few people who recognized the cavalier: the gentlemen tipped their hats, the ladies smiled and bowed their heads, and the man responded with formal courtesy.

He is clearly every bit as ill at ease as I am, Ricciardi thought to himself. What could the cavalier possibly want from him? A vast array of different possibilities crowded into his mind. The first, and the most upsetting, was that Enrica might not be well, and that was the reason that for so many days now she hadn't appeared at the window; that was especially plausible because Rosa, who lay unconscious in a hospital bed, was the sole contact that the commissario possessed with his own neighborhood, and therefore he wouldn't have found out from anybody else. So perhaps the father had come to give him sad news.

Another thought was that perhaps Colombo had come to demand an explanation for the moments of intimacy Ricciardi had enjoyed with his daughter, without ever obtaining his permission. He had written to her, he'd spoken to her, and he'd kissed her in the street, on Christmas Eve, even if not at his own initiative. Had the family maybe seen it happen, peeking out the window? But that was absurd: seven months had passed since then. That couldn't possibly be the reason. In that case, what had the man come to tell him?

As they entered Gambrinus, each man distractedly headed for his usual table: Colombo toward the little dining room that overlooked Via Chiaia, where he customarily read his newspaper; Ricciardi toward the inner room, which tended to be less crowded and overlooked the main piazza. They both stopped at the same moment and, laughing in an unexpected complicity, opted for the central salon, taking one of the tables off to the side.

Through the plate glass window they could see the corner of the Royal Palace, which marked the beginning of the Teatro San Carlo portico, and a strolling vendor doing his best to sell hazelnuts and sweets; at the vendor's side, visible only to Ricciardi and to his curse, was an old beggar woman who'd been suffocated in her sleep by her own vomit. The beggar woman was slurring out an ancient, absurd lullaby: *nonna nonnooo, nonna vo' fare chesta nenna bella, nonna vo' fare mo' ch'è piccerella.* Who knows what she was dreaming about when she died.

Colombo politely asked Ricciardi what he might like, and ordered two espressos. His eyes, behind his glasses, wandered around the interior of the café; he didn't know where to start, and Ricciardi didn't know how to help him.

Colombo coughed and said: "I have a shop right there, practically at the corner of Via San Ferdinando. You can't see it from here. A haberdashery. Hats. That's not all, of course—also gloves, walking sticks, umbrellas. But mostly hats."

Ricciardi tried to answer, but his voice stuck in his throat. He cleared his throat and nodded.

Colombo resumed: "I hope you'll excuse me, Commissario. I imagine you have a great many things to do. A city like this one . . . A number of your colleagues are my customers, and the things they tell me . . . I notice you don't wear a hat."

The phrase sounded to Ricciardi like a reproof, though it had been couched simply as a question.

"No, I don't. I suffer from . . . migraines, and unfortunately a hat immediately triggers them. I need air. It may be because I come from a town in the mountains."

"I understand."

There was another pause of awkward silence, during which

both men looked at the movement of automobiles, carriages, and pedestrians in the piazza. The old beggar woman, faded but still visible, continued singing to Ricciardi.

Colombo turned his placid gaze toward the commissario.

"You know, I have five children. All children are dear to you, as you'll discover when you have children of your own. I live for them. To give them decent lives, and a future."

He stopped, and Ricciardi waited.

"All the same, it is only natural that one has with some of them, or with one of them in particular, a special affinity. An understanding that requires no words, that can be summed up in a look. In my case, that happens with a daughter. My first-born, to be exact."

Ricciardi was sweating. It was hot out, yes: but he only rarely sweated, no matter how intense the heat.

Colombo continued: "I've sought you out because I'd like to tell you a story. Let me preface this by saying that it is quite unlike me to enter into contact in this manner with a stranger: I belong to another generation. I'm accustomed to a proper introduction, I tend to establish a certain acquaintance before opening myself to confidences. So I will make no secret of the fact that I feel quite awkward about being here."

Ricciardi shifted in his chair, trying unsuccessfully to alleviate his own sense of awkwardness.

"Cavalier Colombo, I beg of you, feel quite at your ease to tell me whatever it is you like. In my work . . . we see a great many things, you said so earlier and you are right. Nothing can surprise us, and nothing could be more uncomfortable than the many sorrowful situations to which, like it or not, we find ourselves witnesses. I assure you that you can speak freely about whatever you please."

Colombo smiled. And his smile, too, reminded Ricciardi of Enrica. How could that be?

"Work is one thing, and one's personal life is something

entirely different. But let's just say that I'm here to tell you a story, if you're willing to listen. I won't take much of your time."

"Please, do tell me this story."

"Now then, let's imagine a girl. A sweet, gentle girl, good-natured, quiet but possessed of great determination. A dreamer, who when she isn't working or helping her mother with the housework, reads romantic novels and dreams of a future not that different from her present: a family, a home. A husband, whom she loves and who loves her. Let's imagine that this girl is waiting for the man of her dreams, for Prince Charming, we might say; and that she's unwilling to settle for anything less than her one true love."

Ricciardi listened alertly, with his heart in his mouth. The cavalier's voice was low and shot through with melancholy; there was no mistaking the tremendous tenderness he felt for his daughter.

"Let's imagine that this girl believes that she's found it, the one true love of her life; and that she believes that the man of her dreams loves her in return. I . . . those who know her understand that if she comes to believe something, she has good reasons. That the man must have behaved with her in such a way as to make her think that he loves her."

Ricciardi felt his stomach tie itself in a knot: "Cavalier, I . . ."

Colombo raised one hand, without looking at Ricciardi: "Commissario, please. Let me finish. This is already hard enough as it is, believe me."

Ricciardi said nothing. Colombo took a sip of water and continued: "But then something happens, or else perhaps doesn't happen. The fact remains that this girl comes to the belief—and as I told you, when she is convinced of something it is no easy matter to make her change her mind—that she was only dreaming when she thought that the man loved her back. Or that for whatever reason, the best thing is to get over it, to forget. And that she therefore makes up her mind to leave. To go away."

Ricciardi leaned forward, his feverish green eyes fixed on the cavalier's face.

"Go away? But where? And why should she go away? Couldn't she . . ."

"Not far away, no. But far enough to make sure she wouldn't have to wait for a glance, a word, or a letter that might never come. I believe it was the right thing to do, you know? But that's not the point."

Ricciardi felt removed from reality, sitting there in Gambrinus talking with a stranger about things he'd have been embarrassed to admit to even by himself, in front of a mirror.

"What is the point?"

"The point is that in the place where she goes to forget about that man, she meets another. Another man, who expresses interest in her and courts her in an increasingly unequivocal manner, until he actually asks her out on a date."

Ricciardi felt the way he'd always assumed someone who had been shot in the chest would feel.

"A date? And . . . and she, what did she say? This imaginary young woman, I mean, what did she tell him?"

Colombo took a long sip of his espresso, which he had until then left untouched. He seemed exhausted by the effort.

"She's torn. She believes that this man, the one that she's met in the place where she's gone, has strong and sincere feelings for her. That he wants to give her what she has always desired in life; or, at least, what she thought she wanted. That he wants to take her away, carry her off to his distant homeland, and perhaps she's a little sad about that, as her *papà* would be sad, very sad indeed, because it would break his heart, though he's willing to accept any sacrifice as long as it would make her happy . . ." He fell silent as he mastered his deep emotion. Then he resumed: "But she can't bring herself to forget the other man, the one she had in her heart when she went away. She continues to cherish that dream."

A tram honked its raucous horn in the scorching heat of early afternoon. Ricciardi felt a tempest raging in his body, shaking every single organ.

"Why are you telling me these things, Cavalier? Why have you come looking for me? If this man . . . if this girl should find what she's looking for with this other person, then what . . . what could the first person even do?"

Colombo focused on the sun-drenched portico of the Teatro San Carlo and on the vendor of sweets and hazelnuts now seeking a place to shelter from the sun, while still continuing to offer his goods for sale to every passerby.

"You see, Commissario, this girl sends letters home in which she tells what she does every day. These letters brim over with joy, serenity, contentment. She's doing well. Very well. And in those letters she says nothing about this man, or the other one. Her mother . . . a wonderful woman, let me be perfectly clear, wishes she had gotten engaged years ago, and was already married or about to tie the knot . . . The other daughter, the younger one, actually already has a baby boy . . . But those aren't the only letters she's writing. She sends other letters, this girl. To someone else, and to that person, in contrast, she truly opens her heart."

Continuing to look out the plate glass window, the cavalier slipped a hand inside his jacket and half-pulled out a bundle of cream-colored sheets of paper, which he then immediately replaced.

"And this someone has had to overcome everything he believes in, his own principles and even his own upbringing, in order to do something he would never have dreamed of doing. Because his baby girl—the first child who ever made him feel like a father and therefore a man in full, the only child who is herself able to understand every thought in his head, without his having to speak a word—is fighting against the idea, if you follow me, of settling for serenity, for the rest of her life."

This time it was Ricciardi's turn to feel a gust of emotion shaking every last fiber in his being. That man had the right to know why loving someone might possibly mean having to abandon them to their fate.

"Cavalier, you ought to know that I . . ."

The man turned an indecipherable gaze on him: "No, Commissario. Not you. That man. Remember? This is all just a story. An imaginary story. Otherwise you and I couldn't go on talking. You understand that, don't you?"

Ricciardi seemed to awaken from a sudden stupor; then he realized that Enrica's father had a point.

"Agreed. We know nothing about that man. We'd have to investigate, just as we do in our line of work. Because sometimes, Cavalier, if you don't know the true, underlying motives, an attitude, a way of acting, or even just the expression on a face can appear entirely incomprehensible . . ." He, too, now, focused his gaze on the vendor outside and glimpsed the old dead woman, fading in the sun, singing her long-forgotten lullaby and vomiting out the wine that had killed her. "That man, you see, has exceedingly strong feelings. Strong feelings if ever there were any. But he's also terrified, because he sees the effects those feelings can have in everyday life. And so he believes that keeping those feelings out of his life, and keeping himself out of the lives of the people who . . . of the people he cares most about, is the best way of doing them good. That's all. That, perhaps, is the reason why he keeps his distance, in the terrible hope that he will be forgotten; and in the certainty that to be forgotten would be the death of him."

It was clear to him just how abstruse his reasoning might seem; but Colombo seemed to have grasped it.

"Commissario, I'm only a shopkeeper. I like to read and keep up with events, and I'm interested in politics, which, these days, with everything that's happening, may be a serious shortcoming. But I stopped studying after high school, and I don't understand much when it comes philosophical speculation. All I know is that Enrica is about to make a decision whose consequences could last forever. I don't know the intentions of the man to whom we've been alluding; all I know is that it's his duty at least to look her in the eye and speak to her, the way that the other man who met her is about to do."

There was a pause. Colombo stood up, reached into his pocket and pulled out a sheet of paper, and extended it to Ricciardi.

"Here is an address that might prove useful to you, Commissario. Perhaps I'm doing the right thing by giving it to you, or perhaps I'm not. But I know that my Enrica would want me to. I hope that you find the correct balance, and that you make the right decision. I confide in your discretion, and therefore in the fact that you will never tell anyone, and especially not her, that this conversation took place. Good day to you."

Ricciardi took the sheet of paper and slipped it into his pocket, stood up as well, and bade the other man farewell with a curt nod.

Then they both left, turning to walk in opposite directions.

LXVI

Maione was waiting for Ricciardi outside the front entrance of police headquarters, in the shade of the stone arch. Upon his return from Vomero he was sure he would find him in his office, as they'd agreed the previous day, and he was already starting to worry for no particular reason when he spotted the commissario in the distance, walking toward him with his hands in his pockets and his eyes on the ground as usual; but to the brigadier's empathetic gaze it was clear that something wasn't right.

He walked to meet him, climbing a few dozen yards up the narrow *vicolo* from the building's entrance.

"Commissa', are you all right? I was just starting to wonder where you were, you told me that you were going to go talk to Rispoli first thing and then you'd come to the office. But here they tell me that they haven't seen you since yesterday. Did something happen?"

Ricciardi said nothing, as if preoccupied, his face creased with pain.

"Has something happened to Signora Rosa, Commissa'? When could it have happened? I just phoned over to the hospital a few minutes ago, because when I heard you weren't here I thought she might have taken a turn for the worse. But I talked to Dr. Modo and he told me that her condition is stable."

At the mention of Rosa's name, Ricciardi seemed to snap out of it.

"Ah, you already called over? I was planning to do that

myself, as soon as I got back to the office. No, nothing's wrong. Everything's normal. Come on, let's get upstairs; we need to make arrangements for the last interview we need to conduct, so we can close out this investigation."

"No, Commissa'. I think we're going to have revise our plans. A call came in from Incurabili Hospital, where they've completed the autopsy on poor Coviello, which by the way confirms in every aspect what we already know about his death. They tell me that there's someone claiming the body to give it a funeral."

Ricciardi stared at Maione, a long stony gaze.

"Well, that's something at least. Okay, let's get over to Incurabili."

Incurabili—"Incurables"—was the largest hospital in the city. Its name was in apparent contradiction with its mission, but only because the institution's full name, St. Mary of the People of the Incurables, was habitually abbreviated, and this because it, in turn, was at odds with the frenetic activity that went on there.

Ricciardi and Maione made their way across the atrium, threading carefully through the crowd of physicians, nurses, family members, and those patients well enough to walk on their own two feet. They passed the entrance to the church on their right, from which emerged the sound of mass, and emerged into an inner courtyard; they ignored the broad staircase leading up to the wards and the monumental old pharmacy, and instead proceeded on toward the rear of the building, where the morgue was located.

Just as they were about to step out from the courtyard, they were cordially greeted by the young physician they'd first met in Coviello's workshop: "Good afternoon, Commissario, greetings, Brigadie'. So they informed you that we were done with your hanged man, right?"

Ricciardi took immediate issue with the man's glib tone and

offhanded manner toward the deceased; once again, he gained renewed appreciation for the merciful respect for the dead that Bruno Modo invariably displayed. The words that the ghostly image of the goldsmith had uttered at the scene of his death echoed clearly in his ears: *the bottom of your heart.*

"What is your name, Doctor?"

The physician replied in a haughty voice: "Guglielmo Franzi, Commissario."

"So I would guess that you prefer to be called Dr. Guglielmo Franzi, don't you?"

The young man blinked behind the round lenses of his spectacles: "I don't follow you, Commissario. What are you saying?"

Ricciardi snapped back: "The person you refer to as "our hanged man," sir, had a first and last name, you know? He was called Nicola Coviello. He had a mother, a poor demented old woman who's now all alone in the world, an apprentice that he was teaching a trade, as well as an array of feelings, loves, interests, and ideas. I'd be much obliged, if our professional paths chance to cross again, if you'd refer to the deceased by their first and last names."

The young doctor blushed.

"You're absolutely right, Commissario. I beg your pardon. The corpse . . . er, Signor Coviello, as seemed to be the case on a preliminary investigation, died as a result of strangulation caused by the rope after a certain period of . . . after he . . . after he came to be suspended from the rafter. The groove on his neck showed the marks of the rope, which unfortunately means that a fair amount of time had passed. I would therefore confirm the presumable time of death."

Maione asked: "And there are no signs of struggle, correct?"

"No, Brigadier. In fact, from the marks on the hands and the traces of hemp fiber corresponding to the rope, it is evident that he hauled himself up, without any external support. He must have been incredibly strong. Otherwise, he was healthy, no signs of any advanced-stage diseases: this wasn't done to avoid further suffering, in other words."

But he was suffering, Ricciardi thought to himself. He was suffering, and how. Regrets, despair. Perhaps remorse.

"Thank you, Doctor. There's nothing else, is there?"

"Actually, Commissario, yes, there is. I had that information conveyed over the telephone. As you know, there's a person who has claimed the dead . . . that is, the remains of the deceased. They say they won't leave until they can make arrangements for a funeral and decent burial. I explained that we would have to await instructions from police headquarters, but . . ."

Ricciardi nodded: "Yes. I did know that, Doctor. We'll take care of it. Where is this person?"

The doctor pointed toward the rear of the courtyard: "Back there, by the entrance to the morgue itself. There's a bench, in the shade of the porch roof."

"Fine. Thanks again, and have a good afternoon."

Maione touched his visor in a salute, and followed Ricciardi, whispering: "Nice work, Commissa', you told him what's what, this young punk of a doctor. He's going to have a lot more work to do before he can become like Dr. Modo."

"Doctors as bad as Bruno are born, not made. Let's go, Raffaele. Let's try to understand just when Coviello started to die."

On the bench that the doctor had pointed out to them was a single person: a woman dressed in black, skinny, with gloved hands clutching at a purse in her lap. She wore a hat, likewise black, with a dark veil that covered her face, making her unrecognizable.

Ricciardi walked over, followed by Maione, and came to a halt before her. The heat was terrible and the crickets were chirping loudly in the trees.

The commissario made a slight bow: "*Buonasera*, Signora Iovine."

LXVII

All three of them sat down on the bench, Maione next to Ricciardi and Ricciardi next to the widow Iovine. The brigadier kept glancing at the woman's veiled profile, practically impossible to see except for the sharp, narrow nose, which projected slightly beyond the silhouette of the commissario's own, as if it were a shadow. From the first time he'd laid eyes on her, he'd never been able to rid himself of a deep uneasiness: that skinny figure dressed in black, sitting stiffly outside the morgue, alone, reminded him of death itself.

Without turning to look at her, Ricciardi began speaking in a low voice, little more than a whisper: "I should have figured it out right away. All the evidence was there, you know; and I doubt that either you or he made any special effort to conceal it. But you don't see where you don't look, and I was distracted by . . . by a number of things. Then at last I saw."

The woman didn't seem to be listening. She hadn't moved by so much as an inch, she hardly appeared to be breathing in the indifferent chorus of the crickets' chirping.

"The first clue was the most obvious of all. He'd been the last person to see Iovine alive. We listened to what he told us: the shadow in the dark, a gigantic man; but the last person to see the victim alive is always the murderer. He's the one with the strongest interest in shifting suspicion onto someone else, to give himself time. Not to get away with it, but just get a little more time. The time he needs to finish his work. He knew that suspicion on the other men, the doctor's son, the gangster with the dead wife, would eventually dissolve. He just wanted a little more time."

Someone slammed a window shut high above them. Ricciardi continued: "And he himself, when we questioned him a second time, said that he had recommended a style of ring that would go perfectly on slender fingers like yours. And yet, by his and your own admission, he'd never seen you: you told us that you'd learned his name from some of your girlfriends and that then you'd told your husband about him. How could he have known what your fingers were like? Your husband couldn't have told him, he'd been very brusque, they'd hardly talked at all. And then, when we went to his home, his mother, a poor old woman with a wandering mind, told us that Nicola's girlfriend from many years ago had returned; a woman who had appeared one night, and stuck her face through the door of the workshop with an enigmatic phrase about steamships departing. The same words that he carved into his workbench, the place where he spent his whole life waiting for you, Signora. Waiting for you to come back. The grace for which he completed the ex-voto to the Virgin Mary, the Madonna whose name you bear."

Maione sat there, as expressionless as a Buddha in a policeman's uniform, but deep inside a storm was raging. Ricciardi had explained his hypothesis to him before, but now to hear it in detail, just a few yards from the morgue where the poor goldsmith's body lay emptied of its innards, and in the presence of that lady in black who could easily have been a mannequin, was pushing him to the edge of madness.

Ricciardi went on: "And it was there, and only there, that I understood. When I went to see the heart in flames, devoured by the fire of an eternal love and an eternal pain, the solid gold heart that probably represents the entire fortune accumulated over years of highly respected craftsmanship. The heart at the bottom of which, engraved with enchanting skill, is your name,

Signora. Your name, like a despairing scream. Your name, like a last misbegotten thought."

The crickets fell silent, as if they'd been listening, suddenly attentive. To the bewildered Maione, that sign seemed at once terrible and simultaneously completely natural.

The commissario said, grimly: "It was Nicola Coviello who threw your husband out the window. It was Nicola Coviello, with his incredibly powerful and skilled hands, who picked him up by his belt and the collar of his shirt and hurled him over the windowsill, easily and promptly. It was Nicola Coviello who put an end to your husband's life, obeying an order from you, whether explicit or implicit. I can't prove it and I'm not really interested in doing so; for that matter, given the larger context, it doesn't really matter all that much to our investigation. But I'm sure of it. I just don't know what your motivations were. I want to know. And you must tell me. For justice's sake. To do him justice."

Once Ricciardi was done speaking, there was an extended silence. Maione shot quick glances at the two backlit profiles, carved and motionless, both oddly sharp, the nose jutting forward, almost as if they were the same person: the commissario with a lock of hair dangling over his forehead, his green eyes chasing after his thoughts in the empty air; the woman in black, straight-backed, skinny and still, her gloved hands clutching the handle of her handbag. Time hung over the edge of an abyss that could have been the inferno, full of the dead screaming in the atrocious heat of eternal flames.

Then Signora Iovine moved her hands.

She raised them to the veil that she lifted over her hat, resting it on the brim and uncovering her face.

Maione had noticed how hard her features were the first time he'd met her; a hardness that had crumbled slightly only when she spoke of her son. This time, the face of Maria Carmela Iovine del Castello was completely devoid of any expression; the

424 · MAURIZIO DE GIOVANNI

wrinkles around her mouth and the corners of her eyes seemed to have been carved in marble. Like Ricciardi, she too was staring into the middle distance, almost as if they were both watching the same performance.

The brigadier felt his heartbeat slowing, but now his stomach was tied in knots; he had an expectant feeling, like when you see lightning and are waiting to hear the thunder.

The woman opened her mouth and then shut it again, twice, in search of the right words.

Then she spoke.

LXVIII

We used to go watch the steamships depart. We were little more than children, you know? And we'd go watch people leave for America.

In our neighborhood that was how we spent time together, as if it were an obvious, ordinary thing. A matter of age, proximity, friendships uniting families: a little boy and a little girl, first playing on the ground among the hens pecking up and down the *vicolo*, then walking together in the street, and finally sharing a life together. Nicola and I were destined for each other. That's what everyone thought, and he thought so too. Not me, though. I wanted more.

He would have left for America. Not me, I'd never have left. I thought that to leave meant to accept defeat, and I think the same thing now. Still, I'd go down with him to watch the steamships departing. Until the day that I myself departed.

I never believed that he'd wait for me. I went to live in a town in the provinces, pretty far away, with an aunt who couldn't have children, married to a rich businessman. A man with lots of money. That was where I met Rosario, a few years later.

My aunt had sent me to school. She treated me like a doll, she played at being my mother, she dressed me, fed me, and sent me off to study; but I wasn't playing. Everything, every exam, every new acquaintance only helped me to improve. I wanted to be rich, respected, a fine lady. I wanted to be happy.

Rosario wasn't an aristocrat, he wasn't a prince, but he was ambitious and he came from a good family. And then he was so intelligent, the smartest person I'd ever met. He had a spectacular memory, he only needed to read a sentence once and he'd remember it forever. He could have done anything he set his mind to, and he would have been successful without even trying. But there was only one thing he wanted: he wanted to become a doctor.

He was a good man. I believe that he was a good man precisely because he was so intelligent. He said that wrongdoing makes no sense, it's incomprehensible because it's counterproductive. Because it hurts people, for no good reason.

I trusted him. Things were going well, he was climbing the ladder step by step; I was working to help him, I established a network of relationships. You know, Commissario, to start a great career, it's not enough to be excellent, you also have to make friends, establish relationships. Sniff the wind, and then move in the right direction. I'm good at that. Very good.

So Rosario worked as a scientist and a physician: the things he knew how to do. And he did them very well indeed, he became a sort of guiding light for the entire discipline. And I became the favorite girlfriend of the wives of the powerful, politicians, business tycoons. Gynecology necessarily works through a network of women: and you'd never guess the extent to which women control their men.

When Rosario became director of the chair of gynecology, here in the city, I chose to move someplace other than the old quarter. My parents were dead by then, and I was a different person myself. I couldn't hope to be happy where I had once been so unhappy and so poor.

We began spending time with those in high society. We were young, famous, and rich. There was no limit to how high we could have reached. I dreamed of Rome, and I would have won it one day. There was just one problem: Rosario's heart.

That big, kind heart was sick. No one knew it, they'd warned him to keep his illness a secret because it was the sort of thing that could have kept him from getting certain jobs; but he had to be careful. Sometimes he forced himself to take time off, when overwork put his health in danger. He couldn't let himself rest for too long, or he'd be overtaken by his rivals and he'd lose years. He needed to husband his energies. That was why his assistants needed to be more than just talented, they needed to be able to replace him without doing harm.

Rosario wanted a baby. He really wanted one. To tell the truth, I would have been happy to wait a little longer, but he kept insisting: perhaps he knew that what happened to him might happen.

He had selected two young men to serve as his assistants. They were both brilliant. He enjoyed watching them compete, seeing them intuit things even before he said anything. Then one of them was caught in a scandal, and he was out of the running. Only one remained.

Rosario was always telling me about this Tullio Iovine del Castello, one of the finest students he'd ever had. He always followed in my husband's footsteps, he knew what my husband wanted before he did, he stayed on at work even when he wasn't on duty. Rosario would have sent him off to be the director of the chair of gynecology in some smaller university.

But he never had the time.

Rosario died on the job. His heart gave out, unexpectedly.

You see, Commissario, I never knew that I loved my husband. Not as much as I did. I thought of the day we met as an ordinary fact of life, something obvious. Instead, a heart is a great vase full of liquid: the heaviest things settle to the bottom, and you never see them until you dive down in search of them.

Or until they break.

I was pregnant when Rosario died. He was in seventh heaven, he smiled like a little boy, he'd keep his hand on my belly and explain in great detail exactly what was happening inside me: you see, now this or that organ is forming, now you're feeding it, now it's moving. It was his pregnancy, even more than it was mine. And then one day he was gone.

I had no money problems, but I was alone. My future had been stolen from me. I'd patiently and laboriously constructed an edifice that had suddenly collapsed. Like a beehive built by a swarm, cell by cell, crushed by a boy with a sledgehammer.

I met Tullio. I'd seen him once or twice before, he seemed like a wide-awake, ambitious young man. After Rosario's death, he temporarily took his place at the hospital, but he was determined to stay. He came to see me every day, sometimes more than once. He said that as Rosario's first assistant, he felt morally obliged to keep an eye on my pregnancy, he who had been unable to save his life.

But fate would have it that nothing of Rosario was destined to survive. I had a miscarriage, even though Tullio tried everything to save the baby. In particular, in the days that followed, he reassured me that in any case I could have other children; I didn't understand why he was telling me that, I wouldn't even have wanted back the baby I had lost, especially now that Rosario was gone.

Tullio continued coming often to see me at home. At first, his thoughtfulness touched me, then I realized what he had in mind. He had no doubt about my importance to Rosario's career, and my network of relationships, and now he wanted them for himself.

The idea disgusted me at first, I thought he was a slimy opportunist; then I started to give it some thought. I had spent years developing my network of contacts in the field of medicine, specifically in the gynecological field, and now I was alone, about to lose it all: Tullio would make it possible for me to maintain my prestige and my prominence. He wasn't as brilliant as Rosario, but he was more ambitious, and he seemed capable of following the paths that I myself could show him. It was the perfect solution.

I started working on it, and he was soon appointed director

of the chair of gynecology on a permanent basis. Now all he needed was time to achieve his full stature.

We were married, and Federico was born. I had never felt particularly maternal, but the boy changed me profoundly. I loved him. He was a piece of me, my own life perpetuating itself. Everything that I had wanted, everything I had fought for, struck me as petty and tawdry. My son was the most important thing in the universe.

For Tullio, on the other hand, the child's presence was an obstacle to his ambitions; I was determined not to move away because I wanted to raise him in a stable environment, I wanted him to grow up here. The position Tullio had his eyes on came open when Federico was three years old, and I made sure he wasn't even in the running. He learned what I'd done, and from that moment on a gulf opened between us. Life was pushing us in different directions.

Some time ago I was awakened in the middle of the night by violent pounding on my front door. Two huge men had come looking for my husband. This was hardly the first time such a thing had happened, it was normal for a gynecologist. I told them that he was at the hospital, but they replied that that was where they had just come from, that they had taken their boss's wife there, but he wasn't there.

The next morning, when he came home, I asked him to account for where he'd been, when he ought to have been on duty at the hospital. We had a furious quarrel. At first he denied everything, then he confessed that he was having an affair, that he was in love. Can you imagine? In love. A snake, an ambitious vulture, a cold-blooded reptile who had never experienced a single emotion in his life, had fallen in love.

I wasn't jealous, far from it. By now he disgusted me, I wouldn't have felt a thing if I'd known he was in another woman's arms. But I was insulted at the thought that he'd never spoken words of love, or tenderness, or even simple affection when it came to my little Federico, and that now he was telling me that he was head over heels in love with this other woman. Head over heels, you understand. Can you believe it?

I told him that I'd created him myself, that he was nothing more than a goddamned puppet dancing on my strings. That just as I'd created him I could destroy him, without pity. That he had better not even think of making my son the talk of the town, or of trying to make a spectacle of him, or he'd have to reckon with me.

I thought I'd frighten him. But he shot back a reply without flinching.

Me? he said. *Me*, a puppet? *Me*, dancing on your strings?

You're so stupid, he said. You're so ridiculously stupid. Maybe you could manipulate your first husband. Sure. Because all he wanted was to be a physician, and he went along with your frenzy for social climbing, your thirst for power. But not me. Remember? I'm every bit as ambitious as you are.

I slapped it in his face that he was a nobody, that he could never hope to approach the heights Rosario had achieved. That Rosario had been a genius, a superior mind, and that he was just a grimy little wannabe, a small man eaten up with envy. That if Rosario hadn't died, he'd still be standing in the wings, waiting for his chance.

That was when he told me. I think he'd always wanted to tell me, certainly sooner or later he'd have boasted of how his fierce determination had successfully circumvented every obstacle in his path, including my late husband. Or perhaps he was simply swept away by the horror of that conversation, by my desire to wound him and crush him, by the feeling of omnipotence that people say comes over you when love arrives and makes all things possible.

He would have died anyway, eventually. That's what he said. His heart would have given out. Anyway? I asked. Yes, anyway, he said after a moment's hesitation. What do you mean? Tell me immediately what you mean by that, I demanded.

He smiled, that's right, he smiled and he replied: yes, it was me. Me and no one else, the little man waiting in the wings. I'm the one who eliminated your precious husband, the vehicle of your ambitions. And he told me how he did it.

It was the herbal tea, Commissario. A common, simple, apparently harmless herbal tea of valerian, lemon balm, and chamomile; the tea that Rosario drank twice a day, to ease the tension and agitation of a profession that might threaten his heart. Tullio took over that everyday task, as if currying favor with his boss, assistants do this and much more in that world, and he began adding moderate quantities of extract of digitalis, lethal for someone suffering from heart disease like my husband. Until one day his heart gave out, all at once.

He got away with it easily, Rosario's weak heart was an established fact, and it didn't occur to anyone that his cardiac arrest might have been chemically induced.

And then, he said, I took care of you. You took care of me? I asked. Certainly, he replied: do you think I would have raised and supported another man's child? That I would have tolerated the living memory, the progeny of a man whose life I had chosen to take?

The herbal tea, I said as I remembered. The herbal tea for me, too. I was having intestinal problems, and he, who had been so solicitous about my health, made me an herbal tea of powdered liquorice, to ease my discomfort. What did you put in the herbal tea? I asked him. And he replied, blissfully: Claviceps purpurea, rye ergot fungus, in powdered form. Three days, and the result is a miscarriage, an abortion.

I was looking at the man who had murdered my husband and my baby, Commissario; and at the same time he was my husband and the father of my child. I felt as if I had just plummeted into a nightmare without end. Why did you tell me? I asked him. For what reason?

He said nothing for a little while. Then he told me: I'm in

432 · MAURIZIO DE GIOVANNI

love. And I want to experience this love without subterfuge, happily. Still, I don't want to lose my career, a career I've conquered with so much hard work, and with your presence. So I want you to know what I'm capable of. And I'm sure that you, who have made your own personal success the sole guiding principle of your life, will be very careful not to ruin everything: your son, first and foremost, would be ruined for the rest of his life. And you can't prove any of this. Absolutely none of it.

He was right, and I understood that instantly. I had no other choice.

We'll go on exactly as before, he told me. Actually, it will be better, because now everything will be so much clearer. But with our friends, our relatives, our acquaintances: the same as before.

I stopped sleeping with him. I had a bed made up in Federico's room. I was afraid to leave my son alone, I had no idea what was going through the mind of that lunatic. After a couple of days he came to ask me, as natural as could be, what kind of gift I'd like for my name day. I'll take nothing from your hands, I replied, but he just laughed and said that it was important to keep up appearances, and that included a name day gift, so I might as well tell him what I wanted. And that's when I thought of Nicola.

A few months earlier I'd happened to run into an old friend who still lived in the neighborhood and who I hadn't seen since we were children; I couldn't even tell you how we recognized each other, when we came face-to-face in the street. We'd chatted for a while, and she was the one who told me that Nicola was still waiting for me. That in all these years no one had ever seen him with a woman; he still lived with his mother, who had lost her mind, and he'd set up in business for himself, becoming the finest goldsmith in the *borgo*. Now I understood the reason behind that chance meeting: fate had shown me the way.

I told Tullio that I'd heard good things about this goldsmith, and that I'd like a ring. He was happy to have an opportunity to meet me halfway: he thought he was sealing an armistice of some sort. I later found out that he'd also commissioned a second ring for his whore, but by then there was nothing he could do to offend me.

I went to see Nicola. First at home: but I found only his mother, with the woman who looked after the apartment building. Incredibly, the mad old thing recognized me the minute she laid eyes on me. He's certainly still down in his workshop, even though it's late, the woman told me, and I went to look for him there.

When he saw me I must have seemed like a ghost to him. He told his young apprentice to go away, then he stood up and walked toward me. Lord, what had become of him. It broke my heart to think what we'd been like, as children, when we used to go down and watch the steamships set sail for America.

We talked. And we talked again, that time and the other times that I went back to that workshop, always at night, always when he was all alone in that deserted *vicolo*. He listened to me openmouthed, with a half-smile on his face, whatever I told him. He was just as much in love as he ever had been, in fact, much more than before. To his mind, which had never accepted anything else, I was his goddess, the sole custodian of the happiness he had once brushed up against.

I slowly brought him around to think what I wanted him to think. Tullio had gone to see him, to order first one ring, then the second. And Nicola would go and deliver the finished rings to him at night, at the general hospital. There was no need for anything more. I knew what he would do, even though he had never discussed it explicitly. I wanted it, he knew I wanted it. And that was enough.

One night, the last night we saw each other, he asked me what I would do afterward. If it happened that Tullio was no longer on the face of the earth, if he was made to pay for what he'd done. I didn't have the heart to lead him on, that was more than I could bring myself to do. I told him that I would look after my son, and tend to the honor of his name.

I wouldn't want anyone else beside me, I added.

He said nothing. Probably he understood. I was different from the little girl he remembered, who had been on his arm at the festival of Our Lady of Mount Carmel.

That night he told me that there was a vow to the Madonna he had to keep, a vow he'd made when I left, and that he had made a heart of gold. I didn't want to see it, I already felt soiled enough as it was. I bade him farewell with a kiss on the lips. He was trembling.

I prepared myself to wait. I pulled out the pathetic letter that Ruspo wrote, the one that Tullio had laughed at some time ago, and I kept it there, knowing I could use it when the time came.

I only needed to wait. Because I knew what would happen.

I knew it, at the bottom of my heart.

LXIX

When Maria Carmela Iovine was done talking, it was as if no words had actually been spoken in the whispered monotone that had lulled them until now.

Maione observed the two profiles, Ricciardi's and the woman's, overlapping as if on a coin, both of them raptly following the images that the sentiments and emotions sketched in her account seemed to project in the air before their eyes.

The crickets, as if responding to a command, had begun chirping again. Maria Carmela's hand moved, snapping open the lock on her purse and searching inside. It reemerged, her black-gloved fingers holding a folded sheet of paper.

"He wrote to me. A little boy delivered this sheet of paper to my concierge, yesterday, and then took to his heels. In it he declares what he did, as if I didn't already know. I think he wanted to shield me from all suspicion. He tells me that he doesn't regret it, and that it would have been so much better if we had left together, when we were children. He hopes that I am able to give him a decent burial, even if he did what he did. And then he says that I am the only one, at the bottom of his heart. And he hopes that there is still a place for him, at the bottom of mine."

Maione was overwhelmed by a great sense of pity for Coviello, murderer and suicide, a victim and executioner for love. And he tried to imagine the profound essence of his regret or the beauty of his perennial wait.

The widow Iovine turned slowly and, for the first time, looked at Ricciardi.

"Now do you understand why I'm here, Commissario? I owe him this. I have a friend who is a high prelate, I won't tell you his name; he spoke to a certain parish priest who will offi-ciate at the funeral and ensure that he is buried in a Christian congregation, in the cemetery of a town near here, where no one will ask who Nicola Coviello was, a kind friend and an emigrant in his own birthplace. Who can say, he might even have been right. Perhaps we should have left together."

Ricciardi stood up. His face was a papier-mâché mask.

"Life is full of missed opportunities, Signora. Nothing but missed opportunities. You lived by manipulating men, and you destroyed every man you manipulated; I hope you don't do the same thing to your son, who is as innocent as Coviello was. And I hope that you're able, in the nights that lie in wait, to elude the ghosts that haunt you."

With a curt bow, he moved off. As Carmela Iovine lowered the veil over her face, her lower lip trembled.

For a good part of the way back, they walked in silence. Night was falling, but the activity in the *vicoli* showed no sign of diminishing. The sense of anticipation ahead of the impend-ing celebrations for Our Lady of Mount Carmel, celebrations which would culminate with the burning of the bell tower, was palpable.

As if speaking to himself, Maione said: "There are times, Commissa', I'll tell you the truth, when I'd rather not know why certain things happen. I say: can't we just limit ourselves to finding out who did it, and be done with it? Like just now, for example, we knew that the one who threw the professor out the window was Coviello, right? Wasn't that enough?"

Ricciardi shook his head and went on walking: "Everything is connected to something else. Like a string of pearls. Every single event, everything that happens, has a root, a motive that can stretch back in time many years, as you just heard now."

"I know that, I know, Commissa', and who am I to quibble? Still, in this case, wouldn't it have been enough for Signora Iovine to pull that letter out of her purse and show it to us? That way, we could all have just assumed that it was jealousy that drove Coviello to do what he did. He was still in love with the woman, the woman's husband comes to him to order two rings, he tries to see if the woman will come back to him, she says no, he murders his rival and then hangs himself. Wouldn't that have been simpler, more normal? Easier?"

"But when have things ever been simple, Raffaele? You're not taking into account one important element: the woman's need to stop harboring within her the evil that the professor did to her. Her first husband's murder, the miscarriage of her first baby. She sentenced the professor to death; what Coviello did was to execute him. What good is a death sentence, if no one knows that it has been carried out?"

Maione walked on a ways in silence. Then he said: "Certainly, the signora knew how to do a good job. In point of fact, she murdered the professor but kept herself safe from harm. She won't go to prison, and she'll pay no price for what she did. Certain woman seem kind and delicate, in their starched dresses and their jewelry, but deep down they have souls fouler than any sewer. Others look like sin made flesh and instead they're really just little girls, at heart."

"You're thinking about Sisinella, aren't you? Perhaps you're sorry about the way you treated her, that poor girl? You came dangerously close to slapping her face."

"You're right about that, Commissa', I was just on edge and I took it all out on her; but afterward I thought better of it and went back to see her, to say I was sorry. She was in terrible shape, that coward of a *pianino* player even dumped her, just like he told us he would. And I have to admit that I went by the office and got the ring, the one that the professor commissioned, and gave it to her."

Ricciardi stopped short: "Really? But you know, don't you, that you had no right to take things into your own hands like that? The ring was part of the professor's estate, and therefore . . ."

The brigadier interrupted him: "And therefore belongs to his legitimate heirs, I know, Commissa', I know. But it occurred to me that the professor's real wishes, if Coviello had allowed him to write out his will before tossing him out the top-floor window, would have been to get the ring to Sisinella, so I did what the dead man wanted. And after all, I have to tell you the truth, Commissa': I decided that the widow and her son have plenty of money of their own, enough to live not just comfortably, but in luxury for the rest of their lives. While for poor Sisinella, that ring could spell the difference between a decent life and being forced back into the inferno. Maybe she deserved that chance, what do you think? And maybe the professor might have already given her that ring, or he might have hidden it somewhere, never to be found: who can say?"

Ricciardi started walking again: "Let's just do this, Brigadier Maione: you didn't tell me anything, and I can't remember seeing any jewelry in the professor's office except for Signora Iovine's ring. In fact, remind me to arrange to inventory everything that's in that office, so that the victim's property can be made available to the widow and her son, along with the apartment in Vomero that has, until now, been occupied by Sisinella. All right?"

Maione touched his fingers to his visor. They'd reached the front entrance of police headquarters.

"Yessir, Commissa', at your orders as always. Best regards then, I'm heading home. Tomorrow, I'm taking the day off: I'm going to take Lucia and the kids to see the burning of the bell tower, like every year. You have the day free too, don't you?"

"Yes, Raffaele, I do. Garzo gave me the day off for Livia's party; apparently the whole city is talking about nothing else.

Right now I'm going to write my report, and then I'll go to the hospital to see Rosa until Bruno kicks me out: he just keeps telling me that I'm not allowed to stay in a women's ward."

Maione, in an unusually personal gesture, laid a hand on Ricciardi's shoulder: "Commissa', I'm the last person who'd want to say this sort of thing, but the thing is, Signora Rosa . . . do you really think that we ought to wish for her to go on living much longer in this condition? We don't know if she's suffering, if she's in pain, if she wants to move but can't, wants to talk but is unable. I'm so, so sorry for her. And for you, too, Commissa'. Sir, I wanted to tell you . . . I've been thinking about this for several days now: you aren't alone, Commissa'. No, you aren't, even if Signora Rosa does go to heaven. You aren't alone, as long as there's a Maione family in Piazzetta Concordia."

Ricciardi looked the brigadier in the eye: "I know that, Raffaele. I know. All the same, I can't imagine living without her. Now you go home, and make your children laugh; they have every right, and so does Lucia. These are festivals for a family, and you have a wonderful one."

LXX

Baroness Marta put down her sewing again, and sat listening. She giggled, her fingers covering her mouth like a little girl.

Rosa asked her: "And now why are you laughing, Barone'?"

Marta shook her head, as if caught red-handed: "No, it's just that people, seen from here, can be hilarious sometimes. You'll see for yourself, once you're ready and I'm done embroidering this romper for you. They really can be amusing."

Rosa thought to herself that, in the long days they'd spent together when she was alive, the baroness had never confided in her so freely. There had always been a shadow, some hidden grief in her enchanting green eyes; and the same was true of her young master, who so closely resembled his mother.

The thought of Ricciardi shot a piercing pang through her consciousness; she wondered how he was, who was looking after him now.

Marta giggled again: "You see? You're doing the same thing. Just like all the others."

"What is it I'm doing, Barone'?"

The woman looked at her tenderly, and put the romper, the needle, and the thread down in her lap.

"You do one thing and you think about something else entirely. Instead of worrying about what's really important, you think that something else is what matters most, usually something that is quite insignificant. The world forces you to do that, it must be the air or the scent of the flowers."

Rosa tried to concentrate, but she couldn't seem to understand what Marta was saying. She shot a worried glance at the figure in the shadows, the Baron of Malomonte, but he didn't stir.

"Barone', forgive me, but I don't understand you. Maybe if you could give me some examples . . ."

Marta laughed again, and taking up her work again, she said: "Look, *tata*. Just look out the window a little. Maybe, even if you're not ready yet, you can start to get a glimpse."

In the heat of the July night, Peppino the Wolf thought about Rosinella as he listened to his baby girl.

She was crying. She cried all the time. And deep inside of him, he felt those wails were guilt, guilt for having killed her mother. For having taken away his future, his happiness.

And whoever had murdered that worthless man, the professor, had denied him the possibility to in some way make up for his wife's death.

Of course, it would have done nothing to bring her back into his arms.

Of course, it wouldn't have given him back her laughter.

Of course, it wouldn't have given him back the smell of her skin, on hot nights like this one, nights that seemed never to end.

But at least it would have soothed his rage, the immense crashing wave of rage that never subsided.

Still, the professor wasn't the only guilty party.

The sobs that came from the next room, the small thin wails that never seemed to subside: the confession of the other guilty party, the one who had first begun to kill Rosinella.

He got out of bed. His powerful body, his abdominal muscles quivered beneath a veil of sweat. It was hot. So hot. The inferno is hot.

His mother was a little hard of hearing, and she slept heavily. The wailing of the baby girl wasn't enough to awaken her. He opened the door and approached the crib that he and Rosinella had prepared, months ago. When the future still existed.

She didn't have a name yet, the baby girl. She hadn't been baptized. No one had dared to suggest it, at least not as long as the Wolf had forbidden it. *What do I call you?* he wondered, standing in the heat of the July night. *Who are you?*

Maybe I'd be doing you a favor by suffocating you with this pillow, he thought. Maybe I'd just be sparing you a life with no mother and a crazy father. Without brothers or sisters, in an empty house without laughter. What kind of life awaits you? Perhaps I'd be doing you a favor by killing you here, in your crib. So many babies die in the first few days.

Maybe I'd be helping you, by turning you into an angel.

Maybe you'd go to your mother, and let me get some sleep.

The baby girl sobbed and sobbed.

The Wolf reached out a hand toward the crib.

In the heat of the July night, Guido Ruspo di Roccasole watched as his father struggled with death.

He'd never seen anyone take so long to die, he kept telling himself; and yet he was studying medicine, and he was the part owner of a nursing home that often tended to the incurably ill. But no, he'd never seen anyone take so long to die.

Guido wondered why his father was fighting so fiercely. If it had been him, the minute he saw the first signs of the disease he would have killed himself to escape the pain, the crippling effects, the madness of an atrocious, irreparable suffering.

In the heat of the July night, Guido Ruspo di Roccasole felt a shudder run through his enormous body at the thought of what becomes of one's internal organs as they are devoured by cancer. He'd seen so many, during the long anatomy lessons at the university, as he stood with his colleagues in a white lab coat around the autopsy table; eaten up from within, lesions of an unhealthy color, tortured to death by the unstoppable enemy.

Guido loved his father, unconditionally. His sweetest memories were of his father's aristocratic, sensitive hands tousling his hair, the low, courteous voice, his arms, strong and yet also delicate. The man had been father and mother to him, friend and advisor. For his son, in an attempt to help him, he had even done something mad, written to Iovine, and he'd found himself on his deathbed answering questions from the police about a past that ought to have been dead and buried, even if it could never be forgotten.

He'd been a great man, capable of overcoming immense challenges: the ruin of his university career, the death of his wife, which left him with a small child to look after, the financial difficulties that had followed his grandfather's poor business decisions. Every time, he'd managed to get back on his feet, stronger than ever. A great man.

And now here he was, thought Guido as he sat in the shadows: wheezing in his sleep, his organs devoured by the beast, suffering agonies so unspeakable that he had to kept sedated.

His heart clutched in a fist, in the heat of the July night, Guido Ruspo di Roccasole wept for his *papà*.

In the heat of the July night, Livia couldn't get to sleep.

By now she'd done everything to prepare for tomorrow's party. She was going to dress as a siren, a mermaid. It seemed in keeping with her job: she was going to sing.

She'd practiced, shut up in a little room overlooking an interior courtyard, to make sure she wasn't treating the entire neighborhood to her scales and vocalizations. Her voice was a first-rate musical instrument, but it was rusty from long disuse and years of suffering; it needed to be buffed up to a shine, painstakingly prepared, and carefully tuned: and that's what she'd been doing continuously over the past few days.

Livia had even made up her mind to return to her career as a singer, however things went the next day. Music was too

444 · MAURIZIO DE GIOVANNI

important to her. She'd missed it so much, and that had become clear to her as soon as she had set her mind to trying out a melody.

She'd even begun taking language lessons, because she wanted to do full honor to the song—the Neapolitan canzone—that she would be singing. Don Libero, Ernesto, and Nicola, who had composed the melody and written the lyrics to the song, had instructed her and tactfully corrected her inevitable errors of phrasing. They'd had fun, they'd laughed, they'd pretended to tear their hair out in despair, but in the end, at the last rehearsal, they'd all looked at each other and embraced. Everything was going perfectly.

In the heat of the July night, Livia wondered what Ricciardi would think when he heard her sing. She'd tended carefully to every detail, selected a pattern for the dress that she'd had a seamstress make for her, adjusted the voice and the expressions she'd put on when she sang, identified the exact spot where she'd stand on the terrace, all just for him.

She wondered if he'd remain indifferent that night as well, when the long scaly mermaid's tail would give way to a layer of voile that would speak eloquently of her flesh, and the corset that barely managed to contain her bosom would magnetically attract his gaze, leaving him unable, this time, to resist.

She wondered whether her voice would charm him, or whether the magnificent words of suffering and hope in Don Libero's canzone might drop into the void, fail to enchant him as they would everyone else, with the aromas of food, the sea, and love that would be filling the air.

And she wondered, for the thousandth time, in the heat of the July night, whether Ricciardi would come to her party.

In the heat of the July night, Enrica watched the spectacular show the stars were putting on outside her window. She was terrified.

Tomorrow night she had a date to see Manfred alone.

This wasn't the first time they'd spoken: but by day, just a short distance from the children who were playing or splashing in the water, during breaks from their work, things were different. Nothing could happen, in those conditions. A conversation couldn't even take a particular turn.

She liked Manfred; she had to admit it. He was a very handsome man. His clear, light-blue eyes, his thick blond hair, his well-tended athletic body; and even his voice, soft and deep, with that odd, sharp accent that made his way of speaking so attractive. She sympathized with Carla, whom she still caught, every so often, gazing at him, enchanted, a foolish half-smile stamped on her face, her eyes glistening and darting away the instant she realized that Enrica was watching her.

He had finally shown her the canvas he'd been working on since the day she'd met him. He'd taken her to see it that very afternoon, holding her hand to help her climb up the slope, until they reached the easel overlooking the sea and the laughing children.

With a theatrical gesture he'd yanked off the cloth that had concealed the painting from the curious eyes of Carla and the children of the summer colony, and even from her own; that was when Enrica, with a mixture of surprise and secret pleasure, discovered that the canvas depicted her and her alone, sitting in profile and looking out over the waves of a blue, foam-dappled sea, her eyes lost in the distance.

It was a rapt but characterless gaze, the one depicted on the unsuspecting model on the canvas. Manfred hadn't captured—and how could he have?—Enrica's misery every time she sought two green eyes from across the sea.

In the heat of the July night, Enrica felt a tug at her heart as she thought of Ricciardi. The separation that she had imposed on herself hadn't eroded by so much as a gram the feelings that she had for him. She understood now, on the eve of a meeting with a man who had everything that should make a woman fall head over heels for him, that she would much rather be many miles away, busy embroidering by the window, waiting to feel a pair of eyes on her.

In the heat of the July night, Enrica wept with sorrow.

With two green eyes at the bottom of her heart.

In the heat of the July night, Livia smiled as she dropped off to sleep.

With the verses of a song that she'd sing for the whole world, and for just one man, at the bottom of her heart.

In the heat of the July night, Guido Ruspo di Roccasole stood, picked up the pillow, and, with tears in his eyes, put an end to Francesco's pain.

With the memory of a lullaby sung by his father many years ago, at the bottom of his heart.

In the heat of the July night, Peppino the Wolf picked up his baby girl and rocked her gently to sleep.

With the thought of Rosinella at the bottom of his heart.

Marta di Malomonte smiled at Rosa's smile, and went on with her embroidery.

LXXI

Modo came looking for Ricciardi at the usual hour, when he always ordered him out of the room and off the ward. It had become a sort of ritual.

"If I've told you once I've told you a hundred times, Ricciardi: I can't let you stay here after visiting hours are over. You're a little boy, I'm told; at least you look like one, even though Thunder Jaws and his hangers-on claim that any men not married after a certain age are in all likelihood homosexuals. So out you go."

The commissario couldn't take his eyes off the bed in which Rosa lay breathing deeply. Sitting with her back to the wall, a yard from the bed, as always, was Nelide.

"Bruno, I understand that I need to leave. But what can you tell me about her? Isn't there any improvement, didn't you notice any signs of reawakening, or . . ."

The doctor threw his arms wide: "I can't believe that you're still asking me that question. Don't you listen when I talk to you? I'm sorry to say that there have been no improvements and we can't reasonably expect any. The situation will remain stable, until . . . well, you know until what. And it's not especially useful for you and the woman of marble here to stay and watch her sleep. I know that I can't stop her from doing it, but I can stop you, and I have every intention of doing so."

"Bruno, you know very well that I can't bring myself to leave her. If you only knew how many times she was at my side while I slept, when I was little. I used to have throat troubles, I was a sickly child, and every winter I'd suffer from terrible fevers. Who do you think worried about me, who do you think stayed by my side? Now I owe her the same."

Modo went over to him and forced him to get up out of the chair.

"No, I'm going to have to disagree with you. She wouldn't want you here, watching her sleep. She'd want you to clean yourself up and go out for a relaxing evening. I know that you're invited somewhere, tonight. Go to that party: doctor's orders. I promise you that I'll stay here, with Rosa. With Rosa and with that statue of a young woman from Cilento, seated in that chair. I couldn't tell you which of the two is livelier. At least I can hear Rosa breathe."

Ricciardi shot a look out the window. Livia's party, right. It was tonight. And tonight was also when Enrica had her date with the man she'd met on the island, out there across the sea. And there was Rosa, in a bed, fighting a battle that he couldn't help her win.

He felt alone, now more than ever. Out of place wherever he turned. He stuck his hand in his pocket and pulled out the note that Enrica's father had given him, containing an address and a time. And his thoughts went to Coviello, the poor hump-backed goldsmith who dreamed of taking a ship he'd never boarded. *The bottom of your heart*, his phantom had murmured, its black tongue protruding between its teeth. *The bottom of your heart*.

Take a ship, or not take it. And die for not having taken it.

He felt his heart thud to a halt, and then resume beating.

He looked at Rosa, let his fingers brush her hand.

Cold. How cold she was. He couldn't leave her, he decided. Ship or no ship.

"You need to leave, Signori'."

Nelide's words, spoken in an undertone, almost whispered, exploded in the silence. Ricciardi and the doctor turned to look at her as she said again: "You need to leave. If Aunt Rosa

were awake, she'd slap you silly and send you packing. I'll stay
here. You need to leave."

Modo made a face: "So if she says you have to go, you really
have to go. Otherwise, I'd bet *she'll* slap you silly; on her aunt's
behalf."

Livia's party was a decided success.

Walls and furniture had been abundantly decorated, in hues
of white and navy blue, with draperies of silk and other expensive fabrics to simulate waves and salt spray on the rocks, but also
with splotches of dark red here and there, standing in for coral.

The houseboys and waiters, dressed in traditional fishermen's
garb, were serving the typical dishes of summer in the city: ver-
micelli with clam sauce, and a variety of frittatas made of maca-
roni, onion, and zucchini. An "oysterman's stall," set up at the
edge of the terrace, offered seafood, cooked and raw, and a cook
standing over a kettle full of hot oil was frying *paste crisciute*: fritters stuffed with anchovies, zucchini blossoms, and whitebait.

The guests were in seventh heaven, and they exchanged
compliments on each other's outfits, only to turn away and
snicker at the graceless bodies put on display by the costumes
they'd rented or had made for the occasion. Fishermen, sea
goddesses, Neptunes and Poseidons, oversized mullets and
grinning sharks greeted each other, cantering along to the
music of the conservatory orchestra.

Garzo, dressed as a mythical triton, with his wife as an oyster
on his arm, fluttered from one circle of guests to another doing
his best, but with scant success, to catch the attention of this or
that powerful guest; every so often he exchanged meaningful
glances with the policemen he'd pressed into security duty; they
were sweating in tight, impeccable uniforms and yearning to
sample a glass of the chilled white wine that was flowing freely.

The mistress of the house was the most beautiful and the
most closely observed, by both the male and the female guests.

The mermaid costume, her hairdo, and her valuable jewelry, which set off her magnificent figure, glittered with a light all their own on an occasion when there was no lack of ostentatious display of wealth. A number of her girlfriends had traveled south from Rome, and one in particular, given her highly elevated social status, was the object of furtive glances of curiosity: but the envy and admiration were reserved entirely for Livia.

Sadly, however, in spite of the fact that no one noticed, the woman's eyes betrayed no happiness; they were full of unease as the hours ticked past and among the guests who arrived one after another, each announced by a footman in livery, she had yet to see the one she pined for above all others. If everyone else had vanished and he had shown up in their stead, Livia mused, how much nicer it all would be.

Don Libero and the two maestros, Ernesto and Nicola, were the only ones more on edge than Livia. They were split between an imperceptible anxiety and a sense of anticipation greater even than at Piedigrotta, Naples's traditional musical festival. Soon, Livia would premiere in public, for the first time in the world, what they felt to be their best song ever; would she prove capable of performing it properly, in that out-of-town accent of hers? And would the audience like it—that audience so alien to the working-class public, so quick to nitpick?

The hours passed, and the performance of the song could no longer be postponed. Livia shot constant glances toward the footman at the front door, but never saw anyone new arrive.

Enrica was done getting ready. There was a moon, a full moon that looked like an enormous spotlight in the middle of the starry sky.

She didn't have a suitable dress for a real date: when she had decided to spend the summer on the island, this was the last thing she'd expected, and she hadn't packed anything that would be appropriate for the occasion.

To tell the truth, she doubted she even owned a dress to wear on a romantic date. And she certainly didn't want to give Manfred the impression that she was out to seduce him. And so she'd put on a mid-length white skirt, with lightweight socks, the only shoes she'd brought with her—the black shoes she wore when she took the girls out for an afternoon walk— and a blouse with her gray jacket and a little hat the same color that went with them. She didn't know what would happen, but in her heart she had grim misgivings.

She put on her glasses, picked up her purse, and went out.

Livia went over to Don Libero, who had called the guests to attention.

From the terrace it was possible to glimpse, in the distance, the fireworks from the festival in Piazza del Carmine; the enormous moon hung motionless in the middle of the night sky as if it were part of a painted scene on a cardboard backdrop.

Don Libero recounted the tale of how Livia had asked him for a song—a Neapolitan canzone—to offer as a treat to her guests, and how he and the two musicians present that night had decided to bestow upon her their finest pearl. Don Libero's words brought that intimidating audience to its feet with a roar of applause that contained all the city's love for their great bard of popular music; and in the breathless silence that ensued, there was all the immense curiosity that had been lurking, palpably, since the beginning of that evening's entertainment. Don Libero took an emotional bow.

Livia, on the other hand, had her heart in her mouth. She could feel it beat furiously, and she had to delve into her recent memories to put her finger on her determination to sing at any cost, in the presence or the absence of the man she loved. Clara, her housekeeper, had told her: a heart in love must sing, it has no choice. And neither does a heart in despair.

Don Ernesto took his seat at the piano and struck up the

splendid introduction that Livia had learned so well. There was a rustle of movement at the front door, and her breath practically caught in her chest when she saw a man appear in the shadows, beyond the heads of the partygoers who were crowding close in a circle around where she stood.

Enrica had strolled for several hundred yards with Manfred.

The German officer, who was wearing an impeccable dark suit, had put the girl at her ease and made her laugh with funny stories from his military service. He really liked her when she laughed; she had a natural grace about her that was better by far than ordinary beauty.

Now he was leading her to the belvedere, the overlook with a view of the sea. He reached out a hand and took her by the elbow, casually, as if by accident.

Enrica almost jumped.

Livia tried desperately to determine whether the silhouette that she could just make out in the shadows was that of Ricciardi. Too many people in the way, too far away, too much glare in her eyes from the spotlight trained to highlight the singing mermaid.

She gave up trying, leaving to her heart the powerful wish that it might really be the commissario. She abandoned herself to the music and sang.

Chiú luntano me stai, chiú vicino te sento;
chissà a chistu mumento tu che piense, che ffaie . . .
Tu m'he miso int'e vvene 'nu veleno ch'è ddoce,
non me pesa 'sta croce che trascino pe' te . . .

The further you are from me, the closer I feel you . . .
Who knows at this moment what you are thinking . . . what you are doing . . .

You have poured into my veins a sweet poison . . .
I do not mind the cross I am bearing for you . . .

The very air seemed to stand still.

From the deserted street, left empty by the crowds pressing onto Piazza del Carmine, came not a sound. Everyone was listening to the voice of the siren, every bit as much under her spell as had been Ulysses's crew.

Te voglio, te penso, te chiammo . . .
Te veco, te sento, te suonno . . .
È 'n anno, ce piense ch'è 'n anno
ca 'st'uocchie nun ponno chiú pace truva'!

I want you . . . I think of you . . . I call you . . .
I see you . . . I hear you . . . I dream of you . . .
For a year . . . would you believe for a year,
these eyes have not found any peace?

Enrica, sitting on the bench of the overlook, watched from a distance the glare of the fireworks celebrating the Festa del Carmine, the Feast of Our Lady of Mount Carmel, in Naples, twenty miles across the sea.

From there it was little more than a vague luminescence, but she knew the triumph of fiery flowers in the night sky, and she felt a stab of homesickness for the nights spent with her nose in the air, with her parents and siblings.

Manfred stared at her profile, and decided that the magic of that light, that moon sketching a glowing trail on the surface of the sea, was something no painter could ever hope to reproduce.

E cammino, cammino, ma nun saccio addò vaco,
i' sto sempre 'mbriaca, ma nun bevo mai vino.

Aggio fatto 'nu voto a' Madonna d'a Neve:
si me passa 'sta freva oro e perle lle dò . . .

I walk and I walk . . . but I don't know where I'm going . . .
I am always drunk but I never drink wine.
I made a vow to the Madonna della Neve:
if I get over this fever I shall offer her gold and pearls.

The magic of the song poured out of Livia's chest and crashed down on the men and women listening like a silvery waterfall.

The despairing words of the lyrics, the story of a sentiment frozen in time and space, the plea for the divine grace of liberation from the immense, eternal curse of a pitiless, unrequited love, found flesh and blood in the tones of a profoundly feminine voice.

I never thought I'd written such utterly realistic lyrics, thought Don Libero, with tears in his eyes and a hand on his throat. And he also thought that subsequent singers would find it a challenge to find such powerful passion in his *Passione*.

Te voglio, te penso, te chiammo . . .
Te veco, te sento, te suonno . . .
È 'n anno, ce piense ch'è 'n anno . . .

I want you . . . I think of you . . . I call you . . .
I see you . . . I hear you . . . I dream of you . . .
For a year . . . would you believe for a year . . .

Manfred took a deep breath, and told Enrica's profile what he desperately needed to say.

That he wanted to give meaning to his life. That he wanted a wife and children, children whom he could teach proper values, children who could carry on his name. That he wanted someone for whom he could work, someone for whom he could build and even fight if that became necessary. That he wanted someone to survive for in battle, someone worth coming home to. That he wanted to keep and cherish a ring and a photograph in his wallet. That he wanted to breathe again and look forward, to a bright, joyful tomorrow. That, in a word, he wanted a future.

And that he wanted it with her.

Livia took a deep breath.

The last line demanded a high note, a scream of despair and, at the same time, of hope. The scream of a person in love, a person condemned to love, well aware of how fitting it was to die for love.

She concentrated and shot a quick glance at Don Ernesto, who looked up from the keyboard to give her a nod of happy, emotional complicity.

The silhouette in the partial darkness by the door stirred and stepped forward.

Ca 'st'uocchie nun ponno chiú pace truva'!

. . . these eyes have not found any peace?

Enrica had listened as Manfred spoke, and his words had flowed around her heart like water streaming over marble.

She had sat stiffly watching her city, across the sea. Imagining the sounds and colors of the festival. Thinking of the man she loved, the man she really loved, perhaps in the arms of another woman, perhaps with his eyes turned toward a future that didn't include her.

But in her heart, at the bottom of her heart, there was no one but him. And Enrica wasn't willing to settle for anything less than the man that she loved.

She turned to Manfred to tell him so.

In the frenzy of applause, as all her guests hurried to offer their most enthusiastic compliments and hailed the composers for the triumph of their new, incredible masterpiece, Livia finally had a chance to get a clear and unobstructed view of the mysterious figure. He seemed to have waited in the penumbra for her to finish dispensing to all those present the magical gift of that song. The shadow stepped away from the wall and took a step forward to reveal to her from afar the face streaked with tears and an ecstatic smile.

It was Falco.

The Baroness of Malomonte heaved a deep sigh and turned to Rosa, showing her the romper, finally finished with lovely embroidery: "Come, *tata*. Look how nice. Let's see how you look in it."

Miles away and in the same exact spot, Nelide wiped away a tear with a single, brusque gesture.

The instant Enrica turned to speak to him, because the moon was casting a silvery wake on the sea and the air was full of hope and music, Manfred kissed her.

In the trees, a few dozen yards away, something broke at the bottom of a heart.

And a pair of green eyes, that thought they'd seen too much sorrow and suffering to ever weep, filled with tears.

ACKNOWLEDGMENTS

The wonderful song *Passione*, one of the absolute masterpieces of the Neapolitan *canzone*, was first debuted by the composers and lyricists Libero Bovio, Ernesto Tagliaferri, and Nicola Valente at the Piedigrotta Festival of 1934; I couldn't resist the temptation of moving its creation forward a couple of years to allow Livia—who was pestering me to do so—to perform it at her party. I ask forgiveness and I express my gratitude.

Ricciardi, in order to tell this story, has benefited from the assistance and support of a number of guardian angels.

Annamaria Torroncelli and Stefania Negro, who staged the journey to 1932 to absolute perfection, opening a window on that period from which one enjoys a breathtaking panorama. Difficult to imagine Ricciardi without them.

Antonio Formicola, who, as always, constructed with the undersigned the murder and the context in which it took place.

Giulio Di Mizio, who with Ricciardi has once again seen corpses talk.

Manlio Monfardini, who has been caring for Rosa ever since she first fell ill.

Mariapaola Arienzo, who told Ricciardi all about the gyne-cologist's profession.

Misha Falconio, who suggested the pharmaceutical details of the murders.

Valentina Pattavina, Severino Cesari, and Francesco Colombo, who have tended to the book, wonderfully as always, as their chaotic author chased after his story, losing himself as always in the *vicoli*.

Francesco Pinto and my marvelous Corpi Freddi, without whom Ricciardi would never have existed.

Maria Cristina Guerra, who puts up with—and heroically—the sorrows and complaints of Ricciardi and his author.

As for me, my writing, my desire to tell stories, and my whole life, I send a kiss and a smiling tear to my one guardian angel: my sweet Paola.

Maurizio de Giovanni's Commissario Ricciardi books are bestsellers across Europe, with sales of the series approaching 1 million copies. De Giovanni is also the author of the contemporary Neapolitan thriller *The Crocodile*. He lives in Naples with his family.